iron shadows

Tor Books by Steven Barnes

Achilles' Choice (with Larry Niven)

Beowulf's Children (with Larry Niven and Jerry Pournelle)

Blood Brothers

The Descent of Anansi (with Larry Niven)

Firedance

Gorgon Child

The Kundalini Equation

Streetlethal

iron shadows

Steven Barnes

A Tom Doherty Associates Book

New York

TOR®

IRON SHADOWS

Copyright © 1998 by Steven Barnes

A Tor Book
Published by Tom Doherty Associates, Inc.
175 Fifth Avenue
New York, NY 10010

Tor Books on the World Wide Web:
http://www.tor.com

Tor® is a registered trademark of Tom Doherty Associates, Inc.

Book design by Judith Stagnitto Abbate

Library of Congress Cataloging-in-Publication Data

Barnes, Steven.
        Iron shadows / Steven Barnes.— 1st ed.
                p.   cm.
        "A Tor book."
        ISBN 0-312-85708-X
        I. Title.
        PS3564. I9I76   1998
        813'.54—dc21   97-29840
                                        CIP

First Edition: February 1998

Printed in the United States of America

0 9 8 7 6 5 4 3 2 1

To Toni Annelle Young: for twenty-five years, variously, wife, partner, friend, support, and mother of that most precious being, Lauren Nicole Barnes. Thank you for sharing my life, and God bless you, and keep you, wherever your path may lead.

acknowledgments

To Harley "Swiftdeer" Reagan and Dianne Nightbird, for their support in the adaptation of the Sweet Medicine Sundance teachings, without which the Golden Fire workshop sequences would have assumed a much different character. And for my research partners: Jennifer Jauw, Jamie Charles, and Porsche Lynn. Thank you more than I can say. Others who deserve wholehearted mention: Ina Gregory, Richard Dobson, Stephanie Wadel, Deborah Laughlin, Brenda Cooper, and Razel Wolf.

To Pat Connell, for permission to share his hard-won experience. To Suzanne Vegas, JoAnne Kirley and Karin Waller, Rebecca Neason, Rex Kimball, Suzanne Nixon, Sue and Jeff Stone: all contributed to the evolution of the tale. To Stevan and Kim Plinck, again, for the sharing of home and wisdom. For my editor, the irreplacable Beth Meacham, who waited patiently.

And, most joyously, to Tananarive Due. Much love, and many thanks, for the promise of a new beginning.

Steven Barnes
http://www.teleport.com/~djuru
lifewrite@aol.com

prologue

Sunday August 6, 1995
Los Angeles, California

Screams and acrid, oily fumes choked the labyrinth. A man and woman stumbled desperately through its shadowed twists and turns. Their footfalls echoed like distant gunshots. The woman, a small wiry brunette with an ugly bruise on her left cheek, wore a yellow unisex utility uniform. The man was enormous, but barely conscious. With every tortured breath, the woman tasted her own mortality. Until this moment, fear, at its very worst, had existed as a sour weight somewhere inside her body, a small, gnawing creature burrowing its way through her mind. This was something very different. This was a cocoon spun of pure mortal terror.

She pushed her heels hard against the ground, shoving with all the strength in her superb legs, dragging the man a few more feet into the darkness. She trembled, fighting for control. Soon, too soon, her abused body would no longer respond.

She had dragged him away from the terrible sights and smells on the field above, pulled him deeper into the concrete tunnels, but now her own pain and exhaustion, muscles bruised and stressed beyond their limits, were signaling an end to her efforts. The man could not help her. His left arm and right leg were broken, and he hovered on the brink of shock.

Above her head, pipes hissed and bled warm water. The tunnels beneath the Los Angeles Memorial Coliseum were as warm and damp as a womb. She dropped the clip in her 9mm Glock automatic. At least three bullets remained. What was no longer certain was if physical force, however massive or efficient, would make any difference at all.

She could still hear, or imagine that she heard, the dying shrieks of the most brilliant warrior she had ever known. Ultimately, all his skills had meant nothing. Nor had the fact that he loved his murderer with all of his heart. Perhaps the woman he loved was gone, as if she had never existed at all.

And perhaps, in some terrible sense, the beautiful external shell had been the illusion, her current nightmarish incarnation the reality.

From somewhere behind them rose an echo, a sound like someone screaming down a well. *"Bitch . . ."*

She held the man upright, staggering a few more paces through the gloom. Dim, yellow lights above her flickered and died. She sagged against the sticky wall, mind racing, struggling to devise a way out of the trap. He tugged weakly at her arm.

"For God's sake," he said. "Get the hell out of here." He coughed, a wet ugly sound. She wondered if a lung was punctured. "Without me, you've got a chance."

That was as far as his strength could take him. Neither of them had slept in fifty hours. Both were operating in some resource twilight, stripped of everything except the will to survive. She pressed her cheek against his, cursing herself for waiting so long to love him.

Only now. When it's too late.

Shit.

"Go on. . . ."

"To hell with that," she said, and slammed the clip back into the Glock. A surge of adrenaline swept away the cobwebs. If this was the end . . . if this was death, if the creature coming to take their lives could not be stopped, then by heaven she would die fighting, rather than spend the rest of her life wondering if she could have saved him.

Damn you. Did you even tell him? Have you ever told him?

Even now, you can't, can you?

"Your first instincts were right, you know," she said. She braced her back against the tunnel wall as she pushed her way up to standing. She took the Weaver stance: right arm straight, supporting with the left. Aiming at the corner not twenty feet away. Already, an unholy blue light peeled back the darkness. The temperature was rising.

Death was on its way.

"We should have told Sinclair to keep his damned money. We should have left the Twins alone."

"*Bitch! Where are you . . . ?*" The words seemed more like the hiss and crackle of a bonfire than any product of human vocal cords.

She bent, and ran her fingertips along his stubbled cheek. Despite his injuries, the corners of his mouth lifted in a smile. "You never listen, do you?"

She kissed him softly, her heart breaking. *Say it, dammit. Say it at least once, before you die.*

Tears streamed down her cheeks as she struggled to find her voice. The heat was baking now. Sweat beaded and streaked her face, plastered her dye-darkened hair against her forehead.

"I just wanted you to know . . ." she began to say.

He laughed. "Shut up," he said. "I know. I guess I've always known."

She bit her lip and nodded, her shoulders finally relaxing. She drew a bead on the corner as the floor boiled with flame. It looked as if a pool of blazing oil was spilling down the corridor. She glimpsed a leg, an arm, a face shrouded with fire. Her finger tightened on the Glock's compound trigger, releasing the safety.

I love you, Jax.

Then hopelessly, she fired.

one

Two Months Earlier:
Wednesday, June 7, 1995
Los Angeles, California

Cat Juvell nibbled thoughtfully at the southeast corner of her dry wheat toast. As she did, she peered through the western window of the LAX Excelsior's coffee shop, enjoying the sheer power and grace of a powder-blue

747's approach. She allowed herself a moment's wistful speculation. What passengers traveled in that iron bird? What lives had they lived, what destinations did they seek? And how many had safe, normal families to enfold them?

She was in her early thirties, with an oval face framed by a cascade of small soft blonde ringlets. Her habit of peering out from behind them sometimes made her resemble a mischievous child peeking through a fence. Presently concealed beneath a powdery pink jump suit, her broad shoulders and narrow waist rivaled those of a National-class rock climber or competition swimmer. Neither of these were her discipline of choice. Her taut frame seemed knitted of pure energy, forever on the skittish edge of unraveling. Her birth certificate read **Portia Musette Juvell.** Since her mother's death a decade before, she rarely answered to anything but Cat, and invariably signed or spelled her first name "Porsche."

"Come on, Jax," she said to the man across the table. "What do you think you're going to do with yourself?"

Jackson Carpenter hunched his enormous bulk over his plate, enthusiastically consuming a chili omelet smeared with sour cream. His thick chest and arms filled his leaf-patterned purple silk shirt impressively. In his middle forties, Jax's closely cropped black hair, mild brown eyes and wire rimmed glasses contributed to an oddly academic demeanor, as if he were a hulking, overaged grad student. It was easy to imagine him in his collegian days, the kind of quiet giant oblivious to the entreaties of football and wrestling coaches, never quite able to comprehend the appeal of such violent and exhausting pursuits. This carefully cultivated image seemed even more incongruous on those occasions when he exercised his considerable talent for mayhem.

"I'll find something," he said pleasantly. "Just time to move on, that's all."

"You want your name on the door, is that it?"

Their waitress approached the table carrying a little steel pot. Her smile was as improbably large and bright as her *Hi! My Name is Margie!* name badge. "Your water, ma'am. Is everything all right?"

Cat winked at her. "Very fine, thank you." She removed a glassine envelope from her purse. Tearing the corner off, Cat poured a stream of yellowish powder into the water, and mixed it with a red plastic coffee stick. Ignoring Jax's baleful expression, she spooned the resultant thin syrup onto her wheat toast.

"And what, exactly, is that substance?"

"Butter Buds" she said. "Tastes just like real butter. No fat or cholesterol."

He forked another load of omelet into his mouth. "A pitiful attempt to deny mortality. Why can't you just clog your arteries like the rest of us?"

"Because," she said, "I'm not *like* the rest of you. How's your Myocardial Infarction Special?"

"Yummy."

She pressed her lips together into a thin line, and abruptly changed the subject. "Come on. It's the door, right?"

"Keep your door." He leaned back, watching a 727 take off. The bland blue Eskimo stenciled on its side seemed to wink at him. After Nanook disappeared into the distance, Jax studied the crosshatched shadow pattern on the wall, then watched Cat nibbling at her toast again . . . in fact, he began to pay careful attention to almost everything except the blocky, expressionless gentleman seated in a corner booth on the opposite side of the room. Occasionally, Jax watched the mirror tiles on the east wall, but never the man himself. Or his bodyguard.

Cat's gaze similarly avoided the corner booth. It wouldn't do to have Sheldon Algoni identify them before they were ready to move. It simply wouldn't do at all. And that circumstance dictated a certain amount of genuine slyness. Algoni was a hard, dangerous man, a man who had preserved life and limb via unceasing alertness and unwavering suspicion of anyone not directly under his emotional or financial control.

In a little over six hours, Algoni would leave the United States forever.

Quietly and with a ventriloquist's skill, Jax said: "Perhaps you'd better take a look."

Cat rested her face in her hands and twinkled, as if fascinated by the conversation. She shifted her face enough to flick a discreet glance at the corner. "Son of a bitch." Although her lips were smiling, her voice was unamused.

A third man strode toward Algoni's table. Jax and Cat slumped a little, trying to slip into a shadow. Cat brushed her left ear. In it, invisible in the dim light, nestled something resembling a tiny pink hearing aid. Her other hand fished in her purse, groping for the beeper-sized communication relay.

"We've got trouble" she said. The plastic smile never left her face. She laughed as if Jax had just said something hysterical. "Oh, yeah. Right here in River City. With a capital 'T' and that rhymes with *Oh Shit.* Milton Quest just turned up."

A t the outer edge of the Excelsior's parking lot stood a drab, battered green Volkswagen van. Its fenders were dented and its paint badly chipped, revealing ancient blue primer beneath. It had a California plate on the rear, and a torn, empty plate sleeve in front. A weathered yellow sign on either side read: BAXTER ANIMAL SANITATION SERVICES: "YOUR DOG'S POOP IS MY SOUP" with a cartoonish painting of a frisky, presumably unconstipated pup pursued around a sparkling clean yard by a ravenous vacuum cleaner.

The van's windows were tinted slightly blue, but pressing tightly against the glass might earn you a hint of video screens, speakers, receivers and microphones. You might also glimpse its single occupant.

His name was Tyler Juvell, and his muscular upper body contrasted sharply with his withered legs. A shaggy mop of brown hair hedged a deeply freckled face that sometimes reminded his friends of Mickey Rooney playing Huckleberry Finn. He usually wore a hat of some kind, at this moment an aged felt bowler acquired at a Venice thrift shop. He wagged his head in amazement. The radio crackled again. *"Did you hear me on that? Milton Quest."*

"When you care enough to hire the very best," Tyler said. "Any sign of the girl?"

"No." Cat's voice was edged with static. *"I'm betting Algoni won't let her out of the room."*

"Did he make you?"

"Nope. We've got a good position. Seems to be a summit."

"Can you hear anything?" Tyler asked. "Flight times? Anything?"

J ax reached beneath the table and adjusted the miniature umbrella perched on his lap. The bumbershoot was actually a powerful directional microphone of Tyler's construction. Jax struggled to aim the damned thing without being too conspicuous. Two tables stood between their position and Algoni's. Criss-crossed conversations made eavesdropping a nightmare.

"Anything, Jax?" Cat asked softly.

"I caught something about St. Croix, I think." He paused, head tilted slightly to one side. "I've got a clear impression that they're in no hurry . . . but I think they leave tonight."

Cat touched her earpiece. "Jax thinks he heard Virgin Islands. Maybe late this afternoon."

"*Then they're gone with the wind,*" Tyler's voice said. "*All right. If Quest is involved, we're talking private plane, everything legal but sleazy. Baby Algoni is gone, folks. Can we please call in the cops . . . ?*"

Cat shook her head. "Client was very specific. We're on our own here."

"*All right then. We have one Union thug taking off with maybe fifty million bucks and his lovely daughter. What now, Sis?*"

Cat's eyes narrowed. "All right. We proceed as planned." Her hand slipped out of her purse. "Did you pay off the maid?"

Jax grinned like a shark. "Let's just say I'm busy Friday night. Not everyone is motivated by greed."

"Nor by good taste."

The men in the corner rose from their table, shaking hands all around. In leaving, they passed within ten feet of Cat and Jax, who hunched further back into the shadows and the protective covering of a broad-leaved plant. No one glanced in their direction.

"I'll settle the bill," Jax said. "It's show time." He paused. "This might be the last one, Cat. Let's make it good."

Cat slipped on oversized sunglasses and a floppy flowered hat, obscuring her hair and the merry blue hell of her eyes. "Still say it's a negotiating ploy."

"Nope. I'm serious this time."

"New door, new window, new stationery. My last offer."

"Hah."

Cat slipped away from the table and followed her targets. Algoni, the bodyguard and Quest entered the leftmost of three elevators. As soon as its maw closed, Cat ran past it to the exit stairs, slammed the door back, and bolted up the steps.

In the elevator, Sheldon Algoni stood at ease. A tall man who had been at the top of his rather dangerous field for many years, he found vast comfort in the presence of Milton Quest. Responsibility for the next six hours (critical to the successful completion of his plans to leave the United States both wealthy and in possession of all major body parts) rested in Quest's capable and very expensive hands.

"Slick, Milt." He watched the numbers climb above the elevator door. He'd always liked that, even as a kid. In fact, he had often ditched grade school and spent all day riding downtown office elevators, dividing his attention between backlit numerals and the unguarded wallets of preoccupied businessmen. "We do this right, and I'm gone before they even know there's a problem."

"The attorney general has your deposition?" Quest asked calmly. Quest was a year or two shy of forty. He was trim, tanned, and impeccably tailored. Only X-ray vision could have distinguished the Remington .38 beneath his Biella Black jacket.

"Every word," Algoni replied.

They passed another floor, and Quest spoke again. "I'm not certain it's wise to take the girl. You should send for her later."

Algoni snorted. "That's between me and Felicia's mother. Private business."

"My pardon," Quest said politely. Quest was very polite. But courtesy was not the attribute currently earning his security firm twenty-two hundred dollars a day.

Cat bounded onto the sixth floor landing, turned and headed up to the seventh. She bolted the stairs two at a time, then eased the door open—

And immediately shut it to a hairline.

Thirty feet away, Algoni and Quest shook hands in front of room 715. Quest nodded his head in agreement to some comment Cat couldn't hear, clasped again, then headed back toward the elevators. Algoni and the bodyguard entered the room. The door closed.

Cat punched the transmitter in her purse. Her "hearing aid" curled around the back of her ear, picking up her words by bone conduction. "Jax? Let's go."

Jax Carpenter had just finished paying their bill at the cash register. He touched one finger to his earphone, and then another to the belt transmitter. Oh, yes sir—he read Cat loud and clear.

Time to get to work.

In the stairwell, Cat peeled out of her jumpsuit like a snake shedding its skin. Beneath the outer garments was the rumpled blue and white uniform of an Excelsior Hotel maid, skirt folded up against her blouse. She smoothed it down into place, whispering: "Consider this a lateral promotion. It'll look damned good on your resume."

two

Cat Juvell pulled back on the handle of her utility cart, bringing it to a halt just outside Room 715. Her blonde curls were pinned beneath a white service cap. Her uniform was a little too loose—although she and Jax's Friday rendezvous were the same height, they had differing conceptions of an acceptable waistline. A pair of safety pins fixed that pretty quickly, but she was conscious that her disguise wouldn't withstand close inspection.

The radio button in her ear buzzed. *"Everything in place?"* Tyler's voice.

"I'm ready." She knocked on the door, and then inserted the key. "Housekeeping," she said blandly, and pushed the door open.

Jax knelt in a corridor on the basement level, tying his shoelaces over and over again until two Asian kitchen staff walked past. Then very carefully and professionally he employed a strip of cellulose to open the door marked COMMUNICATIONS ROOM.

He slipped inside. Humming banks of relays and video monitors supplied data and communications service to the entire hotel. All the security lines ran through this room, but after a minute's fiddling with the fire alarm system, he transferred all attention to his primary objective: The in-room video lines.

He opened his black briefcase. Within was a Macintosh Powerbook, a cellular modem and a collapsible antenna. Jax touched his ear.

"I'm in," he whispered.

"Good man," Tyler said. *"Find the video 'in' console, and hook me to the main board."*

"All right." Jax scanned the room quickly. "Where are you, suckers?" He spotted a black shoe box–sized shelf studded with gold-plated RCA jacks. A moment's unplugging and plugging, and he started to feel optimistic. "All right. There. Is that it?"

A garishly designed bedroom appeared on the Powerbook's video monitor. Two masochistically aerobicized actors feigned passion on a circular pink waterbed.

"Oooh!" he said. *"Somebody's* enjoying the liquid soap, but I don't think it's 715." Jax finished accessing the Communication room's main computer console. On it, an automated roster of rooms with active video scrolled. "Just found it. Punching it up now."

His fingers darted across the keys. The Powerbook's active matrix screen darkened, and then splashed with color again. On it, cartoon characters frolicked, singing: *"We're Tiny, we're Toony, we're all a little loony—"*

"Bingo. Tell Cat that we have contact." Dammit, he grinned to himself, Cat was right. He *was* going to miss this job.

Algoni and the two thugs were the only ones in the living room. The larger bodyguard was a swarthy man with a bad shave. Cat immediately nicknamed him Rover. Rover sat on the couch with his boss. The other bodyguard was a big-bellied man with a flat nose and the disturbingly light-footed step of an ex-boxer. She immediately nicknamed the pug Dover. Dover hovered behind a red leather wetbar tinkering with ice cubes and mixer.

She noticed, without giving sign that she noticed, that when she entered the room Rover and Dover moved their meaty hands marginally closer to the bulges in their expensively tailored jackets.

Smiling her widest and most disarming smile, she contrived to inhale and hold a portion of the breath. Her uniform became two sizes too small, breasts pressing against the fabric, hips filling the short skirt to the bursting point.

Cat watched their eyes and saw, actually *saw,* the moment when she exited the "potential threat" category, was expelled from the ranks of general humanity, and became an ambulatory vagina.

Male mammals were so wonderfully predictable.

In her ear, Tyler said: *"All right. Can you hear cartoons? Typical Looney Tunes music? Coming from somewhere in the suite?"*

Cat set up her vacuum, simultaneously peeking around the room. It was a six hundred dollar a day suite, with three bedrooms leading off from the main living area, the aforementioned wet bar, a convertible sofa in the living room, and a breathtakingly smog-shrouded view of Los Angeles.

Music drifted from one of the side rooms, sounds so faint that she wasn't completely certain of its reality or locus. The door stood open a few inches, and Cat went to close it. As she did, she glimpsed a beautiful but solemn little girl, perhaps nine years old, with flaming red hair. The girl sat too close to a fifty-inch television set. Its reflected rainbow tinted her lovely, unhappy face.

The child looked up, and their eyes locked.

Felicia.

A little catch relaxed in Cat's throat. The girl was here, and she was all right. That was the most important thing. Everything else was secondary to that critical fact. Cat winked, and closed the door.

She left her utility cart by the door, and pressed a button on her belt beeper. This part of the job was down cold sober. The rest rested in the hands of the two men she trusted most in all the world.

Jax, you have a go."

Jax plugged a Sony 8mm video player into the feed, and punched the "play" button. "Come on, you sorry sonofabitch," he muttered. "Work."

Up in her room, Felicia Algoni watched Buster Bunny whack the Tasmanian Devil upside the head with a mallet the size of Mount Rushmore. She had seen this cartoon before—she'd seen all of them before. Nickelodeon repeated its offerings only slightly less often than Madonna changed personas. But it was still funny, and it distracted her from Daddy's odd behavior. He had picked her up from Mommy's house three weeks ago for what should have been a weekend trip. Then he announced that they were going to play a little trick on Mommy, and wouldn't that be fun?

They were going to Disneyland, and Magic Mountain, and then maybe to Universal Studios to see the Cylons and the shark and after that they were going to go to every fun park across the country, and send Mommy postcards from each of them, and wouldn't Mommy be jealous? But the fun hadn't started yet, it had mostly been hotel rooms and lots of men in suits, and Daddy hadn't had much time for her at all. Sometimes Daddy didn't seem to know she was alive. And when she said she wanted to go home, Daddy used bad language, and once he hit her, and afterwards he bought her ice cream, and spanked her until she ate it.

After a day of begging to go home, Felicia realized that asking again was just going to get more spankings. Daddy had been in this mood before, and she had learned to wait it out. Something was different this time, but she wasn't sure what it was. She did, however, know that it would be smart to keep her little mouth shut.

And watch cartoons. Over the years she had learned that cartoons were a wonderful place to hide. Cartoons were a place where colors were bright enough, and sounds loud enough to drown out the arguments. To distract her from the terrible screaming and the occasional *thwack* of a strong flat hand striking her mother's face.

The violence was broad enough, over-the-top enough to evoke laughter instead of tears or fright. In fact, it went beyond mere catharsis. Following some ineffable cosmic Looney Tune regulations, smaller creatures always won in cartoon-land. Mice emerged victorious against cats, Road Runners perpetrated mass mayhem on a whole tribe of cloned Coyotes, and the early bird invariably encountered the Conqueror Worm. And, on virtually every occasion, kids kicked adult butt. For Felicia, this world held a strange and warming fascination.

Suddenly, the screen jittered. Felicia caught her breath as a pretty, but hollow-eyed redhead appeared on screen, one recognized in a fraction of a second as Mommy.

This was impossible, as impossible as cats rebounding after anvils squash them flat, but it was also happening right here, right now. The very impossibility of it startled her out of her video violence-induced coma.

"Hello, Felicia?" The woman on screen looked as if she hadn't slept in a week. "Baby, if you're watching this, then I was right—Daddy's pushed you off in a room to watch television while he does business. Nothing changes, does it Hon?" She smiled wanly. "Baby. What I need you to know is that he's not bringing you back to me. I know he probably told you he is. He said it's just a game, but it's not. Daddy's leaving the country with a lot of someone else's money, and he'll have to hide. If you go with him,

I'll never see you again, darling. Please believe Mommy. We don't have much time."

The words just hit like *clunk,* and without having to question anything, Felicia knew that Mommy was telling the truth and that Daddy was lying, as Daddy often did.

Felicia thrust her fist against her mouth, and began chewing on her knuckles. She felt immersed chest-deep in ice water.

"Think about things he's said to you," Video Mommy said, "and you'll know that I'm telling the truth. Now, if you want to go with him, I probably can't stop you. He has too many lawyers, and I'm not even sure where you are. But I hired a nice lady. Her name is Cat. You can trust Cat to take care of you. If you want to come home to me, please open your bedroom door now. There'll be a cart or something right outside. And room for you to hide in it. Just go. Go now, darling. Please."

Then the image of the mother she hadn't seen in almost three weeks died away. Suddenly, Felicia was staring at a duck pretending to be a rabbit in drag, or a girl rabbit disguised as a duck, or some other bizarre bit of interspecies gender confusion. And just as suddenly, she knew exactly what she was going to do, and that decision was both exhilarating and very, very frightening indeed.

Somebody jostled the communications room door, catching Jax's attention in a flash.

Shit. A janitor. Or the communications man, despite the fact that he should have been in the lounge at that very moment, sharing an extended lunch break with one of Juvell Associates' more delectable decoys.

Jax braced himself and gripped the knob, all the muscles in his forearms tensing. The knob stopped turning as certainly as if it had been welded into the faceplate.

Someone of the far side of the door muttered: "Dammit. Jammed again. Well, all right, if I try and the damned thing won't open, they can't blame me. . . ."

A diminishing patter of shoe leather against tile, and then nothing.

"Are you all right?"

"Except for a mild heart attack. What's with Cat?"

"Say a prayer. I think we're rolling."

———

The red upright Hoover glided over the carpet for a third time, picking up non-existent dust and dirt. More importantly, the repeated movements gave Cat an opportunity to display the elegant, golden contours of her superb legs.

Slowing her pushes and pulls down to a languorous edge she smoothed them, made them more rounded and sensual. She turned and smiled at Algoni, not surprised to find that he was already staring at her.

Which was very good, because that meant he wasn't watching the bedroom door behind him as a tiny, frightened girl peeped out. Felicia looked past the men, directly at Cat. Her eyes were glassy with terror.

Cat licked her upper lip as Felicia slipped through the utility cart's skirt, into a cleared space just large enough to hide a nine-year-old girl.

The vacuum continued to purr for a few moments, then Cat shut it off and swayed over to the cart. She giggled girlishly and said "Hope you gentlemen won't mind—I have some other rooms to do, but I'd like to come back and finish here. Maybe an hour?"

Algoni grinned like a lazy tomcat. "I think maybe there's a little more cleaning needs doing, yeah."

They shared a moment's intimate intensity, then Cat said "Hold tight" and pushed the cart out of the room, rolling her hips invitingly.

As she looked down onto the cart, the side curtain parted perhaps three inches, and she could see the little girl hidden within. Felicia's face was ghostly pale, afraid, confused. But she had listened to her mother, and she had trusted Cat.

As far as Cat Juvell was concerned, Felicia was a trouper.

As the door closed behind them, Cat triggered the beeper on her belt. With any luck, Algoni and his men would spend five minutes on vulgar speculation before anyone even thought of checking the bedroom. Putzes. A man with enough blood pressure to operate brain and penis at the same time might actually be dangerous.

A second light in Jax's briefcase winked on. He touched his earphone. "We're on," he said. "Second verse, same as the first."

"A little bit louder, and a little bit worse. Go!"

Jax disconnected the video feed, threw his equipment in the attaché case, and slammed the case shut. He opened the door—

And ran headlong into the janitor. "Hey! Who are—"

The janitor looked as if he would be courting retirement in a couple of years, but he was certainly young enough to raise an alarm. In a single, seamless motion, Jax yanked him into the room and spun him. He clamped his left forearm behind the old man's neck, his right arm circling to cut the blood to the carotid arteries. Jax felt a flash of guilt and shame, but it was over so fast that the older man barely had time to realize that he was in trouble. A moment of panic, a few aborted attempts to struggle, the sudden realization that there wasn't even enough breath in his lungs to scream. . . .

Then blackness.

"Great going, asshole," Jax muttered to himself. "How about next you go ten rounds with Grandma Moses?" He slipped a twenty into the janitor's shirt pocket. "You'll have a headache when you wake up, pal," he said quietly. "I'm really sorry about that. But if you saw the little girl, I think you'd understand."

Then he slipped out of the room, locking the door behind him.

Cat still pushed the cart down the hall, away from Room 715, toward the service elevator. She kept her steps measured, precise. There was no trace of the flirty walk or stance she had used to reinforce her maid persona. Every step took this child a few inches closer to freedom, a step further away from the hoodlum father who had sold out his cronies. The fact that he was endangering his daughter's life had probably never even occurred to him. And for that, for the sake of the little girl cowering in the utility cart, she hated Sheldon Algoni.

As she rolled past the main elevator banks, the door opened, and Milton Quest emerged.

Quest was conversing intensely with a human Oak possessing the general appearance and vitality of a very large, well-laundered and manicured Hell's Angel. He barely gave her a second glance. Cat continued smoothly on her way, paying them no apparent heed.

"Oh, shit," she whispered into her earphone.

"Cat? Do we have a problem? Cat?"

She continued down the corridor, pushing the cart slowly, carefully. She turned her head just enough to watch Quest out of the corner of her eye. He continued toward Room 715, then stopped, pivoted, and gazed after her.

She concentrated on the service elevator ahead. Quest's gaze burned mercilessly into the back of her head. She could almost smell her hair singe.

She was bare meters from the end of the hall when Quest's cultured voice floated after her. "Excuse me. Miss? Could I speak to you for a moment?"

Damn, damn, *damn*. She saw no way out of this. What if he just wanted the bed turned down?

She turned, and immediately began to rummage in her cart, tilting her face carefully away from his gaze. "Yes, sir?"

He strolled up to her lazily, his lieutenant towering and glowering at his side. Confusion pinched the taller man's broad, fleshy face . . . he wasn't sure what his boss was up to. Quest, on the other hand, was almost vibrating, like a teenaged girl bursting with a delicious secret.

Quest put on his brightest, friendliest expression. "We need towels. Could I possibly obtain an extra towel for my room?" His eyebrows arched quizzically.

Cat continued to busy herself, as if worried that she was out of toilet seat covers or wrapped slivers of cheap, scented face soap. Simultaneously, she inched her cart backwards toward the service elevator. Quest continued to close the gap between them, eating the distance with long confident strides.

"I'll need to go to the storeroom for that," she said. "I'll be right back." Only five steps away from the elevator now.

"How about an extra glass?" he asked. "You have cups, don't you?"

The two men were almost on top of her. Quest's pet Oak had picked up that *something* was wrong, but still had no inkling what that *something* might be. He was now close enough to grab her arm.

Cat's heart tap-danced in her chest. She didn't like this, hated what was about to happen, but saw no way around it. She felt some part of her mind float free, so that she seemed to be watching the hallway from some elevated, dispassionate perspective.

"Certainly, sir," she said, looking directly into his face. His grin widened in triumph. "Here we go."

She reached into the cart, extracted a towel—and flung it up into the Oak's face. About a tenth of a second after it hit, the metal-reinforced toe of her left sneaker impacted against his right shin. Agony squirted up his leg like liquid fire. When he doubled over, she delivered a perfect palm-heel strike to the nose: elbow behind palm, short sharp exhalation, turning the hand just *so* at the moment of contact to create maximum agony with minimum effort. Cartilage crumbled. Blood darkened the towel as his nose exploded across his face.

The big man stumbled sideways against Quest, hampering his boss's draw. Not a moment too soon—Quest's hand was already reaching for the .38 automatic holstered beneath his left arm.

Cat rammed the cart corner-first into Quest's gut. He huffed in pain, but flailed back into a balanced posture, and shoved his bleeding biker to the side. Quest yanked at the gun again. As he came up to the aim, she yanked another towel off the cart and snapped it like a whip, as precise and calculating as any Sunset Boulevard dominatrix. The .38 popped from Quest's hand and spun through the air. A long, sliding step brought her into punting range, with Quest's crotch playing pigskin. Quest staggered back against the wall, all professional concerns temporarily forgotten.

Cat looked at the elevator in despair—she couldn't chance the wait. She knelt and scooped Felicia into her arms, pivoting to sprint toward the fire exit. Felicia stared up at Cat with huge eyes, frightened but still silent. Cat touched her earpiece.

"Jax, Tyler. The balloon is up! I'm in the north stairwell."

"Got you covered," Tyler said in her ear. Even as he said it, the fire alarm howled, and the overhead sprinkler system began to flow.

In the hallway behind her, the cold sprinkler water brought Milton Quest to full alertness even as the pain between his legs braided rage and agony together into a single vibrant knot.

He cursed himself for playing stupid games with a bitch like Cat Juvell. He should have known, he should have *known.* . . .

Sheldon Algoni emerged from Room 715. Their eyes locked across the intervening twenty feet, some entirely preverbal communication arcing between them like lightning between thunderheads.

"Shit!" Algoni said. "Felicia!"

"They have the girl. North stairwell."

"Son of a bitch!"

"I'll get her." Quest unhooked a radio from his belt. "Condition Zinc," he snarled. "We're dealing with Cat Juvell. Be on the lookout for her trained dog, Jax."

He forced his breathing to slow, forced the dots and squiggles out of his vision, forced himself to become calm. There was still time to pull this out. Still time to complete his commission perfectly. Still time to wipe that goddamned smile from Cat Juvell's face.

Hell, he reminded himself. He'd done it before.

three

The lobby of the LAX Excelsior swirled in chaos. Alarmed by the fire sprinklers but curious about the lack of smoke, patrons streamed toward the front doors.

The concierge, a fiftyish, well-tailored woman named Nita Vasquez, held her hands up, palms out, attempting to restore order. "Please remain calm," she said. "I'm sure it's a false alarm."

To her left, an enormous black man shouldered his way effortlessly— but courteously—through the human tide. He was quite nice looking in an odd way. In his forties, perhaps, but quite solid. His wire-rimmed glasses seemed a bit incongruous for his size—he rather reminded her of a WWF wrestler moonlighting as a librarian. Most patrons moved in an orderly if moist fashion toward the front doors. This one was heading to the north stairwell. "Sir?" she called after him. "Sir?"

He ignored her, vanishing though the doors. *Dios Mio,* she thought. Panic did strange things to people.

Two men stood on the stairwell above him. They were linebacker size, with a coldness about their eyes that Jax had come to associate with the minions of Quest Security.

The one on the upper stair recognized him first. "Carpenter," he said in a hard flat tone. Jax didn't know the man in front, but recognized the speaker. Big, maybe 260, about ten pounds bigger than Jax himself. The fire sprinkler pasted his shirt and pants tight against a chest swollen from endless hours at the weight bench. Probably steroids on his Sugar Crisps, too. His name was Timothy McGee, Quest security thug, maybe the best Quest had. McGee had bodyguarded Mike Tyson and Sylvester Stallone, and was said to be a world-class whiz at Tae Kwon Do or Hap Ki Do or one of those other sporty Korean imports.

Once upon a time, Jax had boxed Golden Gloves and lettered in wrestling. At the police academy, he had enjoyed Gene LeBell's judo classes enough to beg that living legend for a few private hours of instruction in the hidden laws of physics and the limits of human tolerance for pain. That was funzies, this was different—he hadn't time or energy or testosterone enough for this crap, and zero interest in testing the Mighty McGee's mettle.

Jax leaped up the stair, yanked a taser from his belt and depressed the trigger. Two copper spurs leaped out, trailed by wires.

They hit the first man in the chest. He convulsed so violently it seemed that he drew and threw his gun away in the same instant. He slammed back against the wall, and slid down, twitching. Jax threw the taser aside, and went straight at McGee.

Maybe this guy was Bruce Lee back from the grave, or maybe not. Jax didn't give a shit. Like LeBell had told him once upon a time: "Let the other man's skill remain a deep, dark secret." Jax was betting everything on two widely misunderstood aspects of unarmed combat:

The first is that certain reflexes, once hardwired into the human nervous system, completely bypass the higher logic circuits. If you extend your right hand, even an enemy will be tempted to extend his. If you smile sincerely, most people will, from countless thousands of such responses, begin to smile even if they hate you. And someone conditioned by thousands of hours of stylized combat will respond with a stylized response, given the correct stylized stimulus.

Jax's hands were low and wide. Fists clinched like a boxer's, face tightened into a caricature of a fighting snarl. McGee shifted his balance, flashing a *yop chugi* sidekick to Jax's open chest with blinding speed.

Oh, yes—the second truth about unarmed combat? Simply put, combative *balletomanes,* those whirling and thrusting dervishes so popular in B-movies and strip mall self-defense emporiums, rarely practice their adagios on wet metal steps.

Jax didn't have enough time to get his forearms up to absorb the kick, but when the foot slammed into his chest, recoil sent McGee's supporting leg skidding from beneath him. The *karateka* crashed thunderously back against the wall.

Jax came in hooking to McGee's body. He landed solidly to the short ribs, evoking a gratifying gasp in response. A muffled reverse punch grazed Jax's cheek, snapping his head around. He saw stars, but never stopped. You never *ever* stop once you have them going. Jax rolled atop McGee, throwing a right cross backed by two hundred and fifty descending pounds. The punch connected solidly with the side of McGee's head, banging it down onto the metal step. It bounced back up into Jax's fist, and then down again.

Game over.

Jax levered himself back to standing, and rubbed his breastbone gingerly. Man was good. That kick had been *hard,* and unbelievably fast. If McGee had gained decent traction, or enough room to work . . .

He cleared his mind of extraneous thoughts: He was standing, McGee was sleeping, and there was a job to finish. Jax bolted up the stairs.

At that same moment, Cat and Felicia were making their way down from the seventh floor. Guests flooded into the stairwell, seeking escape. The little girl looked terrified, lost, abandoned, and Cat hugged her close. Cat's arm clamped tight around her as a pale, hard-eyed man in an ill-fitting suit banged back the door beneath them, then snaked up through the crowd, left hand in his jacket. Cat instantly tensed, but with Felicia and the other guests present, her options were limited.

Bad Suit gripped at her arm, and waited until the press had momentarily diminished. He leaned close. His breath smelled like cheese. "No need to hurt you, or the little girl. Just don't make me get ugly, all right?"

"I think your tailor's got that covered."

His lip curled. "I heard you were a smart ass. Don't do anything stupid," he whispered, "and you might get out of this alive."

Felicia's eyes pleaded with her. "Anything stupid," Cat asked. "You mean like this?

She counter-grabbed his right hand and, holding tight to Felicia, jumped down two steps. Her weight yanked Suit sideways and he teetered, eyes bulging, left leg and arm flailing for balance. She jammed her left foot against his standing ankle, and pulled with all her considerable strength. Suit flew past her screaming, cannoning into the wall head-first. He slid down into a boneless heap. Felicia looked up at Cat as if she were Wonder Woman. "Wow!" she said.

Cat smiled shyly. "Did I do that?"

They made it down another flight of stairs, and saw Jax climbing up to meet them. Relief flooded through her like a warm tide, but Felicia recoiled. "A friend," Cat reassured her. "The best friend anybody could have." With Jax at her back, she could *stroll* through the lobby.

The fire klaxon screamed full-tilt boogie as the three of them descended. She punched him lightly in the stomach. "I like the cheek."

He touched the bruised skin beneath his right eye, wincing. "Matches my shirt."

They backed against the cool wet of the stairwell wall. Jax continued to scan as Cat touched her ear button. "Tyler. We're headed to the east exit. Pick us up."

"*Cat. Are you all right?*"

"Fine. Just do it."

Down two more flights. Then they left the stairwell, cut across a deserted office wing and left through another exit door. They emerged into daylight. For a moment Cat felt crosshairs on her forehead, then she spotted Tyler's ratty blue van, and they were moving again.

The van screamed up next to them. Jax wrenched open the sliding side door, and they jumped in.

"Let's get the hell out of here," Cat muttered.

The van rolled away, Tyler expertly working the wheel-mounted hand controls which allowed clever fingers to substitute for crippled legs. As they left the parking lot, they passed a large black car coming the other way. The words QUEST SECURITY might as well have been inscribed in foot-tall Day-Glo script. Tyler played it absolutely cool as the driver and passenger of the sedan scanned them.

It just might have worked if Felicia hadn't poked her head up at that moment. The bald guy in the passenger seat said "Hey!"

Tyler said "Shit," and burned rubber rocketing out onto Manchester Boulevard. Behind them, the black car smoked and skidded through a violent Y-turn and sped in pursuit. The bald man's head gleamed as he babbled into a cellular phone.

"Which way?" Tyler asked.

Cat was about to answer when a stomach wrenching concussion slammed her head against the padded dash. The black limo had smacked into them from behind. She tasted blood and saw stars. She cursed and buckled her seat belt as Tyler thumbed the accelerator lever. Ahead of them, the traffic light turned red. Tyler ignored it and slipped through the cross traffic, attracting hostile glares and a protruding middle finger or two. A scrape of tortured metal told them the limo had cut it even closer.

"What the *hell* are they trying to do?" Jax muttered.

"I think Quest is taking this personally."

"Now why would he do that?

She shrugged. "Some men have this silly attachment to their testicles." She glimpsed a stop sign just ahead, and a semitrailer snailing its way through the intersection. "Here!" she said sharply. "Right!"

Tyler swerved right through a driveway gapping a chain-link fence. The sign above it read Omni Light Craft. The black car was less than twenty feet behind them. It bounced as it hit the driveway lip. For an instant its front tires lost traction, then it gripped the pavement and straightened out. Tyler leaned hard over the wheel, eyes narrowed, lips compressed as he weaved expertly, avoiding a row of Beechcrafts and Cessnas.

Cat wasn't certain, but he seemed to be humming the most famous portion of the *William Tell* Overture.

The black limo fishtailed, its bumper slamming into a little single-engine trainer, missing the prop by inches. A man jumped out of the cockpit, scanning the foot-wide gash in the fiberglass body.

"Think Algoni's handling expenses?" Jax asked thoughtfully. The airplane's owner shook his fist at the cars, and stomped his foot in rage.

"Quest has insurance," Cat said.

"Here it comes." Behind them, a second car accelerated through the gate.

A squat man in grease-stained overalls ran out from a maintenance shed, waving his hands for them to stop. Tyler yanked the steering wheel aside but couldn't slow down, and the mechanic was forced to jump back out of the way. He ran back into the office.

"Cellular!" Cat barked.

Jax tossed her the phone. Cat punched in a number.

When the operator replied *"Los Angeles Police Department, Century Division,"* Cat said. "Police? There is a disturbance at the Omni light aircraft field. Off Sepulveda. Please hurry."

Tyler grinned and gunned the van toward a cluster of Quonset huts.

"Over there," Cat pointed. "We can make a stand—there'll be cops all over this place in a minute.

"I've got it, O.K.?

The van skidded into a spot between two huts, and did a 180. Jax was out of the van before it came to a complete stop, his empty hands pointing toward the sky.

The first black car screeched to a halt, the second one right behind it. Algoni clambered out, face purpling with rage.

Jax didn't move. "Just slow down. Nobody wants anything stupid to happen."

"Give me my daughter."

Inside the van, Cat took Felicia's face between her palms. "Do you want to go with your father?" she asked.

The little girl shook her head urgently.

"Then you don't have to. Stay here. No matter what happens, all right?"

Felicia barely breathed.

Cat exited the van, staying behind Jax. Her black Glock 9mm automatic was at her side, muzzle pointed at the ground. She remained near the door.

Algoni's fists were balled. "I want my daughter, dammit."

Jax's voice remained very calm. "Your daughter doesn't want to go with you, Algoni."

"It's none of your goddamn business. Quest? Why are we listening to this crap? What am I paying you for?

"Yes, Milton," Cat drawled. "What IS he paying you for? How are you earning your money this time? Kidnapping children is sleazy even for you."

Despite the recent insult to his genitals, Milton Quest would not be baited. "Incivility will not improve your position, Miss Juvell. I ask you to produce the child. Let her go with the man who is, after all, her natural father. Then you, your brother, and Mr. Carpenter may go on your way." The "you" had just a touch of heat on it.

Cat glanced back into the van. Felicia's face was pressed against tinted glass, washed almost to the image of a ghost. She was shaking her head an imploring "no."

"I don't think so, Milton," Cat said calmly.

"Get her," Algoni said. His voice was so cold it was almost reptilian.

Jax stood calmly in the gap between the van and the first limo. His hands were empty, but there was something about him that filled the space.

"Shoot that sonofabitch," Algoni pleaded.

"Jax is unarmed," Cat said. "Milton, do you really want to kill him in cold blood?"

Quest considered the possibility for a few moments, then shook his head. "I . . . wouldn't recommend it, Mr. Algoni."

Jax smiled thinly. "Are those police sirens I hear?"

The distant wail grew slowly, steadily, louder.

Quest didn't like this at all. "Mr. Algoni. I suggest that we leave the field. Legal means may secure your daughter's custody." Algoni tried to take a step forward, but Quest clapped a restraining hand on his shoulder. Despite his emotional reserve, the anger in Quest's voice was blistering now. "Another time, another place," he said softly.

"Cowards. You fucking—" Algoni took one stiff-legged step forward, and then another one, and threw a punch at Jax's nose.

Once, long ago and in another life, Algoni might have been genuinely tough, and strong, and fast. But for too long he had relegated the simple pleasures of battery to younger, hungrier men. Jax avoided the punch without ever taking his eyes from Quest. He took the second punch on his arm, and kicked Algoni's leg from beneath him so that the big man thumped butt-first on the concrete, hard enough to crack something.

Still watching Quest, Jax said softly, "Want to try again, Algoni? I hear you're six and oh with your wife. Ready to move up in weight?"

Sobbing, Algoni heaved himself up and swung again. Jax moved his head perhaps three inches, simultaneously pumping a left hook to the gut, so short and quick that a blink would have obscured the action.

Algoni dove face-first into the asphalt. He put his palms against the ground, and tried to push himself up. He managed about six inches before his trembling arms betrayed him. Crimson drooled from his nose and mouth, and he collapsed, managing to turn his face this time.

Quest snapped his fingers, and his driver dragged Algoni back to the car. The injured man spit blood and mumbled "Damn you. Fuck all of you. Why am I paying you, Quest?"

Quest spoke, his voice almost overwhelmingly reasonable. "To get you quietly out of the country. We don't want to be here when the police show up. Mr. Algoni—do you want your associates to know where to find you tonight? We must leave. *Now.*"

Algoni suddenly seemed to remember where, who and what he was. Despite his reddened face, he actually paled. He glared at Jax and Cat, but self-preservation finally won out. "Dammit," he growled. "This isn't over."

"Yes," Cat said. "It is."

His gaze was venomous. Perhaps he thought he saw Felicia's face through the van's tinted glass. At any rate, he spat his next words in her direction. "I didn't want the little bitch anyway. Tell her mother I hope this cost her plenty." He wiped blood from his cheek, glanced at the smear on his hand. "Plenty."

Jax's smile was benevolent. "Do the words *'pro bono'* mean anything to you?"

"Fuck you!" Algoni screamed.

"Well bend over, you sweet silly thing."

Quest hauled the increasingly apoplectic Algoni into the car, and ordered his driver to back up. The sedan behind them pulled back in coordination. Quest leaned out of the window. "Another time, Miss Juvell. Mr. Carpenter."

Then both cars peeled out, snaking swiftly into traffic just as the first of two police cars appeared. Sirens shrieking, the police shrieked to a halt, and then headed after the two limos, which were already accelerating past fifty miles an hour.

Jax sagged against the van, breathing a deep and utterly sincere sigh of relief. "That . . . was too damned close."

Tyler leaned out of the window. "I need a change of shorts," he said. "Think Uncle Miltie will get away?"

"Sure," Jax said. "Maybe the tail car takes a fall, but he'll get his client away, don't even doubt it. Right Cat? Cat?" When he turned around, Cat was gone.

Jax whipped out his pistol, running around to the passenger side of the van. The door was open. Christ! While he was distracted, someone had slipped in behind him and . . .

Then he saw. Cat was in the van, clutching Felicia to her chest. The little girl huddled against her savior, sobbing.

Cat Juvell saw nothing except the little girl in her arms. "It's all right," she said over and over again. "It's all right, now."

Felicia's grief turned every breath into a struggle. "He never wanted me," she said. "He just wanted to hurt Mommy."

"Shhh."

"I hate him. I hate him."

"It's all right." Cat kissed Felicia's strawberry hair. "You're going home now."

The girl hardly seemed to hear Cat. "Why did he say that?"

"Say what, honey?"

"Say that he didn't want me?"

Cat squeezed her. She glanced up at Tyler, and something passed between them. At that moment, Jax felt completely excluded from their world.

"Sometimes," Cat said. "Sometimes daddies are like that. Sometimes they just are."

Jax watched them both, something heavy and cold stealing some of the victory from the moment, and he barely heard the approach of the other sirens, or the squeal of brakes as the police cars slid to a halt behind him.

four

Santa Monica Beach was unusually quiet for a late morning in early June. A couple of bicycles rolled along beneath the sign suspended from the second floor window of JUVELL ASSOCIATES. A short round black man in a three-piece suit floated along almost languidly on purple in-line skates, eyes closed, popping his fingers as if jazzing to some internal melody.

Cat watched him from the window. She didn't know his name, but he rolled by about this time almost every day. He could have been a nutcase, or a stockbroker on an early lunch break. She just didn't know. He was always skating, always alone. His eyes were usually closed, his plump face suffused with an odd sweetness, as if completely involved in the effort to extract every possible moment of pleasure from a life which would, too soon, wind down into darkness.

She turned away from the window and her own thoughts. In the middle of the room, Brenda Algoni hugged and held Felicia desperately close, as she had for the past five minutes. Mother and daughter were crying. No one spoke. Jax busied himself with the cappuccino machine long enough to produce a tall latté. Tyler sorted and arranged the same stack of papers again and again, vaguely embarrassed by it all.

Under other circumstances, Brenda Algoni would have been a devastating beauty. Irish and Italian blood mingled in her veins to produce a flame-haired, emerald-eyed woman with gentle Mediterranean features. Her dress, shoes and hat were a shade of chocolate so deep they were almost black, as if she had suffered a death in the family—and perhaps she had, at that. Death, and resurrection.

Her face was fashion-model thin, and her body had obviously endured countless sessions of high-intensity aerobics to maintain that level of tone. Sadly, she projected none of the easy confidence which often resulted from such physical dedication. It was as if she had conditioned and maintained a show animal for the pleasure of an absentee owner. Cat tried not to let herself think too deeply about what this woman's life had been like prior to the divorce.

"I thought I'd never see you again." Mrs. Algoni pressed her lips against the warm hollow of her daughter's throat.

"Mommy." It was all that Felicia would say, but she said it over and over again.

Brenda Algoni finally stood, honked, and wiped at her nose with a flowered handkerchief. "I don't know how to thank you," she said simply.

An awkward silence followed, then Tyler said, "Money works just fine."

"Hush," Cat said without heat. "This one was tricky, but we rarely get to reunite a family."

Jax nodded above his coffee. "Just take care of Felicia. That's an adorable little girl you have there."

Mrs. Algoni froze for a moment, staring coldly at Jax. Then some switch seemed to throw in her head, and she relaxed. *We're among friends here,* that little inner voice seemed to say. Her generous mouth curved in a smile.

The smile was genuine, but Cat had glimpsed what lay behind the mask. She hoped a dark and very private corner of hell was reserved for one Sheldon Algoni.

Felicia took Cat's hand. She gazed up, and they locked eyes. For the last twenty hours, Felicia had stayed at Cat's side, the two of them holed up at the Santa Monica Travelodge on Pico Boulevard. Cat hadn't wanted to stay at her Malibu apartment—there was always the outside chance that Algoni would convince Quest to do something stupid. But with Algoni gone to the Caribbean or other points south, it was safe to meet in the office.

"Thank you Ms. Juvell," Felicia said shyly.

"Cat," she said.

"Thank you, Cat."

Her mother smiled at all of them. There wasn't a lot to be said. Monies had been paid, contracts signed, assignments completed. Yet there was still something undone, and if none of them could put their fingers on it, perhaps it remained to be completed another day. "Good-bye, Mrs. Algoni," Cat said firmly, letting her client off the hook.

"I don't care about the money," Brenda Algoni said firmly. "My husband will be dead in a year or so. To hell with Witness Protection, or whatever he's arranged. He can't live small. He'll make a mistake. My father will find him, and kill him. I couldn't be responsible for his death, so I couldn't tell my father or the police what I knew. It had to be you."

She paused, and her eyes defocused a little. She was looking at something, a distant or future scene. Cat felt a trill of apprehension brush her spine. "Someone will get him, and it might get out of control. It might not be clean." Her gaze focused on Cat, and with shocking suddenness, she felt the awesome force of this woman's will. "Felicia might have been hurt. You gave her back to me. I want you to know that I owe you. And I hope that you give me the chance to repay you." There was steel behind those words.

"Perhaps so," Cat said. Suddenly, the steel was sheathed with silk. Then velvet. And then, apparently, gone. Mrs. Algoni smiled again, suddenly as shy as her daughter. Without another word, they left.

Cat breathed a heavy sigh of relief, and collapsed into a chair. "Yow."

"That was . . . entertaining." Jax said. "She's a piece of work. I think Mr. Algoni had better spend his money *fast.*"

"Speaking of money," Tyler said. "We're actually in pretty good shape here." He held up Mrs. Algoni's check, rubbing it with his thumb as if checking to make sure that the ink didn't smear. "Always assuming, of course, that it actually clears the bank. If we don't get sued by the Excelsior, we're only three thousand bucks in the red."

"Sued? Us sued?" Jax said. "How could that happen? Only Quest would guess we triggered the fire alarm—and *he* isn't going to tell."

Tyler made a face. "Algoni might make a long-distance call from the Caribbean. . . ."

An entirely predatory expression spread across Cat's face. "In which case I will offer our services to Mrs. Algoni's father."

Jax laughed. "Ooh. Can you say: 'pro bono?' " When the merriment died down there remained a kind of easy silence between them, an oasis of shared satisfaction, a feeling that, if only for a few moments, all was right with the world.

Cat broke it first. "You did good, Jax." Her eyes shone.

"You too, Kitten."

She liked looking at him, wishing for the millionth time that their relationship weren't so damned complicated. Why couldn't she just let it *happen,* like any normal . . .

Tyler's voice snapped her out of it. "None of that, you two. Cat, please: no mushy stuff. Do you recall that this thug is leaving us at the end of the month?"

Jax grimaced. "I gave you the best years of my life. Is this polite?"

"Integrity supersedes civility." Tyler said. "Children, we have to consider our next job."

Cat bounded out of her chair, and perched over his shoulder. "And what do we have?" she asked.

"An invitation," Tyler said. "The question is, do we bite or not?"

Tyler held up a six-by-six square of pale yellow cardboard, engraved with black letters. It read:

You are cordially invited to a gathering of very special people, to be held the evening of the 9th. See and Believe!!!

No photography or video, please.

On the bottom of the invitation was printed a row number and seat designation.

Cat plucked it from his hand and held it up to the light. "Well—what do we know about this?"

"Well," he said, "It came with this book in a package yesterday morning." The book in question was a two-inch-thick hardcover with two smiling, pixieish, dark-skinned Asians on the gold cover. They stood, very relaxed, on a raised platform addressing a worshipful crowd. Male and female, they wore matching denim suits and projected something which

Cat found herself categorizing as ruthless compassion. Odd. The name of the book was *See and Believe*.

"It's at Long Beach State's football stadium, and according to their office, it's been booked this evening by a group called 'The Golden Sun.' "

He looked at each of them in turn. "Heard of them?"

Jax picked up the book, flipped it open at random and ran his finger down a page. "Aren't they the sex gurus? Dr. Ruth meets the Dalai Lama or something?"

"Exactly. Deprogramming, anyone?"

Jax shook his head. "I don't think so. Not this time Cat. Leave it alone. Not really my kind of work."

Cat shrugged. "We don't really know what this is about. What is this?" she asked. There was a long piece of paper attached to the invitation.

"A check for a thousand dollars."

Jax squinted. "Just for attending a football game?"

"It hasn't been signed yet. It's dated tomorrow—and it's drawn on the account of Dr. Maxwell Sinclair. This fellow is very real, and very rich. Nice as this check is, I think we ought to meet its big brothers. What say ye?"

Cat considered for a moment, and then raised her hand. "Aye." She paused. "Jax?"

"If Sinclair has deep pockets, might be a good way to clean up the bills. End this thing clean, you know?"

Cat nodded. "I wish you wouldn't talk like that, but . . . we go?"

"We go. Keep our eyes open, ears open, and tomorrow the Good Doctor signs the check." He thrust his arm into the air. "Aye. Tyler?"

Tyler wagged his shaggy head and chuckled. "What the hell," he said. "Take the money and run."

five

Friday, June 9

The Long Beach State University football stadium was packed shoulder to shoulder, back to chest. Rectangular banks of sodium arc lamps flared in series above the bleachers, creating an artificial noontime on the field. A broad rectangular platform with a gold skirt stood five feet off the ground at the fifty yard line. Two standing microphones were rigged in the middle. In front of this were three rows of thirty folding chairs. All were occupied.

To the left of the stage was a huge pile of wood, and on the grass to the right, plate-sized silver disks and some kind of fluorescent tape marked out an enormous X.

Cat and Jax edged their way through a crowd of expectant, adrenaline-inebriated young people, who cheered as if celebrating the end of a war. Cruising through the crowd were several dozen security men and women in golden uniforms, their expressions friendly but watchful. Just ahead of her, a blond Valkyrie of a security woman took a camera away from a girl, and give her a voucher stub in return. The girl pouted, but offered no serious resistance.

Cat and Jax slid on. She noted that the Valkyrie's shoulders were only an inch lower than Jax's. Cat whistled to herself. These folks were *serious*.

Venders walked through the crowd, selling little log-like confections called "Twin Cookies." Jax paid a dollar for one, unwrapped the cellophane, and took an experimental bite. He shrugged and handed the other half to Cat. "Tastes kind of gummy. Uncooked, like a molasses-peanut butter cookie."

"You keep it."

Jax carried a largish brown bag leaking grease stains shaped like Australia and Greenland. Cat carried a gift box just big enough to hold a cantaloupe.

They found their way to the correct row, and the right seats. Jax squeezed his bulk in and opened his brown paper bag, extracting a fistful of homemade popcorn. He offered some to Cat.

She turned her nose up in disgust, and then focused her attention back on the field in front of her. "Quite a show."

Jax nodded without speaking. "Isn't that Darryl Hannah over there?"

Cat shrugged. "Don't know, but I think I saw one of the Jackson Five."

That piqued Jax's interest. "Which one?"

"Zeppo, maybe." She shrugged. "Why?"

"Thought I could get the skinny on Mike's nose job. Wait. Something's coming. . . ."

The lights all over the stadium dimmed to half, and then a quarter, and night fell. Spectral golden spotlight fingers probed the clouds above them.

Slowly, Cat became aware of a steady *whoop-whoop-whoop* propeller sound. As yet, no aircraft was visible.

In the seats in front of them, a chunky young man in a beige TWIN CITY sweatshirt leaned over to speak to his girlfriend. He probably wanted to whisper, but against an ocean of sound, a whisper was an impotent weapon. "God," he said. "I can't believe I'm actually seeing them *live.*"

"As opposed to seeing them dead?" Jax muttered.

Cat elbowed him in the ribs, and leaned over. "Excuse me," she said. "I'm Cat, and this is Jax—"

The boy grinned, as friendly as a Pomeranian. "I'm Raymond. This your first time?"

Her smile was dazzling. "Yes. I've never seen them before. A friend said we just *had* to come."

Raymond beamed. "Right on! Change your life, man."

"Really?" Cat's voice sparkled with genuine curiosity. Turning that faculty on and off at will was one of her greatest people skills. "And how did it change yours?"

He leered at her. "Every way you could think," he said, "but you know, especially in the sack."

His girlfriend, who looked just a little too young for Cat's comfort, blushed and looked pointedly at the ground. "Oh, Raymond—"

Raymond seemed perfectly ready to swing the bedroom door even wider, but the distant rotor sound suddenly increased. "Wait . . . there they are!"

For an instant the spotlights probed only clouds. Then with a roar, a gold and silver helicopter crested the edge of the stadium, swooped up, and then settled toward the field. The theme from *Rocky* blared from the loudspeakers as the copter's landing gear touched down. The crowd cheered thunderously.

Cat wrinkled her nose. "Music's a touch incongruous for a pair of sex gurus, isn't it?"

"Dunno," Jax said thoughtfully. "Makes me want to pound some meat right now."

The attendees seated in the folding chairs covered their faces, as the props billowed dust in every direction, a thin brown cloud that momentarily obscured their view. As the dust began to settle, the helicopter door opened. A ramp extended to the ground, but the doorway remained empty.

The entire crowd seemed to hold its breath, and there was almost complete silence. Then two figures emerged.

"Joy and Tomo," Jax said, and she was surprised to hear a bit—just a bit—of genuine interest in his voice.

They wore some kind of blue one-piece suits with large gold buttons and high collars. Both wore their black hair straight back, to an inch above the shoulders. Viewed through the binoculars, it was difficult for Cat to distinguish their ethnicity. Asian features—yes, she could make those out. But the skin was a little too dark, and nose too broad—African? American Black? Perhaps, but certainly lighter than Jax.

No, the attempt to analyze simply fell on its face. She estimated their height at no more than about 5' 8" but they moved like dancers, carried themselves as if they stood ten feet tall. The stadium shook, rocked, roared with stomps and claps and cheers. Vast waves of approval crashed against the field and rolled back stronger instead of dying out.

"Brother and Sister?" she asked Raymond.

"Twins," he answered.

They walked down the shallow gangplank, hands linked and raised to the crowd. Regally, they strode to the foot of the raised wooden platform, where they paused, and shared a glance. Cat had the clear impression that they were giggling.

The music changed from its pugilistic theme to Queen's "We Are the Champions" and the two of them bounded up the steps. Joy made it to the top first, and snatched the microphone from her brother. There was a little sibling byplay as they pretended to fight over it.

Reading body language is a strange discipline, one part observation, and nine parts sheer intuition but over the years Cat had learned to trust her hunches. And right now, despite the obvious good humor of the byplay, instinct told her Joy was the dominant twin.

Why, then, did her eyes return again and again to Tomo?

"*We* are the champions," Joy cried triumphantly.

"All of us," Tomo continued. "Because we have the courage—"

"To throw away our fears, embrace the power, the *beauty* which is our birthright." They played off each other perfectly, picking up each other's lines as easily as an old vaudeville team. Cat wondered if it was stagecraft, or that little extra *something* twins were reputed to have.

Tomo continued. "Each and every one of your hearts told you it was time to come—"

"Together. To rise—"

"Beyond yesterday's limitations, and together—"

"We will stoke the fires within you, and bring you the pleasure—"

"The peace—"

"The success and power you want, you dream of—you deserve!"

The crowd went absolutely berserk.

"We consider all of you to be family," Tomo continued. "Chosen family, more important by far than the circumstances of your birth."

"We stand with each other," Joy said. "By each other, and for each other—and together, we cannot fail."

"We love you—you know that. And even now our ushers are bringing you unto us. . . ."

Very carefully and quietly, Cat had lifted her package up onto her lap. The "no photography" warning on the invitation had immediately triggered her evil streak. Just cussedness, she guessed. Just an aversion to anyone telling her she couldn't do something.

Inside the package was a compact camcorder, peeking out through a one-way mirrored hole. She hoped the autofocus was working.

"Come unto us," Joy said. "Put your faith in us, and you *will* be healed, I promise you."

Again (and it seemed to Cat for no really good reason) the crowd cheered.

"Pretty standard stuff here." Jax murmured. "Pretty bland. Nothing racy at all . . . nice turnout, though."

Tomo stepped forward, and another difference between the twins became apparent. Joy was the powerful one, filled with passion, her arm motions sharp and almost militaristic. In contrast, Tomo's gestures were rounded, gentle, almost effeminate.

"Come unto us!" Joy called. "Please come to us. Become ours, let us heal you."

Cat made a snap decision, based on nothing but gut instinct.

"Here," she whispered to Jax. "Take this, work it for me."

"Where the hell are you going . . . ?"

She was already heading down onto the field, joining a steady stream of afflicted winding their way toward the stage, merging with the group from the folding chairs.

She saw the usual lame and halt. Bandaged arms and legs. Crutches, eye patches, slings. One unfortunate boy bore the glistening pink scars of a burn victim.

Hell. What would she say if someone stopped her? Migraines, she decided. She had this killer, corkscrew-in-the-cranium, ratfuck-your-concentration migraine, and goddamn it, if Tomo and Joy could help her with it, she would throw her Bufferin away and buy a sunflower caftan *tomorrow*—

Or maybe she would have Tomo unknot her carefully tied Fallopian tubes. Maybe she could make that sound plausible, if she could invent a reason it shouldn't be a capital offense to deliberately bring a child into a world like this—

The line seemed to congeal as she hit the field, as supplicants were funneled into a column two or three abreast. As they approached, Tomo laid his hands upon them. Even from her remote vantage point, they seemed extraordinarily gentle hands.

And from that thought, without warning, her mind leaped and flared into a burst of anger. The sheer power of the emotional surge shocked and dismayed her. There was no rational reason for it except that . . .

Hell. These people were coming to him, trusting as children, and these bastards were abusing that trust, were asking people to have *faith* in them. And when, inevitably, they couldn't deliver, each personal night would grow just a little darker and colder.

The idea that so many hearts had opened, so much trust had been extended to these sharks, offended her deeply. She jumped line, and worked her way a little closer.

It wasn't the easiest thing in the world. Security down on the field was tougher than that in the stands. Down here on the grass, the gold-suited young centurions weren't smiling. Down here, they carried short batons in draw-cases at their belts. Some new emotion began to well up inside her.

She wasn't offended now. Now she was afraid, and for no reason that she could determine. The security people functioned primarily as crossing guards, assisting people in the line. Why then was she wary of them? They were only doing their job.

Something swept through her, a sudden, almost overpowering sensation that she didn't *belong* here. Cat wanted to be somewhere else— she didn't know where, just anywhere but here. She forced herself to continue forward. Pure panic response. Claustrophobia, agoraphobia, maybe

Churchill's phobophobia. Something clawed at her chest like an animal, made her feel tight and gassy in the belly, something was just *wrong*.

Up ahead, Tomo laid his hands on an old woman. Even through the crowd noise, even through Joy's steady platform spiel, Cat distinctly heard the woman sob. It was a broken sound, as if some thick viscous bubble of pain had percolated up from a ventricle and burst at the surface of her heart. Cat caught a flash-change in the woman's face. Something had happened. At first, Cat thought that she seemed impossibly *younger*. No, that was wrong. Not younger, but something even stranger. For just a moment, she had somehow *transcended* age, become a thing more of spirit than flesh.

For just an instant, Cat saw another woman behind the rheumy eyes, within the withered body. The wrinkled skin and age spots were still there, but something else was there, as well. The innocent, almost effervescent laughter of a young girl. Shimmering in those wrinkle-rimmed eyes were spring tears, brimming with the joy of sunshine following a terrible winter. Shining in her face was the promise of love.

All those things appeared in that withered crone, for just a moment, just a few seconds, just long enough to make Cat doubt her own senses. Then they was gone, and once again the old woman stood, hunched in Tomo's hands. Upon her wrinkled brow, Tomo bestowed the lightest butterfly of a kiss that Cat had ever seen.

Cat's anger burned brighter.

"Excuse me—!" a very tall, gold-suited security man called, and turned toward Cat. His motion was puppet-loose, his eyes intense, his shock of pure white hair a contrast with the extreme beauty and clarity of his complexion. His arms seemed firm but not freakish—this was no bodybuilder—but he projected a disorienting amount of physical vitality. His wrists were abnormally thick. Cat had the instantaneous sense that she knew this man. More to the point, that it would be prudent to stay away from him.

Cat hared the other way, seeking cover in the crowd.

She didn't understand why or what, she just understood that she had to get closer to Tomo. She had to get close enough to feel . . .

Feel what? Whatever there was to feel. To find the fraud here, to sense the sham. Innocent people were being hurt. How many of them might miss a chemotherapy session, might avoid consulting a physician, might disregard ominous X-rays because this pretty-boy laid his manicured hands on them?

As Cat slipped between two supplicants, she saw a man sob, and throw his crutches to the side, shrieking "I'm healed!!"

Yeah, sucker. And how much did they pay you to do that?

Joy's voice rose dramatically. "Come to us, one and all. You need not believe in us, believe only in your own senses—"

Right. Believe in yourself. That was something Cat Juvell understood about as well as a human being could understand anything. *Hysterical re-mission, shills, herd behavior. Nothing we haven't seen before.*

At that very moment, Tomo looked up. She thought that he was darker than he appeared from a distance. Their eyes locked, and Cat was swept with a feeling uncomfortably like sky-diving down a chimney stack.

There was a moment of contact so extreme that Cat thought she was going to drown. There was something infinitely comforting in those gray-black eyes, something kind beyond any ordinary sense of the word. He smiled, and in that smile there was something from which her conscious, calculating mind retreated.

It was music, it was a kind of comfort that she didn't, couldn't allow herself, not now, not in her adult past, not *ever.*

She heard a very still, very clear voice.

I can heal . . . , it said.

Are you mine?

She felt her shields peeling away, felt herself stripped naked and trembling before him. But instead of anger, or lust, or even triumph, she felt nothing from him save a deep and embracing love. Aching eons of time and a terrible, unsuspected weariness fell away from her. For a glorious instant, for the first time in her life she was fully understood and cherished and—

Then Tomo turned back to the woman kneeling before him. Cat was alone again, abandoned, vulnerable, buffeted by the crowd, the breath stolen from her lungs, the wind from her sails.

The crowd surged around her. She felt so small and frail that she might have imploded.

Suddenly the music quickened tempo. Colored lights fanned across the field, leading toward—a bed of coals. She couldn't get close to it, because a low fence had been set up, and here the security people formed a solid line. In the center of that line stood the thin, white-haired, thick-wristed giant. And despite herself, she understood that the security corps' major concern was the safety of an eager, surging crowd.

Tomo and Joy shared a quiet laugh. Tomo turned and mounted the stairs again. Two gold-robed acolytes knelt and slipped his shoes off, then performed the same service for Joy.

Still buffeted by the crowd, and cursing the fact that she wasn't six foot six, Cat snaked her way through, until she was at the front, pressed against the security rope.

The music was almost dancelike now. Rocking, a driving beat with a Latin flavor, a synthesis of Billy Joel and the Miami Sound Machine. Tomo and Joy stepped down from the stage toward the coals.

The crowd roared in rhythmic clamor, as if they never wanted it to end. "See!" they said. "And believe. See! And believe."

Cat didn't just hear them. She *felt* them, all around her. It reverberated inside her, lifted and carried her in its hands, and the air seemed to thicken.

The spotlight snapped onto Joy, whose arms were spread in cruciform.

All right. What was this? Cat didn't like the tremor in the internal voices, knew that all this choreographed chaos had put her on the emotional defensive. She wished that she was absolutely anywhere but in Long Beach.

Joy screamed the next words. "See!"

And Tomo echoed her. "And Believe!"

To the rhythm of the music, swelling and bursting and timed perfectly with their movements, they descended, bare feet pressing firmly against the bed of blazing coals.

The night wind shifted. Hot air slapped Cat's face, made her squint. She wasn't moving now, could only stare. The rest of the stadium had disappeared. The entire world had dwindled down to just Cat, Tomo and Joy, and the coals.

One at a time, the supplicants began a swaying dance step. Two at a time, they followed the Twins in a faith walk across the blazing coals.

And the chant continued. "See. Believe. See. Believe—"

Cat longed to follow them, to abandon rationality and simply trust in something, *just once, just once in your life.* . . .

But didn't. Longed to strip her own shoes off and dance across the fire. You'll be free, *free of your fears, free of the pain.* . . .

But couldn't.

Across the coals, the rhythm and the lights and the heat combined in an odd trancelike effect. Although her feet remained planted where they were, her mind seemed to float above the embers. She felt outside of herself, someplace strange and remote, adrift on a murky sea of sensation.

One step at a time, they walked across the fire.

No. *Coals,* Cat told herself. She was breathing hard, too hard, and remembering her physics. Wood doesn't transmit heat well. The Ledenfrost principle protects the feet of the faithful. That, and the layer of sweat on their soles. "Hell," she muttered, and was aware that she wasn't quite believing her own words. "Tony Robbins does it better."

As they came to the end of the bed of coals, the supplicants began to file off alternately to the left and right. Joy and Tomo continued to stand, facing the pile of wood.

The crowd was utterly silent.

Joy and Tomo just *stood* there on the coals. Their feet should have scorched, for sure. Cat could feel the heat from where she stood, strong and hot enough to fry her curls. *Jesus, that's not right, is it . . . ?*

Then Joy reached down between her feet and scooped up a handful of burning embers. She held them in her cupped hands.

"Damn," Cat whispered to herself. What was this . . . ?

Joy threw the coals into the air as if releasing a dove. They arced down over the pile of wood. They flared with light, bright, brighter, brightest, enough to sear the eyes, so bright she was unsure whether the embers or her own mind finally exploded into a scintilla of tiny stars. As they arced down over the pile of wood, it erupted into flame.

All Cat's inner voices and observer-mode cynical repartee fell utterly silent. She gawked like a six-year-old at her first magic show.

Cat hadn't noticed before this moment, but a set of wooden stairs had been erected in the near side of the blazing pyre. Incredibly, Joy and Tomo now climbed it together. It blazed beneath their feet. Their clothes didn't singe. Their hair didn't curl and brown. Their skin didn't sear.

At the very top, they raised their hands together, in triumph.

All around Cat, and all through the stands, the crowd broke into wild cheering, and Cat felt more alone than she had in her entire adult life.

six

"You're too close," Cat said to Tyler. "You always sit too close to the screen."

"You've been saying that since we were kids," he replied. His freckled face was about a foot away from the thirty-eight-inch wall-mounted video monitor. "And which one of us needs contact lenses?"

Cat snarled at him pleasantly, and returned her attention to the screen. Watching the rally through the camera lens was a hell of a lot less disturbing than attending the actual event.

"I don't know," Tyler said again. "Heat reflective clothing?" The video was shaky and amateurish, but explicit enough to clearly detail the previous evening's events.

"That is definitely Joy and Tomo up there on the bonfire." Jax was sunken deep in a leather recliner. In the last hour he had downed two bourbon-and-waters. She never saw him take a sip, but every time she glanced around, the fluid level in his glass was a little lower. This was his third, and she was determined to catch him sipping. So far, no luck. "Shit," he said for the tenth time in the last hour. "Those flames look real."

"There are ways to get around that," Tyler mused. "I could talk with some friends in Hollywood. Specially treated wood can produce a low temperature flame."

Cat remembered the waves of heat which washed over her. How her cheeks had almost blistered. How she had been forced to avert her face. Her skeptical response was frozen in her throat.

"What about air?" Jax said. "How can they breathe? There shouldn't be any oxygen up there, should there?"

"Okay, I'm stumped." Tyler said. "I don't know how they did it." He spun his wheelchair around. "All right, Cat. You were down there. What are we missing?"

On the tape, Joy and Tomo stepped down from the bonfire. The Bell helicopter awaited them. They were more than holding hands; Joy seemed to be leaning against her brother. Maybe she stumbled a bit: Cat wasn't cer-

tain. A tall, white-haired man took her other arm. The thick-wristed security man. There was certainly no bounce in her step. When they waved
good-bye to the crowd, weariness cloaked Joy like a shroud.

This display had cost them. If it was mere fakery (as it had to be), why
the exhaustion?

The helicopter blades increased their speed of rotation, blurred. The
big silver and gold craft vanished into the clouds.

"Jax—do you recognize the tall man?"

Jax shook his head. "No. Should I?"

"Not sure. I think I've seen him before." Her voice had a dreamy, far-
away quality to it. "How did they do this?"

"Not sure. I've got a pal up at the Magic Castle, though."

"Talk to the man," Tyler said.

"I mean—David Copperfield made the Statue of Liberty disappear, and
nobody genuflected."

He turned and looked at Cat, whose expression hadn't changed. "Is
there something wrong?"

She pulled herself back out of her self-induced trance. "No. Nothing
wrong. It's not worth getting upset about."

A stranger's voice said: "Is it worth a hundred and forty million
dollars?"

They turned. Standing in the doorway was a quiet but expensively
dressed man in his mid-forties. His hair was wispy and windblown, his
pudgy face framed by wire frame glasses and a salt-and-pepper square-cut
beard. A melon-sized pot belly swelled beneath his shirt, but he carried it
well. He had that slight but unmistakable gravity of the man who comes
from money. Clasped beneath his left arm was a legal-sized manila envelope.

Cat rose to her feet, and noticed that Jax had preceded her. Tyler
straightened in his wheelchair. "Doctor Sinclair?" Tyler said.

He nodded. "Tyler Juvell?" He shook Tyler's hand, and Cat was pleased
to note that he didn't hesitate to pump vigorously. Too many people shook
Tyler's hand like a limp noodle, as if his arms were crippled instead of his
legs. She immediately liked Sinclair.

"And you must be Porsche Juvell." He looked into her eyes very directly, and shook with a dry, warm hand.

He broke the eye contact just before it would have become uncomfortable for one of them, and turned to Jax.

Dr. Sinclair grinned up at Jax. "From your size," he said. "You can't be anyone but the notorious Jackson Carpenter."

Jax laughed, engulfing Sinclair's hand with his own. "Mea culpa."

"I saw your post-trial interview. Barbara Walters"

"I've regretted that a time or two," Jax laughed.

"Really, how?"

"Two weeks later I was shadowing a guy. Industrial job. Sonofabitch came up to me in the restaurant and asked for my autograph."

Sinclair roared appreciatively. "That's quite a story." Then he quieted, grew more serious. "I still think about that case. The Vasquez case. That was a bad one."

Jax shrugged. "Win some, lose some." The shrug was emphatic, but unconvincing.

Cat chimed in. "That's what the agency is about. We get to win a few."

"I can understand that. In fact, Mr. Carpenter—when Ms. Walters asked you about your military record—"

Jax became so quiet he seemed to steal sound from the rest of the room.

"—and your experiences in Vietnam—"

Cat glanced at Jax questioningly. His eyes narrowed a bit, but he was still calm. "I really don't talk about that much. However, Vietnam is a perfect example," he said, recovering smoothly. "You have to be willing and able to win. Otherwise don't fight."

With remarkable agility, Tyler whisked a chair out and around, presenting it to Sinclair.

"Thank you." Sinclair crossed his legs and slid the envelope from beneath his arm. He set the beige rectangle on his right knee and folded his fingers atop it. "In fact, I understand your philosophy perfectly. I like to win as well. Well, if you don't mind, I'd like to get right to the heart of this. Time is working against us."

"Coffee? Tea?" Cat asked solicitously.

"No, thank you."

"Pen?" Tyler asked, and handed Sinclair the check. Their guest chuckled and signed it atop the envelope.

"Fair enough. Now. A year ago, my younger sister Kolla fell under the influence of these frauds."

"Pretty impressive frauds," Cat said quietly.

"Kolla was impressed. Sufficiently to turn over her share of the family fortune to them."

That caught Jax's attention. "That's the hundred and forty million?"

Sinclair nodded. "Yes. Our father built Sinclair Electronics single-handedly. Computers, laser guidance systems, pacemakers, communications gear. You name it, he built it, and probably patented it. On her twenty-first birthday—six weeks from now—Kolla will sign the papers turning her share over to these charlatans. I believe they call themselves 'The Golden Sun.' "

"Twenty-one years old?" Cat asked. "That's all growed up, Dr. Sinclair. She can pretty much do whatever she wants. Exactly what did you have in mind?"

"I just want to talk with her. Be sure she's still herself. I love her, and care about her. She's always been a headstrong child, and at first this just looked like another of her adventures."

"So," Jax said. "You want us to find her, and get her out?"

"Yes."

Cat modulated her voice carefully. "And if she doesn't want to come?"

"We'll cross that bridge when we come to it."

"Nah," Jax said. "Let's cross it now. Kolla is twenty . . . any history of drug abuse?"

"The usual, I'm sure. Nothing heavy."

"Mental instability? Attempted suicide?"

"No. A morbid fascination for Sylvia Plath. Probably not unusual for college psych majors, though. That's what she was, before she dropped out to join this cult."

"Scientology?" Tyler offered. "Moonies? est? Young Republicans? Star Trek?"

Sinclair chuckled. "No. She's a normal, impressionable, headstrong, passionate girl. The stock is hers to do with as she will. I just want to be certain that she knows what she's doing. That she hasn't been coerced, or brainwashed. I haven't seen my kid sister in a year. Isn't it understandable for a big brother to be worried?"

"I don't know," Cat said. "These things can be pretty involved."

"I'll pay ten thousand dollars. For five minutes of talk."

Before Cat could answer, Tyler chimed in. "Fifteen. Half now, non-refundable, plus expenses."

"Tyler—" Jax said.

"Done," Sinclair said, rising. "Do we have a deal?"

Tyler and Cat both watched Jax. Normally, these decisions were Cat's, but with Jax threatening to leave the firm, his opinion carried a certain weight.

"Why us?" he asked.

Sinclair seemed to have anticipated this question. "The Twins . . . that's what they're called . . . have a Byzantine network of coffee shops, crash pads . . . you name it. Kolla could be anywhere. But some of the locales need a man. They're pretty tough."

"She's the tough one," Jax said modestly. "I'm the beauty."

"And some places need a woman."

Jax straightened in mock amazement. "You *are* a woman, then, Cat? I've heard rumors. . . ."

This time, Sinclair ignored him. "And frankly, there is a strong . . . I might say distastefully pervasive sexual element to the teachings, the environments they create . . . their entire cesspool of a cult. A male-female pair . . ." He let the sentence drain off, the implication clear.

There was a moment of uncomfortable silence, and then Cat spoke. "Jax and I have been divorced for almost a year now. Our present relationship is strictly business. I'm sorry if someone misled you."

Sinclair seemed completely unembarrassed. "I'm certain that camouflage is all that will be required. Do you think that will present a problem?"

The question was entirely reasonable, but for some reason, Cat still felt queasy.

Tyler spoke for her. "No, I guess not. . . ."

"Then it's agreed."

No one spoke up to contradict his assumptions. Sinclair nodded his satisfaction. His expression changed to one of polite curiosity. "Since we're in business now, I was wondering if you would answer a question."

Cat nodded. "Within reason."

"Why did you leave the police department? Not generalities—I've read your public statements about the Vasquez trial. I mean why *exactly.*"

The silence that followed was decidedly uncomfortable. "That was personal," Cat said.

Sinclair pressed on. "I really would like to know."

Jax looked at Cat. Perhaps because she didn't have her *shut the fuck up* expression in place, he spoke. "We knew that psycho slug killed his lover, and her twelve year old daughter. He got off because no justice system can resist eight million dollars worth of legal talent. That and one very special pussfuck who sold his guts."

"Jax . . ." Cat started, but her voice was already resigned.

"No," Jax said. Anger sizzled in his words, but none of it was directed at her. "Sinclair is paying enough. Maybe seeing Milton after all this time . . ."

"Milton?" Sinclair asked politely.

"Milton Quest." Jax paused. "Quest Security. Biggest in the west. Know how he started his agency? He was the original investigator in the Vasquez case. First on the scene. He found the knife and the bloody shoe. He was the first, critical link in the evidentiary chain. Quest actually retired before the case came to trial—he came back to testify.

"Cesar Vasquez . . . that grinning mudpimp bastard. Seen his etchings? His movies? Nauseating. Critics on both sides of the border eat it right out of his ass and then lick the spoon. One of those real cultured bastards—calls himself a 'magical realist' or something. God puts talent in the strangest fucking places. Vasquez can do it all: sculpture, stage, movies, books. Horror stuff. Choreographed a ballet once. Really vile, a cross between *Nutcracker* and *The Texas Chainsaw Massacre*."

"That's . . . a little hard to imagine."

"Tell me about it." Jax was warming to his story now, and his gaze was distant. "One thing I always noticed about his work. Yeah, I saw a couple of 'em. He could create monsters and demons and visions of hell like you couldn't believe—but no *people*. Never any people you really cared about. But God, if his human beings were only clay pigeons, he was knockin' them over with nukes. Audiences left his movies shell shocked. But I remember thinking: 'there's no *people* in his movies. I can remember the monsters, but I can't ever remember the *people*.' "

Jax took a pull of his bourbon. Cat almost didn't notice that he'd done it in front of her. For once, he wasn't playing one of his little games. "Even before the whole thing up in Cahuenga, I remember walking out of his movie, looking at the faces of the people around me, and thinking, 'this fucker is sick.' " He leaned forward. "He's not like someone like, say Stevie King. I always thought that King's best talent is characterization."

"I thought he was just another scare expert."

"Nope. He's a people expert. Take a look at one of his non booga-

booga books or movies. You know—*Shawshank,* or *Stand by Me*—what was the name of the book that one came out of?"

"Was a story," Tyler said. " 'The Body.' "

"Yeah. 'The Body.' No monsters. No killing. Just really great characters. People to believe in. That's why his stuff is scary—he creates people you care about. He understands families, and small towns, and personal hopes, and love. And because he understands it, he knows how to attack it so that it hurts."

"Isn't that sadistic?"

"I don't think so," Jax said. "But that's another discussion."

"I can see you've put some thought into this."

"I've had six years," he said grimly. "Anyway—so Vasquez has horror the likes of which King or Koontz or Barker have never dreamed. But his stuff doesn't really sell quite the same."

"And you have a theory about that?"

"Jax has a theory about everything," Tyler offered.

"Fuck you very much," Jax said pleasantly, and then continued. "Vasquez doesn't understand human emotion. He has no idea what a healthy family is. He doesn't really believe in that stuff. So even though he is brilliant—everyone agrees he's a better writer, a world class director, Christ, he should have it all over King—but doesn't. There's something dead inside that man. I'd seen him on talk shows, in interviews. There's just something wet and rotting inside. And I remember thinking that if that sonofabitch ever got writer's block, children would start disappearing from playgrounds."

The room seemed to have lost a few degrees of warmth.

"Anyway," Jax said. "We had his ass cold, after he butchered his girlfriend, and her kid. You remember how we lost the case?"

A few thought wrinkles appeared in the middle of Sinclair's brow. "I think so, yes."

"The defense accused Quest of being rabidly anti-Latino. Quest denied it all."

Cat sighed deeply. There was no way out of this but through it. "All right," she said, giving in. "Remember now? The defense produced a video tape made at a police convention back in Boise. Had Quest drunk, saying 'wetback' and 'fucking greasers' about twenty times a minute. Jesus, it was disgusting."

Sinclair nodded. "I remember, yes."

"Right." Despite herself, Cat was warming to the role of storyteller. "We lost the case. And six months later, Quest sued Vasquez and his lawyers on some bullshit defamation charge . . . and they settled out of court for two million dollars."

A long, telling pause followed.

Jax smiled nastily. "Within a year, Quest set up Quest Security."

Sinclair looked incredulous. "You're saying he threw the case? Compromised his own testimony?"

"Bingo," Cat said. "Merely by stating under oath that he had no anti-Latino bias. The convention took place a year after the murders—the trial began eight months after that. The defense got him to make that tape. He testified, then they blew his testimony out of the water, thereby corrupting the evidentiary chain, and he got his payoff right in plain sight. End of case. Nobody can touch him."

Another long pause. Sinclair's expression was unreadable. Then he said: "That was . . . subtle."

"Wasn't it, though? Cat and I broke our backs over that case. Vasquez went back to Panama, and he's still making movies. He's bigger than the fucking canal. Quest is rich. We got the hell out. I won't work for a system that rewards trolls like that."

Sinclair nodded understanding. "So now you make your own rules."

Cat shook her head. "When you have principles, you don't need rules."

Another long silence followed, and for a few moments, Cat was certain that they had lost him. Then he smiled. "I think I've found the right people. I trust I'll be hearing from you?"

Tyler grinned. "Step over to my desk, please? We'll need your signature in triplicate, and your deposit. We'll also need pictures, and all of the information we can get."

Sinclair dropped his manila envelope on Tyler's desk. "I think that you'll find most of what you need in there."

The envelope was a treasure trove: Photos of a pretty, dark-haired, full-faced girl in her late teens, with piercing eyes and a pouty smile. Photostats of birth certificates and a diploma from Colorado Springs High School. Copies of eighteen-month-old letters, and a list of names and addresses—most of them in Colorado.

"So . . ." Cat said slowly. "You and Kolla are from Denver?"

"Yes."

"Why are you looking for her out here?"

"These Twins have quite a chain of followers here—as you can see, she sent a few post cards from Southern California before she disappeared. There are other possibilities, as well, and I've contacted other investigators to search in New York and Toronto."

She closed her eyes as if watching a slide show against the inner lids. "What about boyfriends . . . lovers? If the organization is so sexual, I assume she had some steady intimates. Any idea about names?"

Sinclair nodded. "One she'd seen on and off for at least a year, a young man from Pomona, I believe."

"Name?" Jax asked.

"His name is Tony Corman, but that won't be much help. He's vanished as well."

seven

Portland, Oregon

In the final hours of his brief but unusually eventful life, Tony Corman did something extraordinary.

Corman was a deeply tanned, muscular man in his early twenties. He lay semiconscious in a bed on the seventh floor of Portland's Good Samaritan Hospital. His thick brown hair, normally tightly curled, lay slack with sweat. His dark eyes, set in an angelically beautiful face, were usually sharp with curiosity, wide with wonder. Now, pain and the drugs which had failed to relieve it rendered them as dull and flat as old nickels.

On either side of his bed, a nurse held his arms as he struggled to throw off the pale green hospital blankets. The woman on the left, a tall severe redhead named Rosemary, said: "Mr. Corman, please. Calm yourself. You're going to pull your stitches." To the nurse across from her, a short woman with a round pretty face, she said: "Bethany—hold him, please."

Corman whispered the words *"Iron Shadows."*

Puzzlement creased Bethany's cheeks. "What was that?"

"Help me," Corman groaned. "You have to help me."

"Your sister is here," Rosemary said. "She wants to see you, but you have to calm down. Would you like us to send her away?"

Corman's face distorted with the effort to relax. "No. No. Please."

"All right," Bethany said approvingly. "That's better." She stroked his cheek with one tapered hand. Bethany was slender and darkly olive-skinned, with high cheekbones which suggested an oddly attractive mixture of Black, Italian, and Native American. Her touch and voice seemed to reassure him.

"What do you think?" Rosemary asked.

Numbed by a brutally long shift, Bethany found it hard to think. Darn it, anything that might quiet Corman down was worth a try. The ward had rocked with his screams through a long and nerve-wracking night. "Mr. Corman? Would you like to see your sister?"

He nodded as if his skull were filled with broken glass, then spoke as if he had swallowed something corrosive. "Yes."

"All right," Rosemary said. "Bethany, why don't you show her in?"

Silvery morning filled the waiting room, warming the pale saffron floor and walls. An oval-faced, strikingly dark-haired girl sat in a plastic-backed metal chair, utterly absorbed by a wrinkled copy of *House and Garden.* She wore black silk pants and a knit yellow scoop-necked sweater showing two inches of tanned midriff. The sleeves were short with a scalloped frill. Her hair fell to two inches above her shoulders. It was extremely straight, and lustrous enough to reflect the overhead light.

Bethany said: "Kolla. Would you follow me, please?" The girl nodded her head fractionally and rose in one smooth motion. Her black and yellow platform shoes brought her height to just two inches below six feet. Her stride was long and confident.

Bethany rarely bothered to form opinions about the people who passed through her ward. Still, she couldn't shake the thought that, with the loss of perhaps fifty pounds, Kolla could succeed spectacularly as a fashion model. And it was just as evident that Kolla was utterly comfortable with her extra cushioning.

"How is he?" Kolla asked. Her voice was precise, alert.

"Stable." Bethany paused. "To your knowledge, does your brother use any non-prescription medication?"

Kolla's neatly pinked mouth wrinkled in distaste. "Do you mean illegal drugs? Of course not. Why?"

"In some ways . . ." Bethany considered her words carefully. "He seems to be going through some kind of withdrawal. We can't find any reason for his pain."

Kolla's face conveyed only concern and puzzlement, but something, some little butterfly of an alternate truth flitted behind her eyes. Swiftly here, just as swiftly gone. "The accident?"

"The broken leg, yes. We've dealt with *that*. This is something else. You're certain you know nothing about it?"

Kolla shook her head vigorously. "Nothing."

Tony's fevered eyes widened as Kolla entered. Bethany had the sudden, disquieting image of an alcoholic watching a bottle of Jim Beam roller-skate through the door.

Kolla turned to the nurses. "Could I see my brother alone, please?"

Rosemary nodded understanding. "I don't see why not. You can have ten minutes."

"Thank you."

Rosemary crooked her finger at Bethany. Both nurses filed out, and closed the door behind them.

Kolla approached Tony's bedside. He gazed up at her, trembling. Slanting louver light sliced his face into horizontal segments. Kolla trailed her fingertips across his stubbled cheek.

"Does it hurt?"

He nodded.

She leaned close, closer, intimately close, so that her full pink lips brushed his ear. "Have you talked to anyone? Anyone at all?"

His answering whisper was agonized. "No one. I didn't mean to run away. I was coming back." Kolla nodded her empathy and belief. "I just needed time to think."

"You shouldn't have left. It's not safe." She paused. *"She* thinks you've betrayed us."

Tears welled in his eyes. "I'm sorry," he said. "God, tell them I'm so sorry. Please. I would have come back."

Kolla's teeth worried her fleshy lower lip, and her face was filled with uncertainty. "It's all right," she said. "You don't have to be afraid of the Twins. But now, you're alone, and vulnerable. They can't protect you now." She leaned closer. "You know who'll come for you, Tony."

He nodded, ashen.

"Ask their help. Tonight, when you dream. We love you, Tony."

She reached beneath the covers, her fingers trailing down until they reached the fork of his thighs. She stroked until the flaccid organ beneath her palm began to swell.

His body arched, pressing against her hand, and he made an almost inarticulate mewling sound.

Her tongue flicked his earlobe. She whispered to him, with each breath blowing a tiny puff of warm air into his ear. "One last time, Tony." Each word was a kiss. "Have you talked? To anyone . . . . ?"

eight

Despite the daylight, to Tony the hospital seemed all shadow and echo now that Kolla was gone. The soft murmur and beep of the diagnostic equipment seemed somehow oppressive. His eyes darted left and right, up and down, searching. There was nothing out of place, nothing overtly threatening. Somehow, that was no comfort.

His groin ached; nurse Bethany's untimely return had interrupted Kolla's ministrations. Everything seemed to be going wrong. One moment of doubt, a single conversation overheard between mother and goddess, and he was damned. He shouldn't have taken the motorcycle, shouldn't have driven so fast or so far. But he had needed to clear his head. Needed time to think.

What did a few muttered words mean, devoid of context? *The Unveiling. Revenge. Death to the killers.*

Iron Shadows.

He shouldn't have listened. If he hadn't, he wouldn't know things that were none of his business. Did he trust, or not? Was he willing to give up judgment and extend faith, or not? He was such a little man, so unworthy, and had been given such gifts, by a *god.* There were such enormous things to be done, and so little time to do them.

Still . . .

Death to the killers.

Iron Shadows.

The hospital's sterile walls, its placid murmurs . . . somehow they added weight to his unease. The patter of nurses and technicians strolling unconcerned through the halls, obliviously preoccupied with their lives, their loves, their jobs . . . that very normalcy increased his sense of isolation.

He wanted to scream at them: *It's all about to change! Everything! You stupid, stupid people* . . .

But he didn't. He couldn't. Their very ignorance protected them. And as for a small, foolish man named Tony Corman, well . . .

What was it that curiosity had done to that cat?

The hours between three and five in the morning are called the "Hour of the Tiger," sacred to religious sects in places as far removed from each other as India and Central America. It is said to be a magical time, a time when the walls between the physical and spiritual are the very thinnest, when those with the courage to rise and meditate might glimpse the Divine.

It is also the absolute low in circadian rhythms. Between the hours of three and five hospital patients are most likely to slip away, and the slender thread connecting mind and body is most easily severed.

It is the hour of death.

Tony Corman slept, but his sleep was not restful. Again and again he awakened, tossing, as if some unspeakable, half-formed phantasm pursued him through the dark and twisting corridors of his dreamscape.

He mumbled the same words over and over again. Occasionally they emerged clearly, and could be understood as words separate from the steady jumble of sleep-speak.

He said: "Iron Shadows."

The hallways outside were relatively placid. The night shift was always quiet on the ward, and would probably remain so until the next shift came in at seven A.M.

For now, there were charts to examine, and the usual medications to set up and administer, midnight rounds for those patients requiring special care. But mostly, it was a time of peace, when books could be read, music listened to. Studies completed, homework begun.

With so much to do, it was hardly surprising that Bethany Edge, the duty nurse, barely noticed when the overhead lights began to dim and brighten, on an oddly rhythmic cycle mirroring the sixty-two beats per minute of the average sleeping heart.

In Tony Corman's room the EEG and other monitoring equipment hummed at the very periphery of his consciousness. The electronic sounds were always there, part of the regular background noise of any hospital.

Suddenly, the sound began to peak and then fall away on a steady cycle, rising and falling with a curiously organic manner.

Something else, even more curious, began to happen. The air around Tony Corman began to glow. There was no one in the room to notice, and even if there had been, there was sufficient light to obscure the moment at which the phenomenon commenced. At first, a few hairs on his arms stood up and danced, as cobras beckoned to the flute. Then something like a heat mirage began to shimmer about him, a pulsing cloud perhaps an inch deep. At first the disturbance was a wavering without color, merely an optical illusion. Then it crackled, a few tiny pink sparks leaping away from his skin, the sparks diffusing into a translucent mist which occasionally condensed again into sparks—cilialike, barely visible, but sparks nonetheless.

Tony's eyes drew up halfway, the pupils hanging heavily at the edge of the lids. Not quite awake, nor completely asleep. Drowsing, still half immersed in dream. The ceiling lights pulsed dully, steadily. The television screen bolted in the room's upper right corner should have been completely black. Instead, it throbbed with pale colors, flickered on and then died again, as if fed a bare, uneven trickle of power. He wasn't certain at all that anything in the room was real—in his life, dream had come to mingle all too freely with reality.

His hand cast about groggily for the call button, but even as his fingers closed on it, he experienced a tightening in his groin, and gasped.

Sleeping. He had to be sleeping. The sheets around his waist began to bunch up, as if pulled by invisible threads. Bunched and twisted like a handkerchief being knotted into a puppet by an imaginative child. But they didn't form into a rabbit or duckie. No, they formed into something which, every moment, betrayed more and more of the roundness of a human head.

He felt the stroke of invisible fingers, a spectral touch trailing up his erect penis, rolling up to offer the very briefest flash of pleasurable pain from a squared fingernail. A phantasmal tongue offered a lingering, silken caress.

He hung there, suspended between dream and reality, longing to simply slip back into the mists of sleep, unwilling to break the spell, longing for it to intensify.

Corman closed his eyes and fell into blackness, waves of pleasure engulfing his body. His erection swelled, grew hot and heavy as if returned to Kolla's skilled embrace. A vortex of fire and wetness and *God yes oh God oh God, it was so good, so good it was almost . . .*

Almost . . .

Like . . .

The liquid sensation intensified. The sensation went beyond pleasure now, heightening to a place surpassing ecstasy, beyond even pain, as if something were simultaneously draining him and injecting the most exquisite poison. He heard himself scream *yes yes yes yes,* body arching as if everything inside him were one fluid mass, coming to a boil, bursting at the seams. He inhaled, inhaled, inhaled, couldn't seem to stop, the top of his head flying further, and higher, and up and away and—

Ohhh

Myyy

God.

Bethany Edge hated night duty. It was, however, the available shift, and she was able to jury-rig a child care schedule to accommodate it. Bethany was married to an engineer named Tommy Edge, and had borne him two children. Tommy's job on Alaska's North Slope kept him far from home six months out of the year. Bethany found the money less attractive than the consistent activity—a remedy for boredom. The same drive motivated her college studies. She was tired of nights alone without her Tommy, and, if truth be told, had begun to do something about it. Those efforts began with a quiet date with the X-ray tech on Six. Well, the date had *started* quietly, anyway. By the end of the evening, both of them were making quite a bit of noise. She remembered that wistfully, and her memories were making the delicious transition from auditory to kinesthetic when the screaming began.

"*Oh God. Godgodgodgod—*"

Who was that? And what? Nightmares, she would bet. But sweet Jesus, it sounded like someone . . . well . . .

Like someone having one *hell* of a good time.

She stopped thinking and began to walk. Then she ran. The tenor of the scream suddenly, drastically altered, became an agonized contralto. Bethany began to run, envisioning a collapsed bed, and the resultant shower of insurance forms. She fantasized about miscalculated drug dosages and needles slipping out of bruised veins.

Halfway down the hall, she finally noticed the overhead fluorescents flickering on and off rapidly, as if something were tickling the power circuit. Some kind of electrical surges, maybe? At the very moment that thought crossed her mind, the entire hall went black. She stood still, momentarily shrouded in shadows deep enough to swallow thought. Had lightning struck the power lines? A Portland June could be wet . . . hell, *any* month could be wet in Portland, but if it was raining outside, she had failed to notice.

The tubes overhead flickered halfheartedly, then died again.

Bethany walked more carefully now. Something was very wrong, and the screams were coming from right in front of her, all pleasure long since stripped away, leaving only the torment of raw, bleeding nerves. Tony Corman again. He had been quiet for hours, and had never been *this* bad.

A door on the opposite side of the hall clicked open, and a wizened little man in a paper gown emerged. His hair was no more than a few tightly curled white wisps against his black scalp. "What the hell's going on?" he asked, voice shaking.

"Please sir. Return to your bed. This is being handled." He hesitated. "Please," she repeated. He disappeared into his room.

Her certainty seemed to have vanished with him. Suddenly, the very last thing she wanted was open the door in front of her. What she wanted, more than anything in the world, was to go back to her desk, and pretend that nothing at all was happening. In fact, what she really wanted was to crawl *under* the desk.

But now there were two other patients staring at her, wondering why she didn't go ahead and open the door, search out the source of those ghastly wet screams.

Her hand turned the knob.

With an almost obscene finality, the screams halted. The lights returned fully, swallowing the shadows. Bethany stood frozen there, unable to make a conscious decision, watching her hand turn without volition.

A rustle of cloth behind her. She barely managed to turn her head enough to see who or what it was.

The head nurse stood close at her shoulder, a tiny, fifty-year-old grandmother with piercing pale eyes and the driving energy of a jackhammer. Her name was Lisha Maltz. "What the hell is going on here?" Maltz demanded. "I heard that scream down on Two. What was it?"

Bethany still didn't answer. Couldn't answer. And Maltz stared at her. "What's the matter with you? I asked you a question."

"It was Mr. Corman," Bethany said, very softly.

Maltz looked from the door to Bethany, and back again. She pried Bethany's hand away from the knob, and opened it.

The room was dark, save for a wedge of light which broadened as she pushed the door open. Everything looked perfectly normal.

The last thing revealed by the widening wedge of light was Tony Corman.

His naked body arched tautly, his clothes shredded into rags by his own hand. Corman's eyes bulged sightlessly. His hips bucked, as if ridden by a phantom lover. Milky strings of semen glistened wetly on his belly, speckled the sheets and blankets.

He spoke no words, merely kept mewling that awful, broken animal sound. The spasms ripped through him again, stronger and stronger even as they watched, frozen in the doorway. With awful inevitability the screams lead to one final, ultimate muscle-locking contraction—

That terminal convulsion continued for seconds that stretched like hours. Corman's muscles strained against his skin, bursting out as if someone had clipped one end of a set of battery cables to his testicles, and the other to the battery posts of an old Ford truck. And then gunned the engine. Grinning.

The scene was unspeakably grotesque, but became more so as Bethany's eyes accustomed themselves to the darkness. She had assumed that the knot of sheeting at Corman's midsection was just a random twist of linen. Now eyes wide, she realized she was very wrong. The sheets moved with a life of their own, bulged obscenely as if they concealed a puppeteer's hand. They made a bulbous shape, something obscene and insectile, with thin, fibril legs and a swollen abdomen. For a fleeting instant, she thought she detected the caricature of a woman's face in the twists of cotton. The thing perched in Tony Corman's lap, hunched over his genitals sucking and pumping, feeding like a gigantic cotton spider.

Bethany watched as his left biceps muscle tore loose from its insertion point. The trapezius bulging between neck and shoulder, crawled like a snake and then ripped free, knotting like a big fist beneath his skin. Somewhere in his body a bone went crunch-*crack!* and then another *crack!* and another one. Tony Corman virtually levitated from the bed with the violence of his response.

He screeched, clamped his teeth down on his tongue and chewed. Blood and saliva foamed from his mouth, the scream bubbled away to nothing and his body just . . .

Sagged.

Relaxed. All of that awful, terminal tension just suddenly . . . gone. Gone, like a wisp of smoke from an extinguished flame.

The bulbous arachnid sheet-shape flattened out, like a balloon collapsing in slow motion.

Gone.

Maltz slammed the door shut. She spun and gripped Bethany's shoulders. "Call security, dammit." It was a scream, and Bethany was still staring at the door, realizing distantly that Maltz had said those same words twice before. She still stared as Maltz reared back and slapped her across the face with her open palm, the sound of the crack resounded down the hallway almost as loudly as had Tony Corman's anguished cries.

Then and only then was Bethany able to snap out of it, turning and running, running, and she didn't stop at the nurse's station. She kept running until she reached the fire exit, and was halfway down the stairs before she realized that the screams ringing in her ears were her own.

nine

Monday, June 12

Early June is an odd time on Southern California beaches. The sands are gorgeous, sparkling white, dotted but not yet glutted with humanity. The waves churn in toward the shore in their eternal rhythm, a comforting consistency in a world of change. The beach culture had fully emerged from winter's hibernation: the surfers, swimmers, joggers, sidewalk venders, street artists, the roller skaters. The carny pitch men working the pier. The retirees who stroll in their purple shorts and *I Love My Grandkids* T-shirts—those universal senior uniforms proclaiming victory in the game of Life, and an exit from its competitive grind.

Tiles in a uniquely Californian mosaic.

Venice, California was named with her Italian sister city in mind. There are miles of canals which, following a decent rainy season, are actually passable. Gondola rides are reasonably priced and considered, at least by Angeleno standards, an unbelievably romantic Valentine or anniversary present.

A kind of super-compression exists in Venice. In some ways it resembles San Francisco: its twisting warren of streets favors pedestrian above automotive traffic. Tiny cafés sprout in the least likely places. Graying flower children and hippies seem to emerge from wormholes connecting the '90s to the '60s, complete with granny glasses, tie-dyed shirts, and black-light Strawberry Alarm Clock posters.

Cat and Jax ambled through a walking tour of the area, stalking their way toward a coffee shop known to employ Golden Sun members. They soaked in the day, enjoying themselves and the light street traffic, stopping in shops and cafes to display a three-by-five photograph of Kolla Sinclair.

"Let's try this," Cat said, and entered a coffee shop amusingly named *The Human Bean.*

The aroma of roast espresso enveloped them like a warm blanket. The counter girl was a pale little thing with narrow shoulders and broad hips. She compensated for unspectacular physical assets with a hundred-watt smile. Cat ordered a café mocha, Jax a latté.

"Is that on your diet?" Jax asked.

"Chocolate and caffeine cancel each other out," she said piously.

"The perfect food." .

The counter girl introduced herself as Donna and scribbled down their order. She disappeared behind the counter and immediately began arcane manipulations of a steaming chrome machine. Donna used no superfluous motions at all, her every flick of wrist and forearm as economical as a sushi chef's.

By the time that twin streams of fragrant black liquid drizzled down into the cups, Jax had worked his way through half of the framed photos circling the wall.

They were an interesting lot: Tomo shaking hands with President Clinton. Joy harnessed in some kind of a weightlifting apparatus, lifting a Volvo's rear wheels about three inches off the ground. Tomo in a track suit at a Golden-Sun-sponsored twenty-four-hour marathon. Joy seated in a cross-legged meditation posture. Some kind of glossy photographic enhancement gave her a saintlike aura. Tomo holding two small children close, grinning into the camera. Joy standing on a platform, arms raised to the heavens. Tomo giving the benediction at some kind of very posh looking business meeting. And so on, and so on.

In two of the pictures, standing quietly in the background, was the tall, white-haired man. His thick hands were folded in front of him. His expression was attentive but neutral.

Just who the hell was he?

Cat went to the counter and showed Donna Kolla's picture, received a negative response, and paid for the coffee. Jax sniffed his with satisfaction, and then sipped. "Well, whatever else you can say, they make a good cuppa. Any luck with the picture?"

Cat shook her head. "Nope."

"Notice anything odd?" Jax pointed to the wall photos.

Cat shook her head. "Just Tomo's haircut. He looks a little like Moe. I always liked Curly better."

"You know, if they can do something as spectacular as that fire stunt, why aren't there pictures of it? I mean, why isn't it everywhere? If you wanted to promote yourself, wouldn't you put your very best foot forward and build everything else around it?"

She sipped. "You're mixing metaphors, but it's a good point. Let's ask Donna."

They sat next to the window, enjoying the sunshine. A laminated plastic menu was propped between a spice shaker and a honey jar. Cat glanced at it. It listed such delectable items as sunflower cakes and prune preserves, baked soybean curd in New Orleans sauce, and black bean and lentil soup. The scent of fresh-baked muffins wafted sleepily through the room.

Donna finally came back from behind the counter. "Can I get you folks anything? A nice piece of prune cake to go with that?"

"Sounds yummy," Cat ignored Jax, who mimed a gagging motion at Donna's back. "Are all Golden Sun restaurants vegetarian?"

"No, they encourage us to follow our appetites. My guy and I are just vegan, that's all."

"Hmmm. Listen. We went to the last rally—"

Donna's thin legs nearly buckled. "Me, too!" Some of her reserve vanished. With that admission, Cat had gained admittance to a great and secret tribe. The decoder ring was probably in the mail. "Wasn't it just too *much?*"

"Do they always do the fire thing?"

Her eyes were darkly humorous, and that expression transformed her face. Suddenly, Donna was lovely. "Not all the time. But often. They don't encourage us to talk about it."

"Really? Why not? I mean, wasn't there a bootleg tape on *Hard Copy*, or something?"

"*Unsolved Mysteries.* The Amazing Randi did a number on them. The Twins just aren't interested in proving anything to professional skeptics. They do things like that to show us what's possible. But if we concentrate on that stuff, people will miss the big picture. Or try to walk on fire, and get hurt."

" 'We are trained professionals. Don't try this at home?' " Jax said.

"Kind of."

"Lifting Volvos is okay, though?"

Donna giggled. "Isn't she *strong?*"

"So . . . no fire pictures around the restaurant." Cat drummed her fingers against the table top, and pondered, then went ahead and asked the question on her mind. "There's a tall, white-haired man in several pictures. I saw him at the rally, as well. Just who is he?"

Donna's eyes narrowed, as if she was about to share an awesome secret with them. When she spoke, it was in a tone ludicrously close to a jail house whisper. "That's Manfred Gittes."

"Who?" Jax asked. Cat felt a little tingle of surprise at the base of her spine.

"Manfred Gittes. He's their bodyguard, and Aikido instructor. He's probably the best martial artist in the world." Donna grinned and bent closer. "I think he's Joy's lover, too."

Jax shrugged and looked at Cat, who's expression had grown thoughtful.

The front door jangled. Donna turned as a tall, marathon-lean young man entered the restaurant. He would have made two of her. The sallow girl flushed, actually reddened at the sight of him.

He winked at her, and slipped behind the counter.

Donna shifted her feet side to side like a little boy waiting in a long urinal line. "Is there anything else I can do for you?"

"No. The mocha is excellent."

Donna twinkled impishly and excused herself. She went to stand beside the tall boy, busying herself at the cash register.

"Gittes," Jax mused. "Where have I heard that name? I don't read karate magazines."

"He's a professional. Used to do bodyguard work in Europe. Supposed to be excellent," Cat said.

Jax grunted and confined his attention to his latté for a few sips. Then Cat said, very softly, "Don't make it too obvious, but catch a glimpse of what's going on behind the counter."

He found a mirrored award plaque, and watched.

Donna and her boyfriend were standing very close together. Apparently, he busied himself arranging honey rolls, and she was counting register receipts. Except . . . that they were too damned studiedly ignoring each other. The boy turned and gave Donna a brief, steamy look. Then went back to sorting sweet rolls. One handed.

And then Jax saw that Donna was also working one-handed.

"Ah . . . I'd say that their other hands are busy," Jax said.

"Ummm-humm." Cat said quietly, taking another sip.

"Ah . . . are they feeling each other up?"

"Yep." Cat was apparently staring out the window, but she had extraordinary peripheral vision. "And the pace just quickened. And he just got a little wet flush on his forehead. Oh, I'd say that these two are beyond first base. We have definitely entered the digital age."

"His knees just buckled a bit. Now he steadied himself." Jax shook his head. "Jeeze. That was quick."

"Ah, youth," Cat said. She drained her cup. "Makes you wonder, though."

"Wonder what?" Jax asked, sipping.

"Wonder what kind of cream they used in your latté."

Jax choked, but managed not to spray. He glared at her, and discreetly spit the mouthful back into his cup. He got up very carefully, left two quarters on the table, and walked briskly out of the coffee shop.

As they left, Donna and her boyfriend waved merrily at them. One handed.

Cat caught up with Jax, and linked her arm through his. "Beautiful day, isn't it?"

Jax made a retching sound. "Shut the fuck up."

"God," Cat beamed. "I love this job."

ten

Tyler's van was parked across the street from a bookstore near the corner of Selma Avenue and Caheunga Boulevard. The entire trip wasn't as depressing as he had feared. Hollywood was making a bit of a comeback—right now, it wasn't as bad as he remembered it as a kid, maybe twenty years before. He remembered coming up here to buy or sell comic books at the used book store off Wilcox, and actually being terrified by the street denizens.

That was back when he would jump on the bus by himself, or sometimes with Cat, and go almost anywhere. That was before—

He cut the thought off. He really didn't want to go down that road. There was no purpose to it, really.

Anyway, Hollywood was no longer frightening. A little depressing, perhaps. There was too much trash on the street, human and otherwise. Too many adult bookstores and pawn shops. Too many grates across too many empty, dusty windows. Bottle-strewn vacant lots. The movie theaters looked a little forlorn, as if in their very brick and concrete foundations they remembered better, brighter days.

Dawn's Light was one of two book emporiums in the Southern California area known to be owned by Joy and Tomo's followers. In addition to their athletic and humanitarian accomplishments, the Twins were prolific writers. Between them, they had published—mostly in the form of small press efforts—close to three hundred books, dating back to the late sixties.

As far as he could determine, the volume he held in his hands, *See and Believe,* was their longest work. The Twins had written it jointly, alternating chapters. Ordinarily this would have seemed a clumsy approach, but they were of sufficiently similar mind that it worked seamlessly. He had begun reading it the previous evening and, before he ventured into Dawn's Light, decided to continue onward for another chapter.

He opened the book to page seventy-eight, and began reading.

Dissection Day

The truth behind my first public demonstration is a story I relate here for the first time. It occurred in our sixteenth year, while we attended Dorsey High School in Los Angeles. This was the time of our awakening. In our mid-teen years, the changes within us began to accelerate.

Biology class was the third period of the day. I enjoyed the sciences more than did sister Joy, who preferred math and history. Or sports. As I have said, Joy has always loved sports—and they certainly adore her in return.

Our high academic standards earned us a measure of flexibility in our school schedule. I elected to take biology, while Joy selected chemistry that semester. Whenever possible, we attended different classes. Mother drilled this into us, always concerned that we develop as two separate beings, not as one creature with two bodies.

It may seem odd, but I loved that classroom. The teacher's name was Miss Novokow, a plain, unmarried woman of great warmth and intellect. She filled that room from floor to ceiling with little boxes and charts and glass beakers and specimens neatly sorted and pinned to display boards. The room was choked with aquariums and cabinets, microscopes and beakers filled with chemicals of all kinds.

Because she also taught botany, there were several little glass or plastic planter kits rowed with alfalfa, beans and corn sprouts. The room always smelled *green*. Sometimes she would have us press the seeds against glass with black construction paper or cotton so that, as days passed, we could watch them grow. It was wonderful.

I partnered with a girl named Nadine Izumi. She was the loveliest thing I had ever seen, and probably my first love. Her bangs were cut straight across her forehead, and her eyes were a kind of crystalline black. She seemed too fragile for this world, a slender, elfin, almost translucent beauty. I swear that sometimes I could see the sun through her. Nadine was like a deer or a mouse. She would eat with little, absurdly delicate and polite nibbles, pausing at any sound to look around and see if it might mean her harm. Only then would she return to her meal.

She was so beautiful that sometimes I would just stop eating or writing or whatever else I was doing to stare at her.

I'd loved her since seventh grade, but she never really knew I existed. I wasn't a person. I was one of the Twins, and that put me in a different category of humanity. I was Joy's brother. Joy was Tomo's sister. I think that for a lot of the kids, that was just the way they saw us.

But this year, I was Nadine's partner, and we worked together, and laughed together. For once, maybe for the very first time, she was seeing me. *Me,* not just Joy's other half, but Tomo Oshita, who adored her hopelessly. Not just the straight-A student who was too clumsy to be picked for any sport save Murder Ball. (I still twitch when I think about those elementary school games, the balls screaming in at me so fast. Hitting me in the head, in the hip, knocking me from my feet. Banging my head against the backboard. And all the kids, even Joy, screaming at me to get up, get up, when I fell down. Sometimes I hurt my knee, and when I did, I cried.)

I warned you I would ramble some.

Anyway, on this day, we were supposed to choose an "A" and a "B" member of the team. Nadine knew what we would be doing today. Today was dissection day. We'd been building up to it for a month.

I was fascinated by all of amphibian arcana: frog estivation and burrowing frogs and tree frogs, biting frogs and clawing frogs, frogs that rained from the sky. Frog diets, frogs who secrete poisons, hallucinogens and medicines, frogs tiny enough to sleep in your nose or be devoured by carnivorous plants, and frogs big enough to eat snakes and knock men down.

It was all great fun to me, but I knew that one day we would have to do something more with frogs than merely study them.

There was a boy in class named Mike Tyree. He was a huge pale whale of a boy, well over six feet tall. He had eyes for Nadine, as well. Even if she never really saw me as an individual, she liked Tyree even less. He was always trying to get her attention, and it didn't much matter whether it was in a positive or a negative way. Like me, he just wanted her to know he existed.

Tyree had plagued me since elementary school, but I could do nothing. He was just too big. And Joy, though she would stand up for me against most adversaries, couldn't hope to match Tyree physically.

Of course, by the time her other abilities began to develop, Mother's Rules were firmly in place, and neither of us would have dreamed of disobeying them.

On the day it happened, Nadine and I sat at our desk/table arrangement. I guess we were both giggly and a little nervous, filled with the kind of kid bravado that gets us through the worst times.

I remember fourteen pairs of partners, one at each desk. Tyree was partnered with another young thug named Tyrone Carter. Tyree and Tyrone. Ebony and Ivory, living to inflict agony. Think McCartney would mind if I rewrote that?

Anyway, after lecturing us all on the seriousness of what we were doing, each team sent one partner up to the front of the room, made obeisance and received in return a metal tray with swabs, a scalpel with a disposable blade, tweezers, surgical tape—and most importantly, one anesthetized frog.

I was surprised by its size. It was bigger than my fist, with a swollen belly and dull, protruding eyes. A pale mark, something between a leaf-shape and a comma, curved between its eyes, marring the perfection of its greenish brown skin. I could feel its tiny bones through it slack, rubbery cool flesh.

It was an *R. clamitans,* the common North American green frog. It lay splayed out on the little metal tray, pale underbelly exposed to the air. I rested my finger against it. Its little heart beat very quickly.

I remember carrying it back to the table I shared with Nadine. This little creature was about to die, so that I could learn something important about the structure of the world around me. Do I think that this is or was wrong? No. All animals must kill to live. One thing distinguishing mankind is that we must also learn in order to live. It is then no sin to kill if in so killing one learns something important to survival.

What then is the secret of maintaining that perspective so necessary for spiritual growth? We must always remember that the creature on the dinner table, or the specimen table, has given its life for us.

Whether we eat it, or learn from it, we must respect it. Acknowledge its contribution to our own life and growth. And never kill for the dark pleasure of the killing. That way lies damnation.

I remember saying a prayer to the frog's little spirit, asking it to understand why I must do what soon I would do.

Do frogs understand prayers? I don't know. But they are alive, and like all living things, fight for life, and in that fight, feel fear.

Completely absorbed. Those words would describe my relationship with the frog as I carried it back to Nadine.

She stared at me, watching from someplace behind her eyes. Perhaps I should have been more concerned about my partner, should have noticed, but I didn't.

Nadine moved very close to me, shivering. Perhaps she came close to me because almost for the first time, my attention wasn't on her, but on the task at hand.

She watched as I washed its belly carefully with an alcohol-dampened swab. A short strip of tape anchored each webbed foot to the tray.

Perhaps I was humming to myself, or talking to myself, because Tyree, who stood at the table in front of me, turned and snapped: "Are you gonna stab that frog, or talk it to death, moron?"

Quietly, I said, "the frog has to die. I see no reason to disrespect it as well."

He stared at me, and then he laughed, and the whole class was laughing, except for me, and Nadine. She was trembling. Then she screamed in a voice even higher than her usual squeak. "Leave him alone!" It was like a little bolt of lightning shot through the class, rattling the windows and, for a moment, stopping all action or conversation.

I remember that moment. It was one of the best in my young life.

By now she was shaking all over, and Novokow clapped her hands together at the front of the class and brusquely told us all to be quiet. We had work to do.

I remember the last look Tyree gave me before he turned back around. It was pure murder. He had lost, and I had won, and everyone knew it. Judging by what happened later, I think that was the moment he decided to hurt me.

Looking back, it is easy to forgive him. I think perhaps on some deeply subterranean level, we all know the time of our deaths. Some of our hunger for love, or fame, or wealth comes from a desire to achieve goals in an attempt to outrun the engulfing darkness. Perhaps Tyree anticipated the short time remaining him, knew that within weeks a terrible accident would fill all needs and answer all questions. I wish I had known: I would have felt no pleasure in his discomfort.

Instead, as any child might, I gloated.

Novokow clapped her hands again. "A's?" she said. "You have completed your preparation? Raise your hands if you have NOT." Michael Tyree's hand went up, and then faltered.

"All right, then. B's, if you would? You will make the initial incision."

Beside me, Nadine went rigid. "I just can't," she whispered. "I'll hurt it."

"It doesn't feel anything," I said. "It's asleep." Her face was very pale.

I leaned close and whispered to her. "I'll do it if you can't."

When I looked up, Tyree was glaring at us, his expression one of venomous glee. "Miss Novokow?" he shouted, raising his hand. "Miss Novokow? Nadine's refusing to make the cut."

Novokow glared at him witheringly, but came down the row to talk to us. Every eye in the classroom was upon us. After all, if she let Nadine refuse, where would the day's experiment be? Nadine was hardly the first eighth grader to refuse to murder a hapless amphibian.

Novokow leaned over and whispered to Nadine. "You don't think you can do this?" she asked. Nadine shook her head. The class was silent. All ears seemed to be tilted in our direction.

"Won't you even try?" Her voice was very kindly. The wind rattled the blinds a little bit, blowing an aroma from the lunch room. I remember that smell. Coconut and oatmeal. How inappropriate was that happy cookie aroma!

Nadine shook her head sadly.

"If you don't, do you understand that I'll have to give you an 'F,' " she asked.

Nadine was crying now. Tyree and his buddy Tyrone snickered. "Why?" Nadine asked.

"Because if I let you refuse, I'd have to let anyone else do the same. Can't you see that I can't do that?"

Nadine searched Novokow's lined face. There was no cruelty there. I think Novokow had nieces and nephews she adored. She would have said the very same thing to them, I'm sure.

Slowly, Nadine nodded her head. Her eyes looked glassy. When she picked up the little razor-edged scalpel by the wrong end, I said "Nadine!" and she dropped it back on the tray. Breathing shallowly, she picked it up again.

Her entire world focused down to just our table, that tray, her two hands.

Three times she brought the scalpel close to the flesh of the sleeping frog, and three times her hands shook too greatly to attempt the incision. She looked at me again, pleadingly and then up at Novokow, who stood back behind her desk at the front of the room. Her view of our table was blocked by the joint bulk of Tyree and Tyrone.

The first of Mother's Rules was never to lie, or to cheat, but this seemed like a good occasion to break it.

"Give me the scalpel," I whispered. "Give it to me. I'll do it."

She looked over at me with gratitude in those lovely eyes. Eyes that haunt me still. She handed the blade to me—

Before it reached me, Tyree had her hand in his paw. "No you don't," he said, and slammed hand and knife down into the exposed belly of the frog.

The frog *exploded.* Blood and guts went everywhere, splashing up on Nadine's face, in her eyes and her shocked, open mouth. Suddenly she was shrieking and screaming and screaming. Even Tyree was surprised and frightened, because what he had intended as a joke—however cruel—had become something else.

She was on the floor, thrashing, spitting, spitting, fingers tearing at her mouth as if trying to tear her own tongue out. Novokow was over her in a minute, trying unsuccessfully to calm her. "What happened here?" she demanded.

"I . . . I dunno," Tyree said lamely. He seemed to be searching for a flat rock to crawl under.

Nadine was having trouble breathing.

Had I been able to reach her, I might have tried to take her pain and fear into me, as Mother warned me never to do publicly.

Instead, I turned to the dying frog. No one watched me. All eyes were on Nadine.

Its tiny heart was bared by the brutal slash. Incredibly, it was still beating, spurting blood into the ragged wound. Its little eyes stared up at nothing. I pried one finger under its flattened head, looking at the white marking. Part leaf. Part comma. I remember thinking crazily that, considering what had just happened to it, a semicolon might have been more appropriate.

I do not know if it felt pain. I know that Nadine did. I know that I did.

"Nadine," I said. "Look." My voice was very calm. Soft, but there must have been something in it, because the other girls and boys quieted and turned to look at me. Novokow's face tilted up from the shivering girl to gawk at me. Then, somehow, even Nadine quieted and her eyes focused on me. On my hands.

They were cupped.

In them sat the frog with the little white mark. Part leaf. Part comma.

I said: "See? It's all right. He's all right. You didn't hurt him."

The frog sat there. Awake, alert, but unmoving. And unharmed.

No one spoke. I looked around at the eyes of my schoolmates, and saw the fear and awe in them. And knew I had made a terrible mistake.

eleven

Tyler shook his head. This was all a load of crap, of course, but he had to admit that the Twins seemed more and more interesting all the time. He was back in the main body of the van, perched on a cot beneath the side window. The parking meter wasn't paid: Handicap stickers work magic with meter maids.

Through the one-way glass, his video camera rolled. The viewfinder framed a pair of middle-aged women ambling in to Dawn's Light. They stayed for perhaps ten minutes, and then walked back out. They paused in front of the gaudy window display that screamed AVAILABLE HERE: See and Believe—the Oshitas speak!

Tyler put the book aside and levered himself into his wheelchair. He opened the rear doors of the van. The little elevator lift sighed as it lowered him to the ground.

He closed and locked the doors as a blue Chevy rattled past, belching smoke. Tyler wheeled himself across, relishing the flex and burn of effort in his powerful arms. Most people found it difficult to believe how intensely he enjoyed trucking around in his wheelchair. His arms were so strong that the sensation was, he thought, analogous to a runner's high.

Aiming himself at a driveway, he wheeled up and onto the sidewalk, and coasted into the store, setting the door a-jingle.

A very attractive young lady, her hair half blond and half black, worked the register. A second one who reminded him of Nancy's comic strip Aunt Fritzi busily sorted books onto shelves.

Half-Blonde looked down. "Well, hello," she said. She seemed to be looking directly at him—not at the wheel chair. That was odd. More interesting still, the crinkle at the corner of her eyes was downright adorable.

Damn, this job was looking better all the time.

"I'd like to get a copy of the new Oshita book. Would that be cool?"

"Sure," she said, and came out from behind the register. She was wearing a halter top, and her legs were strong and very good. Tyler caught himself humming.

"You really should come to some of the meetings," Half-Blonde said, and then turned, looking at him over her shoulder with an expression hot enough to toast marshmallows.

Hell, yes. I'd also like to smear you with peanut butter and—

He curbed those thoughts. Business first.

"As a matter of fact, yes," he said. "You know, I'd just love to find out more about the Oshitas, and you look like someone who might just be able to tell me what I need to know. I was wondering if you might have time for lunch?"

She twinkled. "Well, I just came back from lunch fifteen minutes ago, but I could take a break." She nodded her head toward the back room. "O.K.?"

Tyler was too busy counting his blessings to reply. Christ, she was gorgeous.

"Kim," she called out. "I'm taking a break with this handsome man, all right?"

The other girl, who must have been "Kim" but looked more like the woman who had never noticed Sluggo was an abandoned child, giggled and said, "Sure, Sue. I'll watch the front."

Sue had a remarkable bust line and freckles dense enough to make her look a little like an adolescent boy in drag. Just a little, though. She also had a kind of healthy switch to her long stride, an acknowledgment that she knew men watched and wanted her. And gloried in it.

Those beautiful buttocks were just inches away from his face as he wheeled after her, back toward the break room.

The back room was pleasantly crammed with the kind of paraphernalia one might find in any book store: posters and paper rolls, damaged shelves, unopened book cartons, stacks of remainders, shipping labels, postage meters, and a mini-sink/refrigerator combo.

Sue pulled up a chair and sat across from him, one leg up on the sink. He could see her inner thigh, and the muscle play within it. She smiled at him sweetly, as if reading his mind—or worse still, not requiring a mind reader's skills to know exactly what he was thinking.

"So. What would you like to know?"

"Well, I've heard so much about Joy and Tomo, but I guess this is the first time that I've talked to someone who actually follows them." He checked himself. "You do, don't you? I mean, actually follow them."

Her laugh was deep and genuine. "Oh, yes. For three years now."

"How long have they been around? I mean, public?"

She leaned her head back, exposing a long and lovely length of silken throat. "Let's see—this is '95? I would guess that they first went really public about twelve years ago. Started doing workshops. You should come to one of the workshops," she said. "There's really a lot to learn. You'd like it."

She laid her hands on his thigh, just above the knee. "How did you hurt your legs?"

"Accident," he said.

She squeezed it, reached up and probed his arm with a forefinger. "Your upper body is so strong. I bet if you had your legs back, you'd really be beautiful. Can you feel anything?"

"Anything?"

"I mean, can you feel this?"

Her hand moved back down to his thigh and she squeezed it again, but this time her thumb was only two or three inches from his groin.

He swallowed "I feel a little pressure. That's all."

"That's all?" There was no mockery, no cruelty in the question. "Aren't you tired of that?"

He felt a door slam down in his mind. For a moment, just a moment, he had let that barrier up and now he was lashing himself for it. "Well," he said. "Some things you can't do a whole hell of a lot about." An edge of irritation had crept into his voice.

She wasn't the least ruffled. "You'd be surprised," she said.

"I saw the healing at the rally," he said. "Or . . . I mean I heard about it. Are you saying that you think the Twins could help me?"

"They help people sometimes," she said, "But they don't do it all the time."

"Why not?"

"It costs them. It takes energy to create change. The rest of us can make energy with love. But Joy and Tomo—they're so far out there that there aren't a lot of people who can keep up with them. And they're not perverts or anything, so I don't think they have much physical sex."

He smiled weakly. "What kind *do* they have?"

Sue just smiled.

Tyler waited, and when he became certain that she wasn't going to answer, continued. "So if I wanted to ask them for help, what would I do?"

She leaned closer. He detected a sharpness in her breath. Nothing unpleasant, almost as if she chewed incense. "You'd have to belong to them," she said.

"What does *that* mean?"

"It is what it is. There is a part of you that knows exactly what that means."

"No, there isn't," he said the words, but was surprised to hear a soft, distant voice whisper *Yes, you do.*

She looked at him a little quizzically, and he knew that the connection was broken. Just like that. There was no anger, not even disappointment. As if she had extended herself as far as she was going to, and for now, he had failed the test.

"Well, what if I want to see?"

"Then you'll see," she said, but the reserve was definitely in control. "Well, I have to get back to my post." She flashed a smile at him again. For a glorious moment, the heat was back.

"You think about what I said," Sue said. "Read the book. And when you decide that you know what I mean, come back and talk to me."

"Maybe I understand now," he said, wheeling after her.

"No, you don't." She looked down at him, and smiled. "But I think that you will."

Tyler looked at the store, and at Sue, back behind the cash register, laughing to her friend Kim. There had been no mockery. The flirtation, the interest, the responses were all honest. He knew that she saw his crippled legs, and yet she saw beyond them, too. Shit. It wasn't something that he could get a distinct fix on.

Tyler started up the van and began to pull away. And he was at least six blocks away before he realized that he had completely forgotten to ask if anyone in the bookstore knew the identity or location of a missing heiress named Kolla Sinclair.

twelve

United State Government RAIN FOREST Archive
Exhibit #2348
Oshita File. DO NOT PHOTOCOPY OR REMOVE FROM BUILDING

Portions of the following report are transcribed interview, conducted on the behalf of the commission to investigate the events of August 6, 1995, hereafter referred to as the Oshita Incident. The interviewee is Dr. Phillip Bluth, who was chief of surgery at Kyoto Hospital from 1946 to 1949. At the time of the taping, Bluth was diagnosed with liver cancer, which had already metastasized to his bone marrow and lungs. He chain smoked during the entire interview. He was in his mid-eighties, but despite the terminal diagnosis, his carriage is erect, his energy good.

Bluth remained in the military until 1963, at which time he left to establish a private practice in Chicago. In 1983 he retired. His wife of thirty years died in 1987, and since that time, Bluth has been fairly reclusive. The interview was conducted on September 12, 1995. He died four months later.

Interviewer: Is it true that you were head of surgery at Kyoto Hospital during the summer of 1948?

Bluth: Yes.

Interviewer: And do you remember presiding over a medical team which separated a pair of Siamese twins?

Bluth: Yes. I remember that. I couldn't forget that.

Interviewer: What was it that was so remarkable about that?

Bluth: Well, they were half-black, and Siamese twins to boot. How many Negro-Japanese ex-Siamese twins you think there are? Jesus, you think I'm too old to remember something like that? If you're the best the government's got, we're in deep shit.

Interviewer: Ah . . . what exactly is it that you found most remarkable about them?

Bluth: *(laughs)* Well, damn. If you looked at the records, you'd know what was so goddamned remarkable, wouldn't you? I assume you can read. Or maybe you went to public school.

Interviewer: Yes. I can read.

Bluth: Listen up, Buckwheat. Siamese twins are identical twins. They're basically one creature, just divided once too often. These twins were male and female. If you knew jack shit, you'd know that that's not supposed to happen. As a matter of fact, a man could deliver babies all day long, and not see a case of non-identical Siamese in a lifetime. It's that rare. But there it was.

Interviewer: So where exactly were they joined?

Bluth: *(pauses, takes a long slow pull on the cigarette. His hand is shaking.)* Well, they ah . . . they were joined along the vertical axis. They had a full complement of lungs and so on. The only problem was the kidney. It was like the boy's kidney had budded, and he got the lion's share. I mean, you can get by on one kidney, but I wouldn't wish that on a Liberal. I mean a fever, an infection, something really major, something that attacks the body . . . and you're up the creek. But the girl didn't have much. The boy had a double dose. (Laughs) Well, anyway, we had to separate them there. And that surgery was tricky. Almost six hours, and a pretty piece of work it was.

Interviewer: Do you remember anything in particular. Does anything in particular stand out for you about the operation?

Bluth: Hmmm. Stand out? Well, there's only one thing that really stood out for me. And that was the birth itself. I wasn't there. The children weren't separated until about . . . oh, I don't know, four months after they were born. I wondered about that, and what it turned out is that they'd been born at home. How in the hell this little woman . . . I mean, she was awfully torn up. Giving birth to those kids outside of a hospital, I mean, Siamese twins, are you kidding? She was . . . she was a mess. We put her back together the best that we could, but I'll tell you, even with the best reconstructive surgery we had at that time, there wasn't much . . . *woman* left of her, you know? She was torn apart. I can't imagine what ever happened to her after that. Never saw a woman holding on to life the way she did. Never saw a woman who wanted to be alive more. She was so beautiful. I mean her face. Like a flower. People say that, but they say it too easy. With her, it was true—but she was also crazy. Raving. Can understand that. Can't even imagine the kind of pain that she was in, but she just wouldn't go out, and she showed up, she brought those babies in to us. She was bleeding, and bleeding bad. I don't know where she had those babies. I had this bad vision some time, of her curled up in an alley somewhere like a cat, yowling 'em into the world. Don't like that thought. But she brought 'em in by herself. And they were sick. Those kids were real sick. Internal bleeding. I think that if they hadn't been sick, she wouldn't have brought them in to see us. I don't know how old they were. A few months? Six months? Eight months? I don't remember. But I think she tried to keep them together. I don't claim to understand what was going through her mind, but I think that if she hadn't thought they were dying, she wouldn't have brought them in to us. She just wanted us to give them antibiotics, but she was out of her head, too. Woman was crazy. We had to tie her down. I remember that. I do remember that. And when she found out what we'd done, that we'd separated those kids, she just went crazier. I do remember that. She attacked one of the nurses. Christ. Never seen anything like it. Biting, scratching, Christ Almighty, almost took out one of her eyes. Took three men to hold her down, and she was bleeding all over the floor at the same time. Damnedest thing I ever saw. I'll tell you something else, too.

Interviewer: What's that?

Bluth: Woman was infected as hell. Jesus. The blood tests came back and she made Typhoid Mary look like Mother Teresa. I'm telling you that according to the blood tests, she was carrying about three kinds of plague, syphilis, some kind of anthrax . . . if she hadn't bolted before those tests came back, we never would have let her out.

Interviewer: Were the children infected?

Bluth: No. Strange about that woman. She was torn up from birth, but aside from that, seemed to be in perfect health. Carrying enough germs and viruses to kill a dozen people, and . . . just nothing.

Interviewer: You said that the children carried no disease at all?

Bluth: *(here, his expression is unreadable. It may be a smile, but if so, it is a nervous one.)* I wondered if you'd catch that. It's the dog that didn't bark. The something wrong is that there was nothing wrong. Our instruments weren't really that good at the time, even when we got good and curious. After the separation, they seemed perfectly healthy. In fact they healed about three times faster than they had any right to. And things quieted down. I guess if the mother hadn't snatched them, we might have figured it out. I remember the lab guys saying they wanted to take more samples, but we never got it. I don't know what happened to the blood samples. *(Here, Bluth looks sharply at the interviewer)* Do you?

Interviewer: No.

Bluth: Uh-huh.

Interviewer: Is there anything else you can tell us?

Bluth: Those little babies. I'll tell you. They were beautiful. You know, I remember that time, all that, you know, Yellow Peril stuff, and talk about Japanese. Negroes had a lot of problems back then, but being Japanese was worse. I mean, I lost a damn good friend at Pearl Harbor. An uncle at Iwo Jima. Didn't have no reason to love 'em, you know. But I was a doctor, and I did the best I could. I always did. There was something so different about this. Those little kids. I just looked at them. There was just something about them, and they looked right back at me, and their eyes were just so . . . black, and soft, and clear. (laughs) I just remember hoping that they were gonna live. I don't even exactly know why. But I just do remember hoping. Did they?

thirteen

Wilshire Division was still situated in a six-story brown building on the Miracle Mile, two blocks east of the La Brea Tar Pits.

Cat and Jax wound their way through the office cubicles, nodding and waving to a few of the familiar faces, trotted up a winding staircase to the third floor until they came to a cubicle labeled CAPTAIN FRED KING.

They knocked lightly and then opened the door.

The man seated behind the desk was harried-looking, but very lean and fit for his age, which looked to be his late fifties. Sparse and graying brown hair pulled back from a high forehead. His skin was weathered but pale, as if he spent too many hours beneath artificial lighting. His desk was very neat, but heavy with scattered paper, as if he had a thousand tiny rooms in his head, and could seal himself in any of them at will.

He was on the phone at the moment, and hadn't really noticed their entrance. "There's a problem here, sir. . . ." he was saying.

He finally looked up as Cat and Jax entered the room. He pointed to a wooden sign that said: TAKE A NUMBER.

"Yes. Well," he said, ". . . the only problem is that you refused to compensate the store for the tapes. Sure, everybody makes mistakes. But you damaged their property, then told them it was their problem."

Jax and Cat took seats. Cat leaned forward to eavesdrop.

"Sir," King continued. ". . . its not your tape. It's *theirs.* Yes, you recorded your images on it, but the cassette still belongs to them. Yes, sir. Well, you can speak to a lawyer, but I think you should offer to settle with them." He lifted his middle finger to the sky. "I think not sir. All right."

He made a kissing sound into the dead receiver, and hung it up.

"Problems, Freddy?"

He groaned. "Just a little video reality."

"There's a contradiction in terms," Jax said.

"Guy named Tad Byrdie taped himself bopping his girlfriend—no big problem, except that he taped it over a rental of *Forrest Gump.* Then this idiot returns the tape to Blockbuster or wherever. Guess what happens when Johnny Jones sits down to watch the Bubba Gump Shrimpworks for the ninetieth time? Why, there's a new scene! And one very unsuitable for family viewing."

"Life is like a box of chocolates," Jax said mildly.

King shrugged, grinning. "When the store complained, asked him to pay for it, he told them to fuck themselves. They closed his account, and he thought that was that."

Jax squinted for a minute, running through possible permutations of the story. "Don't tell me. . . ." he said.

King's smile was almost saintly. "You're way ahead of me. Gee, whiz, a half-dozen copies of the tape got mailed around. Store claims they accidentally rented it out, or, hmmmm . . . maybe it got stolen out of the trash after they threw it away. Byrdie owns a local car lot. Does his own commercials—you've seen them: 'We lose a little on every deal, but make it up with volume?' "

"Right," Jax said. " 'We steal from the other guy, and pass the savings on to you.' "

"You've seen them. Well, as of Tuesday's mail, a half-dozen of his competitors learned exactly how Tad Byrdie achieves full customer satisfaction."

Jax wiped tears of mirth from his eyes. "What a world, huh? Looking good, Freddy."

King probed at a nonexistent love handle. He was a dedicated jogger, and at fifty-eight still ran at least two marathons a year. This despite the fact that he smoked half a pack of cigarettes a day. "Not bad. Heard about the shit out at LAX. How's that working?"

"Not bad," Cat said. "Needed a little damage control. Quest didn't want any problems."

"Fucker," King said emphatically. "Weird shit, huh? Whoever thought? He'll get his one day."

"Hope I live that long."

"Well," he said philosophically. "One good thing came out of it . . . you guys got together."

There was a moment of silence in the office. Cat and Jax looked at each other a little uncomfortably. Cat cursed to herself, wondering if it would have been politic to send out divorce announcements.

Hearye, Hearye, it is now solemnly announced that on this twenty-fourth day of September, nineteen hundred and ninety four, Portia Musette Juvell and Jackson Emory Carpenter have formally dissolved the Holy Union which began just nineteen months ago, placing Jackson back on the dating market, and dropping Portia back into the erotic null zone from whence she came. . . .

No, not a good idea.

So instead, she just said. "We . . . got divorced a year ago, Freddy. Sorry."

Jax's voice was carefully neutral. "Dead issue."

King sighed wearily. If he was embarrassed by his gaffe, he didn't show it. A little saddened, perhaps: Freddy King had introduced them. "Yeah. Dead as Elvis. So. What brings you back to the old digs? Just homesick?"

"Hardly," Cat was happy for change of subject. "We're looking for a maybe missing girl named Kolla Sinclair. Heard of her?"

"Nope. Anyone file on her?"

"I don't think her brother did a missing persons—he doesn't think she's dead on the street some where. He thinks she's inside this quasi-religious group, brainwashed by a couple of gurus who might have connections in the skin business. You still keep up with that action?"

"Must be talking about the Oshitas."

"What do you know?" Jax asked.

"They've cleaned up a bunch of teenage hookers. Run a halfway house off Melrose."

Cat's nose wrinkled as if she had caught a bad smell. "Pimping?"

King shook his head hard. "No. Righteous clean. They may be sex crazy, but they run a clean show. No balling on premises. Several of their little hookers cleaned themselves up, got straight jobs, left the halfway houses. None of them ever had anything but good things to say about Joy and Tomo."

"The others?"

King shrugged. "You can't win 'em all, but the Twins do a pretty decent job. You know, the Golden Sun does a lot of sex stuff. But none of the men and women involved come off the street. They've got Ph.D.s and tech types, and former Marines."

Jax laughed. "No such thing as a 'former' jarhead, numbnuts."

"Semper Fi, my man," they shared a laugh, which turned just a little dark and secretive, and then died out. Jax and Freddy had both served in Vietnam—different theaters, different branches of the service, but same dirty war, and same reticence to discuss their experiences with her. They hadn't met until Jax joined the LAPD.

"What you're saying," Cat said carefully, "is that the people having sex in the Golden Sun workshops aren't off the streets?"

"Oh, hell no. If they had been, some of the moral watchdogs would have shut them down. They help the street kids, but they don't exploit them."

Jax smiled. "Sounds like you like them."

"Seen lots worse," King said. "And what the hell—they put on a good show."

"We noticed."

"I know a half-dozen hookers probably be dead without 'em."

That comment cleared the room for a second. Cat felt impatient. All right. So they were dealing with a couple of saints. Even saints had muddy feet sometimes. "We need a connection. Can you help?"

"What's the deal?" King asked.

"Missing heiress," Jax said. "Brother's piss-scared she's turning the family jewels over to a pair of bunco artists."

King chuckled at that. "Now, *that* could be. Their inner circle is mighty pricey. Coffee?"

"Big one," Jax grinned.

"Cream in your coffee?"

"Not since this afternoon," Cat said.

"Will you shut up?" Jax said in disgust. "Come to think of it, no coffee. I may never drink coffee again."

King's eyebrows formed a quizzical arch. "You guys."

"So," Cat said. "Tell us what you know."

"Well, they take street people and feed them. Restaurant customers and enlist them in meditation groups. College students and entertain them."

"We saw one of their little entertainments."

"They *are* showmen," Jax admitted.

"Their workshops draw mostly a middle-class group, and they have special workshops. Pricey. Strictly upper class and invitation only."

"What happens there?" Cat asked.

King grinned at her. "What do you think? Sex. Lots of it. Their whole thing is built around sex. Hell, they've got their own line of designer condoms. 'Twin City.' Mayor of Minneapolis got a free lifetime supply. Gave 'em the key to the city."

"Got a contact for us?"

"You know," he mused, "I have to tell you, the Oshitas have friends in Hollywood, Wall Street, and Washington. Yoko Ono wrote the forward to their frigging book."

"And?"

"And . . . there's something wrong. I can feel it."

"Wrong? Like what?"

"Hard to say," he said quietly. "You know, whispers. You hear things."

"What kind of things?" Jax asked.

"Well . . . like maybe the Oshitas have enemies. People who'd like to stop them, you know? There's been a lot of talk, and editorials. The *Sixty Minutes* spot pretty much tore 'em a new asshole. Called them fakes and frauds—Some Bible-belt stuff calling them perverts."

"Is that what you're talking about?"

"No." King rose hesitantly. "You really need this stuff, right?" he didn't wait for an answer. "I'll be right back."

He slipped from behind the desk, and into the outer office. The detectives remained seated, waiting. Jax cleared his throat. "I guess we should have told him."

Cat was looking at the floor. It felt like something was stuck in her chest. "Sharing good news is one thing, Jax. . . ."

"Yeah."

She finally looked up, gazed at him curiously. "You asked for the divorce, Jax. I'm not saying you shouldn't have. But . . . if things had worked differently, you wouldn't be leaving, would you?"

There was a flat, hard expression on his face, as if he had been over and over this entire subject in his mind, and had no further interest in exploring it. Cat met that stare for perhaps ten seconds, and then looked away, chewing her lip.

Before she could speak again, Freddy reappeared. He held a thick file folder, but before he could open it, or hand it over, he seemed to catch the changed, charged atmosphere, and bent to look at Cat more carefully. She peeked out at him from behind her blond ringlets, her smile not completely convincing. "Are you all right?" he asked.

"Fine. Contact lenses scratch sometime."

Freddy glanced form Cat to Jax and back again, and then shrugged.

"Whatever," he said, clearly unconvinced. "Anyway, this is what I've got. The Twins got started back in the early eighties, I guess. Used to preach or lecture or whatever in Hollywood. Had a couple of soup kitchens, one downtown, and one off Selma, near the meat market. They did good work. Then in about '86, some transients started turning up dead. Maybe as many as twelve. We had some kind of a stalker, but no one was ever brought in for it."

"Victims?"

"All white males, slender, mid-thirties to forties. They had another link—at least half of them had been to one of the Twin's kitchens."

Jax took the file from Freddy, opened it and slid out a sheaf of reports and a dozen photographs. Most of them were slab shots—photos taken in the autopsy room. A couple were taken while the victim was still outlined in chalk, and one was a blowup of a driver's license. All of the men were as Freddy had mentioned. In fact, the more that Jax stared at them . . .

Brown hair. Lean. Sharp cheekbones. High foreheads . . .

He handed them over to Cat, wondering if she would come to the same conclusion. She did, and more rapidly than he had. "Jesus," she said almost at once. "They look like you, Freddy."

King laughed mirthlessly. "Yep. I thought so too. Spooked me a little. It was one of the things that hooked me, and got me interested in the cult scene, and the Twins. All of these men were found dead where they slept. Couple of shelters, a flop house or two, out on the street in a cardboard jungle."

"How had they died?"

"Never completely sure. There were bite and claw marks, but nothing severe enough to cause death. Little bleeding . . . more like the puncture wounds of a big snake.

"Any venom?'

"No," Cat said. She had already made it as far as the pathologist reports. "None. But lots of broken bones."

"Yeah. Something mangled them, chewed them up in their sleep."

"And no cause of death was ever established?"

He wagged his head back and forth sorrowfully. "Nope, and boy, did we want this one."

Cat laid the folder on her lap, and closed her eyes.

"Did you see the newspaper clipping in there?" Freddy asked.

Cat opened her eyes and dug a photostat out of the folder. The article was short, not much, just an article about a Jason Cleese who had apparently been the victim of a mountain lion attack.

"They don't really go into details in the article, but I know a few things," Freddy said.

"Like what?"

"Happened out in Riverside. I got in touch with Riverside Sheriff's, asked some questions. This guy Cleese used to be part of the Oshita organization. He left about a year ago, not sure why, but he still spoke highly of them—at least, did on that *Sixty Minutes* segment. Then he turns up very dead."

"Coincidence?"

"Could be. But the bit about 'mountain lion' attack? When was the last time someone was killed by a mountain lion in Riverside? Something like never. Damnedest thing. It happened in the middle of the park, close to midnight, he's walking home from work, and—" King put his hands up. "Hell if I know. You call it. Weird shit, that's for sure."

He folded his hands together and sat back down, put his interlaced fingers behind his balding head. "I got interested 'cause there were whispers that he wasn't the only one."

"Is the Golden Sun a cult?"

"Define your terms. Their people are true believers, if that's what you mean. They associate mostly with each other. They only have sex with each other. They have their own jargon, Twinspeak, they call it. It's hard for an outsider to get very far without actually joining, going through all their ceremonies. The story is that the Twins were sent to save mankind from itself. They're kind of Jesus come back to earth, one soul in two bodies. And that sex is the big answer."

"Most of my life," Jax said, "It's been the big question."

"Anyway," King said reasonably, "if you'll keep your wise ass puckered, you might learn something. People close to the Twins say they can do stuff."

"Stuff?"

"Stuff. Do things. Miracles."

"We saw the fire trick," Cat said. "It's just a trick, Freddy."

"Yeah, yeah, probably. But I've had people swear that they can do things that they don't show to the public."

"What kind of things?"

"This sex magic stuff. The stuff that happens at the workshops—it's supposed to be pretty far out."

"Anybody straight ever talk about it?"

"Well, problems there. First, you gotta get an invite. That's not the easiest thing. They're real selective. Then you have to be willing to have sex in front of strangers, maybe *with* strangers, I dunno. Story is that a couple Fibbies went undercover couple of years ago. Husband and wife team. Made it through about two days of this damned workshop. Both of 'em spun out. Husband had a nervous breakdown. Wife was worse."

"Worse how?"

He looked at them blandly. "Story is that she stepped in front of a car. Just . . . stepped out into traffic and *bang.* Didn't try to dodge, didn't scream, nothing."

"Jesus," Jax said reverently. "Kill her?"

"No, but you wouldn't know by looking at her. I think they feed her through a tube in her ear. Anyway, you can imagine with all this strange shit, there are . . . stories. You know, light side, dark side stuff? And bugaboos. Stuff that goes bump in the night. And in this case, it's The Bad People. The ones who want to stop them. Who want to hurt them. Golden Sun groupies hang together so tight because they're afraid of what might happen if The Boogieman got hold of them."

"Yeah, well, that's all well and good, Freddy. But do you have contacts for us?"

Freddy's pale, lined face wrinkled. He seemed genuinely pained. "Call me Cassandra. Nobody ever fucking listens. All right, I've got a contact."

He pulled two books off the overburdened shelf behind them, and then browsed them until he found the right number, and scribbled it on a sheet of paper. "Here's one. Remember a therapist named Debbie Norris? Testified for the state a couple of times?"

"Sure," Jax said. "We consulted with her on the Vasquez thing."

"That's the one. Well, she does some family counseling. I think she's referred couples to the Twins' workshops. Talk with her."

"Will do. And the other?" Cat asked.

He added two names and an address on the paper, and handed it to them. "Second-hand store on Melrose. Heard that one of their ex-lovers works there part time. That's all I got."

"It's a lot Freddy. Thanks."

"No problemo. You kids take care of each other, all right?"

Cat stood. "Thanks, Freddy." When she got to the door, she stopped and turned. "By the way. What did they call these Bogeymen of theirs. You know, the ones who were trying to stop them?"

" 'Iron Shadows,' " King said, and shook his head in disbelief. "Can you believe that shit? They called them 'Iron Shadows.' "

fourteen

United State Government RAIN FOREST Archive
Exhibit #1009
Oshita File. DO NOT PHOTOCOPY OR REMOVE FROM BUILDING

The following is a section of the original publication of See and Believe, *which was deleted for the second edition. Tomo Oshita's handwritten notes follow.*

When we were six years old, our mother took us to our uncle, a Shinto priest named Yamato, a member of the *Ten No Kishi,* or the "Knights of Heaven." I remember him as a round man with small hands. He told us that we were very special children. He said there was a force that governs the universe, and that force is thought of in most Western religions as being Male, but that the Male cannot give birth to life. The feminine gives birth to life. The Male is the active force, the feminine the conceptive force. They work together, and we were born male and female to bring something unique into the world.

We began our instruction there with him, and even after we went to America we continued our education. And a time came when we were no longer the ones being instructed. We were able to give answers where once there had only been questions. We had been chosen, and regardless of how painful that choice might have seemed sometimes, how it might have placed us outside the flow of most humanity, we had to fulfill our destiny.

Often, the only society that either of us knew was that we shared with each other. It was what we were intended to do. What we were born to do. And so we accepted it. If not gladly, wholeheartedly.

(Note: The following has been confirmed as an authentic sample of Tomo Oshita's handwriting)

This is a nice fairy tale. I don't know how to rewrite this to match the truth. I feel a need to be as honest as possible. If Joy and Mother agree, I would like to stay a little closer to the truth. I think that no matter how it may seem on the surface, it is important for people to understand that out of the most intense pain can come beauty. That the worst and most crippling kind of ugliness can birth warmth and understanding. If the power of love cannot transform, then nothing we have done has any meaning at all.

To reach people, you must first achieve rapport with them. The more god-like we seem, the less good we can do. Our followers must understand that not only did we begin our lives on a level similar to theirs, but in many ways were below them. They must see that they hold within themselves a spark of divinity. Then, and perhaps only then, can we make a real difference. Anything short of that seems almost to be gloating.

I would not have it thought that a group of secret elders anointed us. Chose us. Our father, our real father, may be partially responsible for what we are. I dream some time that he will find us, and explain to us why we are what we are. Or perhaps it was our mother. Did something happen to her in the lab? Something involving the germs and gasses? I don't know. Or perhaps, despite what Mother says, it was the Bomb itself. A gift of life from death. A gift of peace from the depths of the most terrible act of war.

fifteen

The Beautiful Folk thrift store was situated on Melrose, three blocks east of La Brea Boulevard, between the Classical Gas used record store and a Handee-Man plumbing supply shop.

Tyler parked the van around the corner on Carlotta Way, then looked back at Cat and Jax. "Well, how do you want to play this?"

"Pretty straight," Cat said. "I think we just march in and present our bona fides. See what happens."

"Yeah," Jax said. "Honesty being the best policy and all."

"Well, that's a first," Tyler said blandly. "You let me know how it all works out. I'm not sure I understand this 'honesty' thing."

The Beautiful Folk was indistinguishable from a hundred other thrift shops in the Hollywood area—clothes were the mainstay; dresses and suits crushed the shelves and racks like refugees jammed into lifeboats. All eras, all styles, all makes and models—all equally abandoned and hoping to find new homes. Because this was Hollywood, there was always a minuscule chance that a trunk purchased at blind auction from Lyons storage might have belonged to a once-popular comedian or talk show hostess fallen on hard times. You never knew. It might contain costumes or jewelry from a stage show at the old Pantages, something unexpectedly gaudy or valuable.

Cat found herself browsing as she entered, wondering honestly how *this* piece would look with *that,* and made a silent promise to return and do a little real shopping later.

About twelve people were in the store. Cat figured that perhaps five of them were staff. Those were the ones who repaired clothes, inventoried, and assisted customers with pumps and sweaters.

Behind the counter, a lovely blond in her early fifties sorted earrings and broches into a red flowered box. She wore a gray pantsuit with oyster trim and a white silk blouse. The pantsuit fit her to perfection—Cat bet the blonde was her own best customer, and damned handy with a needle to boot.

She had the kind of flexible, willowy strength Cat tended to associate with yoga adepts. She smiled brightly, displaying excellent teeth. "Yes?" she said. Her makeup was good, but Cat thought that direct sunlight would probably treat her severely. "Do you need help finding anything?"

"Maybe," Cat said. "We're looking for Chris Zimmer. Would that be you by any chance?"

The blond studied them, her face slightly pinched. "No," She said. "I'm Hannah Appelion, the owner. Why do you want Chris?"

Jax spoke up. "We're doing some research on Joy and Tomo—and were told that we should speak to Chris."

"What kind of research?" Hannah asked.

"We're doing a documentary," Jax lied smoothly.

Truth is always the first casualty, Cat sighed to herself.

"And who referred you to Chris?"

"Captain Fred King, Wilshire Division?"

Some of the tightness left Hannah's face, replaced with a kind of cautious welcome. "Freddy. Sure I know him. He's a good man." She leaned forward, caught at Cat's wrist. "Chris is a little fragile," she said. "Don't push too hard." Her smile seemed a reluctant artifice. "All right . . . over in the shoe section. Tell Chris Hannah said it was all right."

"Thanks," Jax said.

A statuesque brunette was folding clothes over in that general direction. Cat wryly noticed that Jax immediately straightened, and put on his most serious expression. The brunette was a large girl, unselfconsciously *zaftig,* with just the barest hint of rose blush and purple eye liner.

"Excuse me—" Jax began.

The brunette smiled up at him. "No," she said. "You want Chris."

She pointed over another aisle. Barely visible there was a dark, slender, harried looking young man earnestly sorting shoes. He looked like a Ken doll, like a second-tier soap actor, someone a little too beautiful to play the lead, a man who once had absolute confidence in his appearance. The past tense was appropriate. Judging by his humble posture and the worry lines at the corners of his mouth, something was very wrong here.

Cat reached his side first. "Excuse me—are you Chris Zimmer?"

He looked up nervously. Cat immediately went on point. This man reminded her of . . . of what? An addict? Zimmer was too tightly wound, too fragile. His pupils were tiny, like those of a man gazing into the sun.

Subtly, Cat positioned herself to examine Zimmer's inner forearms. Smooth and pale—no scars or marks, but that proved nothing. There were a thousand ways to hide needle tracks.

Jax seemed aware of Zimmer's strangeness, as well. "Wondering if we could ask you a few questions," he said.

The tip of Zimmer's pink tongue flicked out, moistening dry lips. "What? About what?"

Cat assumed her most soothing manner. "The Twins. Joy and Tomo."

The mixture of emotions warring on Chris Zimmer's face was painful to watch. Hope. Fear. Pain. Nervousness. Then resignation. "Oh, ah . . . well, I have to work."

"Hannah said it would be all right."

Again that flickering indecision. He locked eyes with Cat, and she saw something familiar in them. Cat glanced from Chris Zimmer to a full-length mirror behind him, and in that glass rectangle glimpsed her own reflection. There was an odd similarity between Chris Zimmer and the woman in the mirror. As if they were long-lost relatives. The relation was not one of blood. It was something darker than blood.

Cat had the sudden, wholly inexplicable sensation of standing on the edge of something, teetering. A ledge. A precipice. She shook her head, hard.

"She did?" Chris asked. He glanced over at Hannah adoringly. Chris was frightened, but trusted his benefactor completely. Hannah trusted Freddy. And Freddy trusted Cat. Maybe that was too much trust, a chain of goodwill stretched a crucial link too far.

What the hell were they into, here?

Chris came to an uncomfortable decision. "Oh, well . . ." He motioned them toward the back room.

A glass bead curtain separated the back lounge from the sales floor. A few beanbag and straight-backed chairs, a refurbished couch and a four-burner stove filled the space cozily. A little automatic brewer kept water steaming on the stove.

Chris was trying very hard to play host. "Would you like some juice? Tea?"

"Tea, thank you," Cat said.

"Got any Red Zinger?" Jax asked cheerily. "Kinda like that."

Chris' lips curled up in a brittle, somehow pitiful attempt to smile. "Yes, in fact, we . . . ah . . . we do."

Wrong. Something's wrong. This man was on the edge. Chris Zimmer moved around the kitchen almost like a puppet, plastic smile frozen in place.

Chris's hands were busy as he dipped tea bags, but his eyes continued to cast about, as if searching out a potential route of escape.

On the edge. But of what? And why?

He brought them two steaming cups, and for the first time, the trace of a smile touched his face. "Nectar?" he asked, extending a gray ceramic honey pot to them. The substance within was thick and dark, rather like a mixture of molasses and chopped grass.

"Nectar?" Jax asked. "What is this?" He poked a spoon into the pot, coating its tip with a quarter-inch of granular syrup. He touched his tongue to it, and nodded approval. "Sweet."

Chris beamed. "Tomo's Nectar," he said. "Honey, clarified butter, herbs imported from China and India . . . and special ingredients. You'll like it."

Cat shrugged and dipped a spoon in, stirring a lump of it into her tea. After it dissolved, she sipped. Pretty damned good, she thought.

Chris selected a tall, thin glass from a cupboard, dropped in a handful of ice cubes, and poured cranberry juice cocktail over them. For almost a minute there was little sound, as they enjoyed their beverages. Jax set his cup down, and turned the conversation back to business. "We were hoping you could answer a few questions for us."

His head flicked up as if his knuckles had been rapped with a stick. "Questions?" Chris said. "What kind of questions?"

"Do you know a woman named Kolla Sinclair?"

"Maybe," he said. "Do you have a picture?"

Chris stood more upright. With the improvement in posture, Cat saw, for an instant, the confident man hiding inside the brittle shell, the trace of a charisma so strong it rocked her, and made her ache.

Jesus, you're gorgeous!

And what is it that sent you back into the darkness, into hiding? Into that (attic)

where you conceal your beauty from the world?

Attic? Cat caught her lower lip between her teeth. Now *there* was an odd choice of images. Where in the world had *that* come from?

Jax showed him the snapshot. He studied it, and then nodded. "Yes. I think that I've seen her, but not for a long time."

"You're sure?"

"She was at one of the workshops, I think. What is this? Why are you talking to me?"

"I heard that you were very close to the Twins."

He stopped, became very still. Cat had the sudden, absurd thought that perhaps he didn't actually live inside his body. That maybe he resided in some place slightly removed and above it. Some small dark room, where people might store boxes and chests and—

Chris was wracked by a consistent wave of little tremors, and Cat had a sudden, disturbing image of a small, frightened animal.

Crawling desperately through a dark, confined space—

Like an attic?

—toward a distant light.

She shook her head. A big sour bubble was boiling, expanding in Cat's guts. She felt lead-bellied, as if she were about to be physically ill.

Chris's laughter was a brittle, hollow sound, like dry sticks snapping at the bottom of a barrel. "Is that what you call it? *Close?*"

"What would you call it?" Jax asked.

Chris Zimmer's mouth twisted in what might have been the saddest smile Cat had ever seen.

This man is hiding. From what? And why? He is here, and these people protect him. We shouldn't have come here. Freddy King's name opened them up—he's the only reason they're talking. But we don't belong here.

"They were my love," Chris said simply. He was choosing his words very carefully. Almost as if reading them off cue cards. "My life. I would have done anything for them. They looked at me, and didn't see what you see."

"What do I see?" Jax asked.

For an instant, Chris mustered a touch of pride. He regarded Jax challengingly. "I know you think I'm weak. That's all anyone . . . ever saw." That pause. On some level deep within her, Cat knew what belonged in that pause, what had almost been said. What had been skirted around.

Something that makes you crawl in attics. Something that either breaks you, or makes you into someone who can survive anything.

Like you, Cat? Like you?

With irritation, she realized she had missed some of Chris's words.

"—like who we are inside is limited by the package. Joy looked into me. Through me. They . . ." Again, that pause, "saw my *Atman.* My fire."

"Your fire?"

"Saw the God inside me. Loved me."

"All right," Jax said reasonably. "We heard you were . . . with Joy. Is that right?"

Chris's eyes defocused, and he was no longer in the room with them. His body was there, but the essential inwardness of Chris Zimmer, his *Atman,* perhaps, was no longer present. Then he returned, and smiled at Cat thinly. "Yes," he whispered.

"Why aren't you still with her?"

Chris Zimmer began to twitch a little at this, and scanned the room as if seeking someone to help him avoid that particular question. "She doesn't think it would be fair to stay with one person. She . . . told me that when we started. She has to share herself. I know that wasn't her idea. I know."

Cat thought that Zimmer said "she" a little oddly, with a little pause before each iteration. Little webs of muscle and pale blue veins shifted beneath his milky skin. Zimmer was almost angelic, too fragile to be truly handsome. Some people love fragile things. Joy must have adored him.

But other people see fragile things, vulnerability, as something to break, to . . . possess.

In the attic?

Cat looked at her cup, and realized that her hands were trembling. She bore down on herself, shut the response down, didn't let herself feel it. Now wasn't the time. Don't feel, no matter what the cost. *Hide, no matter what the price, right Chris?* A sensation of profound kinship with this wan foundling flooded her like an infusion of fresh, hot blood.

"It was Joy's idea for you to leave?"

Chris's response came in a rush. "No—it was *Hers,*" he exploded. "She doesn't want anyone interfering in her damned plan." The words were gushing out now. "The Unveiling. 'Death to the killers,' she said—"

His face was red, the veins in his neck swelling, and the words rushed out of him as if blown by a head of steam. The change was startling. "Just wait until August, then it won't matter."

"August?" Cat asked, puzzled. "What happens in August?"

"Just wait. I don't care about the world. I don't care about who knows or doesn't know. Nobody can stop them, not even—" He skidded to a verbal stop, staring as if seeing them for the first time. "What do you want?" he asked nervously. "Why are you really here? Who are you?"

For a few moments, Chris had appeared a force of nature, imbued with a strength of will and personality so powerful it was very nearly a physical thing. Now he collapsed, like a child caught stealing, like a tiny hunted thing scrabbling for the safety of darkness, suddenly and horribly aware that it has made a terrible mistake.

"Who are you?" he whispered.

"My name is Jax—"

Chris wasn't hearing him, perhaps wasn't hearing anything at all. "Oh my dear God. You're one of *them.*"

"Who . . . ?" Cat managed to ask, already knowing the answer.

The pale angel trembled. His eyes skipped from Cat to Jax and back again, the horror of some deep and utter betrayal etched on his beautiful face.

Suddenly, and before either of them could make a move, Chris slammed his glass down on the sink, shattering it into a noncohesive mass of razorlike fragments. Crimson drooled between his fingers, blood and cranberry nectar mingling freely.

Jax sprang to his feet. "Shit!!"

Zimmer held his hands up to them. Blood and juice ran down his pale forearms, dripped from his elbows. Cat lurched up, and toward him.

Chris Zimmer jumped back, his face a cunning child's. *I've got a secret. You'd die to know it, bitch.* "You won't use me," he said. "You won't use me to hurt them."

"Let us help you." Cat fought to keep her voice steady.

Zimmer backed further away. "Tell your masters I'd rather *die* than hurt him."

Blood drizzled onto the floor. So much blood.

He's crazy, Cat thought. *Elvis has left the building.* Without taking her eyes from the bloody arms she called out: "Get some help in here, dammit. Get an ambulance."

Jax was trying to get hold of Chris, but he eeled out of Jax's grip, skittered along the floor like a crab with a broken, bleeding claw. He giggled madly.

Hannah appeared behind them in the doorway. "What's happening?"

Forcing her voice to remain calm, Cat said, "Call an ambulance. Now."

Before their very eyes, Chris Zimmer had reverted to a younger self, become a child's broken toy. "Tell them I won't tell. I won't let you take me."

Jax was genuinely baffled. "What?"

"I won't tell," he repeated.

Before anyone could stop him, he shoved a handful of bloody shards into his mouth and began to chew. There was a horrible crack of grinding glass, then his mouth opened and he made a protracted, awful gagging sound. Crimson foamed from his mouth. Zimmer bucked and screamed, gargling in pain and fear and rage. It took all of their strength and skill to hold him down. Jax jerked his hand away as Zimmer snapped at it with crimsoned teeth, then flipped him belly-down so that gravity would fight his attempts to swallow. Chris choked and screamed and fought for death, and all Cat could think of was an animal caught in

(an attic)
a trap, chewing its own leg off.
That, and two terrible words: *Iron Shadows.*

sixteen

The ambulance rolled away from the curb, siren wailing. Hannah Appelion stood in the Beautiful Folk's doorway, arms wrapped tightly around
her chest. As Cat suspected, her face was paler by daylight, hair hard and
brittle with mousse. She seemed to be watching them from the back of a
cave, and Cat wondered at the depth of the darkness within.

Shamed by the raw inadequacy of language, Cat extended her hand. "If
there's anything I can do—"

Hannah reacted as if scalded. "Get away from us. Both of you. Just get
away." Suddenly, whatever it was that lived back in that cave emerged. It
was frightened, loyal. Protective. "What have you done?"

Cat searched for words of comfort, or explanation. Hannah cut her
short.

"You're not friends of ours."

"Chris needs help—"

"He'll get help," Hannah said acidly. "You go to hell. You'll see. You'll
all see, and not much longer now."

"What are you talking about?" Jax seemed utterly baffled.

"Goodbye." Hannah turned her back on them, returning to the store.

The little crowd of gawkers began to dissipate, to return to the surrounding shops, leaving Cat and Jax alone on the sidewalk.

The ambulance siren dwindled in the background.

Feeling somehow diminished, Cat walked back around the corner to
where Tyler's van waited. Jax slid back the side panel for her. She felt
dazed, dizzy, as if she had just belted down several ounces of scotch malt.

Tyler leaned back in his seat, eyes closed, listening to headphones.
His right eye opened as they entered. Silently, he watched them climb in
and take seats—Cat in the front passenger seat, Jax in the back. Cat just
sank herself back against the side of the van and shook her head. Finally,

he asked: "What was that all about? What was the ambulance? What happened?"

"Later," Jax said. Cat wanted to cry, or scream. Nothing would come. "Just get us to hell out of here."

"Where to?"

"We've got an appointment with Dr. Debbie Norris. Let's see what comes out of that."

Tyler nodded, as if realizing that there wasn't any point to pushing it at the moment, and buckled down. Then he started the engine, easing them out into Melrose traffic, and away.

seventeen

The setting sun splashed the sky above Melrose Boulevard with a muddy orange light. A few more pedestrians wore sweaters and coats. A few more hookers and patrol cars cruised the streets. These were the only lines of demarcation between Hollywood days and nights. Otherwise, the entire area existed in a kind of uneasy limbo.

Some of the smaller shops were closed down. The used bookstores, stacked high with paperbacks and tattered hardcovers, had locked their doors. One of the last on the block to dim their lights was the Scented Garden incense shop. It was still operated by Julian and Gracie Rosehill, aging hippies who had weathered several generations of antidrug law enforcement activities. Scented Garden had originally been a Mr. Natural Head Shop. That had been the '70s, when hash pipes, bongs, ice pipes and other paraphernalia could be sold openly. In the late '70s it had metamorphosed into the Natural Way meditation store, selling posters and books on the legal or spiritual means of altering consciousness, with a small case of cigarette papers and coke spoons in the back; in the '80s it became Nature's Door, an exotic export and incense shop which sold drug paraphernalia only if the customer knew exactly what to ask for, and how to ask. The Rosehills had weathered the years, aging slowly but gracefully, but they too had put out the "closed" shingle.

Night in Hollywood was the hour of transition. There had been a brighter day, when people came from all over Los Angeles to see movies at the Chinese, and plays at the little ninety-nine-seat Equity waiver theaters dotting the area, but a queer thing had begun to happen. During the '70s it slid further and further downhill, more and more of the gentle, laughing young flower people replaced by genuine sad-case burnouts, the kind of spooks who crouched mumbling in doorways, who could barely ask for spare change without nodding off.

Free Love had been replaced by paid sex, and even the quality of the hookers had declined. Handjobs just weren't what they used to be. The area had finally become an eyesore, a complete embarrassment—not merely to the local residents but to the millions of people who visited each year. They came seeking the headwaters of the great dream river. Came dreaming of Shangri-La, and returned home remembering Calcutta.

It was this violation of the Grand Illusion that eventually motivated the frantic efforts to change things, to reclaim an era when gilded cinematic figures stood thirty feet tall on silver screens, untouched, untarnished, living antiseptic lives of high adventure and romance. Beautiful celluloid people who would never dream of overdosing in Beverly Hills Hotel cabanas. Or consorting with car-hopping hookers on West Hollywood side streets.

Money alone cannot restore a dream. The initial wave of new dollars sugar-coated Hollywood's rot for a while, but the decay ate its way back to the surface.

Then something odd began to happen. Here and there south of Sunset were little cultural oases where the moral fungus had yet to take hold. Instead of collapsing or fortifying, these little bastions not only held their ground but actually began to expand.

And if the Tinsel Town of the '40s had died, and the Flower Power dream of the '60s proved as transitory as a righteous buzz or a summer romance, Hollywood still attracted dreamers. Some of those dreamers had the craft and vision to create something which would endure, or at least protect its own tiny corner of the world.

Despite private security patrols and endless civic programs, Hollywood and Sunset boulevards continued to deteriorate. But as they did, small sections of bordering neighborhoods developed what might be called a "boutique" personality, preserving little clusters of shops and restaurants, minimalls and little gated neighborhoods where some of the '70s flavor still survived. Not everyone had given up or sold out. Some had dug in.

Hannah Appelion's Beautiful People thrift shop typified one of these latter. Born to Lebanese immigrants in Kalamazoo, Michigan, Hannah sojourned west to California in the '60s to study at UCLA. Blessed with an enormous amount of empathy and a great warmth of spirit, as well as a treble-dose of the we-can-change-the-world fervor which inflicted every college student with an ounce of self-respect or decent hashish, Hannah had followed one radical course after another.

The SDS, Black Power, and embryonic forms of Greenpeace were the first to catch her attention, and for a few months at a time, her heart. Political and personal passions have a tendency to intertwine, and heartbreak in one arena often influences commitments in the other.

So Hannah, as did millions of other young men and women in that turbulent time, engaged herself in the eternal search for meaning. The growing Consciousness movement finally caught her eye. Part of this new wave was chemical. Like many of her generation, she smoked marijuana and its various varieties, extracts and combinations. Like most of her contemporaries, she tried acid and psilocybin. Unlike many of her friends, however, she came to a set of fairly unique conclusions:

   1)   that the drug experiences were real and valid, but

   2)   unless you could replicate them without the use of the narcotics, they were useless.

So she began the long process of seeking the key to her own inner world. She tried floatation tanking (too confining), Dervishing (she vomited), Rolfing (too painful), Transcendental Meditation (interesting—and with modifications, she continued using it for years), est (too expensive—and if she enjoyed having overbearing men call her "asshole," she could have stayed at home and had Daddy do it for free).

Meanwhile, she received a bachelors in philosophy. One weekend, while combusting herbs with her head-tripping friends, she tried to imagine what they would all be like in twenty years, and had an epiphany.

Her friends were nice people, with above-average intelligence, vague commitments, and zero practical skills. Hannah realized that the immense, if mundane, practicality of her parents had its place in the world. In other words, she had glimpsed one of those cosmic truths which most humans avoid until their thirties.

She realized that if she wished to continue her journey of self-discovery, and more—if she wanted to be able to help other people—she first needed to help herself. Only those who had food on their tables could afford the luxury of philosophical speculation. The rest of humanity was too busy trying to fill growling bellies to debate Socrates or Nietzsche. This was a startling realization. Being unusually perceptive, she also realized that many of her compatriots would laugh at her, or merely gawk in disbelief, when they learned of her intentions.

Dropping out of the drop-out culture, Hannah entered UCLA's business school, emerging three years later with an MBA. After graduation, she went to work for Pacific Bell, in an administration position which demanded her left brain's full attention five days a week, but left her in full control of her weekends and her emotions.

On those weekends, and with those emotions, she continued to explore. She attended Esalen, and enjoyed Michael Murphy and especially George Leonard, who coached them through exercises extrapolated from the Japanese martial art of Aikido.

She sought out an Aikido school in Los Angeles, and in 1985 joined the Golden Sun Dojo. It was located near her apartment on La Cienega, on the second level of a strip mall, The school had a reputation in the Aikido community for intense and unusually realistic training. The head instructor was a tall man of preternatural energy and almost hypnotic self-confidence. His name was Manfred Gittes. Arrayed around the walls were an American flag, a Japanese flag, and a picture of a wizened old man she learned was Morihei Ueshiba, the founder of Aikido, with whom Gittes had studied in Japan. And there were also pictures of a beautiful young boy and girl, of mixed ancestry. Their names, she learned later, were Joy and Tomo.

When Gittes looked at Joy's picture, it was with the eyes of a man in love.

For the first few months, neither Manfred nor his assistant instructor Hiroshi (Manfred always seemed to be off on business trips or supervising his three other schools, or visiting . . . someone; Hannah thought she knew who) would answer direct questions about the Twins, although occasional references to them were made.

But one day, after a particularly tough session, when the windows were steamed opaque and her heavy cotton pajama-like *gi* was so sodden with sweat that it doubled in weight, Gittes invited a few of his favorite students to remain after class for a special surprise.

And after the others were gone, he told them to line up against the wall. Kneeling in *seiza* position, Hannah waited, without speaking, for a half hour. Her legs ached, from endless *tenkan* and *irimi nage* repetitions during two and a half grueling hours of workout. Sweat drooled down her face and dripped from the end of her nose. She also sensed that for the six (out of thirty-eight) students who had received invitations to remain behind, there could be no room for weariness or doubt.

After another ten minutes, she heard a car pulling into the nearly deserted parking lot beneath them.

She heard high-pitched voices, laughter, and then two people entered the school.

Her first impression was *they're children!* Then she realized that they had only appeared so due to the extraordinary lightness of their carriage. They had to be in their twenties, and despite the fact that one was male and the other female, they seemed identical twins.

Sensei Gittes bowed to them deeply, respectfully, and the twins returned it. She was a little confused here—they bowed as deeply as one might to a teacher, but Gittes offered them the same extraordinary respect.

He turned to the class. "As I am your *sensei* in Aikido," he said. "So these are my teachers in other areas of life. They came to my dojo in Mill Valley five years ago, and wished to continue their martial instruction. It was my very great pleasure to award them their *nidan* certificates last year. It is my honor to introduce you to Tomo and Joy Oshita."

They bowed to him again in tandem, and then turned to the students.

"The art of Aikido is based on the concept of *Ki,*" Joy Oshita said in a very precise, almost clipped voice. "An inchoate energy which can be directed by the mind and spirit. Most of the things you have learned, which have been explained as *Ki,* or *Chi,* or *Prana,* can be explained as the advanced and proper application of physics. So most students think that is all there is. Master Ueshiba knew that this was not the case. And after we are through here tonight, so shall you."

Manfred's gaze never left Joy. All the stern lines around his mouth and eyes softened. In that moment, he seemed more human than ever. Hannah was instantly fascinated.

Soon afterward, she began her apprenticeship with the Twins. A year later, she quit her job at Pac Bell, and opened the second-hand shop, using her business skills to provide employment for some of the street people that the Golden Sun occasionally adopted and assisted. Hannah no longer practiced Aikido: she had found the source of the truth she had sought her whole life, and was, finally, part of a Great Work.

For Hannah Appelion, life was complete.

Hannah was closing out the cash register. It took her longer than usual: she kept thinking about the way Chris looked as they took him away, mouth stuffed with cotton, the trachea tube projecting from his throat.

She buried her feelings, ignored the uneasy voice whispering in her mind. This wasn't the time, or the place. She needed to get back to her apartment. To consult Her, and ask for Her guidance. That thought gave Hannah comfort. There was always a subtle, delicate, powerful presence in her mind, one which she could count upon in the most trying of times. It would not fail her now.

And this *was* a critical time. Just *how* critical, very few understood. Just a few more weeks, and the world would change forever. So much of the pain and anguish she saw everywhere around her would simply . . . vanish. There would be magic and miracles again, bland Kansas transmuted into a Technicolor wonderland.

The doorbell tinkled. She heard the door open and close. That was odd, but not in itself alarming. She would have sworn the front door was locked.

She looked up quickly, but could see nothing . . . except the door drifted closed, and then went *click.* But if someone had compromised the bolted door, it was someone she couldn't see. Perhaps they had taken a sharp turn left toward the housewares, or right toward the children's clothing, and disappeared down an aisle. She saw nothing at all.

Hadn't she bolted that door?

"Hello?" she called. "We're closed. In fact, I thought the door was locked." Her voice didn't emerge as strong and assertive as she had intended. She didn't like the way she was shaking, either. Hell, at the worst this was probably a late bargain shopper, looking for some odd pennysaver.

Hannah moved around from behind the cash register, past a rack of used paperback books, past pots and pans, and a layout of frilly items. She remembered eight months ago, when Gloria Estefan had entered the shop, hair scarved back and sun glasses in place, and spent forty-five minutes poking around, finally buying eighty-seven dollars worth of frillies. Hannah thought Ms. Estefan was very polite, but looked a little tired.

"Hello?" What the hell could it have been? Maybe just a gust of wind. That's all it was, and—

She gasped as a pair of hands grabbed her from behind. She thought, *hoped* that she was held by human hands. God, whoever—*whatever* it was dug so cruelly that she wondered. The force was emotionally crippling. Nothing, she thought—no human could generate or resist a force like that.

Before she could adjust her bearings, something—it smelled like leather—was pulled over her eyes and nose. A sudden sharp pain behind her knees, and she gasped as she was driven to the ground.

She could see nothing.

"The . . . the money is in the register."

There was a short burst of very nasty laughter. "Don't want money," a male voice said. "No. That's not it."

"What . . . ?" she felt more confused than frightened.

"What did you tell them?" the man asked, his voice a hoarse whisper.

"Tell who?" she asked in genuine confusion.

"The man. The woman." Another voice said. This one was female. Harsh.

"What did you tell them?"

"Nothing!"

A sudden, massive explosion of stars and colors, the breach birth of bright nebulae. Then came the pain, stabbing into her head like a broken bottle.

Blood salted her mouth.

"Lie," the woman said. "Every time you lie it's going to hurt. What did you tell them?"

"Tell who?" Hannah moaned. The ringing in her head clouded rational thought.

"The man. The woman," the male voice repeated. "What did you tell them? What do you know?" The voice was droning, almost disconnected from the sudden, shocking violence of the minute that followed. Hannah felt herself scream, heard herself bleed, saw herself beg, knew nothing but a primal, private chaos until she lay on her side, whimpering like an animal. She no longer recognized the sounds she made as anything human.

"Tell us what you know," the woman said. "And the pain will stop."

"Know . . . about what?"

She felt her arm wrenched up behind her back, and she began to scream again. And kept screaming, all the way into blackness.

eighteen

The beach was unusually quiet tonight. Cat turned away from the window, back to where Tyler and Jax pored over a bewildering collage of written notes, surveillance photos and leaflets scattered across a folding table.

Dr. Sinclair sat beside the table, his beige calfskin jacket unbuttoned to give space to his paunch, his legs elegantly crossed and his lap filled with papers. As he thumbed through them, he adjusted his glasses, sighed and hawed.

"Very good," he said finally. "Thorough."

On one level, Cat felt satisfied with that evaluation. On another, she felt as if she stood atop an ice floe, cool but aware that the entire titanic sheet was buckling, with some terrible pressure from beneath.

What's in the attic, Cat . . . ?

Certainly, their first four days had yielded no spectacular success. Not only had they failed to produce Kolla, but at least in indirect result of their questioning, a harmless little mouse of a man was in critical condition.

"We don't know if Tony Corman's death had anything to do with Kolla," Tyler said, "but a telephone conversation with the duty nurse at Portland General said that his 'sister' visited earlier that day. Corman had no sister. We faxed them a photo of Kolla, and, well, it might have been her."

Sinclair nodded approvingly. "I have an agency in Seattle—and they didn't get as far as that. I'm impressed."

"Will you follow up in Portland?"

"Absolutely—I've passed your leads to the Northwest folks. I'd like you to continue in California."

"Your sister might return to Los Angeles," Jax said. "Golden Sun has nodes across the country and around the world. Simple surveillance isn't going to turn much up. We may have to go through the other end, start with her last known whereabouts, talk to her friends, see if she's been in touch with anyone. Frankly, I'd put my money on Oregon. But if you want to continue paying for our services, we'll keep checking."

He brushed at the wispy fringe of gray hairs at his forehead. "I can think of no better investment."

"Well, no one will admit to knowing her. Only one person even said he'd ever seen Kolla—then *he* tried to kill himself."

"Are you suggesting a causal connection?"

"It's tempting. He was terrified of betraying the Twins. Thought that maybe he already had. However, I'm just telling you events as they occurred. I think the Golden Sun is afraid of someone . . . but they're excited about something at the same time."

"Something?" he asked quizzically. "Something like what?"

"I'm not sure . . . but it's due to happen within the next couple of months."

"Do you have any idea what that might be?"

Jax spoke up. "Guy at an ad agency says the Oshitas have purchased major television time in August. Satellite hookup stuff. It could be that they're being extra security-conscious until then. At any rate, if she comes back to Los Angeles, there doesn't appear to be a direct route to finding her. She's got money—she can stay in any hotel she wants. Her last known California address was a condo in Hermosa Beach. That was two years ago. No forwarding address. No friends in the building. The management company doesn't know anything—Kolla just sold out and left."

"In case you wonder," Sinclair said, "you have accomplished my primary objective—which is to get an overview of the organization."

"Pretty wild stuff," Jax tried to smile, but the effort wasn't entirely successful. "They're all nookie hooked—" he glanced at Cat. "And some of them are nuts."

"Oh, yes. The poor fellow at the thrift shop." Sinclair puckered his lips with distaste.

Cat handed their client an envelope. "Through a police contact in Beverly Hills we obtained an invitation to a week-long workshop up in the Santa Cruz area. Starts Sunday. You might want to find a partner and attend. Kolla may be involved on the organizational end."

Sinclair thumbed the envelope open, glanced at it, and then closed his eyes thoughtfully. Without opening them, he asked: "Is that all?"

"Nope," Tyler said. "I checked with a friend in Anthropology at UCLA, and he said about what I figured."

"Which is?"

Tyler tapped the book entitled *See and Believe.* "It's synthetic." he said.

"Excuse me?"

"Well, Joy and Tomo give mucho lip service to having studied all kindsa secret stuff." He flipped the book open fifty pages or so. "Here in chapter three they talk about traveling to Tibet when they were kids, and in chapter six about how one of their great uncles or something was a Hawaiian Kahuna. They blather about sexual magic from connections in the American Indian community. And they say that there's this secret society which underlies all of these separate disciplines, and by joining this very secret society they got access to the real core teachings. This is Lynn Andrews stuff. Rosicrucian mail-order enlightenment. You know, *Mutant Message Down Under.*"

Sinclair raised an eyebrow. Jax laughed. "It's a book by a woman who claims she went Walkabout with the Abos. He doesn't buy it."

"Look at her picture on the dust jacket," Tyler said defensively. "Does she look like someone who could walk a thousand miles barefoot? Jeeze, she's the Pillsbury Doughgirl."

"Are we digressing?" Cat asked helpfully.

"Yeah, well, my friend said that no culture could produce these teachings organically."

"Meaning?"

"Meaning it's pieces of this and that. One part shamanism, one part Taoist stuff. Some Tantra, a little Aleister Crowley . . . it's goulash. Non-organic. They're frauds." He shrugged, and threw the book back onto the table.

"Of *course* they're frauds," Sinclair said impatiently. "The only question is . . . are they dangerous frauds?"

That question wasn't the one she had expected. "Maybe," she said. "No. Taking everything into account, I don't think so. But they might attract some dangerous people. Some crazies. Any cult will."

Sinclair looked at Jax, who shrugged. Tyler snorted. "Is it reasonable to say that you aren't afraid of them?"

Despite herself, Cat felt something irritating growing inside her, like an itch she couldn't scratch. "No. We aren't afraid of them. Why do you ask?"

Sinclair sat back in his chair and smiled. "Because, I wondered if you would consider attending that workshop yourselves."

The question reverberated through the room with the approximate impact of a medium-sized fuel-air explosion.

After about ten seconds of total silence, Cat cleared her throat. "Me and Jax, you mean."

Rather tastelessly, Cat thought, Jax began whistling Prince's "Erotic City."

"Yes. I congratulate you on your work—and I believe you to be correct. It would be natural for Kolla to facilitate at such a workshop. She was working on a psychology degree. I find it likely that she'll be there—or that you will find information which could lead to her."

Cat drummed her fingers on her chair, and tried to ignore the painful tension in her chest. "Our information says that someone else tried to penetrate their organization."

"So to speak," Jax said blandly.

She ignored him. "Have you heard anything like this?" she asked Sinclair.

"Mine is not the first allegation of kidnapping—but the Twins have powerful allies. It has been difficult to get anything done. Then, about a year ago, the FBI sent a husband and wife team in to one of the workshops."

Cat remembered the story from King, but decided to wait and hear Sinclair's version. There might be some interesting overlaps, mismatches or additions.

"And?" Tyler asked.

"They found nothing actionable. Consenting adults, and an educational context. Apparently, the woman was terrified."

"What happened to the couple?" Jax asked.

"They aren't you," Sinclair said blandly. "It wouldn't happen again."

Cat bored in. "What happened?"

Sinclair shrugged. "The man was sexually dysfunctional the entire week."

Cat narrowed her eyes. "He couldn't maintain an erection?"

"Correct."

"Hey," Jax said. "He was a Fed. What was he supposed to do—close his eyes and think of Clyde Tolson?"

"What happened to the woman?" Tyler asked.

"Apparently . . . a week after the workshop, she stepped in front of a car."

For almost a minute, a dull, uncomfortable silence filled the office. Cat cleared her throat. "Excuse me, Mr. Sinclair. Mr. Carpenter and I have been divorced for almost a year."

Tyler tapped a ballpoint pen on a pad of paper, idly constructing a constellation of little blue dots. "And they said it wouldn't last."

Jax sighed heavily. "I think you may be looking for someone else."

"I'll pay you fifty thousand."

Tyler dropped his pen. *"Dollars?"*

Cat paled.

Now Sinclair's smile really broadened. "In exchange for one week of . . . pleasurable work. Play. Call it what you will. Miss Juvell. Can we speak frankly?"

Her tongue felt thick and cold, but she managed to swallow. "I would prefer it."

"You and Mr. Carpenter are both adults," he said. "You obviously have respect and affection for each other, and once there was love."

"That was a long time ago," she muttered.

"Suppose I asked you to risk your lives for that kind of money. Would you hesitate?"

Tyler's laugh was sour. "For about two seconds."

Sinclair seemed honestly baffled. "Is this a fate worse than death?"

"Doctor Sinclair . . ." Cat began, but couldn't force herself to continue.

"Jesus," Jax whispered. "Fifty *thousand?"*

"Above and beyond the monies already discussed."

"Ah, Cat?" Tyler said. "We need to talk here."

She held up her palm to Tyler, trying to buy herself time to think. "Mr. Sinclair. This is a very interesting proposition—"

"So to speak," Jax added. He was struggling not to laugh.

"We need time to talk about this. Privately. May we call you tomorrow with an answer?"

"Of course," Sinclair rose. "I'll leave you to mull this over." He paused at the door. "You know," he said. "Mr. Carpenter was probably correct. The FBI agents were a pair of uptight Feds. I'm quite certain that what happened to them wouldn't happen to you. To a man of your caliber, Jax. Or a woman of yours. Good afternoon."

Sinclair rose carefully from his chair, paused at the door to bow shallowly, and left.

Tyler examined his fingernails carefully. " 'A man of your caliber' Jax? And just what caliber is that?"

"Forty-four Magnum," Jax said in his best Clint Eastwood impression. "And it could blow her head clean *off*."

"Thank you. Thank you very much," Cat said. "We need to have a serious discussion about this one. Get Freddy over here. We need to talk."

"Damned right," Tyler said. "Sounds like an all-nighter to me."

Cat shot Jax a dirty look and his mouth closed almost before it had begun to open.

"I need some target practice," Cat's eyes suddenly went bright. "Anyone for the range? This time of night, should be no problem getting a last minute rez."

"Why not?" Tyler said. "We can have Freddy meet us there. You up for it, Jax?"

"A loaded gun is a terrible thing to waste," Jax said.

nineteen

The thrift shop door opened, and then closed.

A man and a woman exited, entering a dark sedan parked beside an expired meter. The engine coughed and then purred softly, turning over. Its headlights blinked to life. Like a prowling predator, it glided away from the curb.

For a long time nothing happened, except the growl and flash of passing cars and buses, cruising on their way to a hundred thousand private destinations. Then the door opened again. Hannah Appelion appeared, framed in a sliver of darkness deeper than the electric night.

She seemed dazed, uncertain of her location or perhaps even her identity. Her jaw was swollen out of shape. The left side of her face was scraped and torn. Blood drooled from a torn lip. She walked doubled over, hobbling, her left arm clamped tightly against her side.

One blindly groping arm found the knob and slammed the door. Despite her pain, she had the presence of mind to throw the bolt.

Shading her eyes with one hand, she staggered down the sidewalk, each uncertain step followed by another, and then another, no matter how impossible the efforts seemed. The street smoked and coughed at her.

An older couple approached from the opposite direction. She had a vague memory of their faces; perhaps she had seen them in the store. Either they didn't recognize her, or didn't care. They veered around her as she lurched toward her destination.

Somehow she managed to make it a single block, and then another. And another. One laborious step at a time, one breath at a time. She knew and felt that something was broken inside her.

If she could get home, she could get help. At home, there was healing. The Twins would save her. She knew it. She could be healed. No doctors. Doctors meant needles, and loss of control and then she might talk more than she already had, and she couldn't have that.

Like Chris Zimmer, she would rather die.

twenty

The indoor range of the Santa Monica gun club hung with the sour but oddly satisfying smell of gun smoke. Cat stood in her modified Weaver stance: right leg back, right arm rigid, left hand bracing the Browning .45, left elbow tight into her side. The automatic was smoking but quiet in her hand.

Beside her, Jax emptied his black Glock, his hand rock steady against the recoil. Cat preferred the Browning for target practice, but shared Jax's preference for 9mm Glocks on the job. If she could control the Browning, with its rougher recoil, small-caliber accuracy was just that much easier.

At ten meters she was silver-dollar accurate. At fifteen her groupings displayed a bit of spread and drift toward the lower right. After she emptied another clip, she paused to watch Tyler. He'd engaged the wheel lock on his chair, and propped his left elbow on its armrest, his right arm stiff in his own modification of the Weaver. He crushed his brown bowler hat down on his head and emptied his clip, one calm shot after another. Braced as he was, Tyler was more accurate than either Cat or Jax. A little slower getting into position, maybe, but once there, Tyler was extraordinary.

Unlike either of his partners, Tyler had never been called upon to use his skills in the line of duty. In his mind, he was shooting paper. For Cat or Jax, it was impossible to completely forget the human beings who had been in their sights.

They had the range's "C" wing reserved for the next hour, and had already run two hundred rounds apiece through their respective weapons. From the corner of her eye, Cat saw the door behind them opening, and Freddy King entered. He carried a flat black gun case in his right hand. Freddy nodded to them without speaking, took up station on the far side of Tyler, and opened his case.

Nestled there in dimpled foam packing was a .44 Sig Saur, his favorite target piece—a far cry from his duty .38. King was an expert marksman with his service piece—and with a Beretta .22 or his 9mm Luger. He maintained all of these weapons in impeccable condition, and carried them to the range on a rotating basis. Of the four friends, Freddy King probably loved shooting the most. Even at his age, he was faster than Jax and more accurate than Cat.

Cat pushed the overhead button, starting the little winch to bring her target back. The man-silhouette fluttered as it reeled back to them. Freddy examined her grouping and nodded. "Not bad," he said. "You're looking a little bit off today, Cat. Breaking your wrist."

"Well, you know me," she shrugged. "I'm not at my best when there's nothing on the line. It's like playing poker with chips. Put some pennies on the table."

"What about dinner? Winner picks, loser pays? We can make it that real. How does that work for you?"

"Chinese, anyone?" Cat asked, reloading.

"Moo Goo Gai Pan?" Tyler asked. "Twice chewed pork? Golden shower chicken?"

"Jesus. Will you put a lid on it?"

Jax raised his hand. "I'll sit out and call it," he said.

She clipped up new targets, and reeled them out into place. "Thirty rounds apiece," Cat said. "O.K."

When all earplugs were in place, he flicked the overhead lights, and thunder filled the air. The percussive roar rolled and swelled as Cat, Tyler and King emptied their weapons, dumped shells or dropped clips, slipped in speed loaders or new magazines, raised and fired again. Although their speed was uncannily similar, the varying capacities of magazines and loaders pushed their sequence out of synch with each other, so that the shattering din never seemed to stop.

After a minute, the last round had been fired. Tyler was ahead—but only slightly. The urgency of competition took a little edge off his accuracy.

King slapped Tyler a high-five. "Great shooting there, Rollerboy."

"It's all in the wheelchair," Tyler said modestly.

"My turn," Jax said. "Cat? Freddy?"

Fred King held up his hands. "Are you about to get strange on me?"

Cat grinned, removing her Glock from its case and slipping cartridges into its spare clips. "It's 'The Weirds' all right. We shot straight for an hour before you showed up. We've earned a little fun."

"I'm sitting out," he said, and backed away from the firing line.

"The Weirds" were Cat's playtime with Jax. Trick shots, dexterity exercises, and specialty drills. There was little practical application for the kind of shooting they were about to indulge in, but it was a great way to relieve a hard day's stress.

Their weapons clipless and placed squarely on the gun platforms, both Cat and Jax relaxed. They stepped back, took a few deep breaths.

Tyler flickered the overhead lights.

Their hands flashed forward, seized their respective Glocks and with a single motion, flipped them around behind their backs, and passed them to their left hands. Slammed in the clips, and fired left-handed until they were empty. Dropped the clips, passed them behind the back to the right hand, reloaded, emptied, passed the empty weapon back around again. . . .

They did it five times, faster and faster, and the last time, they were almost laughing too hard to complete the action.

Freddy King could only watch and shake his head. They fired holding their weapons sideways and upside down. They took turns shooting across the smalls of their backs. They fired three shots right-handed, switched hands, fired three shots, changed hands, three shots, changed hands. . . .

Finally they cross-laned, firing at each other's targets in a deliberate attempt to foul up the other's groupings. By the time that their targets were reeled back in, they were both laughing so hard they could barely breathe.

Jax lay his empty Glock down and raised his hands. "All right, you got me."

King looked baffled. "So—why do you do this?"

"You know," Cat gasped. "The truth is that with any luck, we'll never fire one of these things at a human being for the rest of our lives. We're pretty careful. But if the need ever arises, its a good idea to have put in the practice."

Jax chimed in. "It gets a little dull doing it every week, every month . . . so we find ways of making things more interesting. Keeps us going. But we do occasionally indulge in 'The Weirds.' "

"Both of you are crazy as blind snakes. But, I love you."

"Aww," Cat skritched his cheek with one short nail. "You say that to all the markspeople. I'm hungry. Let's nosh."

twenty-one

Bits of rice and pork had scattered themselves across Cat's living room table, escaping the edges of the paper plates, and the frantic scooping motions of plastic forks. A grain or two had dropped to her chocolate pile rug, and would probably remain there, plotting insurgence, until cleaning day. Cat's fingers were a blur of chopsticks. "Forks are for round-eyed barbarians," she said.

"Which description fits you perfectly," King said.

"Round-eyed perhaps, barbaric never. Besides, it just doesn't taste the same off a fork."

"It's part of the old Chinese curse," Tyler said through a mouthful of noodles.

"What's that?"

" 'May you live with interesting tines.' "

King threw a packet of hot mustard at him, scoring a near-miss. Then he laughed and rubbed a stomach full of sweet and sour chicken and hot and sour soup (Jax's favorite combination, but he would always complain: "you'd think they could make something either sweet, or sour, or hot, and let it go at that, but noooooo. . . .").

They had caravanned from the Santa Monica gun club out to the Malibu Apartment complex, which was technically a mile south of Malibu, but offered all the view and beach access at two-thirds the price. The three-bedroom she shared with Tyler was on the fourth floor, with a spectacular ocean view and wood-burning fireplace. The kitchen was a blaze of steel and glass, and the rest of the apartment was soft with earth tones and filled with low-maintenance ferns.

"So," Freddy said. "Let me see if I've got this right."

"Please do," Cat answered.

"If you go to the workshop, you and Alley Oop will have to boff for a week."

"Not exactly the way Grandma would have put it."

"You'd be surprised where Grandma put it, once Grandpa got her warmed up." He belched, and a fine, satisfying belch it was. "So you go to an all-expense-paid orgy for a week, learn how to bang each other's brains out—"

Jax picked up the flyer for the workshop. "Excuse me." He read. " 'Engage energetically at the level of the second chakra.' "

"Did I offend your sensibilities?"

"Deeply."

"Fuckin' sorry." He yawned, smoothing back his salt-and-pepper hair with his palm. "Anyway, you guys engage in some world-class corkpopping, and get paid fifty thousand dollars? Is that right?"

"Well . . ."

"Gee," he said sarcastically. "Tough decision there."

"It's not that simple," Jax said in frustration.

"No," Cat said. "It isn't."

Tyler was sitting back, watching all of them. "Say what's really on your mind, Freddy."

"I think you're scared as hell."

Cat bristled. "Of what?

"The fuckin' Boogieman. What do you think? Each other. I think you're still in love. I think you're afraid you'll find out."

Cat scowled. "I'm not that easy to manipulate, Freddy."

King leaned forward, grinning. "Then try this on for size, campers. A man ate glass. One FBI agent half-dead, and another one insane. Then that guy Cleese out in Riverside. The transients."

"We've got another weird one for you," Tyler said. "Guy named Corman up in Portland. Linked with the Oshitas. Injured in a traffic accident—"

King blinked. "Stepped in front of a car?"

"No," Tyler said. "This was pure accident. On a motorcycle, blew a tire coming off the freeway. That isn't what killed him. He went into some kind of convulsion. Heartbeat up to two-twenty, tore half his own muscles loose, broken bones. Supposed to be a real mess."

"Poison?"

"Not that toxicology could find. But he listed the Golden Sun as his next of kin. Showed up on the database, thought you should know."

"Jesus," Freddy said. "When did this happen?"

"Oregon, four days ago. Like I said, I've been watching the computers for Oshita links ever since we've talked. I'd be surprised if I don't come across a few more."

"After years of peace," King said, "suddenly two bizarros in one week, and maybe a missing heiress."

Tyler templed his fingers and closed his eyes, ruminating. "Observation," he said finally. "A situation remains static for a protracted period, then suddenly begins to change."

"Speculation," Cat said. "Some new element has been introduced."

"Or a new phase entered," Jax offered.

"Co-rectamundo," Tyler was warming to his subject. "Now. What do we know? The Twins have purchased major satellite time on August Sixth—some announcement. Some major something."

"Iron Shadows?" King muttered.

"So . . . maybe the Twins are trying to do something, and someone's trying to scare them? Pick off the vulnerables?"

"Or the Twins are cleaning up loose ends?" Jax offered.

"Either way—or if it's something else altogether, there's a girl in there, and her brother wants to know if she's safe. If you were asked to stroll through fire, or quicksand, or a pool of rabid piranha, you'd go straight into it. Something's going down, and you may be the only chance this girl Kolla's got. So you tell me, dammit, what is there besides fear that would keep you out of that workshop?"

Cat said nothing. Freddy King plucked up the last egg roll, dipped it in hot mustard and took a bite. A half hour ago, they'd been crisp. Now they were chewy. He chewed, watching his friends watch each other.

"Is there?" he said softly. "Anything at all?"

No answer. He took another bite.

twenty-two

Cat, Jax and Tyler walked Freddy around to the parking lot, saw him into his car and closed the door carefully. Jax leaned over. "Thanks," he said. "Thanks for helping us think this one through. It's a bruiser."

Freddy King's craggy pale face was serious now. "You know, you kids will do what's right. I know that."

He took Cat's hand. "There's nothing wrong with the two of you," he said, looking directly into her eyes. "It's this fucking world out here, you know. You tried to keep crap like the Vasquez case out of your heart, out of your business, but you just can't. I let it tear up my thing with Margie. Hell, I never even tried again. At least the two of you had enough sense not to let it mess up your friendship. You know how *sane* that is? Got any idea at all?"

Cat leaned down and kissed his cheek gently. "You take care. And thanks. And Freddy . . . ?"

"Yeah?"

"You tell *anybody* about tonight's conversation, we skin you and roll you in salt."

He laughed, and pulled out of the lot.

Cat and Jax walked Tyler to the elevator. "I'll be up in a while," Cat said to him. "Got some thinking to do."

Tyler was strangely quiet, just looking from one of them to the other, and then a strange, lopsided little grin touched his freckled face. "You call it, Sis." He rolled into the elevator car, and let the door shut.

It suddenly seemed to occur to Cat that she stood alone with Jax, and she took a half-step away from him.

"So," Jax said finally. "We're gonna do this?"

Cat nodded slowly. "It's business."

"Yeah," he agreed. "Just business. Now. Excuse me, I have to get very drunk." He started to turn.

Cat caught his arm. "Not too drunk," she said, surprised at the strain in her voice. "You never know when you're going to need all your strength."

"Oh. Hah hah." He waved at her without turning around, and walked off toward his Bronco.

Cat watched him go. Jax seemed somehow . . . smaller than he usually did. More vulnerable. She remembered that particular version of Jax Carpenter too well. She had hoped never to see it again. God. Why was she doing this? She was just going to hurt herself. Hurt Jax.

Hurt Tyler.

And for what?

Because there's a girl out there who might need your help, a voice said.

Is that all? Of course it was.

But then there was something else, a single moment when a man she had never met looked at her, and something she had kept closed her entire life had opened up, and he had made a promise without words.

I can heal . . . he had said.

Are you mine?

And most disturbingly, because the thought barely seemed to originate in her own mind: *What's in the attic, Cat?*

A tan sedan was parked across Pacific Coast Highway. Within its darkness, someone watched.

Those eyes watched the four people exit the apartment, watched them go their several ways.

Those eyes watched the woman stand alone, arms wrapped around her chest.

"Porsche Musette Juvell," the watcher said. Then repeated the three names as if darkly amused. The woman turned, and walked along the highway. She cut across and headed down to the beach. Nice walk by the waves to clear your head, dear?

The observer picked up a cellular phone plugged into the cigarette lighter, and punched in a number. When the line was answered, the observer began to speak.

twenty-three

In a shadowed room devoid of furniture, a blind, aged woman slept restlessly upon a straw mat. She was not in the hands of enemies—on the contrary, those entrusted with her keeping loved her more than life. If her quarters were Spartan, it was by her own request. The room was warm, and clean, but bare.

She dreamed.

It was the Bad Dream, an old woman's dream, the one which had haunted her for what now seemed a hundred lifetimes. In that dream, she was young again, not the withered creature who could barely move without an assistant at each arm. Not the hag who had no more control over her bowels and bladder than a newborn infant. Despite the extraordinary resources available to her, the flesh was weak,

The flesh would not last much longer. Perhaps, just perhaps it would survive long enough. Yes. Even lost in dream, she smiled at the thought.

For the dream was always partially lucid. She was always *aware* that she was dreaming, even if she was unable to influence its course or imagery.

In it, she was a student once again, working to protect her country. In it, she prepared sterile solutions and washed glass beakers, and gave respect to the great men who labored diligently, that her beloved homeland might claim its destiny.

In it, she stood facing away from the one window which looked out on the city, washing glassware at a tiny sink when the terrible moment came. In that moment, the world became so bright that she saw the bones through her suddenly translucent hands. Then she was slammed into and almost *through* the wall, and a wave of fire dissolved her world into chaos and pain.

Can you dream of blackness? Of void? She thought so, because there followed a time of darkness, womb-darkness, death-darkness. The darkness of a dream of dreamless sleep.

After an unknown time she awoke, bleeding from a thousand cuts. It was horror beyond imagining even to consider what might have entered her body through those myriad wounds, to think what burning, crawling doom seethed in her veins, seeking her heart and brain and lungs like termites seeking the core of an apple tree.

In that dream, she pushed her way free of the ashes and crushed timbers, of the mangled bodies of the kind and dedicated men who had employed her. Numbness and a kind of mindless lethargy swelled within her like a gray tide. She stood on an endless, featureless plain of despair, where land and sky met along a misty horizon. She was drowning in a sea of discordant sound, pierced only by the small voice which said: *your children.*

After an eternity of struggle she managed to claw her way free of the wreckage, and emerged into a grim world which had transformed from thriving city to boneyard in a single blinding instant. The screams of the dying and the faces of the dead killed what remained of her heart.

And in that dream, finally, she came to the house where she had left her children in the care of her beloved mother. Her children, the most important things in all the world, were gone. The house was gone. The street was gone. All that remained was a single wall, and on that wall were two outlines, seared there by the terrible fire. She raised her own burned hands and touched the black ghosts, touched the images of the children she cherished, now reduced to something very close to nothing.

Daughter Joy. Little Tomo. Gone.

And for the ten-thousandth time, she heard herself giggle. A small sound, at first, which swelled and filled her, and blotted out what remained of her mind. Her fingertips brushed the charcoal remnants of the creatures she loved most in all the world. Powdery brown black flakes smeared onto her fingertips. She blew on them. The powder floated to the wind, like dandelion spores.

"Iron Shadows," she giggled. "Iron Shadows."

The woman stirred, eyelids flickering to expose the cloudy, sightless eyes. Thin parched lips made animal sounds as she neared waking. Then she sank once again, as if some dark, hungry creature wrapped her in ravenous arms, and drew her once again into the depths of her blackest fantasy.

———

The dream reran itself, as it did more and more frequently as she neared the end of her life. There was flying glass, and a wall of fire, the screams of the dying and the charred flesh of the dead.

For the ten-thousandth time, she wandered through the wreckage, and found the charcoaled smears of her children, blasted into the ragged shelf of burned brick.

Sometimes the dream ended there.

This evening, it continued on, into deeper nightmare. She experienced hunger such as she had never known, grief at the loss of everything which had been her world. There was no end to the shattered lives, the hollow, haggard faces.

Legions of the dead walking the shattered streets of her city, their flesh melted and dripping from their faces like tallow. She saw piles of burning bodies, the meat-stink of them a choking, acrid blanket rolling close to the earth for dreadful, endless miles.

She remembered the uniforms of their pale conquerors. Even if they brought food and medicine, they also brought domination to a people who had never known defeat. Her hatred of them blossomed, opened like some sick-sweet flower in her heart.

She wanted to die. Surely the flying glass which had sliced her skin had carried invisible death with every tiny cut. Surely, she had not long to wait.

She curled in her one room shack and shook, and cried, and rolled helplessly in her own sour wetness, praying for death, but did not die. Knew that she was sick inside, sick in a way that she could not understand, that should have brought death to a thousand women. Somehow, she did not die. In every piece of shiny metal, every fragment of glass or mirror she passed as she stalked the streets in endless search for food and meaning, she saw the reflection of a woman similar to the one who had survived that bright, horrible day—only more alive, burning with some inner fire. And knew what she had to do, as soon as desperation lowered her remaining inhibitions.

Ultimately, hunger consumed morality. She earned money through the only avenue remaining to her: selling her body to her conquerors. The men who rented her saw a whore. In her mirror, she saw a warrior queen, waging a lonely war. She laughed herself to sleep at night, knowing that within her body burned a terrible secret, one which might kill the foreign soldiers where her dead husband's bombs and bullets had failed.

She laughed herself to sleep, and cried herself awake. Every new dawn increased her conviction that it was not death that grew within her. Not death, but something far, far worse.

And she remembered the day she met the man. The black man from America. The one with a scarred face, who said she was descended from gods. The man whose laughter was as deep, cold, and inhuman as an Arctic night.

twenty-four

Without knowing exactly *how* she completed her trek to the Sunset Arms apartment complex, Hannah did so.

She staggered up the stairs, each step a torment. She fumbled in her purse until she found her keys. Her fingers felt numb. Her elbow wouldn't bend. She remembered being beaten, and kicked. But she wasn't certain what else had happened. What other insults had occurred. It just hurt everywhere.

Hannah leaned her head against the security gate, gaining strength before she managed to try again. This time, she successfully slid the key into the lock, and opened the black metal grille.

To her blurred vision, the hall looked infinitely long, and threatened to recede with every step she took.

One more step. Then another. The left hip ached, and she didn't remember why or how the damage had been done. Even now, Hannah had difficulty remembering exactly what she had said to the bad people. The people who, she was certain, worked for the Iron Shadows. She couldn't remember, but felt that there was something wrong. That there was something very wrong. Why would the Twins' most dire enemies let her live? What did they really want . . . ?

At her door Hannah stumbled again, fumbled for her key, and then finally managed to open it.

She fell more than stepped in, and kicked the door shut.

She needed privacy. Darkness. Sometimes, in darkness there was safety.

Why did they let you live?

She dragged herself to the most sacred corner of the room. Upon a small rug rested a hardwood table inlaid with ivory and silver. The only object on the table was a trifold golden picture frame, holding images of her dearest loves, of the most important things in her life, the Twins. Joy. And Tomo. One to each side. The most precious picture was in the middle, a snapshot of the three of them together. Joy and Tomo smiling, their arms around a devastatingly blissed-out Hannah.

"Tomo," she whispered. "I need you now."

Her hands shaking, she lit two sticks of incense, and placed one in each of two tiny sculpted holders.

It took her three tries to coax flame from the childproof lighter. She sobbed in frustration by the time the first curls of smoke rose from the scented sticks.

As she had been taught long before, she struggled to steady her breathing. She needed to stay strong. There was danger, and she needed to warn those she loved.

Why did they let you live?

The voice in the back of her head was just a little stronger now, a little clearer, and she couldn't answer the question. She could only trust her conviction that there *was,* in fact, an answer. That she must once again place her reliance in the two beings she trusted above all others.

She knelt on bruised and swollen legs, closed her eyes, and sank her breathing to the root of her belly. There was a void within her, black and deep, and in that hallowed emptiness lived peace, and no pain. In that place lived a pulsing light. She had always known that place, had found it in other meditations, even before the Twins, before the blood, and the joining, and the real magic.

Before she learned to fear what might lurk in the darkness beyond the light of their love.

Iron Shadows.

As she had been able to do since becoming one with the Twins, she began to shape the light within her, watched it spin out its light, extrude its threads, and extend out into the blackness.

"Hear me, Tomo."

When contact was made, she would be completely open, completely revealing, so that everything that she knew or was could be read by the ones she trusted.

She felt her whole body jerk, as if fibers connected to the center within her—the place called *Hara* in her Aikido classes, *Tan Tien* in Chinese. *Manipura* in Sanskrit—that psychic and physical center of a human being—were jerked taut suddenly, and her face flushed hot.

She opened her eyes, and sobbed in sheer delight. The incense smoke sparkled, as if invisible necklaces of laser light shone through the spiraling wisps of jasmine and cedar. The threadlike, sparkling beads seemed to connect the spot below her navel with the pictures of Joy and Tomo. She was fascinated, all pain forgotten now. The connection was so strong, so vital. As she watched, the tiny threads wound around each other, melted into each other and thickened. As they wove together into stronger strands she felt her body jerk, felt the connection deepen, felt herself falling into a comforting void.

"Oh, God, Yes." She had made connection. Someone was there. She could spill out her fears, share her woes. She felt her mind probed, felt all of her secrets giving themselves joyously.

What is your pain, my child? A strong and comforting voice asked her.

Hannah Appelion opened her heart, and gave herself humbly, without reservation, in the manner befitting a mortal suppliant approaching the throne of her god.

twenty-five

Sunday, June 18

Alaska Airlines Flight 4407 touched down at San Jose Airport at seven minutes past three o'clock in the afternoon. It was an uneventful flight, rather quiet, in fact, lasting just over an hour. For most of its length, Cat and Jax never spoke.

They walked through the passenger concourse, close but not touching, almost as if separated by a glass shield.

The Avis shuttle picked them up promptly, ferrying them to the lot where they rented a red Pontiac Grand Prix, threw their luggage into the back, and drove slowly past the guard booth.

It was a five-minute drive from the Avis lot to a nearby shopping plaza. Tyler's van was parked by the two green dumpsters in the northwest corner. Jax pulled alongside, and killed the engine.

Tyler leaned from his window. Today's hat looked like a blue Frisbee with a fuzzy Ping-Pong ball at the peak. "What kept you?"

"How long have you been here?" Cat asked from the passenger side.

"About twenty minutes. We timed this pretty well." Tyler had left Los Angeles at nine that morning, driving up separately . . . they had no reason to think themselves under observation, but better safe than sorry. The workshop organizers had specifically requested flight information, and someone might have met them at the gate. . . .

Cat got out of the Grand Prix, and stretched hugely, yawning. Jax opened the van's door and conducted a last-minute check of Tyler's equipment. Tyler handed Jax a metal box the size of a pack of cigarettes. "Put this in your trunk, would you? Maybe the tire well."

"Got it."

Finally, Tyler handed Cat a necklace and earrings. "All right," he said. "The necklace is omnidirectional. I can filter for breathing and heartbeat. I should pick up everything within fifty feet."

She examined it. "Where's the off button?"

"What?"

"The off button."

"There isn't one. *Not.*" Tyler grinned and showed her a little switch on the clasp.

Jax returned from the Grand Prix with a Bay Area map. "We're all set."

Tyler took one of the maps, examined the route laid out with hi-liter. Then he said: "All right, let's test this stuff," and turned on the directional antenna. The tracer implanted in the undercarriage gave them a good steady beep. "I'll stay about a quarter mile back. I've got a good trace on you."

Cat nodded, still rather inward and quiet. Finally she laughed quietly and said, "Well, let's get this show on the road."

Tyler pushed his hat to one side. "Hey, Jax . . . you be good. That's my only sister."

Jax waved and got in on the driver's side. He rolled their car out in front, and then very casually said, "The accident where Tyler lost his legs. Was your father driving the car?"

Cat looked at him coolly. "I don't like to talk about it," she said. "You know that."

"You can tell me that much."

She sat, staring out the window at the people living their ordinary lives, gliding in and out of the shopping center parking lot. Living normal lives, going home to cook normal meals for normal families. "Yeah, all right. Daddy was driving. Daddy always drove. Let's get the hell out of here."

He pulled out of the lot, and into the street.

They took the 17 freeway south. Cat navigating from the map. A radio monitor hooked to the dash board crackled. *"Jax. One, two, three. Reading?"*

"Just fine," Jax said.

"Hey, Jax—nervous?"

Jax's necklace was of ivory carved to look like shark teeth. A broken tooth near the clasp concealed the on-off switch. Jax turned it off.

For a few minutes they drove along without words, then he said: "Cat. Just wanted to say . . . I wouldn't have chosen something like this. Maybe on some level I always hoped we'd get back together—"

She wasn't looking at him, acted as if the scenery flying by outside her window was the most interesting thing in the world.

"I know. This is business, Jax. That's all it is."

"I guess I was just hoping we could make the best of a bed situation. Bad." He corrected himself quickly. "Bad situation."

She turned lazily to regard him, her mouth twisted tightly, not entirely concealing a wry smile. "Absolutely," she said. "Deal."

twenty-six

They headed up into the Santa Cruz Mountains, along a winding, increasingly rural highway. They stopped for dinner at a restaurant called Louisa's. Jax ordered a steak, with a side of biscuits and gravy. On arrival, he pronounced them excellent. Tyler had chicken-fried steak and green beans. He chewed and poked at it without much appetite.

Cat was pleased to order a feta cheese pita sandwich, and nibbled at it when it arrived. She noticed Tyler's lack of enthusiasm. "Are you feeling all right?"

"Sure." Tyler cast a wary eye at Jax, who was galloping through his steak at mach speed. "Jeeze. You might want to order another of those. I don't want you to come after me if you're still hungry."

Jax grunted, his mouth too full to comment.

Cat wagged her blond curls. "Your colon must be the Graveyard of Lost Cows. Ever heard of salad?"

"If God hadn't wanted us to eat animals," Jax said piously, "He wouldn't have made them out of meat."

From the restaurant they drove up through narrower, poorly maintained roads. Occasionally they could look down into deep valleys, on rectangular garden patches and tiny wood or sheet metal houses hooded by the deepening shadow.

"All right, Tyler," Cat said. "Drop a little further back now. We're within a few miles, I reckon."

"Got you," he answered over the radio link.

They turned right onto a winding road which took them up the side of the mountain, and Cat said: "All right—there's the Arco sign. Count one point seven miles from here, and it's on the left."

They slowed, driving more carefully now. The gloom made it difficult to spot landmarks, but Cat located a wooden sign to their left reading "Serenity Camp."

"Slow down," she said. "I think that's it."

They drove up a narrow dirt road shaded with eucalyptus. A half mile up the narrow drive widened again, and they passed a set of wooden A-frame cabins.

Beyond the cabins was an oval driveway around a heart-shaped plot of grass, in front of an enormous three-story white mansion. Ivy spread up its walls, thickening into a pervasive mat of green near the third story.

A few couples wandered around the drive and grass, arms linked cozily. Jax rolled his car window down. "Excuse me—do you know where the head office is?"

A tall woman with generous hips and a huge smile said "Right over there. Who are you? I'm Cindy—this is Wedge," she pointed an elegantly

manicured fingernail at the man beside her. Wedge was a skinny rascal—
Cindy made two of him. But he was hyper-alert and energetic, shaking
Cat's hand like a little machine. Picturing the two of them in bed together
was a hoot.

"Hi. Porsche and Jackson."

"See you in the dining hall," Cindy winked. There was a delicious
abandon to her stride, something hypnotically free about the sway of her
hips as she strolled away. Cat watched Jax's attentive gaze, icily amused.

"Research?"

He pulled his wire rims low on his nose with a forefinger, peering at
Cindy's generous foundation. "Well, we're embarking upon an adventure.
Heaven knows what rigors will be demanded of me. Just want to be pre-
pared for all contingencies."

"Uh huh."

They found the head office, which was situated in the living room of the
mansion, a circular pillow-strewn space just left of the main doors. The re-
ceptionist was a petite brunette with a boyish figure and an eager smile.
"Ah!" she said when they introduced themselves. "We've been expecting
you. I'm Jeanette," she said, pointing to a gold-rimmed badge pinned over
her heart. "How was your flight?"

"Fine thanks. We're maybe a little tired. Like to get settled in as
quickly as possible."

"No problem," she said, and handed them a series of forms to complete. Some of them were standard, with payment coupons and non-
disclosure agreements, and others which established the exclusive nature
of the intellectual properties to be offered over the next week. Other sheets
inquired into health histories, stating that the workshop was decidedly not
for people with preexisting mental conditions.

There was another form recommending safe sex practices, a sample
three-pack of Twin City condoms and a Joy's Pride dental dam, along with
a note that such contraceptives, as well as a number of more esoteric latex
novelties, were available at their Sex Shoppe, located in cabin six. Another
sheet marked off hiking trails, and included a warning to beware of loose
footing—recent heavy rains had eroded some of the paths.

The last sheet prescribed the suggested dress and attitude for the initial evening's meeting. *Dress Hot!* it said in eighteen-point cursive script.

This is your first date with the sexiest human being you've ever seen in your life!

Cat signed the forms without comment. Jax noticed that her smile was thin and tight. After triplicate autographs, Jeanette handed them an inch-thick, spiral-bound green manual with a plastic cover. The front sheet was embossed with the gold foil letters GOLDEN FIRE WORKSHOP against a beautifully ornate line drawing of male and female flying horses frolicking in the clouds. Cat was pleased that Jax managed to keep a straight face.

Jeanette bounced from behind her desk and led them to the third cabin down the hill. They drove a few feet behind her, Jax eyeing her stride appreciatively.

Their lodgings proved to be a single-story log structure with broad wooden stairs and a worn railing. The sign above the stair read SERENITY HOUSE in grooved lettering. Inside the front door was a short vestibule, with a door to either side.

They parked their car in front, and Jeanette said, "I hope that you'll be comfortable here. Ordinarily, you'd have roommates across the hall, but this workshop was undersubscribed—that's why you were able get in on short notice."

Cat smiled. "I'm sure we'll be fine."

Jeanette smiled back, a secretive, sensuous expression. "You two are a beautiful couple. I think you'll have a wonderful time." Inside, the cabin was wooden-floored simplicity, with windows on three sides, a dressing mirror, two closets and a dresser. There were two bunk beds pushed closely together, and a tarp-shrouded shape in the corner. "Every room has a Love Machine."

Jeanette pulled a protective cloth from a black hobby-horse-type device. It looked like the mutant offspring of a motorcycle and an ObGyn examination table. Jeanette grinned at them provocatively.

"Try it out," she suggested, and closed the door behind her before either of them could make a comment.

"Well," Cat said cautiously. "I guess we better unpack."

Jax ran his fingers along the device's leather and black metal tubing. "The *Loooove* Machine." He said, his voice as oleaginous as a game show announcer's."

Cat glared at him. "The only difference between men and boys is the size of their toys."

Jax opened his mouth to speak, but Cat narrowed her eyes. "Don't even go there," she warned. "Don't even start."

twenty-seven

An Hispanic couple in their late thirties lounged on two of the eight deck chairs set on the mansion's broad front porch. The woman was exotically beautiful and comfortably chubby. The man was muscular but similarly thickened through the waist. They talked in low, musical tones, and their gauzy clothes should have been chilly, considering the evening shadows. They had the same relaxed, comfortably erotic air of the couples strolling across the heart-shaped lawn.

Cat just waved them a "Hi," and went on in. Catching her reflection in a window, she barely recognized herself. Who was this tart in the stockings and high heels, the length of perfect, elegant leg exposed by a scandalously extensive slit in her robin's-egg blue dress? She *never* wore this much makeup, or spent the better part of an hour perfecting it. Blush, eye shadow, liner and lipstick, playing all of the little games of shade and texture that she ordinarily scorned . . .

She cut her eyes sideways at Jax. His thick chest swelled the white silk buccaneer shirt, and if his waist wasn't bodybuilder thin, it was tree-trunk solid. He moved beautifully, his athletic background and years of military and police service evident in every relaxed but animal-alert motion. With every step, his thighs swelled the seams of his black leather pants.

The dining hall was a comfortable, low-key environment. A dozen couples were dressed for romantic rendezvous, a collage of cotton blouses, leather chaps and clinging silken togas. Some wore little more than secretive, intimate smiles. She glimpsed the lecture room to their left, a circular, pillow-strewn area.

To the right was the dining hall. The heady aroma of hot bread and steaming vegetables called to them. Jax loaded his plate with fried chicken and salad. Cat opted for fruit and a yogurt and chive-topped potato.

A curvaceous middle-aged woman with dark red hair and a Betty Boop face joined them on the line. "Hi!" she said. "I'm Caitlin. Are you in from L.A.?"

Jax laughed. "That obvious?"

Caitlin positively bubbled. "Absolutely. Something about the walk . . ."

Very subtly, she angled closer to Jax. With a dance-like step, Cat interposed herself. "And you're from . . . ?"

"Grand Rapids, Michigan. But I know a lot of the West Coast Group. Have you tried the punch?" she said, indicating a steel decanter next to a basket of rolls. "It's great. Twin Punch, we call it. They could make a fortune marketing the recipe." She poured them each a cup of a dark red, sweet-smelling fluid.

Cat jumped in with both feet. "Do you know Kolla Sinclair?"

Caitlin closed her eyes in thought. Her eye lids were tinted violet. Nice shade, Cat thought. "No . . . wait. Maybe she assisted at one of the workshops. Come on. Sit with us."

She wouldn't take no for an answer, and tugged Jax's arm to guide him over to the table. Cat tagged along, sighing.

"The group is so varied now," she chattered. "See over there? Mary Clark." A thin, pretty girl, with her hair pulled back in a bun. "Her father owns half of Miami." Caitlin searched the room. She picked out the stocky Hispanic man who had lounged on the porch. "And . . . there. Ronnie Valdez."

Jax perked up. "Hey! I remember him. Pitcher for the Cardinals. Tore his shoulder, didn't he? Said it would take a year to heal, and he was back in three months or something . . . ?"

Caitlin smiled mysteriously. *"All things are poss-i-ble,"* she sang in a surprisingly low and pleasing voice. Cat recognized the fragment of ancient gospel song. *"Only be-lieve."*

She sat them next to a tall, well-marbled man in his late forties. "My husband Russell," she explained.

Handshakes were exchanged all around. "Hey," he said. "What brings you here? You married or Freedancing?"

"Married," Cat said. "Separated, actually. We're trying to work things out."

"Bless your hearts."

Jax smiled along, but his attention was focused on a table with red place mats. Jeanette and five others with gold-rimmed name badges ate there. It was a little eerie to watch them: every forkful or sip of Twin Punch occurred in some odd kind of synch warp, their movements almost choreographed. They might have been sextuplets. And something else caught

Cat's attention—they were feeding each other. At first she thought it was just something playful, but then she realized that the gold badges were in precise male-female pairs, and members of each pair were taking turns supplying their partners with forkfuls of chicken, salad and pasta.

"Ah . . . we don't feed ourselves?" Cat asked.

"Not tonight. They want to jump you in feet first," Caitlin said.

Jax plucked a grape from the pile of fruit on Cat's plate and popped it into her mouth. She took it with her teeth, and severed it neatly in half. All right, two could play at *that* game. She neatly cleaved a chunk of chicken from the breast on his plate, and speared it with her fork. She dipped it in gravy, rolled it fastidiously against his muffin and held it up to him.

Jax accepted the gift. "Yum," he said gravely.

"Russell?" Cat asked. She paused as Jax fed her a forkful of salad. "Do you know Kolla Sinclair?

Cat tried a sip of the Twin Punch, and found it a little too sweet. Orange juice, cherry juice . . . and something *thicker.* Yes, that was the adjective. She rolled a few drops on her tongue, trying to place that last taste. A little like Tomo's Nectar, perhaps, but that still begged the question. What was that *taste . . . ?*

Russell accepted a dollop of cornbread from Caitlin, and gave his mouthful a few thoughtful strokes before answering. "Name's familiar, but I'm not sure." He looked at her with new interest. "Who talked you into coming here?"

"Dr. Deborah Norris, in Beverly Hills. We'd been seeing her for awhile."

Caitlin nodded. "Oh, yes. She wrote an article on the Twins. It was pretty fair-minded."

A sudden ringing sound rose above the din. One of the staff members rose. He wore an orange T-shirt labeled RUSTY, and he was six feet of teeth and freckles. "We'll be meeting in the course room in ten minutes for evening orientation. Everyone on time, please."

Several of the attendees began to bus dishes.

Caitlin nudged Jax. "Nervous?"

"Maybe a little."

"Good," Russell said. "Joy told me that feeling is your body getting ready to act."

"You've met her personally?" Cat asked.

"Not personally. Yet. But they communicate with us."

"How do they reach you? E-mail?"

"Oh, they talk to us in our dreams," she said, her voice soft and far away. "They can find us through our dreams. They can see what we see. . . ."

Caitlin patted his hand. Russell made an "eek" face, and changed the subject. "Anyway, dreamtime is as real as this," he said, thumping the table.

"Your lives will never be the same after this week," Caitlin promised. She winked at them, then stacked her plates atop one another and left.

Cat and Jax continued to feed each other, Cat absorbing snippets of the conversations around them.

A man was saying: "—after I learned the fire breath—"

And a woman: "—third level orgasm—"

A young woman with an Oklahoma drawl said: "Lasted almost an hour . . ."

A balding man at another table said to his neighbor confidentially: "My entire body felt like one big penis—"

Jax peeled a little piece of potato, placed it on a skewer and held it out to Cat, his expression studiedly neutral. "His entire body?"

"You're well on your way." She worked the steaming chunk off with her teeth. And grinned. But in the very back of her mind, something nagged at her.

Guava? No. Papaya . . . ?

You've tasted it before. But where?

On their way to the course room, Cat and Jax wandered a bit, took side trips to a bathroom and a little book shop under the main staircase. They found three phones, and blessed each with a wafer-thin induction mike. The bugs were good for broadcasting the conversations a few hundred feet, and each was keyed to a separate frequency. The booster, secreted in the trunk of their car, would pick up the signals and rebroadcast to Tyler, parked in a turnout about a mile away.

"Look at this," Jax said. His expression was amused. He was browsing a book titled *Dreaming with the Twins*. "Russell's right. They claim they can reach their followers through dreams."

"Wake me if I talk in my sleep," Cat said.

They entered the rotunda.

Twenty couples were scattered around the room, most lounging on large round cushions. The room was decorated only with flowers and a compass wall chart on a stand-alone easel. Floor-to-ceiling windows looking down onto the heart-shaped lawn and the forest surrounding the entire estate.

"Not exactly what I expected," Cat said.

"What *did* you expect?"

"Dunno. Maybe Turkish decor, wall-to-wall bedroom, vats of cocoa butter. Stuff like that."

A slender, limber brunette of perhaps thirty-five bounded into the center of the room. "Evening! Welcome to the introductory Golden Fire workshop."

The room broke into coordinated applause. There were cat-calls, and a few whistles. She curtsied for them flirtatiously, waving "hi" to some familiar faces in the group. "I'm Karen Tucker. It is my very great pleasure to be one of the two chief facilitators at this workshop. I'd like to introduce Simon LeFarge, my co-teacher. We'll be teaching and working with you for the next week. Our other team members will introduce themselves tomorrow."

Simon was too thin for Cat's taste, with prominent Amerind cheekbones and laughing eyes. His voice was pure Bronx, but conveyed such infectious energy that it was almost musical. "The most important thing we can do," he said, "is create a context for the week. Joy and Tomo teach us that all that exists in the universe is energy and information. Pattern. Time, space, matter, all are ripples in the quantum field."

Karen continued. "All of you have had moments in your life . . . in your relationships . . . when you felt totally alive. Completely connected to the flow of life. We're here to help you find more of those moments."

Cat's sensation of discomfort increased. It seemed that those last words had been specifically directed at *her*. She noticed that most of the rest of the attendees leaning forward eagerly. She shook off the odd feeling of persecution and concentrated.

"In the performance of any demanding discipline—be it sports, the arts, or the art and sport of making love, the very first goal is the achievement of the 'flow state.' Unfortunately, it is invariably true that conscious awareness of your own existence diminishes access to this critical state."

Nothing to argue with there: From her own karate training, as well as her occasional, frustrated forays into drawing and painting, Cat knew this to be valid.

Still, hearing it in this context made her feel a little uncomfortable. That feeling of discomfort oddly manifested first as a percolating sensation in her stomach then rippled up her spine like a big lazy snake. She shook it off, and concentrated.

Karen picked up where Simon stopped. "Around the world, almost any philosophy which speaks of such things suggests that the intensity of an orgasm is in direct proportion to the amount of ego released at that moment. In other words, the more *you* are here, the more passion is *not*. Passion is the release of the ego walls, the burning away of your personal history."

They were bouncing back and forth off each other in a manner imitative of the Twins. Not the same level of ease, perhaps, but with practiced and professional fluidity.

"Which of you have had moments when it seemed that the walls between you and your partner completely disappeared?" Simon asked. "When the world disappeared?" He paused, and some vast amusement suffused his face. "When the earth moved?"

Several hands went up. After a pause, Jax's hand rose. After a moment, Cat's joined it. Jax looked at her curiously. She felt a little as if she were floating. Something in the overhead lighting seemed a little off. Incense hazing the room, perhaps?

She seemed to be floating away, above them, listening to the words because they spoke to her, not because they related to a job.

So, Cat thought. What if that were true? What if she *had* been too present, too conscious? If so, what would it imply about her marriage? And especially her sexual relationship with Jax? Some small voice in the back of her mind whispered, *It's true. You were always there. On guard. No man could reach you, because you were always watching. You never gave any of them a chance.*

No. Not just anyone, she thought. *You gave some of them a chance, but only the ones who didn't mean anything to you, the ones with whom there was no prayer of a relationship developing.* She turned her attention to the man sitting beside her. *You never gave Jax a chance. And you owed him that, didn't you? You owed that to yourself.*

The insight was startling, and disturbing. Where the *hell* had that bit of introspection come from?

The lecture had faded from her consciousness, and she was surprised to find herself bobbing back to alertness. Karen was saying: "So . . . are there any questions before we break for the evening?"

Caitlin's hand went up. "The handouts said to wear a 'northwest' costume tomorrow. What does that mean?"

Karen pointed to the compass chart behind her. The cardinal and non-cardinal directions were marked out with red and green grease pencil.

"Sexual energy is the core creative force," she said, pointing to a label at the center which said: *Catalyst energy.* "It manifests as body, mind, spirit and emotion." For each of these she indicated a position: West, North, East, and South. "Often, we forget that it is this formless force, and confuse one specific manifestation for the energy itself.

"We'll be using a lot of techniques to break you out of your ordinary patterns of dealing with your bodies, your partners, your sexuality," Simon said. "The Northwest is the area of control, here, midway between body/west, and mind/north."

"The questions of submission and control are central to sexuality, but rarely addressed directly," Karen said. Cat spiraled back to a somnambulant stupor, listening with her heart and not her mind. Her heart understood Karen's words precisely. Her mind, retreating back and back away from her, into some unexplored cavern within her soul, screamed in protest.

A dashiki-clad black woman with a short tight Afro mirrored Cat's thoughts. "You want us to do S and M?" she asked stridently. She wore a little pink name badge that said MOIRA.

Simon laughed. "S and M, B and D, L.S.M.F.T. . . . whatever floats your boat, babe. You don't have to do anything—but you may find yourselves wanting to try things you've never experienced before. What we want is for you to step out of your ordinary patterns. Look at yourselves. When was the last time you dressed like this for each other?"

A few of the couples glanced at each other sheepishly.

Cat looked down at herself, at the stockings and high heels, the dress slit up to her thigh, and realized that even when she and Jax had dated, she had never really dolled herself up. Her attitude had always been: *This is who I am. If you like the package, okay. If you don't, well, that's okay too.*

She knew that Jax's entrance had drawn appreciative murmurs. Even now some of the other women evaluated him, checking out his body language. Probably wondering how amenable he might prove to be to a lit-

tle midnight homework, a bit of improvisation upon the day's erotic chore-
ography.

That thought itched at Cat like ants under the skin. Oddly, she wasn't
certain whether that irritation alarmed or relieved her.

Without thinking, she reached out and brushed his leg with one finger, comforted by the warmth and solidity. Then she caught herself and
pulled back. *Watch it, dammit,* she said to herself. *This is business.* Scanning,
photographing with her mind, Cat began to evaluate the faces.

"Ask yourself," Karen said. "Why do you withhold your beauty and
power from each other? Don't you want to soar together? Don't you long
for nights filled with poetry and magic? What stops you? And more important—are you willing to make a commitment—not to each other but
to yourselves, to reach inside and find the essence—"

"That part that used to come so naturally. We ask you to leave
your egos—"

He glanced significantly at the Valdezes.

"Your preconceptions—" and here, clearly, he was looking at a very
young couple, probably the youngest in the room. The girl giggled and
laid her head on her partner's shoulders. They wore badges saying JUDY and
MAC SIMPSON.

"—and your agendas—"

And here, unmistakably, he looked directly at Jax and Cat. She
squirmed.

"—outside the gate. Tonight, we want you to write your Giveaways."

For the first time, Jax raised his hand. "Excuse me? I don't understand
the term 'Giveaway.' "

Karen gave an understanding nod. "Giveaways are all of the things you
would have to lose in order to access that core passion within you. Everything that stands between you and the energy and aliveness you used to feel
so naturally. The doorway back to your freedom is your sexuality. Sexuality is a spiritual thing—enlightenment through an appropriate gender
mirror."

Several of the others nodded at that, but Cat had fuzzed on that last
comment, completely losing the meaning.

"Sexuality is an emotional thing. And an animal thing. In the privacy
of a bedroom, in the safety of your most intimate relationships, there
should be no shame, no fear. . . ."

Karen came close to Simon. The whole room seemed to grow smaller.

The lights dimmed. They embraced. She didn't kiss him, but their lips were very close, and their abdomens touched. They synchronized their breathing. He held her firmly around the waist

"When you do that," Karen murmured, "You make magic."

He spun her in a little dance step, and the light behind them suddenly fractured. It seemed to have been splintered into sparks for an instant, or . . .

Cat shook her head, hard. No, now it looked as if cilialike, luminous threads connected Karen's abdomen to Simon's. Another trick of the light, no doubt, but both of them shook and laughed, and Karen suddenly broke into a violent full-body shiver. "Brrr! *Well!* That's enough warm up." They sat very close to each other on the couch and the lights stayed low. The odd lighting effect stayed the same for about twenty seconds, and then began to diffuse.

"The orgasticness you seek is a very real energy," she said. "If your imaginations were playing tricks," she said, and her smile was pure mischief, "perhaps you suspect you saw some of that between me and Simon."

"Nahhh," Simon said, and they both laughed, sharing a private joke. "One of our most important exercises is called 'The Prey.' It is based on the idea that what we want more than anything in the world is to feed our hungers—our physical, spiritual, emotional, and most importantly, our sexual hungers."

"Relationships die when one partner feels the other is trying to consume her. That she mustn't let her guard down. Has to stay protected."

"There are magical traditions—black magical traditions—where the magician literally *does* feed on the partner's sexual energy. This is the root myth of vampirism. But here, we're talking about the union of two magicians, two people who come together to make magic with equal power and beauty. A meeting of allies."

"Between them, they create energy. And they should imagine that the energy is an actual creature."

"Imagine?" Moira said. "I thought we were here to learn *real* magic."

Simon flipped the compass chart, revealing a blackboard on the reverse side. He wrote the word IMAGINATION with widely spaced letters. Then he inserted hyphens to convert the word into I-MAGI-NATION. "This word does not mean 'make believe,'" he said. "What this word means is that I the Mage—in other words, I the magician—will, with my power and clarity, create my own world. My own 'nation' if you will. I-MAGI-NATION.

It is a word of power, and don't ever forget it. We have to believe it to create it. If you can't say it, you can't have it. Even the Bible says: 'First came the word.' " He stopped, and gazed at each participant in turn. The spiel was ridiculous, corny, but those damn irritating ants had burrowed deeper, were now clambering up Cat's spine. At that moment, Simon had every eye, every ear in the room, and the impact was devastating. "There it is, people."

Karen continued for him. "Right on," she said. "Now, the more powerful—"

"And dangerous," he added.

"—the animal you hunt together, the bigger the thrill. Judging by what some of you have told me, you've been hunting mice."

Chuckles broke the room's tension.

"Well, I don't hunt mice," she said, and leaned forward, her smile predatory. "We're going to help you develop your feral personal. Sexually, we are feline. What this entire workshop is about is the creation of a cat-like body, and a cat-like mind. I'm a jaguar," She said and stretched languorously. "And Simon is a leopard. When we hunt together—and I *love* hunting with him, we never go after anything less than a deer."

"My ambition is a Cape buffalo," he said.

Karen raked her nails silkily down his arm, the tip of her pink tongue brushed her upper teeth. She wriggled in a decidedly feline fashion. "Raowww!"

"Dig it, people, you put everything into your sex life—it is an encapsulation of everything you are—your physicality, your love of self and other, your ability to concentrate, your ability to relax, and your imagination. You and your partner are touching eternity here."

"If sex is so great," Judy Simpson, the youngest woman in the room, said rather timidly, "Then why do so many people think it's sick? Why do churches and other people try to make it wrong?"

Simon held up his hand. "Three separate issues, which are woven together," Simon said. "Most people think sex is sick because they learned about it within a sexually dysfunctional context—their own homes. In other words, they learned guilt. Most of us have some negative associations with sex, or sexual words. That's one of the reasons why we use the Sanskrit words 'lingam' and 'yoni' for the male and female organs—they have no cultural charge in America. They're neutral without being antiseptic like 'penis' and 'vagina.' "

"Lots of people will twitch at 'cock' and 'pussy,' " Karen grinned. Judy looked swiftly at the floor, flushing.

"Anyway, some think sex is wrong, or sick, or dangerous because they learned about it in an abusive context. Rape, incest, molestation, violation of the sacred right of a child to ripen at his or her own pace."

Cat had stopped breathing.

"Then when is it appropriate for a child to have sex? Sixteen? Twenty-one?" Moira asked.

"According to the Twins, you are ready for sex when you are ready to take complete responsibility for your own mind, heart and body."

"And when do you know that?" Mrs. Valdez said. "I was ready at fourteen."

"Were you really?" Karen said sharply. "Could you put a roof over a baby's head? Could you put food on the table without trading your body or selling drugs for it? A person who can do these things, and has learned how to focus her physical, mental and emotional energies to work within her social matrix, honestly, with self-respect, to earn a living—that person is ready for the responsibility of sex—and not before.

"That means some people are ready at fifteen—and some aren't ready at fifty. To have sex with someone before they are emotionally mature is a form of abuse—whether they say they 'want' it or not. And abused children often grow up to be abusers—not out of malice, but from fear and damaged judgment. Sex, for them, becomes a means of control—and in their world, they either control, or are controlled. They often need to determine when a relationship begins and ends—and when that initiative is denied them, they can become extremely depressed, or even violently possessive. It's not about age, its about maturity."

"Anyway," Simon continued. "Churches call sex evil for two reasons— one is that the sex drive is a direct doorway to ecstasy, and most religions try to harness your ecstatic urge, say that you can only reach the Divine through their system of ritual. And, of course, sexually transmitted diseases and unwanted pregnancies are genuine social destabilizers—some of the imprecations operate like warnings against eating pork in the Jewish and Muslim faiths. They are actually hygienic rules, but are put into the context of 'sins' to reduce arguments with the young and ignorant."

"How could masturbation fit in there?" Mrs. Valdez asked again. "There's no risk of disease or pregnancy, so why does the church call it evil?"

"Good question," Karen said. "But certainly any religion that doesn't encourage its congregation to grow will die out. So most nonreproductive sex is discouraged. Oral and anal sex fit right into that category. Once again, hook this basic drive to things which are socially useful. And there, the church is providing a social function. There is probably an inverse relationship between the age at which a society first allows its children access to sex, and the level of material wealth of that culture—in other words, the longer they make you wait, the more education or financial stability required to earn access to sex, the harder people will work. Men, especially young men, will do *anything* to get laid. Tell them that going off to fight a war will make them sexier, and they'll march right off. Tell them that earning a million dollars is the way to get their nards drained, and they'll do that. Great for the tax rolls."

"Then are you saying that it is good for society to tell us sex is bad? Or to control our access to it?"

"Yep. It's very good—*for the society.* And also good for people who don't want to take individual responsibility for their own emotions, their bodies, their futures. But for those of us who want to understand magic— sex is the doorway. Every religion, every society understands this. Now we want you to understand it, too."

Simon inhaled sharply. "Wow! I hadn't intended to get that far into it tonight."

"Forgot to bring your hip boots, did you?" Karen grinned.

He held up his hands. *"Mea culpa.* All right. I'm done for now."

Karen laughed. "Remember, people. No restraint between each other. Come tomorrow in a Northwest mask. And make a list of the things you would have to give up to have full access to your passion. Any fears, negative beliefs, personal history, resentments—anything at all that keeps you from being the most outrageous, orgastic, experimental, exhibitionistic, voyeuristic lovers you can be." She leaned forward. "It's your bedroom," she said. "This is your chosen mate, your mirror, the other side of yourself. You can buy clothes at K-Mart. Only *God* gives you a body. Which are you more ashamed of? It's the best friend, tool and toy you're ever going to have. And guess what? We're gonna teach you how to use it." She blew them a kiss. "Nighty-night."

twenty-eight

Jax followed Cat out onto the porch. Other participants filed past them, nodding their greetings. He leaned against the railing with her, staring out into the darkness. "So . . . ? What do you think?"

"Twelve staff. Twenty, twenty-five acres main camp. Generator. Maybe a helicopter pad to the east. Kolla seems to have joined a pretty well-organized group." She turned and looked at him in the darkness. Her eyes were huge. "Is that what you mean?"

Jax ground his cigarette out in an ashtray, then flicked the butt out into the darkness. "Yeah, sure," he said. "That's exactly what I meant. See you back at the cabin."

Cat watched him walk away, fighting the urge to call after him. She found a corner of the railing, shadowed, and touched her necklace. "Did you get all of that?" she whispered.

Tyler's voice came to her in her earpiece, a little flesh colored lozenge the exact size and shape as a popular brand of hearing aid. *"Loud and clear. Was it good for you, too?"*

"Yummy. Anything on the phone lines?"

"Not yet. Conversations normal. The limpets are operating fine. Somebody called home to check on a parakeet. Somebody else checked their message machine. I can't tell you what the conversation was, but call your stockbroker, have him dump that Apple Preferred. I'll keep monitoring. You guys just have a wonderful evening, all right?"

"You bet," she said, and switched her necklace off again.

Cat walked back toward their cabin, completely lost in her own thoughts. Halfway there, she was possessed by the sudden sensation of being observed. Almost . . . *studied.* She looked out into the trees. The light from the camp died out within a hundred feet. The stars were obscured by clouds. There was just no illumination. Godzilla could have lurked out there, and as long as he declined to ignite his dorsals or breathe fire, they'd never see him.

She tried to shake the feeling, couldn't, and finally returned to to Serenity House. On the steps, she stopped and looked out into the darkness again. Wondering.

twenty-nine

Jax sat on the edge of the bed, stripped to the waist. He stretched the thick muscles banding his upper body, then continued to scribble on a yellow tablet. His wrote in a remarkably dainty hand, one which matched the wire-rimmed glasses perched on his nose.

"What's that?" Cat asked.

"Just working on my Giveaways."

"Oh, for Christ sake. Turn in a blank sheet of paper, will you? They're just going to burn them—not read them."

"What if they ask what our Giveaways are?"

"Come on, Jax, don't lose it, okay?"

Jax sat, waiting, as Cat went into the bathroom. He could see her moving through the crack between door and jamb. A flash of tanned skin. A perfect body. He tried to write, but his hand shook. He put his pen down, and rested his head in his hands. Water sounds stopped in the bathroom. Cat appeared in the doorway in pajamas. Not sexy. Not overly baggy. Just comfortable.

She examined the sleeping arrangements. "I see you pushed the beds together."

"We have to maintain appearances," he said a touch defensively. "Don't worry. I won't take advantage."

Cat turned off the lights and slipped into bed beside him. "Big day tomorrow," her voice, in the darkness, seemed a much younger woman's. A child's, perhaps.

"Yeah," Jax said.

There was a long pause, and Jax wondered if she had dropped off to sleep. Then she said: "Jax. You said you'd felt that."

"Felt what?"

"Felt that place where everything just . . . melts away. Was that true?"

He sighed heavily. "Yeah, it's true."

Another pause. "How many times?"

"Three," he said. "I remember every one."

He wondered if she was going to go any further, had just decided that she wasn't, and had closed his own eyes when a small voice asked: "Were any of them with me?"

He wanted to lie. Hoped he would have the strength to, but ultimately, couldn't. "Every one," he said.

It was just a dream, one that Cat had endured before. In the dream, she prowled through an attic. It was filled with dusty things: knickknacks and gewgaws and all those other words for old crap that nobody cares about.

Strange. She seemed herself, but simultaneously a child. She climbed as if she was looking for something, but didn't know what.

She sorted through books, and old records (not CDs), and dolls, and stuffed animals, and old dog collars, and other things. With each of them, another feeling arose, a fluttering emotion that had no name, one which seemed to be calling her, turning her.

She spun slowly, trying to seek it out. Another feeling warred with the first: Whatever this was, she didn't really want to find it. She dug anyway, looked through the packages and shelves until she found the thing that called her. It sat alone on a little pedestal, a jewel box, covered with dust. She felt both excited and afraid.

Her hands touched the box, and she knew that it was something more than its four walls, top and bottom. Something else, but wasn't certain what. She did know that she couldn't open it. Something was needed, a key perhaps. Cat had been searching for it a long time. The key was here . . . somewhere. She wouldn't look for it now. Tonight wasn't the night.

Not tonight. But soon.

Cat woke up, for an instant unaware of her surroundings. Malibu? No . . . Santa Cruz. Yes. Serenity Camp. And next to her, Jax Carpenter's enormous bulk, snoring softly. The snoring stuttered, and he groaned, legs moving as if he were running in slow motion, through a sea of molasses

Or Tomo's Nectar?

She rubbed a palm over her forehead. It wasn't that hot, but she was perspiring. She dimly remembered a disturbing, elusive dream, its fragments even now slipping further away from her into the oily sea of night.

Jax groaned again. He was dreaming, too. Jesus—this was a bad night for both of them. He muttered something, and she leaned closer to hear. It sounded like he said: "Mister Q. Hot-dog. Gooksbane. Caltiki. Wizard's here. I'm here. I'm coming . . ." but then he shuddered, and the words faded away.

Cat sat up, watching him. She had heard those names before. But where? Then she remembered: another dream, long ago, during their marriage. Jax had drunk too much one night, and had terrible nightmares. Had called out names, and screamed: *"Get your sorry asses out of . . . Charley! Charley!"* and then sank back into a restless slumber. In the morning she had asked him about those names. About that dream. And he had glared at her, and said that he didn't want to talk about it.

And they never had.

She pulled the blanket up around his shoulders, and heard his breathing normalize. He was at peace again, but she had to wonder: After all this time, why in the world would that old nightmare return?

Why now? Why here?

thirty

Monday, June 19th

Tyler Juvell woke up in sections. Every bone in his body felt Superglued to its neighbors.

He hadn't spent the previous evening between sheets, at a comfortable inn. He'd spotted a Big Six Motel thirteen miles back, well outside the booster's broadcast range. Unfortunately, he wouldn't have been able to pick up the signals or monitor the phone lines from there. So for now, he camped in a rest area turnout. It wasn't too bad, actually, except that in a couple of days he would smell like a woodchuck. A generous supply of antiseptic lemon-scented premoistened towelettes would keep him marginally clean for seventy-two hours. After that, well, even woodchucks would stay upwind. The rest stop's lavatory featured a single grimy sink from which brackish water trickled in a sluggish brown stream. Beggars couldn't be choosers.

As he busied himself with a breakfast of instant oatmeal and powdered eggs, Tyler flipped on the monitor to see what the tape recorders were picking up. He recognized the first voice he heard: A man's voice. Simon's.

"—the first thing a child does when you take off his diapers is touch his genitals."

Almost reflexively, Tyler scratched his crotch, then chuckled at himself. A pair of teenaged joggers bounced past him on the road, knees high, spines erect. Tyler took a slightly disconnected pleasure in watching that, happy for them, hoping they were enjoying the morning air. The healthy legs.

Karen's voice followed. *"But Society can't allow you direct access to ecstasy. Every form of approved pleasure takes 'work,' costs 'money,' turns the social wheels."*

"What we want," Simon continued, *"is to put you back in touch with that core energy, that most primal source of pleasure. Once you have that, its possible to accomplish anything else in your life. You are—"*

"Free!" they both said at once.

"How exactly does that work?" Tyler didn't recognize the voice. *"You're saying that sex is the source of everything?"*

"No, it's not. Life energy, life force is the source of everything—sexuality is merely the most powerful and readily available manifestation of the energy."

"Freud says it's the most powerful."

"I don't believe he actually said that, and if he did, he was an ass. Survival is the most driving energy. Nobody will trade his next ten minutes of air for a blow job. Nobody stops in the middle of a forest fire to fuck. But just as soon as the immediate threat to life is over, sex is the next thing we want. So, we have this incredible, driving energy which consumes us, dominates our dreams and thoughts, and fills our artistic symbology—"

Tyler was chuckling to himself as he plugged a water heater into his cigarette lighter, waited for the steam to rise. They were getting into it a little heavy already this morning, he thought. It was crap, but entertaining crap.

"Look at Madison Avenue—if they can't sell a product with anything else, they

sell it with sex. Sometimes I think that they are working hand in glove with the church: One hand makes you guilty to think about sex directly, the other sells it back to you in myriad disguises."

"What do you mean?"

"Well—how many computers, cameras, cars, and other things are designated the 'SX,' the 'EX,' the 'ZX,' the 'SE' or some other rather obnoxious subliminality?"

Tyler stopped, narrowed his eyes. Jesus. Amidst a forest of bullshit, a slender blade of truth. Well, he couldn't take that too seriously. No real reason to start respecting these people. After all, even a broken clock is right twice a day.

Karen went on. *"Passion and orgasticness are the source of all great art, all moments of genius. All such moments involve complete connection to the action. The dissolution of the subject-object relationship."*

"This involves the complete engagement of all the senses," Simon said.

Tyler hoisted himself up into his wheel chair with practiced ease. He spent six hours a week in the gym developing his upper body strength. He was proud of that. Dammit . . . that made him think about the girl in the bookshop. He knew she was right. If only he could walk. If only his legs were as developed as his torso. . . .

He brought himself up short. Nothing lived down that road, except pain.

"—on the medicine wheel, hearing is in the west, taste in the south, sight in the east, smell in the north, and touch in the center of the wheel. Our entry will be through the north."

Suddenly, Cat's voice came thought he speaker. She must have triggered her necklace's throat mike. *"Catching this, Tyler?"*

"Loud and clear. Morning, Cat. What I hear right now is about as organic as Kool-Aid."

Jax suddenly chimed in. His voice was subdued, and Tyler figured that they were seated in the back of the room, away from the others. *"What about the smell thing?"*

"What smell thing?"

"Going through the sense of smell as the primary route to passion. Isn't that a little thick?"

Tyler shrugged. "Dunno. Olfactory nerves bypass the frontal lobes. They're co-terminous with brain tissue. Makes sense. Sniff away, children." He hoisted his coffee. "Mazel Tov."

Don't touch," Karen said.

Cat lay naked but for bra and panties, her hands tight at her sides. Jax hovered over her, a feather in one hand, brushing it one slow inch at a time along her skin.

"*Feel.*" Karen brushed her fingers softly along her own arm, shivering as if mesmerized by the contact. "Feel the touch of the feather as it moves smoothly and easily down your body. This is a time for you to feed your skin. There is no need for you to do anything. Just be. Relax. It's not going to hurt you."

Cat swallowed, fought her tendency to tense up, to lock her muscles in unyielding contraction. Her eyes didn't see Jax kneeling above her.

She wanted to grab him and hold him. She wanted to run away from him. Being able to do neither, she just locked her muscles tight, head to toe. Her chest ached, the room spun, and—

"Cat, wait. Breathe!" Karen said, alarmed. "Breathe! What's going on?"

"I don't know." Jax's voice was tightly controlled. "She just stopped breathing."

"Breathe, okay?"

She felt fingers and warm, supportive palms pressing into her abdomen. The dual sensations of embarrassment and humiliation were overwhelming. *This is business, this is business, this is business.* She silently repeated that over and over again, a litany which failed to calm or reassure. If she'd attended purely as a participant, she'd have been halfway to the airport by now. She couldn't handle this. She felt certain that everyone in the room was staring at her, laughing at her, could gaze into her and read secrets hidden even from herself.

She glanced around, chagrined to realized that no one was paying her the slightest attention. No one cared about her little internal drama. Each was enmeshed in his own world, lost in his own sensation.

Nineteen other couples worked on blue foam mats, positioned around the rotunda and out into the library. Each couple performed the identical exercise: The women lay quietly while the men offered and experienced sensation. Together they explored the sensual complexities of a human body: its warmth, its textures, its scents. And sampled, very delicately, nonsexually, its tastes.

She closed her eyes again. Karen's fingers pressed against her abdomen. Cat experienced an eerily vivid tactile illusion: Karen's hands were actually *sinking through* her, not stopping at the skin but penetrating down into her organs and her spine. Her body arched. Something inside her seemed to take a breath, reacted like a latch coming undone. There followed a sensation like a big warm knot unraveling. Her lids fluttered open and she saw Jax above her, his face broad and warm.

"You're all right now," Karen said.

"Where in the world did you learn that?" Cat asked.

Karen smiled secretively. "Tomo taught me, in a dream." She moved on to assist another couple.

Cat gripped Jax's hand. "Can we try this again?" Wordlessly, Jax nodded. Of course they could start again. And again, and yet again if need be. Jax was the most patient man she had ever known.

He brushed the feather over her thumb, caressed it slowly, lovingly, then moved on to the second finger. Very gingerly, he explored its hollows and ridges, then those of the third finger, the fourth, and finally her small finger. The back of her right hand and its palm, the tingling sensation of warmth and an odd . . . *unfolding* sensation mingling, so that the tension flowed away from her like warm water swirling down a drain. Up the forearm, to the elbow, to the upper arm, playing over the slight definition of the biceps muscle, and up to the shoulder. A little knot of tension there, something exacerbated by the last trip to the gym, but releasing now under his ministrations.

Down her chest, brushing softly against the swell of her breast, and then its tender underside. Down her stomach. A wisp of air caught in her throat, trapped there like a sparrow. Then she relaxed again, setting it free. The feather spiraled down to her waist and hips, and her entire body shimmered with pleasure.

Following directions printed in the green manual, Jax trailed the feather down her right thigh now. Down to the right calf, slowly to the ankle and the instep and arch. There, Jax abandoned the feather and substituted tiny puffs of warm, moist breath. The pattern of inhalation-exhalation was indescribably delicious. Then he focused his attentions upon her big toe, second toe, third two, fourth toe, and small toe.

He laid her leg down and moved to her opposite side, beginning anew. As before, the exquisite process commenced with her left thumb, and proceeded to her other fingers, up the arm, down the shoulder to the chest, the stomach, midsection, and down the left leg to her toes. Each inch was slowly, gently, lovingly brushed. If she shuddered, he noticed. If she caught her lower lip between her teeth, Jax dutifully recorded that information. If her cheeks reddened, Jax would not forget. He was learning her, mentally cataloging every iota of information about how she moved, how she responded. He was drunk with the power—and the opportunity—to pleasure her, even if these were only the first tentative baby steps.

Jax hummed happily to himself.

The feather's butterfly caress smoothed her closed eyes, and flowed with glacial patience down her cheeks, her scalp, her jawline, the slope of her neck. He rolled her carefully onto her stomach, and repeated the entire process using feather, fingertips, lips and the very slightest tip of his tongue.

She began to float away, to drift off into another world, into some place without tensions, without gravity. There, warm and utterly safe, she drifted above the iron flow of her life.

Drowsing, drifting on the misty edge of dream, Cat saw herself laying down there on the floor. She floated further up, until she brushed the ceiling.

Her face was turned to the side, a slight, sleepy, childlike smile on her face. Cat drifted up a little higher.

From this perspective she wasn't merely observing a very fit blond woman twisting in slow-motion ecstasy under the ministrations of a gentle brown giant. Instead, she witnessed an endless procession of Cat Juvells, a series of overlapping blurs, stretching back into her past. The illusion was dreamy and kind of pleasant. The entire mansion, and everything occurring within it was but a single moment on her time line. Yesterday existed as a distinct entity, and the yesterday before that . . . each Cat Juvell encapsulated in a bubble of time, stretching back like an infinite string of pearls. She knew she could investigate each of them separately, as if the days and moments of her life were an endless series of souvenir paperweights, those little glass bubbles encasing idyllic underwater scenes and bits of plastic snow.

From her elevated perspective she replayed the previous day's drive, and the flight from LAX, each encapsulated separately. She saw the dinner with Freddy King, and the friendly competition on the range. And the day earlier, she saw—

A sudden, stunning flash of red and white. *Pain.*

Again, she watched Chris Zimmer eat glass in the back room of the thrift shop.

Cat recoiled, shocked by a flood of guilt and shame, and the unexpected intuition that there was something else, something maybe . . .

Further back?

Like in an attic, perhaps?

That she needed to look at, needed to think about. But for now, she replayed the pitiful spectacle of Chris Zimmer. The scene contained an important piece of the puzzle—

("She doesn't want anything interfering in her damned plan. Death to the killers—")

But Cat couldn't peer into it, couldn't focus herself there. The pain drove her back out.

But now, soaring back, and up . . . up, the entire event devolved to a tiny speck, floating far beneath her. It didn't hurt so much now. And if she floated back a few minutes before the event took place, why, in this position there was no sensation of guilt or shame at all. The whole grisly business was just a little black and white picture of a terrible event, something which hadn't even happened yet.

It shouldn't have happened at all. Cat knew that now, knew that she should have acted on her instincts, that some Golden Sun worshippers were marginal, barely holding on by their fingernails, and that they were afraid. But there was no way for her to have known that at that time.

Forewarned is forearmed.

All right. Curiously, thinking these things made it easier to go back down and look at the entire event. Questions had been asked, and an emotionally damaged boy had injured himself, apparently for fear of betraying Joy and Tomo. This was unfortunate, and a reoccurrence was to be avoided at all costs, but she couldn't hold herself responsible.

It was just an incident, just things that had happened to her along the days of her life, and when you had learned the lesson, it was safe to release the emotions.

A little chill ran through her at that thought, and she repeated it to herself, uncertain of its point of origin: *when you learn the lesson, it is safe to release the emotions.*

In her dream state, she drifted back along the line of Cats toward the present moment.

She snuck a peek at the line of Cats extending in the opposite direction, toward the future. They progressed only a short way before disappearing into a kind of foggy indistinction.

She slid back down into her own body.

The music was ending. Karen's soft, sharp voice asked them to wake up and conclude the exercise. Cat rolled over onto her right side and sat up. Her womb felt heavy and sweet, as if filled with warm honey. She melted against Jax and held him, arms linked around his neck tightly, his heart a slow, hot thunder against her cheek. Thank God, the big lug didn't ask what was wrong, or make a joke.

He just held her. For right now, that was enough.

When Jax's turn came he lay on his back, eyes closed, his entire magnificent body exposed and vulnerable to her. The thick square plates of his chest rose and fell like the gears and levers of a great machine. She brought her hands very close to him, and basked in the envelope of warm air surrounding his body. If she moved her hands an inch further away, the air cooled to room temperature—until she relaxed, at which time she once again felt his heat. The greater her relaxation, the further away she could move her hands and still experience the sensation.

Her palms glided along the warmth until she reached his briefs, and the limp heavy shape nestled within them. Her hands jumped . . . the increase in heat was almost shocking. She could back off to eight inches, then nine, and still feel it. Jax was so intensely *vital* that the air around him damn near boiled. She kept her left hand there, hovering over his crotch, but floated her right three inches over his chest. What she experienced then had to be an illusion, it *had* to be, but she could feel his heartbeat. The air above his heart pulsed. Cat brought her left hand down until she was only an inch or so above his underwear. First a wave of heat, and then combed cotton brushed her hand.

Jax's lips curled in anticipation. From the little basket at their side she selected a bottle of clear oil. She screwed the cap off and tipped it against her finger, rubbed the film with her thumb. It felt like liquid silk. She touched her tongue to it. Cinnamon.

Very gently began to work them into his skin, feeling the insertion points on his muscles, the hard-won strength of arms and shoulders, the great muscular pylons of his legs. She shivered. Jax was a *beast*. She glanced at his absurdly delicate wire-framed glasses, folded now and laid carefully to the side. She brushed her fingers against them affectionately. Something about them, some realization tickled at the back of her mind.

And became suddenly clear, so clear that she wondered how in the hell she hadn't seen it before. Jax wore them to prevent himself from being so imposing, to keep himself at a slight remove from the rest of humanity.

It was all too easy to be blinded by Jax's external character: the quick, childish wit and facility for physical confrontation. Jax knew that most men viewed him as a mountain they couldn't climb. Women as an animal they could not control.

But you controlled him, didn't you? You had the power to say yes and no, to keep your legs open or closed, and for almost two years, you really ran his game, didn't you?

And if she was honest, wasn't there a flash of hot dirty triumph in knowing she controlled a splendid beast like Jax? In that moment she gained an insight into his separateness, his sense of humor, his massive body. Jax had built himself a fortress to keep the world at bay—but Cat Juvell had been joyously admitted. And once welcomed into his heart, she could have done anything to him. And had.

In some ways, that realization was one of the saddest moments of her entire life. But at least there was honesty in that sadness. A cry of understanding. This being, this physical creature, in the prime of his life, would inevitably decline. She saw it now—or more accurately, could, in studying his body, feel that truth in her heart.

In some ways, only an athlete can truly understand physical mortality. Beyond the age of thirty, physical conditioning is much like sculpting ice in the Mojave desert. Daily, you busy yourself in clever little disciplined ways, striving to create a thing of beauty from an increasingly diminutive block of frozen water. If you are at all honest, you understand that the efforts are in any ultimate sense futile, but still you strive to find those moments of elegance and power. Eventually, the sun will steal all sense of form, and the sands will drink deeply, leaving only the memory of grace.

Freely, without reciprocal obligation, Jax had offered her his transitory light, offered heart and body, and offered them so completely that even after their marriage failed, he was still her confrere and friend. Still he loved and supported her. He made no secret of the other women in his life, but never used them as weapons against her. He could even laugh about his bed mates—occasionally, they could laugh together.

Oh Jax. What did I do to us?

What did He do to us?

That last thought startled her. Who the hell was *He?*

thirty-one

Karen clapped her hands. "All right. If you would all please rise."

Cat emerged from her trance, knees a little watery. Jax rolled over onto his side, his entire body glistening with oil. Driving, erotic music crooned from the hidden loudspeakers. It was a fairly eclectic selection, starting with the rather obvious choice of Ravel's *Bolero,* moving on to Bonnie Raitt's "I Can't Make You Love Me" and even, rather surprisingly, Brooke Benton's seductive "So Close."

All of the participants were encouraged to join with their partners and dance.

At first, Cat and Jax moved in a formal kind of box step, but Karen appeared beside them and pressed their bodies together. "You can get a little closer than that," Karen said. "I don't think he's going to bite. Nibble, maybe."

Cat folded herself in closer to Jax, laid her head on his chest. Her body felt stiff and somehow sore. God, where had all of this tension come from?

"Women typically display their beauty," Karen said, returning to the front of the room. "And men their power."

Simon chimed in. "In order to break the chains of habit, we need to reverse this. Women need to express their power, and men their beauty."

Simon took Karen in his arms, and they began to dance.

"Follow the energy," Karen growled into her throat mike. "The woman in her beauty, the man in his power—"

Cat and Jax were surrounded by a sea of liquid motion. That odd *floating* feeling came over her again. She felt slightly feverish. She shook her head in a fruitless attempt to clear the cobwebs. Karen and Simon moved together so well, so beautifully, that it was intoxicating.

"When was the last time you revealed yourselves to each other?" Simon asked.

Cat and Jax continued to dance. The overhead lights dimmed. A spotlight focused on Ronnie Vasquez and his wife. They drifted into a languidly sensuous rubato. The light embraced Judy Simpson and her golden boyfriend. Mac Simpson was too spastic to be mistaken for Fred Astaire or even Ray Bolger, but moved with such sheer exuberance that he was a joy to watch.

"Slow down," Karen said to the boy. "Feel the beat inside you. Move *with* her, not *at* her."

The boy nodded, slowed, and the pair slid into a graceful cadence. The light embraced Cat and Jax, who still danced stiffly.

"Remember the first time you touched? The first time you saw your gender mirror," Karen said. "She is the woman in you, Jax. Cat—he is the man in you. Move for him, Cat. Show your softness."

She backed away from him a half step, and gazed up at Jax, searched for any mockery, any demand. Only love lived in his eyes. Something inside her melted. It was impossible to determine in which moment the inner music began, but suddenly she was swaying like a blossom in an autumn breeze.

All her life, dancing had been an uncomfortable challenge. She had always experienced music as something outside her, something to be pursued and wrestled into submission. Never a part of her. But now . . . her body embraced the melody, opened to it, swelled with it joyously, as if until this very moment she had been deaf to its call.

Now—Simon Says . . . tease each other. Go ahead. Slowly."

Jax reached out for Cat, began to unbutton. His fingers touched the swelling under her blouse, that divine union of firm and soft that triggered so many conflicting emotions, made him feel strong and oddly weak at the very same moment. He remembered every inch of her body, but kept those memories shut away carefully, tried not to dwell upon them. That way lay madness.

He yearned to cup her breasts. He expected to see a warning shake of the head, or a cool, distant expression. Instead, Cat swayed languidly, eyes half lidded, swaying to the music like a leaf drifting in a stream. Her skin was flushed and hot.

"Stay with it. Touch the clothes, but not each other."

Jax's hand froze, just over her breast. She smiled at him slyly.

"Most people are too eager to touch."

"We use five 'T' factors," Karen said. "Tease. Titillate. Tantalize. Taunt. And Teach."

"Use them."

The air had boiled down to a syrup. Cat blinked hard. When she closed her eyes, she saw an image of Jax, and the air around him shimmering like an erotic will-o'-the-wisp. She opened her eyes: nothing, save a Jax who grinned confidently as he unlaced his shirt.

His fingers were clumsy and unfamiliar, the task almost impossibly hard. He pulled the silk shirt up over his head, and the flow of the air against his bare skin felt so good, so damned good. . . .

A fleeting thought: that this was *too* good. He was burning, the sense of connection between them was simply too much for flesh to bear. Surely, he would now die. Then another thought, of a similar feeling during a drug experience at New Mexico State, twenty-five years before. Just an experiment, but his body and mind had collapsed together to a point so bright and heavy that it tore a hole in his universe.

This was similar, and he kept waiting for Cat to pull back from him. It might not happen now. It might not happen until they were making love, but it had always happened, *would* always happen.

Then with a sensation much like a breath of cool air, the fleeting doubt was gone.

Cat seemed all circles and softness. She moved her hips to him, rolled and pulled back, approached just close enough for her heat to pluck at him, and then retreated. Jax groaned.

Jax got his shirt the rest of the way off and threw it to the side, not giving a damn where it fell. He danced for her.

Cat giggled, but it was a fascinated giggle, an entranced giggle, as if she was looking at Jackson Carpenter for the very first time.

His was an unmistakably male, strutting, arrogant dance. She retreated, feeling small and very feminine yet somehow in control of the entire interaction—a response which would have astonished her not seventy-two hours before.

With some small corner of her mind not totally involved with the gorgeous male animal in front of her (and not astonished that she perceived Jax to be exactly that. God! The ridges of his stomach, the flat plated muscle of his chest, the breadth of his shoulders, the corded power of his arms. The breath raced in her throat until she was spinning out of control) she heard Karen say:

"Now—switch. Women, show him your power, men—show her your beauty."

She was delighted and surprised to hear an utterly spontaneous growl vibrating deep in her throat. It was feline, primal, challenging. She circled Jax without blinking. Their hips still moved to the music but their torsos had dropped low, and their eyes locked.

This was mating ritual. It was more, and her conscious mind still hadn't quite realized it.

It was also on the same energetic level as . . . what? Sparring? Or cats playing? Yes, that was it. A male and female . . . tiger. Playing. Testing each other, claws in, fangs used only slightly. Testing to see if the prospective mate is worthy.

He stalked her. She stalked him right back.

Wow. Cool.

"You are two animals. Catlike mind. Catlike body. The two of you, stalking. You don't feed off each other. The two of you create a third entity, a being on which you will feast."

Touching. Dancing. Laughter. Tension growing in the room. The music lead them, teased them.

Simon separated the men and women into two groups. "The men will sit at the edges of the room. The women will dance. As we said before, the Prey is the single most important exercise of our discipline. The premise of the Prey exercise is that the two of you are not feeding upon each other. When sexual energy is imbalanced, one partner needs to possess the other, or to feed upon the other. Rape, abuse, control . . . all these things feed upon the partner's energy. They deliberately increase fear, and use its dark energy to break the partner's boundaries.

"What you will do here in the next hour, is play together. The two of you will create a third, energetic entity, 'The Prey.' You will dance for each other. The women will start, and form a ring, which will circle so that every woman has the opportunity to present herself to every man. If you find a greater warmth, a greater attraction, and all parties agree, you may engage with the new partner. Do you understand that? But all parties must agree, and it must be done with beauty. So . . . you may begin."

The women formed a center ring, most of them in their underwear by now, a few in thong-like swim suits. Jax sat on the couch, his broad flat hands resting upon his knees. Several of the women were beautiful. At least two moved with the facility of professional dancers: that perfect syncopated balance of hips and thighs, the rolling undulating motions of the stomach, the muscles so lightly covered with fat that the *rectus abdominus* moved visibly beneath the skin.

The music began.

This was not a piece of top-40 low-cal technopop. This was something synthesized with an Afro-Arabian flavor, something that tickled the base of his spine, but possessed a melodic quality reminiscent of Vivaldi. It was electric. Caitlin swayed before him, her eyes narrowed. It was too easy to see the beast inside this beauty. She was a panther who had donned a transparent woman suit. He shook his head, trying to banish the mirage. Instead it persisted, and grew more convincing still.

The rest of the room around Caitlin dimmed. Jax knew that it was insane, knew it to be hallucination, but thought that he could see her whiskers. Could almost feel the bite of her chisel teeth. He knew how her belly-to-belly purr would feel, how it would be to press her naked flesh moistly against his own. He growled, a low harsh sound at the back of his throat.

He longed to mount her from behind, to feel the soft heat of her buttocks pressed against him, to hook his claws into her to hold her fast, to grind into her and watch her back arch as she howled with pain and pleasure. With each passing moment, it became more and more difficult to remain seated.

Take her.

*Take her **now**.*

In another moment he would have been on his feet, on her, *in* her, but she laughed and broke the contact, and moved to the man next to him.

The next woman who moved before him was named Sophia, of dark lustrous hair and generous hips. Sophia was almost old enough to be his mother—but she was still firm, her breasts still full, hips still rounded. She swayed, and again, where ordinarily a woman of Sophia's years would hold no interest for him, here, he felt something deep within him open receptively. The women in that circle transcended their individuality, became in their unique diversity Everywoman. Some were old. Some young. But the quality of "woman" that he sought, that every man sought, was a universal as old as the sea. While any given woman, thin or fat, beautiful or plain, possessed this quality only for a while, the quality itself was infinite. In comparison, the measure of a man, no matter how large his holdings, no matter how great his abilities, no matter how staggering his accomplishments, is always finite. Jax's mind spun with a brief and fragmentary insight into the core nature of *maleness* and *femaleness,* and the seemingly inevitable trauma of their interaction.

Afterward, he often fought to find that elusive insight again. Sometimes, in quiet reflection, he remembered a small piece which made sense: Infinity is too large a concept to grasp, and as a reaction we often accord the infinite a trivial portion of our attention. The male aspect deals with numbers—huge numbers, vast numbers, yes. But any number which can be counted, added, or subtracted is less than the infinity which birthed it. The male part of a human being, or of humanity itself, craves infinity for completion.

Jax wanted to crawl up into Sophia's arms, lay his head on her breast and let his cares drift away. Her smile was a warm and comforting thing, one that seemed to say: *You're not ready for me yet. Another few years, my brother. You are still too bound to the physical.*

Sophia moved on.

The next girl was Judy Simpson. She was barely eighteen, and he wondered about the wisdom of her attendance. He thought of Felicia Algoni, for whom he had risked his life, only days before. Suddenly she looked like a younger version of this woman. He remembered Mrs. Algoni's reaction to him, and made an ugly guess about Felicia's relationship with her father.

Judy was just learning, a flower just opening her petals to the sun. He suddenly realized why he saw her as a flower, and how a flower formed a terribly apt metaphor for child abuse. There was no way to test a new bud's sweetness without tearing some of the petals away.

Perhaps Judy's first sexual experience had occurred only months before. She still bubbled with wonder and joy, still reveled in her power as a woman, was still drunken with the response she evoked from men.

Then came Cat. He'd watched her from the corner of his eye, as she moved and swayed for the others. There was something in her dance he'd seen but once before . . . at their wedding reception. . . .

Tyler, some old roommates from UCSB, friends from the station, a few of her neighbors . . . those had represented her connection to humanity. And in the safety of that company, overcome with the intoxication of that day, she had let her hair down, opened herself in a way she never had to Jax alone. She and her girlfriends formed a circle, spontaneously recreating a ritual which was old when the wheel was new Each woman, in turn, entered that circle, swaying, dancing, displaying their beauty not for the eyes of men, but for the appreciation of her sisters, an ecstatic celebration of the feminine.

His memory of her was the vision of a cool flame, shimmering in her gown, spinning across the floor like a drunken queen. He remembered taking her in his arms and surrendering to the vortex. The music controlled them, submitted to them, embraced them, transformed them, lifted them to the clouds.

On that day, that glorious day. Cat amidst her friends . . . but no family. Remember that? No family save Tyler . . .

On that day she was freer, more open and joyous than he'd ever seen her. And there was something of that freedom and exaltation in this. It was different from the kind of self-confidence Cat ordinarily evidenced, the usual brash assurance in her wit or physical skills. It was the freedom of knowing that she was safe to express something ordinarily kept carefully hidden.

Jax fell into her eyes, as if no one else in the room, no one else in the world existed. Cat crawled onto his lap and ground herself against him. He grabbed her legs, gripped her thighs and held her fast while she arched back, entire body spasming with some inner current. He fumbled her blouse open, and when her breasts came free he reached for them with his lips. As he did she arched back a little further so that they were just out of reach, unless he pulled her to him. He wouldn't do that. That wasn't the game.

She rolled her hips, and rose one tantalizing inch, one vertebra at a time. Their eyes met again. He didn't know what was happening to him, to them, but he heeded her call. She wasn't Cat, she was *a* cat, *the* cat, perhaps. She was every wild thing within a woman which could rise up meet that matching energy in a man.

His heart thundered as if he was running a 440, chasing something wild, precious, singular. He could almost catch a glimpse of it now: flashing just around a corner, its shadow-dark, black-flame silhouette barely concealed within a stand of trees.

Cat's tongue darted out to touch the corner of his mouth. He stood up, balanced himself, held her at the small of her back as she melted against him. Her eyes rolled up as if she were seeing something as well, something far away but getting closer with every heartbeat.

He looked through the windows, out into the forest. A living shape fled between the trees. It was bigger than a deer. And behind it, predators stalked in pursuit.

His mouth watered.

The music stopped. The room finally came back into focus. The workshop participants were splayed in disarray. Clothes were scattered everywhere. Bare breasts and buttocks glistened with perspiration. Eyes were wide, unseeing, the minds behind them laboring to pull their focus back into the room. The air was heavy, moist, and hot.

"Your attention, please," Karen said, her own voice strained. "We'll meet back here in three hours. You will form The Prey together. You will pursue it, and bring it down." Her grin was feral. "Good hunting."

thirty-two

Touching. Hands burning. Too much heat now. Burning up. Couldn't control it.

Up the stairs. Doors closed. Shutters drawn. Shadows across the room. Furniture pulled back against the wall.

The two of you create a third, imaginary entity we call "The Prey." The prey is the orgasticness, the ecstasy, the pleasure you both crave. Together the two of you create it, chase it, and feed upon it. Feed your hungers.

Jax took a blanket, stripped a blanket from the bed, and spread it onto the floor, watched it settle there like a magic carpet, slo-mo. Every breath takes an hour. Every heartbeat an eternity.

Heat.

Clothes shed now. So hot. Can't think. Can't think. Jax before her, dressed only in underwear. Tight. Strained, tiny drops of moisture sticky-dark against the light material. She felt her breath catch, knowing that the sight of her, the touch of her, the smell of her was causing him such excitement, bringing him so near to detonation.

They circled the blanket, eyes only on each other.

Don't use the bed for this exercise. We want you raw. We want you wild. We want you completely natural.

Distant crackle of radio sound. Somewhere, another world, someone wants to talk to them. Tyler. Later. Hungry now. Feed now. Talk later.

Hungry. Hot.

Sometimes the cabin was there, sometimes not. If she closed her eyes for even a minute, it was gone, and in its place grew a forest, verdant and primeval.

The forest floor was heavy with leaves and ferns. There seemed no animal life, just the silent forest. Then . . .

A leaf twitched. A vine fluttered, plucked by a nonexistent wind. Leaf and vine, and then fern wove about each other, thickened each other. The plant life danced and merged, melded and heaped until there was a knot the size of a small dog, and then a pig, and then . . . it shifted color, from green and brown to brown and yellow. Solidified. Howled itself awake, and watched as its mate formed from the same matting of ferns and flowers.

Tigers, male and female. Full-sized, adult, magnificent. At least eight feet from nose to haunch. They sniffed each other, stretched, sniffed again and licked at each other's ears and whiskers, then began to run, side by side. Great muscles flexed fluidly beneath sleek shifting, sliding coats.

His hands gripped at her. She pulled him close, bruised his lips and tasted his mouth.

Smell her. Taste her. The very essence of her body will change as she becomes ready. Learn to determine by taste the moment her body opens to you.

Although their eyes were only an inch apart, she spoke without removing her lips from his. Breathing his breath. "I didn't want . . ." she began, and then the words died.

"I don't know what's happening," Jax said.

She kissed him again, felt something in her heart break open, releasing a delicious flood of emotion. "I don't care," she said. She grabbed his shoulders, rolled him beneath her, and climbed onto him.

"You aren't stalking each other—"

She ripped the underwear away, grabbed him, cupped his scrotum, rubbed her thumb gently along the underside of his erection, base to tip. The world was new, all magma, light, and blinding sound. The taste on her thumb was salt-slick and thick as *Goldvasser* liquor. She groaned, opening for him, lowering herself onto him, an inner cry beginning as an embryonic, inarticulate thing and growing until it began to drown thought.

Stalk your prey. The more passionate, the more alive, the more open you are, the bigger, and the better your prey.

She held him inside her now, and they moved together like a single aching organism, two chambers of a single heart. Cat, eyes closed, fingers trailing down his chest, could see the tigers clearly now. They loped stride for stride, in steady, rolling cadence. The woods flashed by them and then . . . then she wasn't watching. She *was* the tiger, and ahead of her, she could see.

An elk. Alert, aware, antlers high. Almost invisible in the brush.

She moaned in pleasure, heard another animal sound boiling up as the strides grew longer, and the fire inside her grew.

This. *This* was what she was meant to do. She lived in two worlds. One was a shadow world of mortal men and women, their bodies locked intimately, a single breath circulating between the two of them, hotter and hotter now. Mouths and groins locked in liquid fire, now moving quick, now resting for a moment, letting the heat quiet, build, and then begin to move—

Her other world, a larger, truer world, was that of the tiger, a carnivore with no thought save the pleasure of the kill. That thought, and perhaps the pride of hunting with the magnificent animal at her side. This was the dream she had created, the world she had chosen to stalk. And the male animal loping at her shoulder was her own flaming reflection, flickering in a golden mirror.

Let yourselves go.

The images and sensations wheeled around each other, faster and faster. The tigers. The elk, fleeing now. Jax, beneath her, his arms encircling her, rolling her on the blanket so that he was above her, taking her hands and pinning them to the ground. She screamed in protest, then branded that scream a lie by pumping her hips to meet him, match him, lengthen the arc of his thrusts.

Men. Hold back if you want a woman to give herself completely. Bring her to orgasm three times before you let yourself go.

She felt something break inside her, like a bubble within a bubble within a bubble, each peak lifting her, leaving her suspended above a pit but still barely able to find her way back to ground—and then the next bubble like molten lava ***bursting,*** lifting her. In a voice that was not her own she begged him to never stop, never ever—**God!** And then another ***explosion,*** a swelling grinding, sweet-sour nova and the world went red—

And then a glorious, crystalline white that was all color, all sensation melded together—

And . . .

—she was in a place she had never been. And knew nothing but lumination. And a *catness,* a *felinity.* And heat. She gripped something, and something gripped her, and—

A moment when she lost the *I,* became the feeling, and it was here, and it was happening, and a brief glimpse—

Tigers leaping

The elk screamed. Claws. Heat. Blood.

Feeding.

Then only heartbeats, sighs, shared breath, and light without end.

thirty-three

Finally and with no small difficulty, Jax remembered his name.

He lay on his side, spooned with but not touching Cat.

He couldn't see her face, knew nothing except but that he yearned to touch her, wanted to talk to her, wanted to say and share things. He reached out to touch her . . . and felt her pull away from him. Just a half inch, but enough.

Enough.

The air was cool. Jax pulled a blanket over her, and quietly sat up. He stood, the floorboards cool against his naked feet. He slipped a robe over his damp shoulders, and left the room.

———————

Rain sprinkled from an overcast sky. More than a drizzle, less than a downpour. He tried to organize his thoughts, and couldn't, quite.

Jax sat in one of the cabin's porch chairs, and pulled a cigarette out of his robe pocket, drawing on it. He let the smoke trickle from between his lips.

He was out here alone. No one else. Behind him, the sun streamed coolly through the clouds. Jax lowered his head into his hands, struggling to collect his thoughts.

Thoughts of Cat, laying in the room behind him. Laying on her side, gloom shadowing without concealing her physical perfection. Cat, eyes closed. A single tear streaked her cheek.

It was the first time he had ever seen her cry.

A mile away, Tyler sat in his van, masked by the swelling shadows. He gazed into the radio. From time to time one of the telephones would buzz. Someone would talk. Most often business, or someone calling home to speak with family or friends.

He wondered what Cat and Jax were doing.

He hated wondering about it.

"Shit," he said sourly, and gazed out the front window of the van, and watched the rain bead against the windshield. Listened to it patter against the roof, a lost and lonely sound.

thirty-four

Jax chewed every bite carefully, as if afraid of swallowing a chicken bone. Each mouthful was of infinite importance. Most of the other couples were there, sharing a delicious intimacy. He waved to them, explained why Cat was not with him. She was taking a nap, he said, and winked salaciously. He piled his plate high, and sat by himself.

A glowing Caitlin tried to engage him in conversation. Her dark red hair hung limply, and the violet tint on her eyelids was faded almost completely away. She looked freshly . . . scrubbed. Jax barely responded to her conversational sallies, and after a few vague answers, she abandoned the attempt.

After about fifteen minutes Cat appeared in the doorway. He watched her, not allowing himself to feel. The corners of her mouth lifted in tentative greeting, and he managed a nod in return.

She filled her plate, and came to sit next to him. Jax scooted to one side for her, but continued cutting and chewing without saying a word.

Without speaking, he finished his meal. The food, already bland, tasted like wet papier maché. Jax pushed himself away from the table and bussed his tray. Cat followed him from the room.

She caught up with him out on the porch, as he lit another Camel. "You're smoking a lot, aren't you?"

He looked at her dully, incuriously. A meaningless smile curled his lips. "Guess so," he said.

"Are you all right?"

"Yeah," he said. "Just fine."

Cat chewed at her lip. "Jax . . ."

He cut her off. "It shouldn't have happened. I don't know why it happened."

He got up and walked a few feet away from her, sat on the rail again, tried to find a point off in the night darkness to study.

She touched his arm gingerly. "Jax—"

His head snapped around sharply. "Listen, Cat. I can work with you. I can fight beside you. When you're hurt, I can patch your wounds. If you were a guy we could be buddies." At that, he almost chuckled. Almost. "But you're not, Cat."

"Not what?"

"Not a guy. You're not my buddy. I love you, and I always have. And you never let me in. Never." The last word hung there in the air between them like a dead thing twisting on a wire. "And just for a moment there, in Serenity House, you did. And it was better than anything I've ever known."

She sighed. "That goes both ways, Jax. We both sit on our stuff. Maybe that's why we're such a pair. How much have you ever talked to me about Vietnam?"

"You know everything important," he said.

She examined him curiously, as if wondering if he really believed that remark. "Then who was Mister Q.? Gooksbane? Caltiki?"

He closed his eyes. "Friends," he finally said. "Would it have made a difference? Would you have felt closer to me? More committed to us?" His voice was flat, brittle.

"Jax . . . ?" she tried to look in his eyes, but he turned away. She trailed her fingers along his arm, then gripped him. "We're supposed to listen to our feelings. Our instincts. All right. I feel that we've both had walls up. It wasn't just me, Jax. It wasn't. And believe it or not, I think I've taken down more than you have. Maybe I had more to begin with. But don't think I haven't tried, Jax. Don't think I didn't get tired of peeling away one layer after another . . . and still feeling no safer with you. No closer to you." Her voice thickened, almost broke, and then she caught herself. "Please, Jax."

For a long time the night pressed in on them, then Jax found the strength to shrug it off, and said, "All right. You want to hear something?"

"If you want to, Jax. Not if its just to make me happy."

He took another deep drag, and exhaled it slowly. "And yes, I do." The moonlight shone dully in his eyeglasses. "Remember what I told Sinclair, about commitment? About the will to win?"

She nodded.

"You want to know the moment I knew we were going to lose, over there?"

Again, but more slowly now, she nodded.

"I was in-country, pretty deep. We were losing sentries, and not just losing them." He lit another cigarette. This time, his hand was shaking. "We'd find them in the bush, with their eyes torn out. They were laying on their stomachs, and Charley'd dug knife holes in their backs. And then they'd put the eyeballs in the holes, staring up at us. Do you get it?"

Cat shivered. "They were saying that they have eyes in the backs of their heads." She wrapped her arms around herself, shivered against the cold. "Jesus. That was when you knew?"

He shook his head in irritation. "No. Not then. Later. It was our response that told me. Brass wanted us to do something just as disturbing when we killed their people. But they didn't want us 'losing our basic humanity.' So you know what they did?" He exhaled another long plume of smoke. "They talked to the news people over there. The CBS people used to put these black and white eye stickers on everything, everywhere, you know, their cameras and mike packs and shit. Well, they got a couple thousand CBS Eye stickers, and passed them out. Then when we took out a VC, we were supposed to put these stickers on the back of his head." He wasn't talking to her any longer. He wasn't even *with* her any more. "That was when I knew we were going to lose. That all of the death, and all of the sweat was for nothing. Just nothing. Because we didn't have the *will* to do what it took."

He took a long drag on his cigarette, and breathed it out into the wind. "As soon as we leave here it's over, isn't it?" The words were delivered utterly flat. "Isn't it, Cat? Don't lie to me."

He looked into her eyes. They met his without blinking. In that moment he felt that he would die to hear the right words from her, knew that he mustn't let himself feel that way, now or ever.

"Yes," she said. "You're right. After we leave here, it's over."

Jax spun the cigarette out into the darkness, watching the trail of sparks as it went, despising himself for the act of littering. "Thank you for sharing," he said.

He turned away, gazing into the woods. "All right," he said. "It won't happen again. We can handle this, right?"

"Right," she said, and linked her arm through his.

"All right."

His eyes were fixed on a point somewhere out there in the dark. He had to find a spot to look at. Someplace to fix his attention. Unfortunately, he couldn't make it stay there. He cursed and found another spot, anything to take his mind off the feel and smell, the physical reality of the woman leaning against him, the slender ribbon of fire who had molded herself to him, who had run with him on a bloody quest.

"Jax?" she said. "I just lied, and I can't do that to you, to us. I don't know what's in the future. The only way I know how to live is one day at a time. One moment at a time. It's the only way I know. Can you wait until tomorrow for tomorrow's answers?"

She smiled up at him and he snorted in exasperation. "You're pretty powerful there, lady."

"And you're pretty beautiful, Tiger."

His eyes narrowed a little. "Cat?' He said. "What kind of animal were you. You know, when we were making love?"

"Tiger?"

He nodded. "Both of us. By any chance, were we bringing down an elk?"

Cat slipped her arm from his, turned, and looked out into the woods. "Shit," she said softly. "This is kind of weird."

C at and Jax reentered the course room, only about thirty seconds before a gong rang to summon the tribes for the evening session.

The door slid shut behind them. Then there was laughter, and conversation from the course room, and little sound in the rest of the mansion.

There was even less sound in the surrounding woods. Little but crickets, and night bird sounds. And a dull mechanical whirring, like the sound of a high-speed camera, somewhere out in the darkness.

thirty-five

Wednesday, June 21

Cat felt deliciously childlike. That *might* have had something to do with the costumes they were wearing: in her case, a plaid Catholic-school skirt purchased at a second hand store. Jax wore shorts and a button-down shirt with a ridiculous plaid bow tie. Everyone in the room wore a similar costume, something evoking a younger, more innocent and inexperienced stage of life.

The night had been a comfortable one, although she realized that Jax had been careful not to intrude upon her side of the bed. It had taken a while for her to wind her way to sleep, but when it came it was thick, deep, black, and apparently dreamless.

Caitlin's hand was up.

"Yes?" Karen said.

"We had an incredible time last night," Caitlin said, "but we remember what you said, that the woman should be given three orgasms before the man comes. That requires a lot of control, doesn't it?"

"Actually," Simon corrected, "Three orgasms before he even *enters* her."

Not surprisingly, *that* triggered an enthusiastic chorus of "right ons" from the women.

Karen held up her hand for quiet. "Now then . . . every woman has a different body type, and so does every man. Depending on that body type, the approach to pleasuring her changes."

Karen wore a pink skirt with a poodle stitched onto the seam. She sat in a straight-backed chair in the front of the room, and raised her skirt with a smile that would have done Becky Thatcher proud.

She was bare underneath, a circumstance which might well have surprised Tom Sawyer, although his older chum Huck might well have known how to deal with the situation. Although she affected a girlish simper, there was actually nothing remotely coy about her actions. She tilted her hips so that her pubic area caught the light clearly. With thumbs and forefingers, she carefully spread her vaginal lips.

Jax was surprised to find himself thinking that the pink folds, displayed so, looked rather like a butterfly.

"I'm a Deer Woman," she explained. "Do you see the folds here?" she pointed carefully. "And the way the lips form part of the clitoral hood? That means my G-spot is about two inches in, and . . . I need a lot of oral stimulation."

"Any volunteers?" Simon laughed. Several hands shot up, but it was a joke, and quickly understood as such. Most people were taking notes, some drawing little diagrams.

"How can you tell that?" Ronnie Valdez said.

"The Twins received this knowledge from their teachers, and transmitted it to us. Human beings haven't changed much in the last million years. There are a few things which are simply the truth. Don't believe what we're saying—test it and see."

After Karen invited anyone who wished to take a closer look, she got up and Simon, who was dressed in patched jeans with a straw hat and fake freckles painted on his cheeks, casually dropped his pants. "I'm a Horse man," he said blandly. "You can tell by the thickness of my lingam, and the low angle of the testicles—"

"Jesus," Jax whispered to Cat. "You can't tell a book by its cover, can you? One-man fire department—" his lewd monologue coughed to a halt as Cat elbowed him.

One at a time, every man and woman at the workshop sat in the chair.

Simon and Karen examined each in turn, saying things like: "Bear Man" "Wolf Woman," "Horse," "Coyote," "Dancing Deer" and so forth, categorizations of size, length, thickness, position of folds and appearance of vagina or penis. The green textbooks bore a number of very specific pictures, some of them obviously cropped from pornographic magazines, but others from medical texts and two apparently taken by professional photographers. The overall effect was not titillating but rather clinical and fascinating. Jax was fascinated by the discussion of clitoral positions and G-spots, the variations in times of the month, the differing approaches to satisfying different types of woman.

Then it was his turn. Shrugging, he went to the front of the class, and dropped his pants.

Karen went down on one knee in front of him, peering at his genitals with purely professional interest.

"What do you think?" she asked Simon. "Horse?"

"Well . . ." Simon came closer too. Jax thought that they were going to whip out calipers and measuring tape, perhaps cry "Eureka!" and categorize by displacement. "Well, the thickness suggests horse . . . but not quite that long. . . . Bear?"

"I think it's a noncardinal direction. I say Pony."

"Pony?" Cat asked, straight-faced as Jax returned to her side.

"Hah-hah," Jax said. His collar burned. "Milady?"

Cat strode up like a queen. She raised her skirt regally, and sat.

"That," Jax said, without bothering to consult his notes, "is definitely a Wolf."

Simon raised a quizzical eyebrow. "Does she howl?"

"Howwwww!" Jax let out in a burst, and the room dissolved into general hilarity.

Cat glared at him, but, with immense dignity, lowered her skirt and returned to her place beside him.

She cut her eyes sideways at him, coughed politely, and then whinnied.

Every female body type needs a different kind of stimulation, has a different hunger," Simon said. "What makes it even harder for men is the fact that a woman's hungers change over the course of a month."

"How about men?" Jax asked.

Karen shrugged. "What about men?"

"You've been spending a lot of time talking about pleasuring a woman—just looking for a little parity here."

She shrugged. "Frankly, there's a lot less complexity. In comparison to women, men are like balloons—you just blow them up until they explode. Women are more like a combination safe. The trick is that the combination changes from one time of the month to the next, so you have to have *really* sensitive fingers, and listen to the tumblers."

"Too mechanical," Simon said. "I like to think of women more like hot fudge sundaes. They need to be . . . *savored.* Tasting a woman will tell you everything you need to know, including and especially, the moment at which she will open to you, when she is ready for lovemaking. Sour tastes indicate fear, or lack of health. Now. Giving head to a man is easy to demonstrate, as we saw before lunch—"

"Helped *my* appetite." Jax whispered.

"But it's much more difficult to demonstrate the proper technique for a woman. The body hides the action."

Karen held up her hand again. "Before we go on, remember that although the individual techniques, the body types, the masks, the games, The Prey exercise—these are intended to raise the energy, the sexual *chi.*"

While she spoke, Simon had picked up a curious object—a clear plastic rectangle stencilled with an image of female genitalia.

"What in the hell is *that?*" Jax whispered.

"Don't ask, don't tell," Cat whispered back.

"Now with this, we should be able to see the proper technique quite clearly. The man places his upper lip *here,* and his lower lip *here,* and the tongue has this curling motion against the yoni. . . ."

Jax's jaw dropped open. Simon continued to demonstrate with considerable skill, and sufficient length and pliability of tongue to unravel a sweater.

"Take notes," Cat whispered. "There'll be a quiz later."

"Written or oral?"

thirty-six

Hours later, at nearly six o'clock, Jax found himself standing next to a weathered pine tree. He stared at an ant traversing the gnarled canyons of its bark, frowning. He touched his necklace. "Tyler. Can you hear me?"

"Oh, yeah, Kemo Sabe . . . loud and clear. What's going on."

"I'm talking to a tree."

"Talking to the tree?"

Jax sang it softly. "I talk to the trees, but they don't listen to me. . . ."

"With a voice like that, who can blame them? What's this bit about?"

"Well, they said that the more natural you are, the more intense your creative flow. But that nobody is really natural in society, because we're always concerned about looking good, or worried how people will react to us.

"Yeah, so?"

"So . . . go out in a forest, and hang out with a tree. What they said is that the way you are just with the tree is your natural self. Then if another human being shows up, to notice the way you shift, the act that you start to put back on."

"How's it working?"

"Oh, I'm the natural me, all right."

"Yeah, natural fucking crazy."

"How are the phone lines?"

Tyler's voice became conspiratorial. *"Something's coming down. Not sure what it is, though. Everyone's excited."*

Jax laughed. "That's their normal mode around here."

"No," Tyler insisted. *"This is different—"*

Without warning, a sudden, shrill cry of complete anguish split the air. Jax jerked around. At first all he could see were trees. Then another kind of vision kicked in, the kind he had perfected long ago, in another world. The trees separated; his visual field deepened, and he caught a flash of motion over to his left. Another scream—this time recognized as a woman in pain. And a flutter of cloth, about a hundred yards distant.

"Problem," Jax said tersely. "Talk later." He ran very lightly for a man of his size, scurrying through the trees along a narrow dirt path.

Below him, perhaps eighteen feet down a shallow incline, a woman sat with her back against a tree. Six people clustered around, murmuring concern and offering aid. Kneeling before her, and temporarily obscuring her face, was Cat. Cat's tensed mouth relaxed into welcome as Jax scrambled down the incline.

The injured woman was Caitlin. Her teeth clinched at her lower lip, her face pale and sweaty. Cat knotted the arms of a sweater around Caitlin's right thigh. Blood pulsed in an ominous rhythm from an ugly gash in her lower calf.

He scanned the scene, noted the dislodged soil up the slope, broken roots, gaps in the carefully set flagstones along the path. The sequence of events was clear: rain-weakened soil had given way. A tumble down the incline, a sudden, terrible impact on a rock, a slide, a second impact as a dislodged rock crashed home.

Jax skidded to a halt. "Cut?"

"Smashed. We need a stretcher down here, get her to the hospital. She's going into shock."

The injury was gruesome. The shin bone was splintered, an inch-long fragment actually piercing the skin. The entire lower leg was swollen and blackening. Caitlin's lips were ghastly white. "Help me," she whispered. "Please."

Jax peered up the grade, and saw one of the other men already climbing for help—nothing for him to do but try to make Caitlin comfortable. She held his hand with desperate strength, eyes closed tightly shut until there was a commotion up at the road, and several of the workshop assistants appeared, Simon and one of the others trundling a stretcher.

"Be careful," Cat said. The warning proved unnecessary: They handled the injured woman with professional skill and care. An agonized wince rippled across Caitlin's face as she lay back onto the stretcher, watching nervously as the injured limb was lifted into place. Her fears were groundless—they couldn't have handled the leg more carefully if it had been filled with nitroglycerine.

Caitlin wiped a bit of dirt away from her face with a shaking hand. "It hurts. . . ."

"Not for long," Simon said gently. Jax couldn't put his finger on exactly what this was all about, but in some way Simon actually seemed *excited* by the injury. There was no fear, no real alarm.

"What hospital is she going to?" Cat asked.

"We don't need a hospital. Everything's going to be fine."

"What does *that* mean?"

Simon ignored her questions. Caitlin was carted up the hillside gingerly, each step taken with extreme care. Twice the loam gave way and they slid back six inches or so, but with no major mishaps, they quickly gained the road. Caitlin sobbed, her cries echoing through the trees.

"They're not taking her to the hospital?" Jax said, disbelieving.

Cat was furious. "I don't know what the hell's going on, or what whacko beliefs these people have, but that woman needs help. Come on."

The course room was sheer commotion. Karen and Simon were taking questions from a very disturbed workshop. Finally, Karen raised her hands, palms toward the crowd, seeking silence. "Believe me—Caitlin will be cared for. Please. Trust us. Now—we have a surprise after lunch. Please just enjoy your lunch, meet back here with us at . . ." she glanced at her watch. "Two P.M."

Cat stared at Karen as the group began to break up, and cursed savagely. "This is the *height* of irresponsibility."

"So what do you want to do?" Jax asked.

Cat radiated anger. "I was starting to like these people. Now I think they're fruity. Sinclair is right—if his sister is with them, God knows if she can think straight. We need to play hardball here. Tonight—we find their records room, and plunder. No more soft-shoe."

"Good by me."

Without another word, Cat headed out of the course room, and was halfway back to Serenity House before she stopped. Her face was tilted a few degrees skyward. She was as still and alert as a deer.

"What is it?"

"Listen," she said, and a moment later he heard the steady whir of a helicopter's rotors.

"Medevac? Jax asked. "Maybe they're not as crazy as we thought?"

Cat's expression was unreadable. "No. I don't think that's it."

The whir grew louder, almost deafening, and a moment later a gold and silver Bell executive transport copter appeared over the southern horizon. For about seven seconds it hovered above the trees, then glided down toward a group of outlying cabins to the east.

"Looks like the same helicopter that brought the Oshitas to the stadium."

Cat nodded agreement.

"Check it out?"

"Let's"

Cat stalked carefully through the woods, heading east. Her eyes swept left and straight ahead. There was no need to look right—she had complete confidence that Jax had that quadrant covered. The first obstacle to confront them was a rude, low wooden fence. To the north was a dirt road and a wire mesh gate manned by two attendants—easily spotted, cautiously circumvented. These two, a bulky young black man and a wiry woman with a carrot-red Moe Howard cut, looked serious and alert, as if they actually had something worth protecting.

She could make out a second, chain link fence through the trees. On the far side of the fence was a concrete helipad, and the chopper descended onto it with the delicacy of an enormous grasshopper.

As they inched closer, Cat was able to make out Simon and Karen standing near the helipad, each carrying a bouquet, their faces wreathed with smiles.

Before the overhead rotors ceased to revolve the side door opened. As she had expected, Joy and Tomo emerged.

The first thing Cat noticed was that they were more relaxed, less theatrical than at the California rally. Be that as it may, they were no less regal. Each wore a kind of nylon saffron jumpsuit criss-crossed with zippers up the sides. They carried themselves with the kind of physical energy generally reserved for professional dancers and Olympic gymnasts.

Even at this range, it was difficult to make a good guess at their age. They had to be close to fifty, but didn't really look out of their twenties. At some angles, they resembled teenagers.

Karen approached them. Cat could just hear her words over the dying engine hum. "We have a problem." Cat crawled closer, was now only fifteen feet away, behind a densely flowering bush.

Joy smiled tolerantly. "There are no problems. Only opportunities to experience life."

"All right," Simon said. "What we got here is a compound *opportunity*."

As Cat watched, Joy and Tomo were ushered along a packed dirt path, through the low fence and up the hill toward the mansion.

Cat looked at Jax, who shrugged his big shoulders and headed after them.

Tomo's voice said "It is important that the local nodes be coordinated for the broadcast."

"Everything's fine," Simon said. "Tickets have sold out for three sections so far. Have you made the arrangements in New York? In Tampa?"

Joy spoke. "We just finished in New York—we're on our way home tomorrow. Thought we—"

"Would swing by and talk to your people if we could."

A sudden sound of footsteps, someone running from the helicopter along the path, crunching gravel and dirt underfoot. Cat turned and peered back through the underbrush, but couldn't see more than the general form of a woman. "Do your attendees know the Twins are here?" At first she couldn't quite see the speaker, then Cat found a gap between branches.

Through the branches she saw a tall, strong-looking woman, heavy but not fat, with a strikingly lovely face and medium-length, very straight black hair.

Kolla.

Jax nodded hard. "Bingo. She's traveling in the Twins' personal helicopter. Lady's connected."

"If she's handing over 120 million in assets—well, even counting inflation, that buys a lot of juice."

The entire contingent entered the mansion. Cat watched as Vasquez's wife tried to follow and was politely turned away.

"How do we get in?"

"*We* don't," Cat said. "I do." She pointed up to a small, open window on the second floor. "Boost me."

Jax lifted Cat up, and she grabbed onto the edge of the roof.

She balanced precariously for a moment, and then scrambled up, crawling around the shingled edge and up to the second-floor window. It opened into some sort of storage loft, packed with boxes and old equipment. She snaked along the dusty floor, trying not to sneeze. At the other end of the loft, a window looked down onto the larger, open area of the course room. The windows were closed, the drapes shut. The doors were closed.

The Twins sat yoga-style on two red cushions. The senior acolytes sat around them in a semicircle. Caitlin lay on the stretcher, the pants on her injured left leg cut and peeled away. Caitlin's pant leg was sodden with blood. Her face was ashen. She was gamely fighting shock and pain. Her face was grimy with sweat. The flesh around the break was badly swollen. "Caitlin," Tomo said. "You have been our loyal student for years, and have brought many sheep into the fold. I am sorry the honor I bestow comes only at the cost of such pain."

Caitlin gritted her teeth. "Pain is a thing of the body. I am spirit."

Tomo nodded soberly. "You are spirit." He reached down, encircling her leg with his right hand.

"Shit!" Caitlin screamed.

He kept his hand on her leg, and threw his head back. Cat saw his face now, and it was ecstatic, far away. "Inhale," Tomo said. "Exhale. Inhale—"

Cat blinked her eyes, hard. Something was wrong with the light in the room. Maybe it was her contact lenses. The air around Tomo seemed to *sparkle* as he exhaled. Cat shook her head, hard. This was crazy, absolutely crazy. The light around Tomo paled, as if *bending* somehow. A gauzy zone of golden light seemed to seep out of his skin. It flickered, shifted toward blue: the azure of evening skies, of perfect oceans, of precious gemstones. A scintillant whirlpool danced and swirled.

Cat's breathing yearned to pulse in rhythm with his. Again, she experienced the sensation of the entire world melting away, flesh and bone dissolving, nothing remaining but—

She blinked again. The blue light condensed into tendrils: tiny, delicate threads really, like superfine wires in an incandescent bulb. The radiant strands floated out and branched through the air.

Karen and Simon were chanting now. *"Inhale—"*

Caitlin performed as requested, and a network of tiny glowing airfilaments entered her nose. She convulsed, her entire body arching as if a low-level electric voltage ran through her spine.

"Ohhh!"

Caitlin gripped the back of the bolster, and Cat watched as every muscle in her body contracted into an ecstatic rictus, fingers gripping into the leather. She screamed as if in the grips of the most savagely powerful orgasm in history.

The glow continued to travel down her body. She shook, muscles still locking, eyes rolled back. Every muscle in Caitlin's arms stood out in painfully tight ridges, in contractions powerful enough to lift her lower body from the bolster.

Cat couldn't breath.

The blue glow continued to crawl down Caitlin's body, until it reached the injured leg. Even from Cat's position above them, she heard a distinct crunching, crackling sound, and Caitlin's cries ratcheted up into a more rarefied level of agony. Tomo shifted slightly to the side and—

And Cat saw the impossible. The damaged leg began to *untwist,* the protruding sliver of bone melting away like ice beneath a blowtorch. The swelling receded, and flesh knitted with a sound like fat frying in a pan. Blood still smeared the recently damaged leg, but the wound had simply healed.

Just like that.

Impossible.

The blue light faded. Tomo heaved for breath. His skin glistened with sweat, as if he had just completed a hundred-yard dash.

"See," he gasped, chest heaving. "See, and believe."

As the light died away, Caitlin's body dropped back down to the bolster. Slowly, her muscles relaxed, leaving her at peace. She moaned slightly, a feline, almost postcoital purr. She looked up at Tomo, her eyes wide and worshipful.

She reached out for his hand, took it with trembling fingers and kissed it. He gently drew his hand away. "Caitlin. This is most important, and you must listen to me."

"Anything." At that moment, if he had asked her to crawl across a mile of broken glass, she would have gladly agreed.

"Do not tell *anyone* what I have done for you," he said.

She seemed confused. "Why not?"

Joy answered for her brother. Her voice was strong, but not unkind. "It is good for doubters to think us charlatans. The genuine demonstration is only for the faithful."

Tomo nodded. "And our enemies must not know our true strength."

Caitlin stiffened, comprehending immediately. "Iron Shadows," she said.

"Iron Shadows," Tomo repeated. He reached out his hand, and without looking, or even really appearing to notice, Joy took it in her own.

———

Dazed, Cat rolled silently onto her stomach, starting up at the ceiling. She felt utterly afraid, lost, in a place mortally strange yet somehow terribly familiar.

The attic. The dark shadows and shapes loomed at her, whispered at her. She was no longer the woman Porsche Juvell. She was a younger child, barely nine years old, crawling in an attic.

Crawling. Hiding . . . and searching. She was . . . hiding? Hiding from what? And why? Searching for what?

There was something behind her in the darkness. She curled up, trying to sleep, trying to hide, trying to pretend, and it didn't work. It wasn't the attic, but the chest studded with diamonds and pearls was here, and she was hiding. She was searching for it.

Drawn to it, driven away from it. Totally confused, feeling like a machine with its wires crossed, completely alone and afraid.

And something was coming. She could hear it. The attic's trap door was smashed once, twice, three times by something, something that couldn't be resisted. She heard a voice but couldn't recognize it, or distinguish the words. Light flooded up from beneath the door. Cat saw a hand, fingers of a hand gripping the door from under it, and heard the thunderous cries, and she searched more frantically and finally found the chest, the sparkling chest, and one key after another she used, and opened it, and she did, and within was a little golden heart—

thirty-seven

Tomo stood, his legs wobbling a bit. He managed to slide back into a chair. His fixed smile stretched thin as Caitlin was carried from the room. He closed his eyes, and then with evident effort, said, "It is time."

Joy's face was pinched with concern. "Are you strong enough?"

He swallowed, then nodded slowly. "Yes. But now, please."

Two of the others brought a white ceramic jug forward.

Joy extended her arm over the pitcher, and rolled up her nylon sleeve. Her face wrinkled in concentration. Then the dark, perfect flesh of her forearm began to roil, actually ripple as if *liquefying*. Joy arched her body, nearly swooning as blood first trickled, then streamed.

She screamed, the cry ululating cyclically. Blood pumped in a dark gout, drizzled down into the pitcher, and as it did, Joy shuddered with pleasure.

A pint. Two pints.

"Joy . . ." Tomo whispered, fingers digging into her shoulder. She turned, her eyes huge and glassy, as if she didn't recognize him at all. Moaning, she tried to pull away, to return to the pitcher.

"Enough!" he yelled.

Joy's face was suddenly younger. "No . . . more. Please. More."

Tomo laid his hand on her arm. The bleeding trickled to a stop. His hands shook as he enfolded her fingers with his. "Enough," he said.

They locked gazes, and she struggled against him for a moment. After a few moments of fierce resistance, she fell back into her chair, gasping. The bleeding slowed to a trickle.

"Tomo . . ." she whispered, and collapsed against him.

Tomo looked at the pitcher as if it were a living, loathsome thing. His voice shook with anger. "Take it. Leave."

Simon whisked the jug away. "Yes, sir."

"All of you!" Tomo roared. "Leave!"

Without a question or backward glance, they filed out of the room. Joy collapsed against Tomo as the door locked behind them.

"I need you," she whispered.

Tomo nodded. He unbuttoned and peeled aside her blouse. Her body was flawlessly beautiful, but his evaluation of it was clinical. An enormous scar ran vertically along the left side of her ribcage, from four inches below the arm pit almost to her hip.

Tomo stripped off his own shirt. The scar's mirror-double marred his own right side.

Joy gripped at his hand. "Please." Her voice was weaker now. Cat could barely hear it. He helped her to a couch, and slid in beside her. The hard edges of the two scars rippled and liquefied, then melded hungrily, seeking each other like lovers' lips. The separated Siamese twins joined again.

Joy groaned. Her eyes closed, and then opened wide, suffused with a red light that spread, washing through her entire body, spreading into Tomo. When it reached him, it became golden. It split into twin threads, wound up his spine, up to the crown of his head, out of his heart, and back into her, completing the circuit.

She shuddered, clutching at him like a little girl, and he smoothed her head, healing.

"Thank you, brother," she whispered. "In all my life, this is the only time that I feel whole."

He stroked her hair tenderly. "It is my pleasure."

Cat trembled. Her mind felt filled with smoke and cobwebs, as if it was short-circuiting. If she didn't do something quickly, she would become physically ill. The storage room's dark spaces were closing in on her, and as she crawled out, the world whirled like a crazed carousel.

She crawled out through the window and jumped down lightly, landing on bent legs, Jax steadying her with fingertips. She wrapped her arms around her shoulders, her knees sagged.

"Jesus," Jax said. "You look shell-shocked. What happened?"

When she looked up at Jax, it was as if she had never seen him before. The woods, the trees—everything seemed new, utterly unique, as if the world had suddenly revealed itself to her.

"Not now," she said. "And not here. Come on."

thirty-eight

Cat strode across the graveled parking area between the cabins, concentrating on reaching their car. Just a few more steps. Just one step after another. That was all it would take. Already at the driver's door, Jax watched her, his dark face creased with worry, his customary sardonic smile completely gone.

Before she could open the door Caitlin ran up, trotting across the gravel on her impossibly healed leg. "Listen," she said breathlessly. "There's no dinner tonight. Free time until nine. Want to meet us in town? Rib place named Red Ryder?"

Cat grinned, tried not to stare at the leg. *Oh, it wasn't as bad as it looked. . . .* "Say seven o'clock? We want to do a little shopping."

Her husband Russell perked up. "Mind if we tag along?"

Jax winked at Cat, and then coughed politely. "Well . . . we want a little time alone."

"Got it," Russell said. "Well, you kids have fun."

Several other couples were driving out too. Cat and Jax smiled broadly at them. But as soon as their car cleared the main gate, their expressions went dead sober. A mile down the road, a battered green van pulled in behind them.

Jax's hands gripped the wheel hard. Whenever it was safe, he found himself looking over at Cat, who was staring straight ahead, all civility and cheer a vanished mask.

The Starlight Motel was a midrange beach cabana on the outskirts of town. Both rental car and Tyler's van were parked in the crowded lot.

Up in Room 29 Tyler set up a speaker phone. After an extensive and uncomfortable debriefing, they finally made their phone call.

I've never seen anything like what Tomo did," Cat said. "They aren't fakes. What I'm trying to say is . . . I just won't betray them."

"I'm certain that you saw a very clever trick," Sinclair's voice came back over the speakers.

"It wasn't a trick."

"I don't want to debate you, nor do I want you to do anything unethical. But I am still worried about my sister."

"You don't have to worry about the Twins," she said. "Golden Sun is scared to death of something, and its not Joy or Tomo."

"What, then?"

"Something outside," Cat said. "People. Something. They call it 'Iron Shadows.' "

"And you believe this?"

Tyler spoke up. "There is evidence that someone is trying to hurt their people. A few stories. Disappearances."

"Miss Juvell, I am surprised to find that you, of all people, would be vulnerable to bogeyman stories."

Jax's voice was cold, clipped, precise. "If she says she saw it, she did."

When Cat spoke next, it was with a certain cool detachment. "If you would like us to return your retainer, we will do so. I'm sorry."

"Miss Juvell, I am sorry if I gave the impression of mistrusting either your intentions or perceptions. I tell you what. I offered you fifty thousand dollars, plus expenses, for a face to face meeting with my sister. . . ."

Jax snorted. "This isn't about money. We're not trying to hold you up, Doctor."

"Nor did I think you were. Please listen to what I have to say. I will allow you to keep the advance money, as well as expenses, and pay you twenty-five thousand dollars if you will get her on the telephone for me. Simply give me your personal guarantee that she is not in the presence of other cultists."

Tyler whistled incredulously. "Twenty-five thousand? For a phone call?"

"Yes. A phone call. You have a cellular phone, of course."

Even Jax was taken aback. "Jesus," he said. "Cat?"

She sighed. "All right. Yes, of course we have a cell phone. We can try that. Dr. Sinclair—you'll stand by at this number? We may only get one chance."

"For the next twenty-four hours," he promised, and hung up.

Jax, Cat and Tyler studied each other. "Well," Tyler said. "We can guess that if she wanted to talk to her brother, she would have been in touch. So how do we do this?"

"I think maybe we should try the truth. These people don't need more problems. They've got all the problems they need."

"Iron Shadows?" Jax asked.

"Iron Shadows," she said.

thirty-nine

"I've got a question for you," Cat poked a plastic fork into her Chinese chicken salad. Jax had rounded up some takeout food—after two days of healthy cuisine, he swore he was suffering a serious grease deficiency.

Jax chewed at a rubbery French fry. "All right. I'll bite."

"What would happen if real miracle workers surfaced?"

Tyler's attention was immediately caught. "You mean, like Tomo?"

"I mean, someone who could blow the Amazing Randi away. Someone who had an agenda very different from that of organized religion?"

"It could smash the church."

"That am a distinct possibility," Jax said.

"If they taught a religion of personal ecstasy . . . it could be the most powerful event in human history."

Tyler leaned back in his chair. "There she goes."

"Where *are* you going with this?" Jax asked.

"Aren't there people who would feel threatened as hell by Joy and Tomo? Mightn't some of them want the Oshitas discredited . . . or even dead?"

"All right," Jax conceded. "What about Iron Shadows?"

"I don't know. Maybe a myth. Maybe another group. Maybe . . . something else," Cat said. "I am only certain that I know fear when I smell it. Tyler—call Freddy King, see if he's found anything linking Chris Zimmer to the earlier deaths. Or maybe the Portland case."

"Got it."

"Something's wrong . . . and if someone or something is threatening these people, they might need some help."

"Something?" Jax had seen her in this mood before, and knew that it was futile to interrupt her. He could disagree, and just walk away from the whole thing, but there was no changing her mind.

"I never believed in the supernatural before," she said thoughtfully. "A door just opened. I have no idea what might walk through it next."

Cat opened her overnight case, slipped out her Glock, checked its clip and action, and shoved it back into the case.

"But if these people need help, I say they're going to get all the help I can give."

Jax suddenly realized that tension had knotted his gut into a hard sour lump. With every passing second, the sensation grew more severe, almost painful. He was perceptive enough to recognize that it was no physical ailment. This was fear, pure and simple. In a low voice, he said, "Cat . . . I don't know that I can go back there."

"Why not?"

"Two things. First, the blood they took from Joy. What the hell do *you* think they do with it?"

She looked a little gray. "I think they put it in the food. But why?"

"Haven't you felt a little strange at times? Almost drugged?"

She nodded. "From the first day—but never strongly enough to be certain. Something in her blood. . . ."

And in Tomo's Nectar?
And what about those yummy Twin Cookies?
Jesus.

She lowered her head for a moment, and then snapped it back up. "All right. We bring our own groceries. Not another bite of food or sip of that 'Twin Punch.' But Jax. I don't think that they mean any harm. I think it's some way of creating a bond with their followers. If you know what I mean, there's a Christian precedent for it, at least metaphorically."

" 'Take, drink, this is my blood'?"

"Implies something about early Christianity, doesn't it?"

Tyler glanced at the ceiling. "Oh, man . . . and me without my lightning rod. Don't even go there, okay? So you stock up on Cheetos and Calistoga. Any other reason you don't go back, Jax?"

"Tomorrow . . . they want us to swap partners."

Tyler whistled. Cat looked blank.

"And?"

"Is that all you have to say? Is that all it meant to you?" He took her by the shoulders. "Read my lips. *I don't know if I can do this.*"

Cat's expression never changed. "You're either with me, or you're not. Either way, I'm going back."

Tyler cleared his throat. "Is this about the job? Is it even about Iron Shadows? You're getting pulled in, Cat. You're in love with the Twins."

"I told you what I saw, Tyler."

"I know what you saw. What we don't know is what it means."

"Not now Tyler. Jax," she said. "Are you coming back or not?"

Jax sat, staring at his hands. When he looked up, his eyes were haunted. After a moment, Cat sat next to him. "What is it?"

"Nothing," he muttered.

"Jax . . ."

He looked positively miserable. Jax turned and said to Tyler: "Could you . . . ?"

Tyler nodded, and wheeled himself to the door. He looked back a final time, and then left.

Jax waited almost a full minute after the door was closed, then sighed massively.

"So, Jax—what is it?"

"The whole time we were . . . married . . . all I ever wanted was to touch you. And I never could."

She barely breathed. "Jax. There are things I've never told you."

"I've guessed some of them," he said. "But let me finish. I may only be able to say this once." His eyes those of a large, wounded animal. "You and Tyler the only things I've ever loved. You tried to love me, and I just couldn't reach you. Now, by some miracle, we found each other."

She leaned her head against his shoulder. "That we did, Jax."

"Logic is logic," he said. "But maybe something inside every man wants to believe that those sounds, that heat—is only for him. Silly, I know. Maybe I don't want you to find out that it's not me, you know? That you could find . . . yourself with someone else. Silly, I know."

"Jax," Cat said. "Its just sex. Love is . . . something else." She reached up and kissed the corner of his mouth. "There's something going on here that's bigger than we are."

"Two people's problems don't amount to a hill of beans in this crazy world . . . ?" He managed a ghost of his old smile. "Sure." She sighed in relief and leaned her head against Jax's shoulder. "You're Ilsa, I'm Rick, and Serenity Camp is Casablanca. We'll get through this. I promise. And then we'll see." He kissed her squarely. "This *could* be the beginning of a beautiful relationship."

forty

Thursday, June 22

Jax stood outside Harmony House, dressed in a cowboy vest with no shirt, denims, and a pair of boots that added two unnecessary inches to his height. He clutched a white rose in his right hand. He felt as if someone had ladled boiling acid into his guts. He was going to puke at any moment. But please. Not *this* moment. Another moment, somewhere down the line. Maybe tomorrow. Just let him get through this, and he'd be fine.

Caitlin opened the door.

She wore a sheer negligee, and he had to admit that the view was terrific. He could see no trace of damage to the wounded leg. Everything looked just fine, although he confessed an urge to make a closer inspection.

In the interest of science. In fact, in spite of his best efforts to hold onto his moral outrage, blood seemed to be flowing out of his superego and into his id with alarming speed.

He stared down at the rose, not quite remembering where it came from. Perhaps it had grown out of his palm.

"I . . . brought you a gift," he said.

She reached down. Her fingertips walked Jax's zipper. "So I see," she grinned. Then pulled him into the room, and closed the door.

Cat fought to keep her mind centered, keep her breathing under control, to use the tools she had been given over the last few days. She caught sight of herself in a mirror. Something had happened to her. She was all frills and lace, stuff that she had bought at Victoria's Secret a week ago, laughing at it, considering it simply part of her disguise.

And now, looking at herself, she *liked* what she saw, liked the softness in a way that she hadn't in a long time. Maybe ever.

The lipstick was expertly applied, but this time she had done it for her own pleasure, not for the effect it might have on someone else. She liked the woman she saw in the mirror. That woman was in charge of herself, and confident enough to own herself, strong enough to protect herself. She didn't need emotional androgyny or a cocoon of fat to keep her safe.

Cat simply *adored* what she saw, and the woman in the mirror returned the adoration gladly.

There was a knock at the door. She breathed deeply, tightened her tummy a bit, and answered.

Simon wore some kind of pale gold cotton shirt which gave volume to his shoulders and chest. His right hand held a red rose. His left was behind his back.

"Simon . . ." she blinked, hard. "I . . . this is a surprise. Why . . . *you* . . . ?"

He brought his left hand from behind his back. It held a small thermos capped with two plastic cups. "Brought us something?"

"I don't need a drink," she said.

He laughed, brushing past her into the room. "No, no alcohol." He paused, and gave his best Lugosi imitation. "I don't drink . . . wine." And he laughed again. He unscrewed the cap, and poured.

"Here," he said. "Twin Punch. All of the ingredients are hand-picked in India, flown here special. They came in this afternoon—you must have heard the helicopter. Brought some new base. It's much better than the frozen. I thought you might like some."

Now that she thought of it, the memory of the drink and its heady spice, that exotic taste which wound through all their meals, nauseated her. She managed to keep her smile, and accepted the cup from him. "Let me take out my contacts," she said, and brushed her lips against his cheek. Then she went into the bathroom, taking the cup with her. She ran the water in the basin as she poured the red fluid down the sink.

She reappeared a minute later, smiling, and holding an empty cup. "So who decided that you and I should play?"

"It was Tomo's suggestion," he said, draining and then depositing his cup on the night stand. "The Twins made the matches. Based on what we told them—and the way they read the energy."

He crossed the room and took her hands in his.

She didn't know what she expected, but the depth of kindness and acceptance in his eyes surprised her. They reminded her of something. Of someone . . .

Of Tomo, the moment their eyes had locked back in Long Beach.

"Don't be afraid, Cat."

"I'm not afraid." But as she said that, the sour feeling she had always associated with fear began to build in the pit of her stomach. It dissolved, blending into that slight intoxicated sensation she had experienced all week. Odd. Why? She hadn't had any of the punch. . . .

"Don't be afraid of the truth."

Very gently, he gathered her into his arms, and they melted into a hug. "Feel my breathing," Simon said. In the embrace, she felt his abdomen flutter against hers, almost like a bird's wings. She marveled at the delicacy of the touch. "Follow my belly with yours. Be with me."

She followed the tidal roll of his inhalations and exhalations, and felt her body open to him, with no preamble or hesitation. The world was melting. She had experienced this sensation before, earlier in the workshop, but she fell into it more readily now. It was the sensation of losing her individual identity, or becoming somehow the *essence* of a woman rather than an individual. That she was bonding to the *essence* of a man, not the specific incarnation named Simon. And from that perspective it mattered not at all that she barely knew him, because those two essences knew each other, had always known each other, and felt only ecstasy at the opportunity to blend once again.

She hardly even realized when he began to untie the bow on her negligee.

The universe was molten. She was back into that place, beyond herself, within herself. She wound her fingers into his hair as his mouth caressed her, and felt all vestigial doubts dissolve. She stood above him and he knelt on the floor, his fingers toying with her, his mouth exploring. From the corner of her eye she caught a mirrored image of herself, of them, together, and wondered who this god and goddess might be.

At some point he rose, and kissed her. She tasted herself on his lips and tongue. With strength she would not have credited his slender body, Simon lifted her into his arms, and held her for a few seconds. She closed her eyes, and felt herself a child. She linked her arms around his neck as he lowered her gently onto the bed behind them.

At first he just looked at her, his face above hers, his eyes wondering and joyful, then rolled himself against her, one slow inch at a time, their bodies joining so gradually that finally she impulsively pulled him closer. They twined there, their bodies making shadowplay on the wall behind them. Their heats and textures and hearts merged. They did everything and found everything and reveled in every sensation together. Cat forgot who and what she was, lost all sense of her history or future, and for an exquisitely long moment there was only the Now, forever and ever.

And it filled her.

forty-one

Cat giggled, her head snuggled into Simon's chest. She bit at him, growling, savoring the light salty dew of perspiration.

"God," she said. "I haven't done anything like this in years."

"Like what?"

"Well, you know. I hardly know you."

"That's the whole point," he whispered. His fingers twined in her hair. "That separates sex from the context of relationship. Let's you see it for what it really is."

She grinned a little, privately, and snuggled back against him.

"You have something," he said. "A strength. A shining I've only seen in a few people. You could teach this."

She felt a very quiet space open inside her. "You don't know who I am," she said. Then added "What I am."

And from very far away she heard him say: "Cat . . . ?"

But she wasn't with him. She was inside herself. In the attic. In the world of the dreams that coiled and fought within her like serpents.

She held the diamond-crusted chest in her hands. Behind her, she heard the force, heard him slamming at the door, heard the lock splinter, and watched her shaking hands open the chest, and saw the tiny golden heart within.

The trap door opened, and something monstrous came in. It wasn't human. It couldn't have been, even if, for just a few instants, it masqueraded as human. It couldn't. It's hands were too large, and its smile too broad and vicious.

"I love you," it said.

The fear inside her exploded, rose up like a tide. She fumbled with the box, with the precious box, and when it opened, she saw the glowing heart, and knew what the monster wanted, and knew that she could never let him have it.

Its bulk was almost through the trap now, and into the attic, and she cast around desperately for a place to hide the precious chest, and finally did the only thing that she could.

She swallowed it.

Then the vast, rubbery bulk of the creature was through the door and into the attic, and her world was—

It doesn't matter," Simon was saying.

With shocking suddenness she saw herself, naked, gripped in the arms of a stranger, and she froze. What was she *doing* here? What in God's name had she done?

"You should talk with the Twins—" he was saying, and then felt the change in her. "What is it?" he asked.

She sat up, and pushed his hands away. "I have to go," she said. "I have to go *now*. Where's Jax?"

She got up, looked down on this stranger with whom she had just shared intimacy, and shivered. Something was happening inside her. Her heart was sliding apart and re-forming. The sensation was ghastly. Some essential shift in her nature, some ineffable damage to the intrinsic structure of her personality had been done over the last few days. The entire house of cards was tumbling. And although she understood that it would re-form into something new, she wasn't, couldn't be certain what that newness might be. And feared it.

She knew who Cat Juvell was, and even if she didn't always like that woman, at least she understood her. This new person . . . who the hell would *she* be?

A fear as deep and consuming as death overwhelmed her. What was she *doing* here? God.

Cat threw on her robe. Her hands shook so badly that she could barely knot the belt.

"You should talk with the Twins," Simon repeated.

"I can't," she said. "I just can't." She was gripped now, utterly panicked. "Leave me alone. I can't—let me out of here!"

Then she was out of the door and running, paying no attention to Simon's cry behind her: "Cat—please!!"

The grass beneath her feet was slick with dew. Cat slipped, almost fell, caught herself.

She ran across the camp to Harmony House, and threw the door open.

In its shadowed interior, Jax and Caitlin lay intertwined and still. Peripherally, she perceived Caitlin, but didn't exactly *see* her. The woman existed in some kind of visual limbo, beyond the focus of Cat's attention.

"Jax," Cat said.

He sat up quickly, pulling the blanket with him, exposing Caitlin's breasts and thighs. They were mere meat, and made no impression on Cat at all.

"I'm getting the hell out of here."

Simon appeared in the door behind her. "Cat—calm down."

"Don't try to stop me," she warned.

"Wait just a minute," Simon said. "Let's chill out. Can't you talk to us?"

"No," Cat said, shaking. "I just need to leave."

Simon slammed his hand into the wall. "Caitlin. Go find Kolla."

Even through the panic, Cat heard that name. "Who . . . ?" she managed to whisper.

"Kolla," Simon said. "She's really good. She counsels for us. You're having a little schiz break," he said.

She's a psych student.

There were too many different voices in her head, and she couldn't fight them all . . . but perhaps she could decide which one to listen to.

"Cat . . . ?" Jax was saying. His voice was urgent. His eyes burned, held hers.

She had to hold on. This was the moment they had worked for, fought for. She just needed to hold on for another few minutes, and they were home free. She could do that. For Kolla. For Tyler and Jax. For herself, dammit.

Cat felt like a trapped animal, but she was managing to keep going, something of which she was enormously proud. "Kolla? All right. I'll talk to her. Alone. Just me. And Jax, and Kolla."

Caitlin threw on a robe and ran out. Jax wrapped his arms around Cat, holding her tight. She shuddered uncontrollably.

The job. Remember the job.

Jax breathed softly in her ear. "Let's go back to our cabin, Babe."

Cat dressed slowly, trying to regain her composure. She slipped on slacks and shirt, breathed into her fingers to calm them. She looked at herself in the mirror. The woman on the far side of the glass was beautiful, but haunted.

Jax had doffed his vest and now wore a black ribbed-knit pullover with his jeans and boots. "What happened?"

"I don't know," she said. "Something opened in my head, and pain crawled out." She looked up at Jax. "Am I sane?"

"What?"

"You know me better than anyone except Tyler. You tried so hard to love me, and I never did anything but push you away. I've tried so hard for so long to bury all of my feelings. What kind of idiot lives that kind of life and then comes to a place like *this?*"

He smiled at her kindly. "Maybe an idiot who knows it's time to change, and sees a way to do it." He leaned forward and kissed her.

She wrinkled her nose at him. "You looked like you were doing fine with Caitlin."

"Closed my eyes and thought of England. How do we handle this? Are you sure you're all right?"

"I'll handle it."

The door opened and Kolla Sinclair entered. Her straight dark hair was pulled back with a rubber band, and she wore a cotton dress belted with a golden braid. She wore sandals, and her strong toes were cut squarely, nails painted a pale pink. She smiled at them very professionally. It was an open, happy expression, one which projected a warmth missing from her brother's pictures. "Hi," she said. "I'm Kolla. I heard you were thinking of leaving. Do you want to talk about it?"

"I need your help," Cat said.

"Anything. It's easy to get spun out in this work. I'm here to help you get it back together."

Jax came closer. "Could we have five minutes of your time?"

Kolla's enthused expression became one of confusion as Jax handed her the compact flatness of their cellular phone. She stared at it as if it was a snake. "What is this?"

"We'd like you to talk to someone," Jax said. "Someone who cares about you."

Understanding dawned on Kolla's face. "My brother put you up to this, didn't he?" She jerked the phone from his hand. Her face was pure contempt. "Maxwell. Are you there? This is a new low, even for you." She listened, teeth gritted. "Jesus. I can't believe you. Why don't you just leave me to hell alone?" Then she slammed the phone back into Jax's hand.

"He's your brother. He just wants to be sure you're all right."

Kolla snorted. "Max has never given a shit about anything but himself. And who the hell are you?"

"He hasn't seen you in a year, Kolla—" Jax said.

Kolla's contemptuous expression cut him off. "What bullshit is that? He saw me last month at Mom's birthday party."

Jax's mouth opened, and he squinted hard.

Cat's mind raced. "Last . . . month?"

"Of course," Kolla snarled. "What did that bastard tell you?"

Reality and realization crashed in on Cat like an avalanche, but before she could answer the lights went out, in the cabin, and all across Serenity Camp.

forty-two

Blinded by the sudden darkness Cat said two words: "Bird dogs."

Kolla's voice, so strong and certain before, was shaken. "What's going on?"

Jax moved fast, getting his automatic out of his suitcase. Cat was even faster, had her Glock out of her purse before he snapped the case shut. Twin clicks as they pumped rounds into their breeches. A floorboard creaked as Jax started to turn, but before he could finish the motion, the front door flew open.

Sudden light blinded them: some kind of high-powered hand lamp. The burst of illumination was agonizing. In the instant before it struck, Cat had distinguished the shape of an automatic pistol, and knew that its barrel was trained on Kolla. These men were ready. They undoubtedly had backup. They knew the game being played, and she did not. She could only wait, and hope.

The first man through the door said: "Carpenter. Drop the gun, or Miss Sinclair is dead."

Jax's voice was sulfurous. "Shit, shit, *shit.*"

"Jax," Cat said. "Do it."

Jax dropped his clip, and put the pistol on the floor. Cat followed suit without being asked.

"All right," she said. "Now what?"

Hands cuffed behind them, and under control of two guns, Cat and Jax were moved out of the cabin and down the road. Kolla was held very professionally, her mouth covered with silver duct tape, "because she may not understand the seriousness of the situation," the taller man said bluntly. The second man wasn't a man at all—she was a woman, a hard looking redhead with close-cropped hair and a bodybuilder physique.

Their captors moved very easily along the tree line, avoiding the occasional flashlight beams as workshop participants ran blindly outside their cabins, puzzled by the lack of light.

At no time did Cat see a good opportunity for a break. Any attempt at escape would surely have placed Kolla Sinclair in deadly jeopardy. The only thing either of them could do was just wait and see.

They stumbled down the incline to the foot of the road, where a Chevy minivan awaited them, its engine purring. A second man was behind the wheel, eyes shifting from the windshield to the rear view mirror, contemplating their escape route.

First Cat, then Jax and Kolla were shoved unceremoniously into the van. Her hands bound behind her, Cat could do little to control her fall, and grunted as her shoulder slammed against the inside wall.

The engine's growl increased, and they began to back out of the driveway, gravel crunching beneath its wheels.

"The cell phone, right? You triangulated us off the cell phone." Cat asked, her voice tight with self-loathing. "Jesus, I've been stupid."

Their guard didn't look at them. Cat rubbed her fingers along the handcuffs. They seemed strictly regulation, but without a lock pick or a key, that information was useless.

"Iron Shadows. Damn. All the time you've been out there, watching. Right?"

The redhead looked at her as if she were a fecal specimen, thick fleshy lips pulled into an inexpressive line. "Just shut up," she said.

Cat did a quick kinesthetic scan, and missed the weight of her necklace. Another blow. However small an edge it might have been, it was something. She looked at Jax regretfully. "Privacy is a bitch," she said.

"Some of us don't care about it as much," he said noncommittally. She followed his eyes. Under his shirt collar, she saw the string of carved *faux* ivory, and breathed a sigh of relief. So he had broadcast his activities with Caitlin to Tyler. Sleazy, Jax.

But sometimes, thank God for the sleaze factor.

"Maybe it'll all work out," she said.

The redhead chuckled. It was a nasty sound.

They drove for almost an hour, but the darkness of the roads, and the number of switchbacks made it almost impossible to determine exactly how far they traveled.

Jax watched the road as they cruised, and once, as they turned left onto a dark street, she heard him say: "Miller."

Finally, they pulled through a gate and up a road. Through the front window, Cat glimpsed a cluster of shacks and abandoned buildings, and ahead of them, a mountainside.

The woods around them were dense with redwoods, scrub oak, and what looked like giant manzanitas. Worn conical cement towers sat cracked and disused at the outskirts of the camp, and Cat's wary mind registered: *lime kilns.* They were near a mine, no doubt abandoned. Damn good place to hide a body or three. This was looking better all the time.

The minivan stopped in front of a low wooden barracks. Their captors pushed them out onto the road. Cat yelped: "Hey! you can be polite." Jax lost his balance and fell to one knee in the dirt. He glared up at their captors, and lurched back up onto his feet again.

Jackson Carpenter losing his balance? Yeah, right. She hid her grim and humorless smile. It never hurt to have your enemies underestimate you.

Kolla was pushed ahead of them, and through the open door of the barracks. Cat and Jax followed.

Cat paused in the doorway, resisting the redhead's impatient shove. She needed a moment to allow shock, and rage and sick self-loathing to cool into something more manageable—that particular emotional combination was pregnant with suicidal possibilities.

Waiting for them in that barracks were Doctor Maxwell Sinclair and Milton Quest. "Well," Cat said. "Milton. Dr. Sinclair. This is a revelation."

Quest made a motion which was very nearly a bow. "Miss Juvell. Considering the circumstances, a decided pleasure."

She turned her attention to her former client. "Why, Sinclair?"

Dr. Sinclair met her gaze with sour disapproval. "I think, on some level, I always knew that you would prove unsatisfactory."

"You used us."

Kolla made a furious sound behind her gag, and the redhead wrenched her arm into tighter control. Kolla's eyes were incandescently furious.

"You sent us in to find her. How did you know she would come to that camp?"

Jax spit out the words. "He didn't. He must have hired other teams around the country, going to other workshops. Maybe putting the screws to some Golden Sun folks. Jesus, no wonder they believe in Iron Shadows. As soon as he got a nibble, he concentrated his efforts."

"What was it all about?" Cat said. Their odds went from bad to worse as a huge man, bigger and bulkier than Jax, entered the room. Milton Quest's bodyguard, the Mighty McGee. He looked at Jax the way a hungry dog might study a pork chop. She knew what had happened between them in Los Angeles, and that McGee would be burning for a chance to regain his honor. Jollier and Jollier.

"Tara," Quest said. "I think you can remove the gag now."

Tara was the redhead. She ripped the duct tape from Kolla's mouth, taking a chunk of lip with it. Blood trickled from the torn corner.

"You bastard!" Kolla hissed. "How dare you! You don't know what the fuck you're messing with."

Quest's smile was simply bursting with curiosity. "And what exactly is that?"

"Wouldn't you like to know?"

"Ooh. Well. I'm certainly frightened now."

She sneered at him. "But I *can* tell you that you will be so sorry. So very fucking sorry."

There was something in Kolla's words, her carriage, which had attracted Milton Quest's attention. *She's not scared, and he wants to know why.* "So," Cat said quickly. "What now, Doctor? Are you going to kill your own sister? Get your hands on her money?"

"Miss Juvell, if I were you, I would be more worried about my own neck, and let the siblings work things out for themselves."

"Why kill her?" Jax said thoughtfully. "Mental incompetence might do as well."

Sinclair looked at Jax with newfound respect. "Please, continue."

"You're a psychiatrist. Drugs . . . maybe a little electroshock to scramble her head."

Cat snorted. "You've established a nationwide search pattern for the poor child. And found her at some freaky sex orgy, stoned and almost brain-dead. You'll be named conservator."

"Sadly for you, Mr. Quest has assured me that securing your cooperation in such a venture is quite improbable."

Jax nodded at Quest. "Thanks, Milty. I owe you."

Quest grinned. "Pleasure was mine. I warned you there would be another time."

"Did you have something special in mind?"

"Oh, heavens yes," Quest said. "Nothing but the very best for my old friends."

Kolla Sinclair's eyes widened, and she was suddenly defocused, lost in a distant land. "Tomo?" she said.

Dr. Sinclair shook his head pityingly. "As you can see, Miss Juvell . . . the truth needn't be stretched very far."

Cat watched Kolla carefully, wondering.

forty-three

Tyler drove slowly, carefully, struggling to get his bearings in the dark. For the first half hour he had followed the kidnappers' van at a safe distance, staying just out of sight. But with all the twists and turns, the little logging and mining roads and back trails splitting off from the main road . . . he had lost his visual contact, and now was trying to get a directional fix on Jax's necklace.

If they stayed in one place, he could cruise around and eventually find them, but judging by the tenor of the conversation, Cat and Jax just didn't have a lot more time.

"Miller" he heard Jax say, and a knot of tension in his chest relaxed. He looked at his map. *Miller? Miller Road.* There it was. A tiny blue line, heading up deeper into mining country. He had missed the turnoff completely.

Tyler turned his van around and started his search over again.

forty-four

Kolla Sinclair swallowed. Her eyes stared sightlessly. Again she said: "Tomo?"

She cocked her head sideways, as if listening. It was eerie, and McGee was the first one to admit discomfort. "What the hell is this about?"

"Some kind of act," Quest muttered. He sounded as if he were trying to convince himself. Kolla was acting like an automaton, scanning the room. Her unblinking eyes fixed upon an ancient wall map, labeled: *World Limeworks.* She studied it.

And she said a single syllable, as if it were the final word in some internal conversation. "—thoughts." she said.

"What was that?" Sinclair said. "Did you say something?"

Kolla blinked twice, hard, and then turned to face her brother. She smiled coldly. "You'll find out."

forty-five

Cat watched Kolla closely as she pulled against her bonds, fidgeting in her chair. The girl's coordination appeared to be deteriorating rapidly. She rubbed her hands across her forehead twice, seemed to forget that she had just done it, and repeated the motion with trembling hands. She reminded Cat of Chris Zimmer, just prior to chewing a handful of glass.

The behavior had first begun about midnight, approximately two hours after the abduction. As the night wore on, the effect became more and more apparent, until by three in the morning, a single word raced through Cat's mind again and again:

Junkie.

"Please, Max," Kolla pleaded. "Please let me go back. It's not too late."

He shook his head. Quest had carefully supervised their shackling, then taken his client away for some kind of parlay. They returned to the barracks after an hour's absence. Cat would have paid good money to know the precise content of their conversation. Probably haggling over the price of their deaths. That sounded about right for Quest. In their absence, McGee had rested his enormous bulk on the edge of a table, just two feet away from Jax, watching him with carefully feigned disinterest.

She knew that only one thing protected them from his fury—Quest's insistence on professionalism. Petty revenge would simply not be tolerated. For a man like Quest, it was all business.

"I don't think so, Kolla," Sinclair said. "Sweet sister. All of this has been a nightmare," he said gently. "I promise you won't remember anything from the past year. Allll . . . gone away.

"You don't understand," she answered.

Almost solicitously, Milton Quest unchained Kolla, assisted her to her feet, and helped her to the door. Her hands were still taped in front of her, but at least, Cat thought philosophically, she could scratch her own nose. Cat's hands were still cuffed behind her. *It's the little things you miss.*

"This is where Miss Sinclair leaves you. Say good-bye to Miss Juvell, Miss Sinclair."

Kolla locked eyes with Cat. "You're a good woman. You had no idea who my brother really was. Don't worry. Everything will be all right."

Cat felt oddly comforted by the words.

Tara jerked Cat to her feet with a single surge of her weight-pumped biceps. Cat deliberately sagged against her to test the redhead's strength. She was pleased to note that, while strong enough, Tara's balance was fairly dreadful. *That* was useful information. Then Tara turned Cat over to another of Quest's troops, and took Kolla's arm.

"Take her to the van," Quest said. "I'll join you in ten minutes." Tara nodded and jerked Kolla's arm, escorting her from the room.

The sliver of moon was low in the sky, casting a silvery pale light over the entire camp. A pair of condemned prisoners, Cat and Jax were escorted by Sinclair, Quest, McGee and a mountain-sized Samoan named Moses toward a gated twelve-foot hole in the mountainside.

Quest unlocked the gate and flipped a switch. A line of naked bulbs glowed to life along the tunnel, providing fifty feet of gloomy illumination.

Moses politely helped Jax avoid an overhead beam in the tunnel's mouth. On the far side of the fence was a heavier steel gate. The center section of it had been lifted out long ago, leaving a space wide enough for large ore trucks to move through. A rusted iron track ran down the middle, now long overgrown.

"Lots of old lime mines up here," Quest said merrily. "Deep. I figure there's a good chance they'll never find you at all."

—N*ever find you at all.*"

Tyler was at the bottom of the hill. Judging by the conversation, the narrow winding driveway led up to an old lime mine. Well. He had found them. What the hell to do now? He didn't know where the nearest constabulary was. Worse, he no longer knew exactly where he was—he'd completely lost track of roads and road signs, following the signal exclusively.

By the time he went and returned, or could coach a carload of cops through the labyrinth of back roads, it would all be over.

Shit.

There was no way to sneak up that road. Not with his legs the way they were.

He hated himself at that moment. Hated himself, but never stopped thinking.

Quest prodded Cat ahead of him, still rather theatrically solicitous. "Cat. I really am sorry about this. I hope you can see it's nothing personal."

"Of course. Neither was the kick in the balls."

"Exactly," he agreed warmly. "We're all strictly professional. Watch the pothole, please. Such nice ankles. We wouldn't want to twist them. By the way—your brother, the gimp? I notice you haven't threatened us with his heroic intervention. That's wise."

"Wise?" Jax asked.

"If he doesn't know what happened . . . if he never knows, we may not have to kill him. I'm not an unreasonable man."

"No," Cat agreed. "You're quite reasonable, if the price is right." She tested her handcuffs again. Tight, and firmly secured behind her back. Given fifteen seconds, she could get her hands to the front. But Quest wasn't going to give them fifteen seconds, was he? Their footsteps echoed down the artificial tunnel. It finally widened out about fifty feet further down, until they were in the domed vastness of a limestone cave. Rings of rectangular electric lights cast odd, clownlike shadows on the walls. Most of the stalagmites had long been broken or crushed, but some of the stalactites spears still jutted from the ceiling like the filed teeth of cannibals. She knew little about such caves except that over millennia, rain and ground water had dissolved the carbonate rock which forms limestone and dolomite. She knew that the results were often spectacular: chimneys and gours and deep potholes, arena-like galleries, hidden streams and chambers so vast that the strongest flash beams ultimately illumined only darkness.

The walls of this cave had been crushed and eaten away by mining equipment. In fact, she suspected that this cave had only been discovered after extensive labor. She wondered how it might have appeared to the first human eyes: ceilings and floor clustered with calcium daggers, perhaps hordes of bats fluttering in panic at the intrusion. She wondered if those miners had grasped its beauty, appreciated its grandeur before they began to destroy it.

She wondered if this would be the last thing she ever saw.

In the middle of the chamber yawned a deeper bit of shadow: a pit of some kind. Perhaps a bubble formed in the original casting of this mountain, or a fissure eroded by water, or the product of human engineering . . . it made little difference. Once upon a time, for safety or perhaps esthetics, it had been boarded up. Now it yawned nakedly. Cat intuited that it was also unpleasantly deep.

Cat stepped a little away from Quest and looked down the pothole. The edge of her foot dislodged a stone, rolling it over the lip. It fell forever into blackness. Quest halved the distance between them. She wanted to back up, but couldn't: She had run out of room. There was nowhere to go but down.

"So tell me, Cat," he said. "Will I have to kill your brother?"

Sinclair stood behind Quest. Quest's bodyguard, McGee, was between the two of them. Moses, the giant Samoan, watched Jax. Cat nodded her head at Sinclair. "I want *his* word."

"Mine?" Sinclair asked innocently.

"Yours," she said quietly, looking him directly in the eye. Her back was to the pit. Sinclair was less than a full step away. He could take a step forward, give one good shove, and she would be gone. "If I can convince you that Tyler doesn't know anything about you, or Quest, would you promise to leave him alone?"

Sinclair studied her face almost tenderly, and then he smiled. "No," he said. He put his hands on his hips jauntily, legs apart and balanced. Ready to push.

"That's what I thought," Cat said. She watched his eyes. Watched with her vision defocused, taking in the whole man. Waiting. Waiting. Where was it . . . ?

There.

Sinclair pushed. Hard.

Unfortunately for him, Cat wasn't there. With perfect timing and eye-baffling speed she crouched, dropped so quickly it was as if she disappeared. Her shoulder rammed him between the ankles, scraping and almost breaking her nose on the rock floor as she did. Sinclair pitched forward over her back, too surprised even to scream. As he did Cat pushed forward and up almost to full standing, gritting her teeth with the strain. Sinclair performed a somersault worthy of an acrobatic clown, and disappeared yowling into the pit.

He screamed for a long time, followed by a sound like a sack of wet meal thudding into a cement floor.

Cat stood, her face scraped, a little trickle of blood starting from her nose.

No one said a word. Quest looked a little pale, and something approximating respect shone in McGee's eyes.

She gulped breath. "Quest," she said. "It's over. Nobody on our side has died. Snatching the girl could be considered deprogramming or something. You didn't know what kind of slime her brother was. He pulled a gun. I killed him in self defense. Don't get in any deeper than you have to."

"Jesus, Cat" Quest said. "Where'd you learn a move like that?"

"Power Rangers," she said. "Watch it every day. What do you say, Milton? Deal?"

Quest mopped his forehead with a handkerchief, then folded it and deposited it carefully in a pants pocket. "Well. You know, I do owe you one. You told Sinclair about me, and he hired me to keep tabs on you. Whatever you told him about me, it worked."

"I could do your infomercial." She forced her mouth to smile.

"Unfortunately," he said, stepping back and raising his gun level with her chest, "there is entirely too much at stake."

"What's done that can't be undone, Milton?" she asked.

"You don't get it," he said. "I know the doctors Sinclair planned to use. I have Sinclair's statement concerning his sister's instability. There's over a hundred million dollars at stake. All I need is time to think. I'll get my hands on it."

"I have faith in you," Jax said flatly.

"Unfortunately," Quest said, "I can't say 'wait and see.' You won't be here." He raised his gun.

"Milton," Jax said. "Two favors?"

"Maybe," Quest said. "What?"

"First—the truth about Vasquez. You rigged that, didn't you?"

A slow smile spread across his face. "Let's just say I knew the camera was running. I got damn near two mill out of that, and I sleep just fine. Anything else?"

"Could I kiss Cat goodbye?"

Quest stared at him, and then at Cat, and his laugh echoed through the limestone cavern. "I'm a sucker for romance. Go ahead."

Cat stared at Jax. "I don't believe you," she said.

He shrugged, hands still tight behind his back. "The handcuffs?" He asked Quest.

"You want to kiss her or feel her up?"

"Is that a trick question?"

"Sorry. The cuffs stay on."

Cat looked up at Jax, and for the first time in memory found it difficult to meet his eyes. "I'm sorry Jax," she said. "I'm so sorry for everything. When I think what we could have had together . . ."

Jax gazed back, lips set into a deadly serious line. "Shh," he said. "What the hell. We'll always have Serenity House."

They kept the straight expressions for almost three seconds, and then they both laughed, and laughing, hands cuffed behind them, kissed.

That kiss was so sweet, so giving, all of her warmth and passion right there on her lips, at the tip of her tongue. Jax thought it was almost— *almost* worth dying for a kiss like that.

Quest thumbed back his hammer. "I guess that's it, kids."

CRUNCH.

A grinding crash behind them, amplified by the sudden wail of protesting steel. The strained whine of a laboring van engine echoed through the limestone cavern. Headlights weaved drunkenly through the tunnel toward them.

Cat and Jax broke the kiss and swiveled to see—

Tyler's van. It plowed raggedly through the gate, lost traction, then caught it again and roared down the tunnel, scraping sparks from the sides.

Everyone stared, gaping, and for just a moment, no eyes at all were on Jax.

McGee's head was turned, and Jax jumped, head-butting him in the temple, ramming the thickest part of his own skull into the thinnest part of McGee's. McGee grunted, stumbling back, and his pistol flew out of his hand. . . .

Skittered across the ground toward the pit—

Everything happened in slow motion. Like a football tackle using a body-block, Jax hurled himself at Moses back-first, driving with his legs, and the two men went down together. The Samoan's head snapped back against the cave wall.

Without an instant's hesitation, Cat threw herself at McGee's gun, wincing as her shoulders hit the ground. She hunched her body like an inchworm, gaining ground at the cost of skin until her hands were on it, and her fingers wrapped around the grip, fumbling—

Quest overcame his shock, and took a shot at the van, spiderwebbing the front window with cracks. Tyler ducked, kept going and a second shot blew another hole. Without his visual guidance, the van crashed into the tunnel wall, wheels spinning.

Quest turned back to Cat—

Who was on the ground. Wrenching her shoulder, hands cuffed, aiming across the small of her back she ignored the pain, thumbed back the trigger and fired at Quest.

Quest stumbled back, shocked more than scared. Cat fired again, missing again, but took McGee right in the chest.

Milton Quest panicked, running in a zig-zag pattern down the tunnel toward the van. He edged past the damaged vehicle, cursing. Outside the tunnel, his men were yelling in confusion. He glared once, back at the pit, his face twisted by rage and self-loathing. Twice, he had allowed this bitch to turn the tables on him. This was the last time, though. He had the men and the resources, and he had the girl Kolla. He would take his time killing Cat Juvell, Jackson Carpenter, and the Gimp, and then he would make himself very, very wealthy.

Limber as an eel, hampered only by her bruises, Cat worked the handcuffs from behind her to the front, and picked the gun up again.

Jax and Moses were down in a tangle. She didn't have time to worry about him: Jax was a big boy.

"Go on!" Jax grunted. "Get the son of a bitch!" Moses tried to struggle his way up. By the flashing lantern light Cat watched Jax ram his shoulder into his opponent's solar plexus and then whipsaw the Samoan with head butts, back and forth and back, until there was no more resistance. Jax stood, took a step back, and kicked the unconscious man in the temple as hard as he could with the tip of his right boot. Bone cracked.

Cat squeezed past the van, peeking in. Tyler gave her the O.K. signal with thumb and forefinger. She blew him a kiss, and then ran like hell down the tunnel after Quest. Maybe forty seconds since the first disturbance. She was probably only ten seconds behind him, too soon for him to organize any kind of trap. Still, the darkness at the head of the tunnel loomed ahead of her. How many men did Quest have?

She cared, and on another level, she didn't. Maybe she wouldn't even kill him. Dammit, he had motivated the very best kiss of her entire life, and she owed the bastard *something.*

Tyler poked his head up in the van. Wow. He knew that he would be starting something when he went into the mine, but he hadn't anticipated all of *this.* The decision to run the van down and into it had been relatively easy—pure blind instinct. The rest had followed pretty automatically.

And thank God he had arrived in time. Being shot at was a unique experience—he always wondered how it would feel, and now he knew. No fun. Nope—all noise, and a sensation that something has burned the air around you, and a sudden realization that Yep, life is like *seriously* finite. But now, as he backed the van down the tunnel, he was happy to have done it. There was nothing else at all to have done.

The rear-view mirror was out of alignment, and Tyler couldn't see well. He was stuck here—the van wasn't going anywhere without a tow truck. He cursed his driving, cursed his legs. He *had* to get out. There had to be something more that he could do to help.

Jax struggled to get his cuffed hands around to the front. He exhaled and sucked his gut in hard, then realized that he was doing it in the utterly asinine belief that that would somehow make his butt smaller. Nonetheless, he squeezed his hands down past his hips, and then paused, gulping air and exhaling again as he pushed them down past knees and calves, over ankles and heels, and finally free.

His wrists were chaffed and sore, but he was alive, and Cat was alive. Judging by the sound of the van's engine, even Tyler was alive, bless his little pointy head. Moses was unconscious or dying. Sinclair and the Mighty McGee were both dead, and his whole life was suddenly a whole lot simpler.

"Shit," Timothy McGee said. "Fuckin' Kevlar's terrific, isn't it?"

McGee rolled to a sitting position, shaking his head. He pulled his shirt open and examined his bulletproof vest's ribbed paneling. He grinned at Jax, and dusted himself off.

"Well," he said. "Your hands being cuffed and all, I guess this won't be the kind of fun I was hoping for—"

Without rising to his feet, McGee pivoted on his left knee, kicking Jax in the head with his right foot. It was so fast Jax didn't even catch the preliminary motion. Jax, caught rising from his knees, hands cuffed in front, barely had a chance to roll with it. The shock ripped through him, snapped his head back with concussive force and blinding pain. Stars and planetary fragments replaced vision.

He tasted blood.

"One good thing about this, old buddy." McGee bounced to his feet, and did a little Ali dance step. He hip-faked right, drawing an abortive block. Then he jumped left, kicking again. Absurd, aerial kicks. Sucker kicks. No one in his right mind would use techniques as flamboyant as these in real life. Techniques like these required too much balance and flexibility, left you too vulnerable for far too long. Only an idiot or someone brainwashed by kung fu movies would even think about it—

Unless they were fighting a dazed man with cuffed hands.

McGee laughed. "Shit. No fun fighting with your hands tied, is it?" He was giggling like a little boy now, really enjoying himself, reveling in the chance to use all of these ridiculous techniques in an actual combat situation. Jax couldn't catch his breath, couldn't get his wits back about him.

"Had some fun on that fire escape, didn't you?" A blur fast kick to the groin. Jax barely had time to turn just a little sideways before it dug in. He thought something in his thigh muscle tore.

A second kick dug into the ribs. He thought he felt one go—he hadn't seen the kick, and couldn't ride it. Oh, Christ, vision was swimming, his leg was hurt, and he couldn't get air.

One chance, he thought. This bastard is just so damned confident. One chance.

McGee grinned. "God, I've been looking forward to this. Ever since we got this assignment, I knew it would eventually come down to just you and me." A hard roundhouse kick to the outer thigh. Jax's leg almost buckled. "Just you—"

McGee spun, kicked on the other side, digging the reinforced steel toe cap in. Jax rode it just enough to keep from being crippled, but the pain was awful.

"—just you and me."

Jax grabbed at his own thigh, mewling with pain. Hunched over. Turned just a little sideways, leaving his solar plexus exposed.

And Timothy went for it, spinning, cocking his heel, stabbing the leg in for a paralyzing blow.

Jax cupped his wrists, grunting with the shock as he caught McGee's leg with the handcuff chain, six inches above the ankle. Even with perfect timing, the pain was awful. Hanging on for dear life. He trapped the leg between the cuffs and the circling fingers, spun, dropped to one knee and pulled as if performing a *seoinage* shoulder throw, using McGee's leg for leverage instead of his arm.

McGee's face blanked with shock. He had never seen a technique like that—and because he couldn't anticipate it, and didn't realize what was happening until the last second, there was no way to counter it. He spun, his knee slamming into Jax's back as he hurtled over the shoulder. McGee landed on rock with sufficient force to jar him momentarily senseless. As he hit, his combat-trained body did what he had trained it to do in thousands of practice sessions:

Slap and roll out. He executed the break fall perfectly, and then rolled . . .

. . . right over the edge of the pit. There was a single instant where he realized his mistake, when the cosmic absurdity of it hit him, where he understood that he shouldn't have indulged in all of the extravagant acrobatics. His mouth formed a word, as if he wanted to share a sudden perception, some profound insight into the nature of existence. Then he disappeared.

McGee screamed half the way down. A wet, spatulate echo wafted up from the darkness.

Jax limped to the edge of the pit, wiping his face with his cuffed hands. He spat blood, watched the droplets disappear into the pothole, heard them spatter against the sides.

An oddly incongruous emotion swelled inside him, and after a moment's reflection Jax realized that the feeling was one of profound gratitude to be alive. He looked up to the ceiling, arched higher than the greatest cathedral built by the hand of man, mighty with its ringed stalactites, and felt an almost religious sense of awe. "Lord," he said quietly, "You know, I'm usually pissed that you made so many stupid people. But in McGee's case . . ."

forty-six

Cat stalked through the shadows, chained hands holding McGee's automatic in her manacled hands. The mining barracks were unlit except for the low, dingy shack where she had waited while Sinclair and Quest negotiated her death. Quest wouldn't return there. The window's wavering light was a baited hook she refused to swallow.

A sound to her left caught her ear, and Cat immediately pictured Quest and a gagged Kolla. Instinct and experience demanded that she remain hidden.

She crouched between two shacks for a moment, waiting. Her heel rubbed down against something pliant. She reached back with one hand, and her fingers brushed against a coil of rope.

All right, she told herself. We use what we find. Moving as quietly as she could, she wrapped the rope once around an empty oil drum, and then set a few smaller cans on top of the drum. Then she played out the cord across a narrow lane between shacks, to another deeply shadowed spot, where she crouched and waited.

She waited, ears straining for any clue, any sign. When she finally heard, or thought she heard the very slightest twitch of sound, she tugged the rope.

The drum jerked, and the cans tumbled. A man-shaped shadow arose from a hiding place just twenty feet away, and darted in for the kill.

Cat took a bead and squeezed her trigger. There was a flash of sound and a roar of light. A limp chunky figure flopped back out of the shadows and slid to the ground. Tara, her head misshapen by the shot. Damn, it wasn't Quest.

Click. Behind her.

"Don't even think about it," Quest said. "Drop it." The gun fell from her fingers.

"Turn around," Quest said. His voice seethed with venom. "I want you to see it coming."

Cat turned. Quest had her dead in his sights. Two men behind him also had weapons trained on her. She felt nothing but a hatred to match his own, and the will to survive. Or, if survival were not an option, to take this bastard with her.

"No fucking around this time. First you, then Jax, then I find the gimp and do him *slow.*" He raised the gun.

Suddenly, with no intervening sound at all, a very bright light pulsed behind Cat. The color drained from Quest's face.

"Please." A soft male voice. "No more violence. Certainly there has been enough."

Cat turned, shielding her eyes. Tomo stood, framed by that light, which came from some source behind him. Whatever it was, it was like an arc lamp, or a magnesium flare, something almost beyond visual tolerance. Perhaps truck headlights.

Perhaps something else.

"Where is our sister, Dr. Sinclair?," Tomo asked. "Is it Dr. Sinclair? She is ours as well as yours. Why not let her choose her own path?"

Another sound, this one behind Quest, originating in a shadow. The whimpers of a terrified girl. Kolla. Now Cat saw her, struggling to rise to her feet. She tried to move past Quest and toward Tomo, but the security man stopped her.

"What did you addict her to, asshole?" Quest said. He had backed away from Cat, away from Tomo, and his pistol wavered between them.

Using all of his strength, Tyler crawled out of the side of his van, and then out between its wheels. He was shaky from glass cuts and impact trauma, but had made his way twenty feet outside the mine to the first shelter, a stack of old wooden flats.

From where he lay, he could see the light, see what was happening. The mountain air was calm and cool enough to carry every word.

"Nothing but love," Tomo was saying. "Love which this poor world so desperately needs. Let her go, Dr. Sinclair." Tomo looked smaller than he would have expected, but very calm, even faced by Quest's gun. Another of Quest's men had reached the center of the camp. He also shielded his eyes from the light, and aimed his gun at Tomo.

Cat started to move, and Quest slammed his gun into her head. She went down hard.

Quest only took his eyes away from Tomo for an instant.

"Stay the fuck away from me." His voice quavered, nearly cracked. To his men, Quest said: "If he moves, shoot him."

Quest pulled Kolla toward one of the cars parked near the mountainside. He pushed her ahead of him, got in, and tramped on the accelerator.

Tomo blocked the drive. Quest went straight at the small figure—

The light shifted as Joy stepped out from behind her brother.

The very air around her *burned.* She was a woman of fire, in a shimmering, incalescent envelope, as if her very rage could ignite the world.

Tomo held up his arms, palms out toward his transformed sister. "No!" he screamed. "Joy, no!!"

The coruscation expanded. It flowed around Tomo without hurting him, but where it touched the grass, plants shriveled. When it touched Quest's car the engine exploded, literally blew out the hood and puffed into the air on a pillar of smoke.

Struggling to her feet, Cat was thrown back violently against a shed. She weaved like a punch-drunk boxer, barely conscious, then what little strength remaining in her body vanished, and she collapsed.

Tyler stared, transfixed, numbed by the sight, his mind forced into some dark corner where it refused to function.

One of Quest's men raised his gun, fired at Joy—

Nothing happened. She wasn't looking at Quest's murderous employee. Her attention was on the car, but still, just *nothing happened.* The air glittered with sparks, as if the bullets were running into something, some impenetrable force emanating from her without conscious control.

Slowly, she turned to look at the gunman, her face twisted by a cold and hungry smile. The blazing sphere intensified until her outline was lost within the flame. It crackled, turned bluish and condensed back into the form of a woman. Tomo watched, horrified.

"Joy. No, stop this!!"

His sister shrieked, and the light fluxed through the colors of the rainbow. Then Tyler saw something which nearly shattered his mind. The very dirt at her feet began to swirl, and Joy was enshrouded by a dust storm, a tornado of whirling particles, expanding and contracting with a heartbeat pulse, obscuring the woman herself. When it expanded, something was forming in there, the dust knitting into fibers, dark protuberances laced with that flashing fire, ghostly and ethereal at first, but then solidifying into flaming tendrils snaking out from a point at the base of her belly, just above the hips.

The tentacles lashed out, twined around Quest's man and lifted him shrieking into the air.

Tyler caught a glimpse of the expression on Joy's face. It was pure, savage, almost sexual pleasure.

She spoke, her words reverberating across the camp. "You would dare to injure one of *mine?* Iron Shadows!" She screamed, and tore the man to pieces even as he screamed his death cry. A circlet of flaming blood sprayed in all directions.

Tyler watched Cat laying unconscious on the ground, and Joy turned to regard her. He felt the impact of her will, her power, like the blistering air from a blast furnace. He saw Joy's hatred open to swallow her and knew that his sister was dead.

"No!" Tomo screamed.

Joy's eyes blazed.

Suddenly, Tomo was between them. "Joy! No!! She is not evil. They were her enemies, as well."

Joy's head twisted to the side. Tyler wondered if she even recognized her brother, if she had any idea at all what he was saying to her. She made a low, miserable sound, keening with the need to kill.

"Joy," Tomo said urgently. "She tried to help Kolla. Do *not!*"

Joy spun away, turned her back on Cat, and the keening sound whipped up into a hurricane of frustration. The hunger in that sound was more terrifying than anything Tyler had seen so far.

Joy strode through the flames directly to the burning car. The fire had no effect on her at all.

Except—the yellow ball of light around her was flickering, darkening. As the flame ate at her, the protective sphere went orange, and then deepened toward red. Metal shrieked as Joy wrenched the car door off its hinges. Milton Quest, still alive at the wheel of the car, stared at her, gibbering.

She ignored him. Joy held her hand mutely out to Kolla. Kolla fell sobbing into Joy's arms. Kolla was twice her size, but Joy carried the girl out of the car as if she were a feather.

In the car behind her, Quest finally seemed to emerge from his trance. He stared at Joy, moving beyond his mortal terror to something closer to rage. He raised his gun.

Joy didn't even bother to look back, but when he fired at her, tiny sparks of fire appeared just behind her head.

Joy's lips pulled back from her teeth. She smiled like a shark.

The car exploded, a blast that looked like an odd combination of napalm and an electrical fire, sparks and fat, jellied sizzling blobs of *something* flying in all directions.

Milton Quest screamed, dying.

The very ground burned around Joy, but the fire parted for Tomo as he approached, and took Kolla from his sister's arms

"Joy," Tomo pleaded. "Stop this. Stop this now."

Joy pivoted. She seemed utterly consumed, intoxicated with her deadly gifts.

Three cars were parked by the mountainside, three cars, and then Tyler's van wedged in the mouth.

Without knowing how he knew, Tyler suddenly understood what was about to happen. He looked around desperately, and spotted a tubular section of concrete pipe twenty feet away, laying near a pile of broken slabs. Desperately, he crawled toward them, cursing his useless legs.

Joy *screamed.* . . .

As Tyler backed his legs into the pipe the first car, a blue Pontiac, exploded. Flame mushroomed out with a roar, and steel twisted into melting junk in the blink of an eye. Joy's shield went a little darker, and she trembled. She stared at the second car, and the fire lanced out of her. The car roared up, pirouetting into the air and then thundering down in what seemed like slow motion. From a showroom special to a pile of flaming junk in a shattering second—

Then she turned her face to the mouth of the tunnel—

Tyler saw, just for an instant, Jax's face pressed up against the bars, low to the ground, beneath his wrecked van, trapped in the tunnel, staring out at them—

Then the face was gone—

And the van exploded, a fireball rolling out of the mouth of the tunnel. Tyler screamed, crossing his arms to cover his face as the mining camp blazed white, and then red, and then went black.

forty-seven

Jax Carpenter limped down the tunnel toward the light. Something glowed out there in the darkness near the cabins. He couldn't quite make it out, but something about it terrified him. He hurt from the blows he had taken, and was worried that McGee's pounding might have torn a thigh ligament, but he kept going.

Tyler's van was jammed, skewed in the tunnel mouth. Jax was going to have to figure out a way around it. Yes—he could crawl under it, if necessary—

He peered out through the grill to the left of the van, and his eyes widened.

It was Joy, blazing like a gasoline-soaked mannequin. Impossible. Alive. More than alive—she capered like a drunken mime. Someone took a shot at her, and then a man was lifted into the air by—

God, his mind wanted to freeze-frame. Quest's man hung there, as if thrown up into a spider web and suspended in impossible defiance of gravity. Impossible. But there it was, right in front of Jax. Then steam and flame exploded out of him and he just *burst.*

Jax was transfixed, unable to move. Tomo argued with Joy. Something happened at a car, and another shot rang out in the night. Joy had the girl, Kolla, and then the car exploded. Blew up, and Jax could hear a man's scream. Quest. God, that was Quest, and he just kept screaming after logic said that the man should be *dead.*

Tomo took Kolla from Joy, and Joy surveyed the camp, and found the cars, and the first one detonated. Jax flinched as the wall of heat struck him. And then another exploded, and then—

Jax came to his senses, realized where he was and what was about to happen, and wiggled back out from under the van, rolled to his feet and fled back down the tunnel. He ignored the pain in his leg, ignored the fire in his lungs, forgot everything but the fact that he had only a few seconds before—

Jax saw light, and felt something hot and hard literally lift him like a leaf in a whirlwind, and the last thing he remembered thinking was *Cat—!*

Behind him, God whispered "death," and ended the world.

forty-eight

Jax awoke in a grave. There was nothing to feed his eyes, no slightest mote of light. His body felt like a bag of shattered bones, and his left arm pulsed fearsomely at shoulder and elbow. Maybe not broken, but they still hurt like hell.

He hitched himself to his knees, still unable to see, but cautious. Somewhere nearby was an enormous open pit. It wouldn't do to survive an explosion, then take a lethal tumble into the arms of dead McGee.

He took a few moments to orient himself. An ocean of boiling blood lent the darkness its only color. He coughed out a lungful of dust, then sobbed a deep breath. Coughed again. The air was still and cold.

Cave-in.

He felt like an open wound. For several minutes Jax hunched on the ground, shuddering, trying to sort out his impressions, and finally decided that the agony meant that he was, indeed, alive.

His head spun. He levered himself to his feet, stumbled a few steps, and collapsed against a wall, banging his head.

The walls closing in on him weren't the worst part. If they'd been the worst, he could have handled that. The worst was the sudden explosion of memories, sounds, smells. . . .

The smell of human blood, torn flesh, thousands of pounds of ordinance, fire, burnt metal and an acrid, fecal stench. He knew that the smells, were memories, and that the same deep source was also birthing sounds. Agonized shrieks. The explosive rattle of gunfire.

Hot Dog. Mister Q. Caltiki. Gook's Bane. All dead.

Because they'd trusted the Wizard.

He didn't know how long he lay there, frozen, curled in the darkness, afraid to move, afraid of everything. Then he began to crawl in a slow circle, humping like a half-crushed beetle.

Flash.

He saw neat earthen rows demarking rice paddies. Above, a blue, almost cloud-less sky. Against that clear blue, an armada of flying metal.

Jax shuddered, fighting for control. He was concussed, and probably fighting shock. He had to move, had to keep going. The last thing in the world he needed was old memories flowing back into the mix. There was here and now, and then there was a past that he simply didn't care to re-member.

Not now. Not ever.

He could see it now, see a wall inside himself, erected long ago, keep-ing memories at bay. A wall of stone, and brick, and . . .

Suddenly the wall was no longer constructed of inorganic material. It was made of grass and shit and . . .

God. There was a human hand, mired into that mass, and next to it, a head in a khaki helmet.

(Gook's Bane)

No body beneath it. Just a head, and the severed stump of a neck. And now that he could see, he saw that the entire wall was made of sticks

(and bones)

and chunks of rock and tree limbs

(and burnt arms)

and bricks and chunks of masonry torn from peasant huts

(and bullet-gouged torsos, the wounds still caked with muck and congealed blood. Mister Q. Caltiki)

Jax fought for control, fought to keep the wall

(dead)

in place, keep it where it belonged, and after a while the heads became rocks, and the arms and legs were only clots of debris, and he was safe.

Safe, in a womb of forgetfulness. He could just stay here, curled up in the darkness. He couldn't do that. He had to rise up out of the fog. He was needed. He had to go. Somewhere out in the world were two creatures with power beyond any rational explanation. Also, somewhere in the world were the two people he loved most. He crawled until he found a wall. He was very careful—there was a pit there, somewhere in his darkness, and he had to stay away from the edge of the pit, the pit was the end of everything in his life, and to tumble into that pit was to stumble into the edge, that pit was the place where he had almost died, once before, a long time before, in another world. It was the depths, it was the darkness.

He felt and heard and watched those words and images running circular riot through his mind, and knew that if he couldn't stop them, he would go mad.

As he watched, one of the stones in the wall grew hair, grew soft round holes that became eyes, grew shiny pebbles gelling into teeth. And it smiled at him, opened its eyes, and winked.

Jax lost consciousness.

forty-nine

Captain Freddy King approached the front gate of the Sunset Arms apartment. He checked his notebook, and found Apartment 34 listed beside Hannah Appelion's name. He hadn't been in the field in years, but this was unofficial business, and he wouldn't have felt comfortable passing it on to one of his men.

He looked a the roster of names on the security buzzer. *H. Appelion* was the third name on the list, next to a numerical code for her apartment.

He punched the number. It rang ten times with no response. He hailed again, and after a long ring, somebody picked up the receiver. The voice on the other end was extremely hesitant. "Hello . . . ?"

"Hello. Miss Appelion?"

"Yes?"

"I am Lieutenant King. Freddie King? We've talked."

The line went dead.

King growled, "Shit," and was about to try again, when a tall, thin Latino walked up to the gate and produced a key.

"Fred King, LAPD?" he said, and followed the man in before he could protest. King ran up the stairs and counted doors until he found the correct room number. He knocked.

After a long pause, a very quiet voice on the other side said: "Yes?"

"I was wondering if you could answer a few questions for me. King, LAPD."

"What . . . what kind of questions?" Damn, that voice sounded frightened.

"About your involvement with the Twins."

"I don't want to talk," Hannah Appelion said. "How did you get in here?"

"I need to talk about Iron Shadows. Have you ever heard that phrase?"

There was a pause, and the door opened about an inch. He glimpsed a pasty face. "I don't want to talk to you. Can't you understand that?"

"We could have this conversation downtown, you know."

"You can't do that." Her voice now had a distinct tremor. He felt like an utter turd. She was correct—there wasn't any reason to consider her really connected with anything. But Tyler had sounded deadly earnest, and that could only mean that Cat was up against it somehow. She had saved his life once—maybe twice. The first time had involved a bag of battery acid in the hands of a junkie. It wouldn't have killed him, but Freddy King believed that he couldn't have looked at the resultant facial wounds too many times before eating a bullet. So, twice. He had taken her under his wing when she joined the department, and the student had surpassed the master. He had never for a moment begrudged Cat her excellence. Rather, he reveled in it. If she needed help, Freddy King would damn well deliver.

He wanted some answers, and this poor sallow thing was it. He could see her face now: pale, frightened. From the aroma, he doubted if she'd showered in a week. Jesus, what had happened to Hannah Appelion?

"As a matter of fact, I *can* force you," he said. She obviously felt safe here in her nest. All right. He would use a little pressure and see what that brought to he surface.

"I can take you down, and ask you the questions there, or I can do it here, in the privacy of your home. And be out of your life in a few minutes."

She was torn. Somebody—or something—had gotten hold of this woman, and done her a number.

"All . . . all right." The door opened wider. "But you don't know what you're messing with."

"Tell me, then," King said. He entered her apartment. Hose the garbage off the floor and it would have been a nice place. Only one small orange light bulb interrupted the gloom, but even by that, he could see that her face was covered with healing bruises, dirty-yellow swellings.

"Who did that to you?" He asked. She flinched away from his examining fingers.

She squeezed her eyes shut and looked at the ground. She mumbled something, but he couldn't quite make it out.

"What was that?"

"Iron Shadows," she said, more loudly now.

"Are the Iron Shadows part of the Twins organization?"

She reacted violently. "No! God. It's the Boogieman. Black plague. Sea serpents, Officer King." An odd touch of sarcasm had crept into her voice. "Don't fuck with Iron Shadows."

The wounds looked painful but superficial. They seemed the results of a very standard ass-whipping to him, but a woman like Hannah might find it easier to believe in supernatural forces than human evil. She rubbed her hand self-consciously across what was evidently a tender spot on her cheek, and winced. Her eyes pleaded with him to leave.

"Are we talking about people or leprechauns?"

Despite her injuries, her eyes blazed. "Mock me if you want to," she said. "You don't know. You can't know. But in six weeks, after the Rally—" her gaze was far away, almost drunken. "They won't have to worry about anything."

"Who won't?"

"The whole world will have to listen. And then everything . . . everything—" Her eyes focused, and she seemed to remember that she was talking to an outsider. "Listen. I shouldn't even be talking to you. You'd better leave. Now."

"Why shouldn't you talk to me?"

"It's not safe," she said.

"What?"

Suddenly, her face twisted, tightened, and the next words exploded out of her. "Out! Get out!" She grabbed him, shoved until he stumbled forward. He was too startled to resist, and a moment later was standing on her front porch.

The door slammed behind him. He looked back at the peep hole, mouth open. "Jesus Christ."

Well, damn, he said to himself, should he get a warrant on this little mouse? Take her down? For what? This wasn't working out well at all. *Everything is going to change,* she said.

What in the hell did she mean by that?

A scream from behind the locked door drove all thought from his mind. King pivoted. "Hannah? Miss Appelion?"

He banged on the door, and got no response at all. Another scream, even more urgent and terrified. King struck the door with his shoulder, then backed away and kicked just above the lock. It yawned open. King stepped forward—

And recoiled at the sight before him.

Snakes, he thought: *Kraken.* Fleshy squid tentacles. Thick, ropy projections, rising up out of the rug. Christ—no, they were *composed* of rug, or cloth fibers, the same sea-green color and texture as Hannah's rug. As he watched, an old chair became denuded, the cloth covering stripped away, cotton batting ripping away, twining and twisting together to create ropes, flowing out in defiance of gravity or logic to ensnare her.

God.

Hannah hung suspended in mid-air, jerking, struggling, one of the ropy coiling things snaked around her waist. By the time it reached her body, it was no longer distinguishable as cotton construction, almost as if it had become something else. Vine-like, yet without leaves; resembling tentacles, but without the suckers characteristic of octopus or squid.

Impossible. Happening.

As King watched, a tentacle arched around and pierced her back. She jerked and he expected to see blood drizzling onto the floor.

No blood. Incredibly, impossibly, Hannah Appelion seemed unharmed. Suspended in mid-air, she swelled for a moment and then contracted to normal size, as if she had absorbed the tentacle.

Her mouth hung slackly. Her eyes were as hard and shiny as ball bearings.

One of the tentacles slammed against King, pinning him against the wall. Hannah stared, her eyes empty windows to some cold and lifeless place. *"What do you know?"* Hannah's voice said.

King felt one of the linchpins holding his sanity in place pop free of its moorings. "Our father who art in Heaven—" Almost as if it had a mind of its own, Freddy King's hand worked its way slowly toward the revolver under his jacket. It felt like his fingers were moving through congealing cement.

"Who else knows what you know?"

"Hallowed be Thy name—"

The tentacle slapped across his face, shocking him from his trance into a more immediate and horrifying reality.

"You will talk to me," the voice said. For a moment, Hannah's eyes

sparkled. Her cheeks grew artificially brighter, and a horribly lascivious smile appeared on her lips. *"Do you find this body pleasing?"*

Hannah's body dangled like a puppet with half its strings broken.

King barely heard his own voice now, trying to wake himself up, to find his way home. "Thy Kingdom come, Thy will be done . . ." His fingers brushed the butt of the gun, then froze, as if uncertain what to do next.

"Tell me what you know. What do you know? Who did you tell . . . ?"

A tentacle crept up from beneath him and between his legs and he felt the pressure on his anus. It pierced him, and he screamed.

He felt the pain, felt his mind surrender another bit of its already tenuous grip. King had the horrible feeling that he could see under the edge of reality, beneath the polite veneer erected above chaos. Something buzzed under there, something swarmed and writhed like a universe composed of billions of living creatures no longer cooperating to maintain an illusion. Everything was coming apart.

His fingers gripped the gun. He pulled it out, aimed it at the center of Hannah Appelion's chest, and pulled the trigger.

fifty

Freddy King sprawled over the trash can, rolled clumsily on his shoulder, and came to a seated position. He set his palm down on the alleyway, slicing it on a shard of glass. He groaned and sucked the wound, tasting blood and grit.

A pale sliver of moon shone between a rise of buildings to the south. He wasn't sure where he was going, or what he would do once he got there. All he knew was that he had to keep moving—motion, in any direction away from the thing masquerading as Hannah Appelion—was an absolute imperative.

The crash of his gun still rang in his head. The bullet had struck her shoulder—and instantly, the tentacles retracted, his impalement had ceased. He scrambled to his feet, ignored the sticky leaking sensation between his bruised legs, and ran like hell.

Cars growled distantly on Melrose, less than a block away. A world away. He had to get himself together. Had to get . . .

His ears buzzed, throbbed. The drone had grown louder since the impossible incidents in the apartment. To the east, a police siren wailed, growing steadily louder. He was . . . he was going to get himself together. He had to get himself together. It hurt to walk. The tissue between his legs was sore. The thing, the damned thing, had hurt him. Forced itself in and twisted, probed. Lord. It had enjoyed his shame and terror. He wasn't certain how badly he was hurt. He felt *loose* inside.

He reached back with one trembling hand, and daubed at the wet place, moaning. If he could only think. Where was his car? Where had he parked it? He couldn't remember. He couldn't remember anything except the sight and sound of the woman suspended in midair, hovering there, twisting and turning. God. Her eyes opening, huge and glassy, their owner lost in the void between dead, distant stars. The mouth moving, the sound emerging as if something were *playing* her like a pipe organ, forcing air out past frozen vocal cords.

More than anything else, he remembered the way the tentacles, the ensnaring fibers turned back into cotton, into sheets, into cloth, and fell away from him. They writhed on the floor, as if with a queasy life of their own. And then began to re-form—

That was all he had time to see, that was when his mind stopped working, when the final underpinnings fell away, were swept away, and he ran screaming from the apartment.

Freddy King didn't really remember much after he left Hannah Appelion's apartment. He had run almost at random, forgetting everything, forgetting that he had driven a car, consumed by a need to move and move and move, with little or no thought for where he was going. Just needing to move, legs and body heavy as lead, putting a lie to his thirty weekly miles of running until his cigarette-seared lungs heaved for breath, and his legs turned into flopping, nerveless things.

He collided with a wall, struggling, trying to reclaim himself, trying to remember who and what he was.

"Fred King," he told himself. Captain, LAPD. Wilshire Division. He had a house in Sherman Oaks, and a sixteen-year-old daughter and a twenty-two-year-old son. He had two ex-wives, a timeshare condo in Maui, and he won an average of eighty dollars playing poker every Thursday night. That was his life, he had built it, and he liked it. Nothing could take away what he had fought so hard to earn.

Not even the impossible.

Oh, God. That thought resurrected the image of Hannah suspended in midair, something inhuman looking out at him through her temporarily vacated eyes. Remembered blood streaming from her bitten lip. Remembered her arms flapping, puppet-like.

Disorientation set in. Where was he? How far had he traveled in his mindless flight? At least three blocks. He sagged down against the alley wall, listened to the distant street sounds, to the thunder of his own heart, wondered what the hell was happening. What the hell was he going to say? He had suffered an hallucination, some kind of a breakdown. But he knew one thing: He had fired his sidearm into one Hannah Appelion, and there was nothing that he would ever be able to do about that. In that one instant, he had utterly and completely damned himself.

Almost thirty years on the force, and the first time he had ever fired his weapon at another human being, it had been an unarmed woman.

"God." He put his head between his hands, cradling it. What had he done? What in the hell had happened to him? In his entire life, he had never even *dreamed* of a problem like this. What happens when you can't trust your own mind? He couldn't remember what had happened—it just *couldn't* have been what he thought it was. That idea was somehow worse than the possibility that he had lost his mind.

Then came a low clicking sound from behind him. Then a sound very like a cough.

He turned his head slowly, expecting to see a wino, or some homeless person slouching through the entrance of the alley. No. Nothing man shaped or sized.

Something different. Very different.

Against the back door of a Radio Shack, a six-foot pile of boxes glistened with some kind of sour night-wet. Shadows spilled across the alleyway in a jumble, cast by street lamps and reflected light from Melrose.

Freddy King peered into the shadows, trying to make out . . . what? Something was there, in the shadows. He could tell. One part of the shadow was deeper than the others. Darker. Like a living part of the dark. He couldn't really see clearly. In fact, he wasn't even sure why he thought something was there in the shadows, but he did. Instinct, or some glimpse that registered too quickly for his conscious mind, told him that it was the approximate size and shape of a large watermelon.

It coughed again.

Fred scrambled back on all fours, unwilling to take his eyes off the shadow, knowing in some distant basic way, that the instant he moved his eyes, it, whatever *it* was, would be upon him. He scrambled back a foot or so, wincing as his palm set down on the broken bottle. Pain sliced through the rising fog of fear. Reflexively, he looked down at the damaged wrist. In the dull light, blood drizzled in a black stream, rolling across the darkness of his palm to the wrist.

He snapped his eyes up, and focused on the thing approaching him down the alley.

It was made of trash, of string, of bottle caps and dust and dirt. It was of protean aspect, continuously losing and remaking itself, as if it were more a pattern than a thing, leaking and grasping simultaneously. It was also growing, had swelled to something about the size of a St. Bernard, but bulkier, with more legs, a confusion of limbs. Eight. Its head was bulbous and swollen, its eyes multifaceted. Predator's eyes. Hunter's eyes. They stared straight ahead, straight at him.

It was coming.

Freddy King scrambled back onto his feet, backing away. He watched with fascination as the creature set one black paw into a pool of oily slime, and the muck was sucked up into the substance of the beast. With every obscenely delicate footfall it left a track of wet slime, a piece of filth. With every step its forepaws absorbed another cigarette butt, another shred of cloth, or in one case, a broken bottle slicked with King's own blood. Its eyes never left him. They were dead, black eyes. Hannah's eyes. No, not Hannah's: They were the eyes of the being which had stared out *through* Hannah's eyes. Not just a being. For a moment, its eyes were human.

A woman's eyes.

It hissed.

Fred King turned and ran as he never had in his life, ran so swiftly he thought he might fly, fled toward the light at the end of the alley, toward life, toward freedom, toward hope, swearing that if he could just make it to the light, that he would give up the cigarettes that tore at his lungs, that fastened leaden weights to his ankles. He would give up everything, just please, please don't make him give up life—

And when the smashing impact hammered him to the ground, he swore that if he could just get back up he would be a better father, a better man—

And when the ripping began, bringing with it the greatest and most exquisite pain of his life he swore that if the thing would just spare him he would find his way back to the church he had abandoned over a decade before. . . .

And when the pain swelled to grow realer and more imperative than any hope for life, he swore that to die, God, just to die and have it be over would be his greatest and most sacred wish.

And *that* wish, finally, his God saw fit to grant.

fifty-one

Cat slipped in and out of dream. She remembered being carried into a car, her sight wavering even then. She saw two Golden Sun acolytes carry Tyler away from a section of concrete pipe. He fought as best he could: knocking one down, bloodying another's nose. But Tyler was weakened by the ordeal, and when two acolytes failed, the two became three, and then four, and finally her brother succumbed.

They were insistent, but oddly solicitous. She remembered Kolla telling them to be careful.

The worlds of reality and dream flowed together in a swirling kaleidoscope of sights and sounds and sensations, but she managed to sort through them sufficiently to interpret one image: Joy, recoiling after the last of her rage was spent. She stumbled against Tomo. He supported her lovingly, tenderly. They slipped into the back seat of a black BMW. The cloud of light around Joy, which had once been white and then steadily darkened, now pulsed with black. She leaned against her brother. The light flickered to dark red, and then to red, to orange and orange-yellow, to yellow, and then to white. And then subsided.

Cat knew, knew on some basic level that she had just learned something of terrible importance, but couldn't maintain her grip on the discovery.

Cat remembered the fireball rolling into the mine entrance. She remembered a flash, just a momentary flash of Jax's face, in the instant before the explosion. And deep within her womb was the conviction that Jax was dead, that she would never see or touch him again. That they had finally run out of time.

The grief was almost unbearable. The air suddenly weighed more than the oceans of the world. She couldn't breathe. Couldn't think. She hovered on the brink of emotional disaster, fending off her total collapse with nothing but the sheer force of her will. That, and her imagination. Jax *might* have survived, she told herself. *Could* have survived. There had to be a way, and if anyone could survive, it would be Jax. And he would escape, and he would come for her. For them. She held that as an article of faith.

But what she knew and what she *felt* were two very different things, and she wrestled with them, heart against mind, until her fatigue descended upon her like a cloak, all of the physical abuse and the fear and the tension finally giving way to healing sleep.

fifty-two

Jax dreamed. He dreamed of a wall of bricks, but couldn't hold that image, although on some deep level he knew he was in a dream. The bricks became less regular, became pieces of stone and metal and trees, and anything that might serve as a barrier. And then when that failed, became a patchwork of other memories, bizarrely like a wall of television sets, each turned to a different channel.

There: a memory flash, something about a summer camp. He remembered running down a hillside, trying to impress a girl. Another screen—getting beaten up by three kids, a crowd of supposed friends watching. No visual memory, but a *feeling* about what had happened later. Weeks later, he had caught each of them, and dealt out rough justice. Another flash: running with a football, crashing through a beefy line of guards. A crowd cheered and waved pennants.

These were early memories, most of them good, another mental attempt to throw up a barrier, to distract himself, to prevent a deeper investigation of . . . what? But one at a time the images shorted out, became snow or test patterns, then flickered to life again, in a full-color, ghastly display, a wall of human heads and limbs, waking up now, broken fingers clawing, mouths chewing silent words, warming into screams and—

Behind the wall was—
Oh, God, he remembered now.
The wall *was* the dream.

fifty-three

Third Corps, Vietnam. October 13, 1971. 1400 hours.

Jackson Carpenter was nineteen years old, a sergeant of infantry who had humped an M-60 through the bush of the Nam from pointless butchery to pointless butchery. The war had become an endless dance of crazed symbiotic leeches, bleeding each other like medieval physicians intent on balancing the humors. Through this contest Carpenter led himself and seven men laughingly known as a fireteam to their betters. They were known to themselves as the "Fired upon, but hopefully not fucked up" team.

He was exhausted from days of marching, yes, but at nineteen fatigue is a small and dreamy thing, vanquished by an hour's nap or twenty minutes rest, or a meal. At nineteen Jackson Carpenter was immortal.

Early that morning, the 101st, the 173rd, and the 25th had crossed the Sun Dung Nai River accompanied by their respective Av battalions. Jackson and team—most notably Mister Q. ("Q" for Cue-ball, an object suggested by the Alabaman's shaven head), Gook's Bane (a tall, gangly Minnesotan with a tendency to get the runs and an absolutely lethal aim), and Caltiki (an L.A. boy whose father published *Famous Creature Features* magazine, and had therefore grown up warped and thoroughly depraved even before hitting the bush), were along for the slaughter without any particular hope that this outing would be significantly more significant than any of the others.

As Caltiki was fond of saying, "We don't take cities, conquer territories or advance battle lines—we just mutilate bodies."

Amen.

Their aerial cover was suspended by the shimmering heat of that awful

place like a swarm of bees. He remembered waiting, sitting, as the helicopters went ahead into a green tangle of tropical rain forest. Above them,
the might of America owned the sky, rained death into the forest. An hour
ago, B-52 bombers had unleashed their thunder. The forest groaned its
death throes with every blazing load. Then attack jets strafed, ripping the
remaining burnt and torn foliage into slaw. Then came the Hueys and Cobras, 105mm howitzers, 155mm howitzers, chewing up the countryside
and killing anything that the arc lighters had left unkilled.

Hour after hour after hour of man-made seismic hell.

Jax recalled the aftermath, the moments after that insane convergence
of destructive forces. Mister Q. had wiped sweat from his pale bald head
and drawled: "Oh, man . . . Ah never get used to the *silence,* you know?"

He was right. It was damned eerie how the entire world seemed to shut
the fuck up after a bombing run. Silence. Nothing to hear . . .

But oh, they could *smell.* Their noses were assailed with the stench of
thousands of pounds of ordinance. The molten scream of metal on metal.
A pungent brew of phosphorous, sulfur, and the oddly vital death stink of
thousands of trees which had grown, in their primal profusion, in that
emerald inferno for years, sometimes hundreds of years, only to vanish in
a rain of fire. Their ghosts clotted his nostrils, raked his mind with their
screams of violation and loss.

They were simply *gone.* One moment the forest was an impenetrable
living barrier, and in the next, as dead as the moon.

This was the first time Jax had been this deep in Third Corps. He didn't
know what the hell to expect, but in some central ways, he had given himself up for dead months before, so it didn't really matter. In an odd way,
that certainty that he was going to die gave him a clarity in the middle of
action that translated into an almost supernatural level of good luck. Not
a bruise or a scratch or a twisted ankle. And the people around him tended
to survive ambushes, firefights, and general fuck-ups notoriously well. All
of this combined to make Jax a natural leader, whether he wanted the role
or not. His men looked to him for guidance on an almost spiritual level.
When he lit a butt, they did. When an officer gave an order, they watched
him to see what his response would be. And when he asked Gook's Bane
why he seemed to pattern his walk and talk and dress on Jackson Carpenter, Bane's only answer was, "Shucks, Sarge—everybody knows you're

gonna live forever. Fairies just favor you, that's all. Figure if I look like you they might make a mistake, rub a little dust off on me, too."

Hard to argue with logic like that.

They had no clear idea what they might be up against, but Intel expected the Viet Cong to have two reinforced regiments in there, which explained the massive display of aerial strength.

Initially they walked north for about an hour, through the blasted forest and onto hard flat ground, opening up into farm country: irrigated ground, cross-hatched into paddies, the rice bowl of Vietnam. The VC, who of course were watching, were of course *always* watching, would have a chance to see where they were headed, and lay their plans. They would meet in their cloistered darknesses, and plot, and send out their messages, make their movements, lay their traps—then of course Jax got the order to reverse field, and they headed back south, hoping to trap Mr. Charles against the river.

It was a good plan, the kind of plan which had worked before. That might have been why it didn't work this time.

Jax remembered every step of that march, as if some movie director in his head had filmed the whole thing, and then squirreled the film away until it was time for a very private screening.

Mister Q. thumped Caltiki on the back. *"Darby O'Gill and the Little People.* Who went from there to fighting Russians and crazy Chinese guys?"

"Sean Connery," Caltiki said. "Try harder."

"All right." Q. slapped his neck with his right hand, killing a whole family of the little black flies that seemed to love his taste and smell. "Had bolts in his neck a couple of times, and did the Yellow Peril routine, looking for the Sword of Genghis Khan. Who was he, and what movie?"

Mister Q. had a running conversation with Caltiki, various bets on the line running from cigarettes to Thai stick to shit details, trying to stump the Monster Master with obscure movie trivia. Jax thought that this bet involved a hooker in Saigon with a reputation for breathing through her ears.

"Boris Karloff. *Mask of Fu Manchu,* 1933."

"Damn!" Q. glowered, and slapped at his neck again.

Jax had divided his attention between the conversation and the landscape. There would be action soon, and it would be hard, and vicious, and there was less and less of nineteen-year-old Sergeant Carpenter that protested that as days went by.

That was part of the disturbing thing (he remembered). It is one thing to be told that They are the enemy, and will kill you if you do not kill them. It is one thing to hear your buddies and officers refer to the enemy in terms generally reserved for rabid animals. It is quite another to find within yourself the part which feels pleasure in their death. Introduction to the part of the deep, primitive mind which revels in destruction causes a reassessment of everything presumed or held dear, all values and ethics. Suddenly the world seems a very different place, a place which cannot be clearly described to those who have not experienced it for themselves. It creates, in those military veterans, police officers, and others who have occasion to kill under license, the strange sensation of being a wolf among sheep. Sometimes it is a saddening sensation. But often, it is almost riotously funny, to realize that some of those sheep think that *they* hold the leash. One could just laugh and laugh and laugh.

And then bite.

As they approached an abandoned farm, Jax's best friend, a brother from New York named Hot Dog, took a round in the temple as their right flank took fire. The squad crouched behind a packed dirt retaining wall, and Jax laced the NVA with long bursts of M-60 fire while the company tried to regroup at the far end of the clearing in an irrigation ditch. Two waves of NVA rolled up to the M-60's barrel and broke on the face of the wall, retreating, leaving bundles of brown-green as a deposit for their efforts, some in a state of twitch and others decidedly non-twitch.

Jackson Carpenter just kept walking.

Judging by the radio traffic, Jax knew that a lot of people had been hurt or hit, but there was too much confusion, the adrenaline was pumping too hard—he couldn't tell exactly what was happening. His company divided, some giving support on the right, the rest proceeding to their pre-arranged targets.

Jax finally took the time to check Hot Dog, although from the first snap of his head and spray of blood and speckled gray-white matter, he had known there was nothing to be done. He prepared Dog himself, taking the

(dog)

tag, placing the second tag in what was left of his mouth and sealing him in the black bag forever. Then he sat quietly by the bag until the Medevac dust-off crew gently shooed him away and took the body. As it happened, Hot Dog went home in an aluminum box with a Purple Heart and DSM to go with a neatly folded flag to a family that probably would have been appalled at the company he kept.

But as night came on, Jax's platoon took up the security on the left side of the supposedly VC-symp village, while the company on the right prepared to go in on the morning, to clean up.

Except for booby traps and a few scrawny pigs, the ten-acre clutch of thatched huts was deserted. Jax took the first watch, was relieved by Gook's Bane just after midnight, and curled up for some shut-eye.

Jax dreamed of home, a little dry patch off New Mexico's Route 66 called Gallup. In that dream, he was a kid again, running the narrow dusty streets, imitating the Friday Night drunken reel practiced assiduously by cowboy and Indian alike, eager for the day that his liver could begin its own one-way journey down that toxic highway.

In the morning, Caltiki told Jax that they were uncovering a massive tunnel complex north of the village, and his squad moved out to provide support.

By the time they arrived, the area was supposedly secured, snipers neutralized, and booby traps disarmed. He remembered being entranced by the incredible underground labyrinth as they mapped it, one section at a time. A few of the smaller men were designated tunnel rats, chosen to explore the darkness. As one of the tallest and broadest in his unit, Jax was out of the running, although Caltiki shucked his pack and went down. He was all teeth and knife, making a thumbs-up just before disappearing into the ground. They were all pretty sure Mr. Charles had vacated the vicinity, but there was more than enough danger to give the venture spice.

As for Jax, he was perfectly happy to take a break, lean back against a hut and enjoy the sunshine.

A shout behind him said that they had found something important. Jax picked his way back to the platoon through a maze of booby-trap wires, and found that they had completely surrounded some kind of low bunker.

The bunker was only a foot or so off the ground, constructed of logs and mud, and it looked like it had two airholes in the thatched top. Immediately, a light went on in his head. *This* is where Mr. Charles had gone: underground from the village, out along tunnels, out of range of the artillery fire. . . .

When Caltiki popped back up, disappointed because he hadn't had a chance to go mano a mano with a fourteen-year-old NVA, Jax's platoon completely encircled the entire amphitheater, every eye alert and watchful.

A lean snake of a good lieutenant named Lopez moved forward and dropped a grenade down one of the holes. Just a smoke grenade, something to show them where the vent holes were.

Then everything went wrong.

fifty-four

When Cat woke next, the rumble of engines and the fluid motion of the floor beneath her told her that she was on a plane or a helicopter. Although she didn't move, full awareness returned rapidly: She smelled and felt the brushed leather against her cheek, and her head throbbed with a hot, leaden pulse.

Tyler snored in the seat beside her. She very cautiously reached out to take his pulse, and was relieved to find it strong. His breathing was regular and healthy, and his little burring snore, ordinarily so irritating, she found the most comforting sound in the world. Jax might be gone forever. The thought of losing Tyler as well was more than she could endure.

"He is quite all right, Miss Juvell," Tomo said.

Little use in feigning unconsciousness. She turned. Tomo sat down across the aisle from her. She picked up enough additional cues to determine that they weren't in a helicopter, as she had originally assumed. The engine's vibration told her they were aboard a jet. The narrow width of the passenger compartment and the plush rug running the center aisle told her that it was a luxury transport worthy of a president or king.

At personal range Tomo seemed about thirty years old. He was darker than he appeared in his picture, as if the black part of his heritage had been African rather than Jax's mixed-blood American. Tiny smile lines in his face gave him a slightly elfish appearance, and his eyes were both sober and mischievous.

"We know the story," he said. "You and your brother were trying to help an innocent. You could not have known the truth."

She pulled her hand out of his cool, firm grasp. "What kind of thing are you?" she said.

"I am the future," he replied. "Your future."

Her voice was stone. "Your sister killed Jax."

He tilted his head. "Excuse me?"

"He was in the mine when she destroyed the van."

He closed his eyes, and Cat had the impression that he had gone far away. His breathing slowed, became imperceptible, perhaps stopped. Then he exhaled strongly, and opened his eyes. He faced Cat with genuine regret. "I cannot contact Jax, and I know he has taken blood. You may be right. He may well be dead."

The words hit her like a hammer blow. Her carefully erected emotional defenses splintered, and she forced her breathing to calm. *No weakness, dammit. Later. Later, you can die a little. Tyler needs you.*

Tomo groaned. "I tried to stop her. Joy gets excited. She is very protective of the things she loves, and when someone threatened Kolla . . . please, believe me. If we had known that an innocent was present, it would not have happened. I am most deeply mortified."

Cat looked behind her. Two golden half-curtains were drawn together across the aisle. Through a gap between halves, she glimpsed Kolla. She was looking at something . . . someone. Joy's back was to Cat, and she was slumped. *Resting,* instinct told her. What she does takes effort. "Rest now," Tomo said.

"Where are we going?"

He gave her a wide and generous smile. "To meet my mother."

fifty-five

Jax was never exactly certain what happened once the grenade went into the ground. He could only surmise that the smoke grenade ignited something down in the tunnels. Perhaps it had landed directly atop a stockpile of explosives. Something with an exposed fuse, or some loose powder. He reached this conclusion because there were two explosions, one immediately following the other. The first was equivalent to perhaps ten pounds of high explosive. At first he thought that a mortar had detonated, and wondered how he had missed the characteristic whistling sound prior to impact.

In a shower of flame and thunder, Lieutenant Lopez was transformed from a decent guy, someone you could joke with, someone who was always willing to share the excellent coffee he regularly received from his wife in Miami, into a bleeding rag doll.

Jax might have had time to sort through what was happening, or ask himself what could possibly go wrong next, but suddenly they were hit on all sides. The Cong had executed a lethally effective ambush: His platoon had aided it by relaxing into a criminally oblivious victor's posture. When death rained down on them, there was little for them to do but die. He watched Mister Q. take a round in the chest, his mouth going wide, expression one more of surprise than of pain. Jax remembered thinking: *His mind knows he's dead before his body's figured it out. . . .*

The next second probably would have taken his life as well, except that in that moment a second explosion dwarfed the first. The ground smacked him like a great flat hand. Jax had a brief sensation of weightlessness, combined with the certain knowledge that his life was over. He felt himself, *saw* himself drifting in slow motion, limbs loose, head back arching back in an oddly graceful posture, the earth wheeling beneath him. He slammed back into the dirt as the ground collapsed in a spider webbed pattern, radiating outward from the central explosion as the entire network of tunnels collapsed, swallowing Jackson Carpenter whole.

fifty-six

When Jax awoke he was covered with earth and rock, completely disoriented, so confused that he didn't even know which direction was up. Nor was he certain if it was day or night—the darkness surrounding him might have been nightfall, or a ton of earth, or blindness. . . .

Or death.

He managed to twist his body, and felt something in his left shoulder give. *Pain.* He heard screams and curses above him. Occasional shots. The sound of running feet. And then laughter and laughing words in Vietnamese. More screams. More shots. And then nothing.

How could he breathe? Something pressed against his face—a board of some kind, a piece of metal or plastic sheeting. Something that created an air pocket. For all of that, he knew that if he were more than a few feet below the surface, he would be dead. From that slender evidence, he concluded that his rude grave was a shallow one.

He lay there for hours, listening. Something wet seeped down through the rock and the dirt, onto his face. He never learned what it was, but knew it to be thicker than water.

Slowly, an inch at a time, he regained the capacity for motion. It returned to him as a spiraling tingle, a savage itching. Pain. The pinprick of returning circulation. But the searing pain brought with it the blessed ability to flex and twist first his fingers, then his aching wrists. He began to claw at the gritty soil.

After an eternity, Jax clawed his way to the surface. He blinked away the dirt and dust, and found himself alive, and standing beneath a starry sky, alone on the plain of tunnels. Alone, but for a wall of the dead.

The VC had not merely slaughtered his platoon. They had butchered the Americans, then stacked the resultant dismembered bodies like cordwood. Their corpses variously missed eyes, tongues, genitals. He remembered the CBS stickers, and vomited.

No attempt had been made to hide this deed. This cairn of death was *intended* to be found, intended to inspire awe, and fear.

The buzzing of the flies, an omnipresent background noise in this tropical paradise, had swelled until there was no other sound in the world. It ceased to be something outside of him, seemed to be the product of his own mind.

He dug through the pile, dimly aware of the sobbing sounds made by someone just behind his eyeballs, aware that he was ankle-deep in blood and intestine and fractured limbs. Not caring, just pulling, pulling. . . .

Until he found Caltiki. Once blue eyes had watched the silver screen, laughing at Ghidra the Three-Headed Monster or crying with fear when Vincent Price's mask shattered in the wax museum, or cheered when Gorgo's mother leveled London searching for her lost child. Now those eyes were gone, and all that remained were gaping crimsoned holes, and torn flesh.

He held the boy to his chest tightly, fervently, in the futile hope that his own beating heart might stir life in his silent friend.

The man named Sergeant Jackson Carpenter walked out into the forest. He staggered, but managed to remain upright, his every walking motion almost completely reflexive. He had his rifle and sidearm, but no compass. For the first hours of walking, he didn't even try to head in the direction of American forces. He was just dazed and concussed, staggering through trees which began to seem like alien things. He was completely lost, but too confused to be frightened.

When he came to his senses, almost two days had passed. He was feverishly hot. He drank water when he could find it. He killed and ate what he could catch, or what he found dead on the ground. He had no sense of trying to survive, only of staving off death a little longer, just a few hours longer.

At night, he huddled in the bole of a tree, wrapped his arms around his knees, and pretended to sleep.

Twice, he came upon Mr. Charles. He didn't remember what happened, only that he had lived, and someone else died. He didn't clearly know much of anything that occurred during that time. In that time the darkness outside of himself and the darkness within joined forces, somehow became the same thing, and in his madness he found a kind of peace, of happiness.

The veil of darkness and mental night lifted a bit at the moment Jax finally stumbled out of that forest into a Marine Recon Platoon. He remembered the way that they stared, then reflexively flinched away from him. He remembered collapsing in their arms and not awakening again until he was in the hospital. But day by day as his body healed, his mind erected a wall around the things that had happened, and what he had done in the forest to survive

A wall of human heads.

Mister Q. Caltiki. Hot Dog. Gook's Bane. They had made the terminal mistake of trusting him, of thinking that he could protect them. Big joke.

Jackson Carpenter had walked out of that hellhole damn near unscathed. Yeah, there was a kind of magic around him. Yeah, the fairies favored him all right. They'd made him a goddamn luck vampire, and somebody needed to drive a stake through his fucking heart.

fifty-seven

Jax awoke with a start, unable to remember when he had lain down and begun to nap.

You're in the tunnel.

Which tunnel?

He hitched himself up to sitting, and then to an uneasy balance on hands and knees. He cursed as his left arm buckled. From shoulder to elbow, the entire limb was awash with pain.

Crawling on knees and right arm, he inched his way around the periphery of the cave. There were two tunnels. One was about forty-five degrees clockwise from the entrance tunnel, and boarded up—that much he remembered. He found the boards by touch, and used that point to orient himself. A foot at a time, Jax crawled the perimeter until he found the main tunnel. He was able to make his way about twelve feet before he found the first chunk of rock. His thick fingers trembled as he touched it. He stopped. Was there something in the dark with him? Wasn't there *something?* There had to be. He shut his hearing down, ignoring the sounds, the terror there in the blackness.

He continued to move until he faced a wall, and backtracked until he found a mountain of jumbled stone, but there was no getting through it. He pressed himself against it, shuddering. He stood there, leaning and resting and wondering what to do next, when the slightest whisper of wind touched his face, cooling his cheeks.

He turned toward that breeze like a flower turning to the sun, and groped out until his fingers touched stone.

Jax began to climb, his useless left arm trailing behind him. The tunnel wasn't completely full. Although the ceiling had given way, it had also grown blessedly irregular. There were fissures to crawl through, and when rock was lifted or kicked to the side, time and again Jax was able to eel his bulk through to another small chamber. He clawed until his fingernails split, sending sudden pain shooting back to his knuckle. He sucked it, tasting limestone dust and his own blood.

Jax pushed rock aside. There was air, moving air from the outside, and that meant that there was a way. He had to find that way, he had to find his way back to Cat.

At some point she stopped being a person, and started becoming a symbol. Mister Q. and Caltiki, and Gook's Bane were gone. He should have died with them, and he had walked away, not dead but damned. He had left his heart in that village, and it had never beat again until he met a small, fiery blond named Porsche Juvell.

Cat was salvation. Cat was life. She was love. Cat and Tyler were family, the only family he had left in this world. *That* was why they had found each other. He could not stop. He couldn't abandon her, not while life remained within him. He worked, he dug, he scraped until he was exhausted. Then Jax rolled over onto his side, and slept dreamlessly, like the dead.

fifty-eight

Friday, June 23

Nearly two hours passed before their jet circled in for a landing, and the sun was still high above the horizon. The landing gear bumped hard on first contact, then gave another soft bump, followed by a smooth rolling taxi to a halt.

Tyler had been awake for the last hour, but he and Cat had exchanged fewer than a dozen words. She held his hand quietly, and in that manner they comforted each other. This was simply too far out of their depth. More than conversation, more even than sleep, they needed time to think, to adjust to a new and frightening reality.

"Jax?" Tyler had said once.

She shrugged. "Maybe. I don't know."

"We can hope," he said. And they spoke no more about it. There was nothing more to say.

The main cabin door opened, and daylight streamed in. Cat made her shaky way to the door, and peered out.

Maybe thirty meters to the north stood a low clutch of gray buildings:

From their appearance she guessed them to be maintenance sheds and perhaps a communications shack for the landing strip. Further out, she glimpsed a few rounded buildings against a backdrop of iron-gray mountains.

Cat felt, rather than saw a presence behind her, and heard Joy's voice: "Please. Descend."

She turned. Joy was the same height as Tomo, the same general build, the same ethnic mixture. But somehow, she seemed larger, as if her energy were explosive to Tomo's implosiveness. Cat's chest tightened. Being this close to Joy felt like walking next to a breathing, talking supernova.

Joy sensed her unease, and laughed. In spite of her trepidation, Cat found it a musical, magical sound. "We mean you no harm—surely you must believe that. If we wanted to harm you, would we bring you all this way to do so?"

"Am I your prisoner?" Cat asked bluntly.

Joy shook her head. "Our honored guest."

"For how long?"

"You have questions," Joy said. "We have answers. After your questions are answered, you may leave."

Cat watched a very tall man exit one of the limousines. She thought that he moved like a well-oiled puppet: extraordinarily graceful, but somehow disconnected from his body. He was over six and a half feet tall—although some of that was his leather boots. He weighed maybe two hundred and fifty pounds—no, she revised her estimate to two forty five. His face was completely relaxed, placid, again, almost as if his body were held in neutral, waiting for his brain to engage. Prematurely white hair. Manfred Gittes.

He held out a slender arm to Tomo, and as they shook, she saw muscular definition leap out of those arms, in an abundance she would never have anticipated. Relaxed, he looked like nothing but a tall, gangly spook. In motion, even a motion as insignificant as shaking hands, he was intimidating as hell.

Joy walked Cat down onto the tarmac, and held her hand out to the tall man. He took it, and kissed the back of her wrist. "Joy," he said. "I am sorry that I was not there when trouble came."

"It was resolved, Manfred," she said, and their eyes met. Something was exchanged, and Cat was puzzled. Were they lovers? Perhaps . . . but that wasn't all she sensed. Collaborators? Conspirators? Perhaps.

But what she really thought of, what really occurred to her, was that these two shared a secret. They were like junkies who reckon themselves the only ones who truly understand the nature of pleasure.

That was it. They were junkies. But for what drug? "Manfred Gittes," Joy said, "I would like you to meet Porsche Juvell. Our guest for the next few days. Ms. Juvell, Mr. Gittes is our chief of security."

Gittes smiled and nodded, and something odd happened: She watched his consciousness, the authentic Manfred Gittes recede behind a thin film of emotional ice. Whatever real contact he had just made with Joy was certainly not being offered to Cat. Instead, a polite, jovial, public persona emerged. "Ms. Juvell?" he said, and extended his hand. She took it, and felt, ever so subtly, *something* flow from his hand into hers. Something that crept around and into her, searching, testing. As if he had extruded a psychic pseudopod and stealthily probed her.

Then the sensation vanished, leaving her feeling flushed and on the very edge of sexual excitement. Cat felt disgusted, even violated, without completely understanding why.

From behind his frozen shield, Manfred Gittes studied her. He *knew* her, knew something about her that comforted him, and she was still completely in the dark. At that moment, she missed Jax more than ever. Somehow. Somehow he had to be alive. And if he was alive, he would find her. And she needed him, now. She was afraid of Manfred Gittes, and that fear clouded her mind.

That lack of clarity was something she simply couldn't afford.

A cargo door opened in the side of the plane. Two attendants carried Tyler out and deposited him in a waiting wheel chair. He waved at her gaily. Several acolytes waited on the tarmac. They wore robes in varying shades of yellow and orange: gold, saffron, a light copper. They smiled broadly, holding flowers. *One big happy family, you betcha.*

Cat strolled to Tyler, smiled her thanks to Tomo then politely but firmly took position behind the wheelchair. "Would you mind? I'd rather do this myself."

"Of course not." Tomo relinquished control, but in doing so his fingers brushed across the back of her hands. It felt like brushing a live wire.

"Down the rabbit hole," Tyler whispered.

"This way to the car, please," Tomo led the way with a brisk, youthful step.

Tyler hummed to himself. "We're late, we're late, for a very important date . . ."

"Exactly where are we?" Cat asked.

"Just south of Bend, Oregon," Tomo answered unhesitantly. "This is our main center."

"Bend?" Cat said, somewhat confused. "We researched you. I didn't see anything about Oregon."

"You wouldn't have," Joy answered. "It's registered under Manfred's name—it's his health farm. We have to have some place to retreat to—"

"—away from the reporters, or even our own followers. We love them, but we need time on our own."

Cat slowed their pace, matching strides with Joy. "What I saw. I mean, what you did back in Santa Cruz—"

Embarrassment curled Joy's mouth downward. "Do you disapprove?"

"No . . ." Cat was surprised at how small her voice seemed. She decided to try the truth. What was there to lose? There was every possibility these two incredible beings could read her mind, anyway. "I just . . . I'm afraid."

Joy touched her arm. "You needn't be. You have done no wrong. You thought you were helping Kolla. She told us what happened. That's enough for me."

Joy turned toward the other car, and spoke with Kolla. "Kolla, darling. I want you to coordinate the satellite linkage tonight. . . ."

Tyler was helped into the second limousine, with Joy and Manfred. His wheelchair was swiftly and efficiently folded, then deposited in the trunk. Despite Cat's protests, she was gently steered toward the first vehicle. This wasn't the time for active resistance. Hell, that time might never come again. "Tomo," Cat said as she got into the cars. "I saw your face back at the mining camp. It seems we were equally shocked."

"Yes," he admitted.

Cat was confused, and didn't bother keeping it from her face or voice. "But—she's your sister."

"True," he said thoughtfully. "But it seems we still have secrets."

Cat searched her heart. "Those men were trying to hurt her. Kill you. Steal from Kolla. I think I might have done the same thing, if I'd been able."

Tomo shook his head sadly. "Violence is not the way," He said. "Love is the way."

———

The limousine pulled slowly down the road. Within a quarter mile, they crested a hill. On a shallow valley below them crouched a clutch of yurts, a geodesic dome the size of a five-story building, at least a dozen log cabins, a sparkling swimming pool and two tennis courts, other assorted log buildings with stone foundations and chimneys, and, on a distant hill, the exact twin of the Santa Cruz mansion. Evergreens, madrones, and Douglas firs shaded the grounds everywhere. The underbrush was thick with pink and yellow monkey flowers, rhododendrons, and sprinklings of false hellebores.

As their limo descended, they passed a group of six acolytes hiking up the hill. They looked tanned and fit, the men stripped to the waist, the girls displaying muscularly bare midriffs. They waved at the limo's tinted windows.

"It's beautiful here," Cat said sincerely. *Jax would have loved it.* She caught herself. *He's alive. Somehow. He'll find us.*

Tomo nodded. "I find great peace."

"I saw what you did for the girl in Santa Cruz. You healed a compound fracture in a few seconds."

"It is not a thing to talk about."

"Yes," she said. "It is."

She looked back through the rear window of the limousine, to the second car, which carried Tyler. "There is someone I love very much, who is injured. Crippled."

"Your brother."

"Could you help him?"

Tomo's reply was very quiet. "He would have to be one of mine," he said. "He would have to ask me."

Cat was silent as they approached the mansion's dopplegänger. The cars eased to a stop. Cat emerged from her car, and Tyler was helped from his back into the folding wheelchair.

Joy and Tomo walked ahead of them. Cat watched the two of them. There was an automatic synchronization about the way they moved. She had a curious sense of experiencing double vision.

There was nothing comical about the implications. Her heart opened to Tomo every time she saw him, and now . . . the single moment of contact between them was electric. She sensed nothing but kindness in this man. But if he was the healer, and Joy was his opposite, the destroyer, then what in God's name lived in *her* heart?

"Paradise, isn't it?" Tyler said flatly.

"What's wrong with this picture?" Cat asked.

There was a wheelchair ramp at the right side of the steps. She pushed Tyler up, and together they entered the main house.

fifty-nine

The decor within the mansion was very different: very Japanese. Rice paper prints of chrysanthemums and snow-crested mountain ranges. To the left, mounted in a glass case, a white silk kimono with blue leaf prints around the fringe. In another, a samurai sword, and in a third, several ancient *sum-i* brush paintings. In cases on either side of the kimono stood a series of tiny, delicate dolls. Samurais and peasants, bakers and fishermen, weavers, dancers and kabuki dancers—the dolls were no more than ten inches tall, with incredible detail, and over a hundred years old. They had to be worth a fortune. Many were porcelain, some of carved wood or bone. Two were exquisitely folded origami, constructed of some pale unlined paper covered with a rough, masculine scrawl.

As they wound through the hallways, it seemed that they were entering another, older world, a world which might have existed before Commodore Perry opened Japan to the Western world.

Gittes touched Cat's shoulder, and for the first time since leaving the airstrip, addressed her directly. "This is a great honor for you. No outsider has ever been allowed to see the Mother."

His gaze was the True Believer's. This man had seen the Truth, and was prepared to die for it. Or kill?

Tyler read the confusion on Cat's face, and spoke for her. "We appreciate the honor, and will strive to be worthy of it."

She gripped his shoulder proudly, but one question still plagued her. "Why?" she asked Tomo. "Why this honor?"

"I choose you," he said. "I see the light in you."

His eyes were as clear as crystal. She felt as if she could peer completely through them into the soul within, and detected no deceit.

She could only nod.

They followed the Twins down the corridor, toward the Mother.

s i x t y

They slid open a sandalwood door with paper panels, which led into a chamber with white paper walls and exposed beams of polished hardwood. Windows in two walls looked out onto a forest of Douglas firs and sword ferns. With balance and precision born of long practice, Joy and Tomo knelt at the edge of a stiff white cotton mat. Following this example, Cat pushed Tyler's chair to the edge of the mat, and then knelt in front of him.

A screen on the other side of the room slid open. Behind it sat an aged Japanese woman. Her face was riven with age, but her carriage was very erect, as though time might have torn, but not bowed or broken her.

"My children," she said.

Joy and Tomo answered in tandem. "Mother. It is good to be back."

"How go the plans?" the old woman barely moved her lips.

"Well," Joy said. It may have been her imagination, but it seemed to Cat that the two women shared a secretive smile. Further, she sensed that Tomo was perfectly aware of his exclusion.

"Who have you brought me?" asked the old woman. Her thin lips turned up into a toothless smile.

Tomo spoke. "Porsche Juvell and her brother Tyler. Both of good heart. I believe she has *potential.* They tried to help one of ours. She was lied to and used by unscrupulous people. I think they could help us. But she needs to know the truth."

Mother Oshita smiled her toothless smile at Cat. "The truth. Can you handle the truth, girl?"

No.

"Yes."

"What is it you want to know? You must *ask.*"

Tyler stumbled over his words. "Where . . . did you learn what you know? I've seen impossible things. How did this happen?"

The old woman stared at him, nodded fractionally.

"It is your story, Mother." Joy said. "It is your decision."

Mother Oshita returned her gaze to Cat, and held her arms out. "Give me your hands, child."

Cat rose from her kneeling position and took two steps, then knelt again. She extended her hands to the old woman, who took them with fingers as dry as parchment. She kneaded Cat's hands thoroughly, dull, dead eyes searching her face. Her fingers reached out to trace the contours of Cat's cheeks, her throat, the ridges of her eyes. Finally she smiled. "We seek friends. Friends who can help us."

"Help you what?"

"Most are followers. Children. You are strong. You could help us in the fight ahead."

Cat was puzzled again. "The fight . . . ?"

"It started years ago. Almost fifty years ago. When I was a girl . . . in Nagasaki."

sixty-one

The old woman fell into a well-worn rhythm and tone pattern—this was a speech given many times before. Still, it was a ceremonial moment, reserved for those who might join the Golden Sun's inner circle. Without turning her head, Cat knew the Twins were watching her closely.

"I was a graduate student at the University. In those dark closing days of the war, every hand was needed. I worked in a laboratory washing glassware and sterilizing implements. The job of the facility was the development of biological weapons."

"Germ warfare?"

"Yes. My husband was a pilot, on assignment in China. I had two children, watched by my mother as I worked twenty hours a day. Our work was vital. I did not realize how vital. The Americans did. I believe that this facility was a primary target on August sixth, 1945, two weeks after my husband's last furlough home."

Cat did a swift calculation in her head.

Behind her, Tyler whispered: "The second atom bomb, Little Boy."

"There was a blinding flash, and I remember nothing until I woke up. I was cut, burned, splashed by the fluids in my lab, surrounded by fire from which my seniors did not escape. Somehow, I survived. From that day, my world changed forever. I stumbled from the wreckage, not thinking of the hundred viral and bacterial agents which had infected me.

"The city was . . . just destroyed. Gone. I cannot even begin to explain what that did to me. I stumbled through the wreckage, looking for my mother's house, thinking only of my children. My sweet Joy and Tomo. And I found them. Or what was left of them."

What was left of them? Cat's mind reeled. Then her first children had died, fifty years ago. And later she had others, and gave them the same names. This was getting creepier by the minute.

Mother Oshita paused, waiting, staring straight at Cat. After an uncomfortable silence, Tyler asked: "What remained?"

The old woman's voice dropped to a low tone. "There, on the remnants of a brick wall, were the charcoaled silhouettes of two children, charred into the brick by the unimaginable heat. All that remained of my family."

"They looked like drawings rendered in black rust. I knelt by them, crying. I called them Iron Shadows."

"Iron Shadows," Cat repeated.

The old woman nodded her head. "So many dead, so many souls destroyed. The war was over and we had lost. I received word that my husband had died, shot down near Shanghai. I was alone in the world. Devastated.

"The war was over. There was nothing but starvation and shame for us, but within me, a small miracle was taking place."

"You were pregnant?" Tyler asked.

She nodded her head. "Yes. Medical care came slowly, first with Japanese doctors, and later, the occupying Americans. By some miracle, I bore no external signs of the hundred lethal agents raging within me. Did they cancel each other out? Was it some effect of the terrible energies unleashed by the blast? I don't know. I did not think. I drifted. I hungered. And I fed my hunger taking any menial job I could find, scrounging for food, aware only that I had to feed the life inside me. Aware that there was something special within me."

She looked at Tyler, radiating sincerity. "I blamed the Bomb for what had happened, but also the men of my own country who had manipulated us into this war. As I looked about and saw such devastation, I knew that if I could, I would keep such a thing from ever happening again. Ever. If only God would give me the strength.

"I didn't know why I had such thoughts. Perhaps even then I knew that something inside me was different. Something special was happening.

"I knew. And when after ten months my child was not born, but stayed within my womb, maturing, I knew. And when at last after twenty-seven months—"

"Twenty-seven *months?*" A ripple of raw shock coursed through Cat, burning like electricity.

"Twenty-seven months. When I finally went into labor, I went to the American naval hospital. I knew that despite what the bomb, and germs, and starvation had done to my body, my womb had borne twins. I named them Joy and Tomo. They were special from the beginning. They even looked different. In a way they were not my children, not my husband's children. They belonged to all of the world. They were the children of God and he had merely used my body as a vehicle." Her voice trembled as she spoke. "It was a message from God."

"The American doctors separated them, but in many ways they were one single creature, a gift of light to the world. Tomo could heal, as you doubtless know by now. And Joy has the powers of a goddess."

"Why did you hide them from the world?" Tyler asked.

"I knew that if the world knew of them it would be afraid. And that until their powers fully matured they would not be able to protect themselves. I would not let anything hurt my children."

Mother Oshita gave an oddly savage twist to those last words, and the hair on the back of Cat's neck stiffened.

"I knew," Tomiko Oshita said, "that they would be my gift of healing to an injured world."

She lowered her face. With the contact broken, Cat felt herself breathe again, but each breath suffused her with an almost incandescent warmth. She felt as if her head were filled with whipped cream. This was all just too much.

"All of the sexual teaching," Cat said. "What was all of that?"

She smiled at Cat blissfully. "It was revealed to me during those twenty-seven months, that my children would need a family to protect them. It took them almost thirty years to reach physical maturity. We traveled the world, learning wisdom, and my children had vision. They read thousands of books, talked with teachers everywhere, and compared it with their inner truth, and found the Way. I hope you can understand our little charade."

"Jesus." Tyler breathed. "Usually, when people are lying, or hiding something, its that they're charlatans. You people are lying to keep people from knowing you're demigods."

"I am tired." Mother Oshita's mouth turned up in a sad smile. "If you are fortunate enough to live so long, you too will understand what it is to be so tired. Now my children can answer your questions." She turned to her daughter. "Joy," she said. "Come to me later."

"Yes, Mother."

The smile broadened. "What a good girl."

Then Mother Oshita withdrew into her shell again, and fell silent.

Cat wheeled Tyler from the room. Tomo walked at her side, gaze fixed directly ahead, as if preoccupied with his own thoughts. "What do you think?" he finally asked.

"I think there's more," Cat said. Despite that certainty, Cat felt intoxicated.

"Of course there's more." Joy caught Cat's mood, and grinned infectiously. "We would like you to join us! Be a part of the wonder as it unfolds."

"Why do you hide your powers behind all of the bullshit?" Tyler asked.

"Not for much longer," Joy said. "Will you join us?"

Tyler's mouth was set in an almost expressionless line. "You said that when our questions were answered, we could leave. I'd like to leave. Now."

Joy and Tomo shared a glance. They emerged onto the mansion's porch, and Cat eased Tyler down the wheelchair ramp. Gittes joined them, accompanied by three members of his security force. Cat was puzzled by this. With powers such as the Twins possessed, why in the world would Gittes need backup?

Unless . . . for some reason Joy didn't want to use her powers unnecessarily. That felt right. Cat remembered her earlier impression: The exercise of her powers *cost* her in some way Cat had yet to understand.

"We are very close to the Unveiling," Tomo said. "We need to keep our secret just a little longer. It is not yet time to expose our true nature to the world."

There was silence for a beat, and then Tyler said: "What if we promised not to talk?"

Joy looked pained. "There are six weeks until the Unveiling. We need you to be silent until then. After that, it won't matter."

"Are you saying we can't leave?"

"Only six weeks," Tomo urged. "You are . . . our guests."

Cat fought to formulate a response, but Tyler got there first. "I think that this . . ." he gestured broadly at the dome and cabins the Twins had carved out of the Oregon countryside. ". . . all of this that you've built, everything that you are . . . it's wonderful. I've never seen anything like you. I would love to be a part of this. But I have to know . . . that I can go, before I could make a decision to stay."

Cat looked at him, torn. This wasn't the time to push it. They were present at the unveiling of the greatest miracle in human history, and all Tyler did was quibble. Irritation bubbled inside her.

"Cat," he said. "Please."

She sighed. "All right, Tyler."

Without another word, she took Tyler's wheelchair and pushed it out of the house. Joy watched, eyes narrowed. Tomo's face was sad.

Cat pushed him along. "Tyler," she whispered, "what are you doing?"

"I don't know," he said. "For now, getting out of here."

"But why? Tyler," she said softly, urgently. "They can heal your legs!"

"There's something wrong," he said. "I don't know, but there's just something wrong. I don't care what they are, or what they offer, listen to yourself, Cat. You're just rolling over for them. That's not like you at all, and it scares the shit out of me."

"But your *legs,*" she said urgently.

"To hell with my legs. If these people are as wonderful as they seem, we can come back tomorrow. I. Need. Time. To. Think."

"Listen, if the Hiroshima bomb created some kind of mutation and—"

He stared at her as if she was a child. "Cat, listen to me. Everything that Mother Oshita said? It might be true. It might impress the followers. It's also bullshit. The bombs we dropped on Japan didn't have any serious mutagenic effects. That's comic book stuff. Radiation will kill you, but it doesn't turn your children into the X-Men. And it sure doesn't make them look Black."

"But all of the viruses—"

"Stop it. Just stop it. Listen to me, Cat: *There is no rational explanation for this.* And that scares me to death."

She wanted to argue with him, wanted to just turn around and throw herself at their feet. And yet . . . and yet . . .

Isn't that exactly what they were counting on? Wasn't that the inevitable end result of seeing their power, and feeling their potential, and hearing their story? Christ, who could resist that?

And yet . . . ?

Tyler was right. Something was *wrong.*

She pushed him down the drive toward the gate, and just before they reached it, two male acolytes stepped in front of them.

This was not the time to fight. There was no way to win, and no way to leave the compound—not pushing Tyler in a wheel chair. "I see," she said.

Tomo's hands were folded in front of him. He seemed infinitely saddened by her choice.

"Please believe me," he said simply. "This is not the way I wanted things to be."

"Take them to the yurt," Joy said.

sixty-two

Their destination was a white canvas dome in the center of the compound, with a raised, crosshatched wooden floor and a circular skylight at the apex. A blue-robed acolyte stood guard at the door.

Cat and Tyler were seated in the center of the yurt. Kolla and a slender male acolyte brought them cups.

"Please," Tomo said. "Drink."

Cat stared at the cup. The fluid within was, unmistakably, Twin Punch. "No, thank you."

"It's just as well," Joy said. His sister's tone was strange, strained. "I think that Miss Juvell should have something more . . . immediate. This is frozen. Still powerful, but not the same at all."

Jesus, she didn't like the sound of this. "Not the same as what?" She also didn't like the sound of her own voice. There was something perilously close to a whimper in it, and she let anger boil up to dampen the fear. "Now wait just one *fucking* minute—"

"Prepare her," Joy said.

Before Cat could respond, Kolla had seized her right arm, and her male counterpart the left. They anchored her to the chair. Kolla seemed pained. "You must accept it," she said urgently. "There's no other way. Don't be afraid—it's the greatest gift in the world."

Tomo took his sister's shoulder. "No. We can't do this. We agreed—only if they ask, Joy. Only if they ask. It has always been that way. They must *ask* to become one of ours."

Joy turned to him, her eyes huge and calm. Tomo tried to match his sister's glare, but ultimately withered. When he spoke to Cat again, his voice was almost childlike. "This doesn't have to hurt, Cat. I swear you won't be harmed."

She had no idea what was about to happen, but terror hammered at her gut. "Tomo," she said. "Please. Stop this now."

Tomo turned his face slightly away.

Joy's eyes narrowed to slits, and then closed.

Although Cat felt as if the room had suddenly grown colder, little beads of sweat appeared on Joy's brow. Then she felt a tickling sensation on her own arm, something that swelled into a maddening itch. She looked down swiftly, and watched, horrified and fascinated as her sweater sleeve began to unravel, exposing her bare arm. The itch died, went as numb as ice, and she thanked God for that—because even as she watched, an inch-wide swatch of her skin peeled back, exposing fibrous muscle and veins. A thin rivulet of blood welled up, and drooled down her arm.

"It feels cold," Tyler whispered. She glanced over at him: The same bloody miracle was occurring in the wheelchair beside her.

Joy raised her own arm. The skin peeled away, exposing a darkly crimson webbing of muscle and tendon.

"OhGodohGodohGod" Cat heard herself babble as Joy approached them, forearms raised.

"There is fire in my blood," Joy whispered. "Mother says it was the bomb. Perhaps the germs. I do not know or care. I only know that I burn, that I am not as other women. And that now . . . I give this gift to you."

The blood drooling from Joy's arms suddenly pulsed as if with sudden, dreadful consciousness. It wove itself together into a heaving black pseudo-pod, questing for Cat's arm.

"*No!*" through the blood roaring in Cat's ears, she barely heard Tomo's cry, but he stepped between them, stepped between his sister and the immobilized Cat. "You cannot do this. It is a perversion of everything we have worked for. They must *ask* for the gift. We agreed, long ago. They must *ask.*"

Joy's face was scornful. "And do all the participants at the workshops ask for our blood in their food? In the cookies and punch? Why draw the line so rigidly, Brother? It is a new time. New times demand new actions." She was breathing like a bellows. Her eyes were bright and hot.

Cat watched the blood hanging from Joy's arms, not an inert fluid like human plasma, but like the crawling darkness of a colony of bees or ants. The dark mass glistened with strange colors, reflected lights that were not there. Cat stared at it until she grew dizzy.

"Diluted blood isn't as strong," Tomo said fiercely. "It doesn't go directly into their veins. We don't enter their souls forever. Joy—do not do this thing."

His sister was clearly torn, struggling with dual hungers: the urge to placate her brother, and the need for control over Cat and Tyler.

Finally she nodded. "We can give them the dilute," she said. "Let them drink. We will see deeply into them, and they into us. But if they refuse to drink—" she didn't complete her sentence, but the implication was clear.

The amoeba of black blood crawled back up into Joy's arm, and was gone.

Tomo turned to Cat and Tyler. "It is up to you," he said. "I can do no more."

Cat remembered the thick, metallic salt taste of alien blood, the sensation of liquid fire flooding into her stomach. Her scream of violation was drowned out by her heartbeat, slowing down further and further, until the universe moved at glacial pace. She remembered being lifted from the chair, and strapped to a stretcher, carried from the room.

Tyler's head lolled back as he sagged in his chair. Cat tried to stretch out her arms to him, but couldn't move them. The roar of blood in her ears filled the world.

sixty-three

Jax awoke. His right arm's joints felt as if they had been injected with concrete, his left felt as swollen as a rotten sausage. He was feverish and hungry. From some hidden reserve he extracted a few more ergs of energy, and began to dig again. He moved rock, climbed a few feet forward, working his way inch by inch through the limestone, coughing from the dust. He was forced to stop until the internal tremors passed . . . then worked on until he was exhausted, and rolled over again to sleep.

He was haunted by echoes of the Vietnam dream, and sometimes lay there in the dark thinking over its compartments, remembering. Occasionally, the sudden flood of memories triggered a panic response there in the tunnel. He screamed, and scraped at the rock, pounded until the fit had passed, then curled up again, profoundly grateful that no one was present to witness his loss of control.

Jax dug.

The cycle repeated again and again. He didn't know how long or how many times. The fear didn't matter, the dreams didn't matter, the hunger and exhaustion didn't matter. All that mattered was getting out, getting through, and finding Cat.

Hunger gnawed at Jax like a live rat trapped in his stomach. He decided to continue moving rock for another count of a hundred, and then take a rest. Before he had counted to thirty, however, he cut his hand on something sharp, twisted, but metallically hard.

The front panel of Tyler's van.

Trembling with excitement, Jax continued to dig until he found the front windshield. Its glass was blackened and melted from the heat. He almost sobbed with relief to see a glimmer of light from beyond. He kicked at the few shards of safety glass which still clung to their mounting like old rotted teeth in a corpse's gums. He crawled through the shattered windshield into the burned-out interior, happy beyond words not to find Tyler's shattered, blackened body. The sliding door was virtually welded shut: It took him the better part of an hour to pry it open, and he was sweating and cursing the Volkswagen company by the time it finally creaked free. There was just enough room for him to squeak past.

The back of the van was a melted mess. The engine compartment looked as if someone had set off a thermite bomb in it. The bumper and license plate were one solid chunk of fused metal. He laughed sourly: For what it was worth, the chances of anyone using the van to connect Juvell Investigations to this slaughter were mighty slim.

Cat. He had to get out, to help Cat.

The morning sun hung over the camp, which resembled a battleground. Blasted cars, blackened buildings. How long had he been in the mine? A night? A day and a half?

Twenty meters ahead of him sprawled a pair of charred corpses. Holding his breath, he examined them, rejoicing once again as he determined that both were male, and neither was Tyler. He felt both unutterable relief, and something close to complete and total panic. "Tyler!" He screamed. "Cat! Tyyyler!"

Nothing.

It was early afternoon before he finally caught a ride. Hitching was an iffy proposition: Jax looked like hell and he knew it. The first potential ride was a faded orange Ford pickup. It slowed, but then the driver got a better look at the thick-chested, dusty, bruised scarecrow at the roadside, and sped up again. The same thing happened three more times, then the fifth car stopped.

It was a teenaged boy, straw haired and somewhat gap-toothed, with wide and curious eyes. He was driving a little blue Chevy compact with a wide pale patch of primer on the side. When he swung the door open for Jax, a pungent cloud of burnt hemp wafted free.

Jax was beyond pain at this point, beyond fatigue. He hadn't smoked grass in twenty years, but when he saw the fat bomber sitting in the ash tray, his mouth watered. "Mind if I have a hit?" he asked.

"Be my," the kid said, and handed it over.

Jax dragged deeply, and held it, and held it longer, amazed how little his lungs protested. By the time he let the breath out, his aches were receding, and he began to remember what it felt like to be human.

He closed his eyes, just trying to sort himself out. Aerosmith's "Love in an Elevator" blared from the tinny radio, and the refrain "Going dowwwwwwn . . ." had never seemed so sincere. Curiously, the terrible speakers were sounding better by the second. He took another hit, and then passed the joint back. The kid took a drag, and set it back in the ashtray. "You look like shit, mister."

"Shit's too kind a word." Jax sighed. "What day is it?"

"Saturday, man."

So. He'd lost a day and a half in the mine. The fatigue ebbed enough for hunger to burn fiercely to the surface.

"What the hell happened to you, mister?" The kid asked finally.

"A mountain fell on me," Jax said.

The kid's lips pursed. He took another short hit, and passed the joint back to Jax. "Kewl," he drawled. "Whatta ya do for an encore?"

Left arm tucked into his belt, Jax climbed up the road to Serenity Camp, hearing nothing, no sound at all.

The entire camp, including the mansion, was deserted. He searched the cabins one at a time. Everyone had simply packed and gone home. The offices were stripped bare, every file empty, the Rolodexes gone. They'd even taken the phones.

Exhausted and disheartened, Jax thumped down on a doorstop. For a while he just stared off into the woods, his mind tuned to a dead station. Finally he thought to go back to Serenity House, the cabin he had shared with Cat.

He banged the door open, and stood there. The beds were stripped, their luggage gone. That meant his wallet, his identification, everything . . . vanished.

He felt completely exhausted, a sticky, stinking oil-slicked tide of despair rising to drown him—and then he clamped it down. Jax crawled onto the bed, face burrowing into the mattress, sniffing deeply. There it was. He could smell Cat, could smell the love they had made together. It was there, trapped in the cotton bedding, and somehow that meant that she was real, and alive, and that there was a chance that they would share that ecstasy again. Someday.

Somewhere, Tyler and Cat were alive.

As were the Twins. Somewhere, there lived a pair of human beings with powers beyond anything he had ever remotely imagined. As far as he could see they were not evil—they meant him no harm. If he could find them, he bet that Cat would be all right. In fact, if he waited long enough, she would doubtless try to get in touch with him.

If he waited long enough.

He remembered Joy, shimmering with heat, with some force beyond anything he could understand, and realized that he had other reasons, reasons that he still couldn't completely understand, for pursuing them.

He had to *know*.

sixty-four

Sunday, June 25

Consciousness ebbed and flowed in a slithering tide. Once when Cat floated up toward some realization of who and where she was, she was curled into a ball, laying on her side, silk sheets cool beneath her cheek. Cool air drifted in from an open window, drying sweat at the small of her back.

Her eyes focused slowly, first distinguishing a human figure beside her in the bed, then divining the blur to be Tomo. He lay watching her. His calm black eyes studied her.

Her veins were on fire. She recognized the same flaming need she had felt down in Santa Cruz, multiplied a hundred-fold. She heard herself whimper. And this was the diluted, oral dose? God in heaven. She searched her memory, fought to remember what had happened in the last hours. Calling out to Tomo. This she remembered. Reaching for him, pulling him, demanding him.

She remembered a time when moments burned like embers, a time in which every muscle in her body sang in unison, every cell rejoiced. And Tomo's calm eyes as he loved her.

Tomo was not smiling. His African features were more pronounced than at any other time she had ever seen him. He seemed to live far, far back behind his eyes, his lips. Contemplative. Perhaps . . . sad.

"I am troubled," he said at last. "We are all children born of will and destiny. I know the task which has been set for me. But sometimes I question."

She groaned and pushed herself halfway up. The room spun.

"Things may have gone too far," Tomo said. He barely seemed to be speaking to her. "There is danger."

"D—danger?" she could barely force her lips to move, fought to get those two syllables from her throat.

"I see something in you," he said with quiet wonder. "Not as strong as what the African saw in my mother, but it is there, nonetheless. I couldn't reach you, Cat Juvell."

She focused her eyes. "The African? Who are you talking about?"

Tomo ignored her question. "It pleases me to give you pleasure. But that's not what I meant. Once my followers have taken blood, or let me heal them, their minds and hearts are open to me—I can travel where I will, unbidden. But . . . there is a private place within you. A place sealed away, that no one can touch. You must have learned it very young."

She felt his pain. He wanted to reach her, this young god wanted only to touch her, and she had denied him? It was wrong—

No, a small voice within her said. *Stay safe, Cat. Stay hidden. You have given everything it is right to give. Your soul belongs to you.*

On one level she felt she was betraying him. But on another, she knew she had not only the ability, and the right but the *responsibility* to protect herself.

And in Tomo's eyes, she saw that he understood, and despite the unfathomable pain, approved. "You are good. And strong. Perhaps . . . you could help me cut this Gordian Knot."

"What . . . ?" His words made no sense.

"Once, there was a man named Alexander," he said. "He was wise and strong, and he conquered his world. And when he entered the kingdom of Gordia, he was told that only wisdom, and not mere force of arms, could win the day. That the one intelligent enough to unravel the most complicated knot in the world would win the kingdom. He looked at it, and knew that it could not be unraveled."

She stared at him, not comprehending. She was suddenly caught by an unexpected rush of pain, of a hunger so powerful that she could think of nothing else for several seconds. Then she composed herself and said: "What could I possibly do for you?" She gasped again, and squeezed her eyes shut. An arc of lightning sizzled through the darkness behind her lids, climbing from the base of her spine into her heart. "It hurts," she whispered. And stretched her hand out, silently asking him to join with her again.

As impossible as it seemed, their second time was better than the first.

sixty-five

Monday, June 26

Forty miles north of Santa Cruz, the manager of the Golden Sun Coffee Shop in San Jose locked the door. His name was Kenny Mickelson. A round, good natured man in his middle fifties, he had abandoned a moderately successful career as a commodities broker to follow the path blazed by the Twins. He found his new lifestyle immensely satisfying, especially the occasional dream visits from Joy. He wasn't entirely certain if they were merely dreams, or actually something supernormal, and didn't care. He had certainly never experienced erotic visions of such intensity before his indoctrination, and they felt as real as any corporeal event.

In fact, as he rolled toward his sixtieth birthday, he enjoyed his dream sex life even more than its waking counterpart—in dream, his body was perfect, he was as randy as a teenager, and his recuperative ability would have shamed a bull rabbit.

It seemed that one part of his mind was always thinking about Joy and her visits, in an endless erotic tape loop, even as the rest of him went about the business of life. He might have been thinking about a special menu item for the following day, and the taste of her lips. He might have been thinking about a display he needed to put in the front window, and the texture of soft short hairs on her inner thigh.

But as Mickelson got to his car, what he definitely was *not* thinking about was the arm that wound itself around his neck, and dragged him down to the ground, face jammed against the pavement with a knee against his back. And he very definitely hadn't anticipated the utter panic and sensation of shame as his bladder squirted warm urine down his leg.

He could see nothing. A male voice whispered a single word in his ear. "Where?"

Then whispered a few more things, and began to apply pain.

sixty-six

Tuesday, June 27

Carla Malone had managed the halfway house in San Francisco for the past two years. She had yet to tire of it, and still felt deeply rewarded knowing the dozens of hearts and minds she had rescued from drugs, homelessness and violent marriages.

She locked her office early this Tuesday, and returned to her room on Division Street. She walked up the stairs of her duplex, opened her door, then chained it behind her.

She switched on the lights, and feeling a renewed rush of pleasure at the wall poster: AUGUST 6, THE GREATEST SHOW IN HISTORY. LIVE AT THE PALLADIUM, AND FREE VIA WORLDWIDE SATELLITE CABLE CORP—

Beneath it was a huge, four-color image of Joy and Tomo. Carla touched it, and then touched her fingers to her lips.

The telephone rang. She picked it up at the second ring.

"Hello?" she said.

"Hello? Miss Malone?" the voice on the other end replied. "My name is Jerry Carson. I'm with Worldwide Cable?" Carson had a good, strong voice.

"Yes?"

"Well, we're handling the linkup here in the Bay Area, and we wanted to do a pre-show interview with some of the local followers, and I was wondering if you'd be willing to come to the studio next week?"

"To talk about what?" she asked, interested in spite of herself.

"All that they've done. The missionary work? The scholarships? The health spa in, Washington, I think it is?"

"Oregon," she said. "Bend, Oregon."

He sighed as if someone had begun rubbing his shoulders. For some reason, she imagined that they were large shoulders. She smiled to herself, and found that she was looking forward to meeting this mister Carson.

"Yes. Bend, Oregon," he said. "Could we talk?"

sixty-seven

In total darkness, a whispered voice. Hands pressed against Tyler's chest, followed a moment later by soft lips. He burned with light; it grew within him. Fluid, liquid light, pulsing with blood, sheathed in warm flesh.

"Do you see the light?" Joy asked. She was the most lovely creature who had ever lived, a creature of song and shadow. His heart could see her, even if his eyes could not.

"Oh God yes. I see."

In all the world, there was only Joy. She had delighted in him, summoning him to her chamber once a day since his arrival, laughing at his protestations of weakness, exalting in the passion she stirred in him.

"Do you feel my fibers?" she asked.

As she said it, he felt something inside him, a tickling sensation as if she had reached up through his genitals, crawling one finger-length at a time up to his throat. His hands spasmed. He wanted to say something, but could only contract, his body floating in an ocean of ecstasy.

"Are you mine?" she asked quietly.

"Don't. Please," he pleaded, but his body responded. God, *how* it responded. The same accident which crippled Tyler's legs had made erotic urges an infrequent thing for him, difficult and delicate to satisfy on those few occasions when he made the attempt. But she pulled response after response from him, drained him and built him up again and again, until he thought he would die a happy, hollow man. Then, laughing, she sent him back to his room to consider whether he wanted to stay with the Golden Sun, to belong to her.

"Doesn't it feel good?" she said, and her sex gripped at him like fingers in a fist, nearly wringing another climax from him. But that sensation was followed by a flash of coolness which delayed his release, kept him hovering on the brink, hovering, hovering, waiting for her to be merciful enough to let him tumble over the edge.

"Are you mine . . . ?"

Some part of Tyler fought, even if he had almost forgotten why he bothered. He had to belong to himself. There was danger here. Danger . . .

But, *God* . . .

"Are you mine . . . ?"

"Yes," he said, startled and frightened by his decision. He stretched his arm out, and touched it to Joy's. It felt like touching dry ice. His skin peeled away.

Later, he screamed.

sixty-eight

Thursday, June 29

This being early summer in Southern California, the night air should have been warmer. Should have been, but wasn't. Jax turned his jacket lapel up as a SCRTD bus roared past, leaving a cold, dirty wind in its wake. He leaned his head against the cold metal of the phone shell, listening to the heartbeat throb in his temples, and gave a prayer of thanks when the ringing terminated with an answering *click.*

"Hello?"

"Mrs. Algoni?"

The voice on the other end of the line was cautious. "Yes . . . ? Who is this?"

"Jackson Carpenter," Jax said.

"Jax!" the delight in the single syllable was unmistakable. "Goodness, how are you?"

"Not so good." Every part of him seemed to hurt. *Cat. I'm coming.* "I was wondering—what you said about help . . . ?"

"Anything," she said, her voice cool, but not remote. Comforting. Mothering. "You brought me my child. What can I do?"

"I'm a few blocks away from you now, on Sunset and La Cienega." He shivered. He wanted to lean into that comforting voice, lose himself in it. He wanted to be a child again. "Could I please come up and talk?"

Mrs. Algoni's door was to the left of the elevator, and she waited for him there, dressed in an exquisitely elegant saffron pantsuit, with open-toed golden sandals with one-inch heels. Her lipstick flamed as brightly as the hair which fell gently to her shoulders. She took his hands warmly, carefully, respecting the wounded shoulder. She searched his face, noting the bruised cheek. "You've changed," she said, finally. "Something bad has happened. Please, come in."

He almost hadn't noticed the sounds of piano keys plinking mercilessly through their paces, but as he entered the living room the music suddenly stopped. Felicia Algoni bounded up from the bench of a Steinway that had to cost as much as a Ferrari. Jax registered that the magnificent instrument was rendered in some stunningly expensive black wood before he was bowled over by four feet of pure energy. Despite his fatigue, Jax hugged Felicia to his chest, and allowed her to wreath his neck with her arms, and burn his cheek with a kiss. Felicia proceeded to recount for her mother how Jax had protected her from the bad men, and how he was, probably, the nicest, strongest man in the entire world.

Mrs. Algoni finally managed to return her daughter to a semblance of calm, and sent her next door to play with a friend. She sat Jax down in the parlor. "Drink?" she asked.

"Please, God, yes," he said fervently. "Bourbon. Straight." His gaze continued to roam around the room. Everything that he saw spoke of money. "That Steinway . . . ?"

"It's a Crown Jewel, in Macassar Ebony," she paused at the doorway, and said with satisfaction. "You like it?"

"Are you kidding?"

The entire room was designed in earth tones, with wood slat blinds and oak paneling, leopard velvet chairs and a coffee table rendered in gold-veined hardwood. The dark marble of her fireplace contrasted with a leopard-spot rug with intermittent floral design, an unlikely combination that somehow worked superbly. He seated himself on a densely flowered couch opposite the piano, sinking into the cushions with a groan. They seemed to leech the tension out of him, and he could have fallen asleep in a heartbeat.

Brenda Algoni returned with a generous shot in an octagonal crystal glass, and a cup of coffee in a speckled blue china cup. She sat next to him on the couch, close enough to look into his eyes, not so close as to intrude on his intimate space.

"So. Mr. Carpenter." She gazed at him. The silence coiled in the air like a snake. "You . . . look like someone died." His chest felt leaden. A clock somewhere else in the house tolled the hour, a stifling, thudding sound. "Did someone die?" she asked, already knowing the answer.

"A friend," he said. His eyes stayed on the floor. "I got back into town, and called a friend with the police department. Freddy King. He was dead. Torn to pieces. No suspect. Two people are insane. Woman named Hannah Appelion, a young man named Chris Zimmer. Up in Santa Cruz, six, maybe seven dead. God." His face sank into his hands. "I don't know what's happening anymore. I don't know what's real. Cat's gone."

At those words, Brenda Algoni's back straightened. "What? Gone where?"

"I don't know. She was taken. I think I know where she is, but . . . I can't face these people without more information. I have to know what the hell they are."

Brenda Algoni's hand twitched, and coffee slopped up against the speckled blue rim, almost staining the buttercup pants. Very calmly, she took a sip. "I don't completely understand."

"You don't want to."

There was silence for perhaps a minute, while she came to some private conclusion. "There is something I can do to help?"

He nodded.

"Please. Continue."

He breathed deeply before beginning. "Your maiden name was Swengel. Sheldon Algoni, your ex-husband, married into your family, worked his way close to your father, Harry Swengel, is that right?

She nodded.

"And the only reason you didn't use your father's considerable connections is that you knew his people would kill Sheldon if they found him first, am I still correct?"

She nodded again.

"In maybe 1965 a man named Duke McCandlish did some jail time over a Teamsters retirement fund scandal. Did his time well, never talked, and then . . . escaped. Ran. Disappeared underground."

"And . . . ?"

"It's no secret that Harry Swengel is connected. Vegas, narcotics—"

She pressed her lips together in a tight, noncommittal line, sipping at her coffee.

"—money laundering, and the Teamsters. If McCandlish did his time, kept his mouth shut, maybe somebody got him out. Maybe those same somebodies set him up with a new identity."

"And you think my father could find him."

"I *know* he could."

"Why do you want this man?" she said cautiously.

"In 1956, Jacob 'Duke' McCandlish was a Marine Master Sergeant, and married a Japanese woman named Tomiko Oshita. They were never actually divorced. He just disappeared. I need to talk to him. There are things I need to know."

"Like what?" she said. She placed her coffee cup on the table, and folded her hands carefully in her lap.

"I need to know what in God's name I'm dealing with." He wanted his hands to stop shaking, but they wouldn't. He felt scared, confused. Ashamed. "I'm in trouble," he said miserably. "We're all in trouble. I don't know how much time we have. Please, help me."

He splashed some of his bourbon down his throat, not really tasting it, just savoring the burn. "It's strange, you know? It feels like I've failed at everything that was ever really important to me."

"What do you mean?" she asked.

"The Vasquez case. God, I wanted to nail that bastard so badly. I had battery acid in my stomach every night. Then my marriage to Cat."

"I know you were married," she said, sipping at her coffee, not looking at him.

"Hard to believe, huh? A woman like her and an asshole like me. Yeah. We were married." His eyes squeezed shut. "I can't tell you what it's like to love someone, and not be able to reach her. Not able to touch her. We just . . . just couldn't connect. She tried the best that she could, but we were just ripping each other apart. We were friends before we became lovers, and we managed to get out of it before the friendship was dead, too."

"So you didn't really fail," she said. "And you came back alive from Vietnam."

"I shouldn't have," he said. She waited, but he didn't elaborate.

He looked at her, miserable but grateful. "And now this. I've lost her, Brenda. I don't know where she is. I don't know what's happening to her. I have a feeling that this is the big one. That this time I can't afford to fail. Maybe, just maybe, if I can make things right this time, it'll make up for everything else that happened. That just maybe, all of the other failures happened just to motivate me this time. Maybe. Could something like that be true?"

The huge man's bulk sagged the center of her couch, and Brenda Algoni reached out to him. His hands were like bear paws.

"You wait," she said, and stood up. She walked to her phone and dialed a number.

"Hello? Frankie? This is Brenda. Listen. I need to talk to Daddy. I need a special favor, and I need it fast. It's for the man who saved my daughter. Yes, that's right."

She talked for a while, then listened for a while, then looked up. "He says he needs something back from you, Jax. He says he needs a place."

Jax thought of Cat, laying in shadows, her body arched, presenting its secrets to him. He thought of the mining camp, and the moment of total destruction he had witnessed, and there was no real decision to make.

On the one hand there was a worthless son of a bitch child thief named Sheldon Algoni. On the other, there was Cat and Tyler, and his own salvation, and just possibly the fate of the world.

"St. Croix," Jax said.

sixty-nine

Friday, June 30

Driving out along I-10 east, you pass through endless outlying suburbs of Los Angeles, and then through Pomona and Claremont, out past San Bernardino, and then to the desert communities. Palm Springs rises up, dotted with billboards of smiley-faced seniors promoting the happy retirement life. On the far side of that desert Eden lie smaller communities, desert scrub, and trailer parks baking in the sun.

Jax drove steadily for three hours. The air conditioning in his car wasn't working right. Sweat rolled down his face and dampened his collar and shirt, but he didn't care. Half a Tylenol with codeine kept the left arm's pain down to a dull throb. It was fractured just above the elbow, and that, along with his other bruises, had evoked unpleasant questions from the emergency room physician. Mythical motorcycle accidents cover a multitude of sins.

He turned off the I-10 at a sign that said "Signal Trailer Park," and steered past it, continuing south up into the foothills, toward the high desert. After about twenty minutes the road became a ratty, rutted thing. It continued to worsen, but before he began to seriously doubt the wisdom of proceeding, he spotted an orange mailbox and turned left.

Although marked with no sign, the area left of the mailbox was a trailer park of sorts. At least a dozen old, rust-gnawed shacks were arrayed around in a pattern resembling a Y laying on its side. A few dusty, rut-faced old men and women watched him incuriously as he drove through. They had an air of exhaustion, of having been completely beaten by life, hollowed out to the point where the only wonder remaining in their existence was wondering why they bothered waking up every morning. Apparently, the Palm Springs retirement dream didn't extend into the foothills.

At the stem of the Y stood three small trailers more or less linked together into a single house. Jury-rigged construction had created something almost, but not quite in balance with itself. A hell of a lot of tinkering hours had gone into this, and it showed.

He pulled his car to the side, crunching beer cans as he did. This place was a rat's nest of old paper, broken bottles, and grease-encrusted TV dinner trays. As he got out of the car, an old man exited the middle door.

Duke McCandlish walked stooped over, as if searching for something in the dust at his feet. Time had withered his once powerful arms and slumped his shoulders. His lips were sunken, as if he had swallowed his teeth. His complexion was a mottled gray. He had a high forehead, and thin brown hair. His protruding cheekbones lent him a cadaverous aspect. His eyes were dull but suspicious. He came to within ten feet of Jax, then halted with thumbs thrust into pockets.

"Yep?" he said.

"Chuck Sipes sent me," Jax said simply.

"You'll be that fella Carpenter." McCandlish wasn't asking a question. "Come on in then. They said you want an hour of my time. I've got that. Got more than that, but that's all you can have."

seventy

The inside of the little round of trailers was cooler than Jax would have expected, and shadowed. Former Master Sergeant McCandlish sat in an ancient overstuffed chair, indicating with a nod that his guest should take a seat.

Jax did. McCandlish didn't bother to offer a drink, or anything to eat.

"Sipes said I should talk to you," McCandlish said. "So I will. Chances are you know all about me, so I guess I have to trust you. If Sipes hadn'ta spoke up for you, though, you'da had that door slammed in your face." His eyes narrowed. "Maybe you'd end up out in that gully, boy. You're big enough, but I ain't going back inside. Too old for that shit."

Jax inclined his head shallowly. "I know you took the fall for Sipes almost thirty years ago. You held your tongue—"

"That's what you did in those days," McCandlish said sharply. "You didn't rat. You didn't talk. You didn't make goddamn teevee movie deals. You kept your fucking mouth shut." He pressed his lips together hard, his eyes sharp enough to slice.

Jax nodded. "That's what you do, if you're any kind of man."

It was the right thing to say. Suddenly, despite the difference in age and race, they were buddies. "Fucking A. You want a drink, Sonny?" Of course Jax wanted a drink. Jax was Duke McCandlish's Kinda Guy, and Duke's Kinda Guy never turned down a goddamn drink. Without waiting for an answer, McCandlish got up, grabbed a couple of jelly jars from a cabinet, and opened a bottle, pouring them each a generous shot. One glass had a dancing Snoopy, and the one he poured out to Jax was stenciled with a Ninja Turtle.

Hero on a half-shell, Jax thought, and took a sip. The stuff was cheap, evil, and potent. He would have to be careful. McCandlish knocked back half of his own glass with a single gulp, looked suspiciously at Jax.

Jax quaffed more deeply. It was like drinking flaming kerosene. "Good stuff," he whispered.

McCandlish chortled heartily.

"So . . . they broke you out, right?"

"Slick as snot!" the old man cackled. "Crawled right through a culvert pipe. Damned thing was supposed to be capped, but Sipes's union boys had the contract." He roared with laughter. "Goddamn! What I would have given to see the warden's face." He laughed, and laughed, and coughed, and then settled down. "But that's not what you wanted to talk about, is it?"

Jax shook his head. "No, not hardly."

"What is it then?"

"Tomiko Oshita, and her children."

Jax might have postulated any of a dozen reactions, and still not expected the one he got. McCandlish stared at him with a slack face, then lurched up from the chair, and stumbled to the door. He didn't make it all the way there before both solid and liquid lunches exploded from his mouth, staining the front steps. He bent there, making wet, awful sounds. For almost ten minutes he crouched out there, staring at the mountains. Then finally he came back in, his face dark and tight. The expression was supposed to be fierce, or mean, but Jax knew fear when he saw it.

"Get out of here, Mister," old Duke McCandlish said. "Get out and leave right now."

"Sipes said—"

"I DON'T GIVE A DAMN WHAT SIPES SAID!" he yelled. "Ain't thought about them for maybe ten years, and if I never have to think about them again, it'll be the happiest thing I can reckon."

Jax thought of reminding McCandlish what he owed Sipes. He considered of the threat of exposure. He thought about twisting the old man's arm off. He actually liked that last notion, but chose another course of action. "All right," Jax said. "But whether or not you help me, I'm going to find them. They've got my woman—" he almost choked to hear himself say that, and didn't really know why in the world he had.

Except, God help him, it was the truth.

"—and my best friend. I know they're not normal. Maybe I'm going to die going up against them. But I have to know. You're the only person who might know what I need to know. You're the only one. Please," he said. "One vet to another."

McCandlish squinted at him. "You were a leatherneck?"

"Army. Went in at seventeen."

"Honorable discharge?"

"Purple Heart." Jax held his breath.

McCandlish poured another slug of whiskey into the Snoopy glass, then sank into the shadows surrounding his chair, a very old and frightened man. The wet rasp of his breathing made the trailer sound like a tubercular ward. *"Semper Fi,"* he said finally. "All right. Not for Sipes. Hell—I don't owe him anything. Yeah, they take care of me, but then they got their pound of flesh, dammit. I got out of the Corps in '53, came home, beautiful wife—" He laughed bitterly. "Two sweet little kids. All I wanted to do was pick up the pieces of my life, get back into it."

"What went wrong?" Jax asked.

seventy-one

Master Sergeant Duke McCandlish met Tomiko Oshita in Osaka, in 1952. She worked in a bath house catering to American servicemen rotating in from Korea, and like many of the girls, she developed regular customers.

Duke McCandlish had never met a woman like Tomiko. She was cultured, refined. Older than the other girls, but still beautiful and reserved, and a Japanese Mixmaster in bed.

"But . . . she wouldn't do it normal, you know? She'd do anything else, and I do mean anything. But we never really did it the way most people do. Hands, mouth, butt—anything else you can think of, and some you haven't. . . ." and he went on to describe a series of acrobatic maneuvers which made Jax wince.

She had two children, mixed blood twins named Joy and Tomo. Joy was always a bit of a distant child, but there was just something about little Tomo that you had to like, and a bond formed between them.

Duke McCandlish had a little money in his pocket, and in '52 American dollars went a long way. He set Tomiko up with a house on the outskirts of Osaka, and they lived together as man and wife while he was stationed there.

Eventually, the Korean War ground to its murky conclusion. When

Master Sergeant McCandlish returned to America, he took his war bride and her twin children with him.

He knew some of her past. He knew that she had prostituted herself to eat, but this was not an uncommon thing for women in war-torn countries. And if there was a reserve within her, it was a place locked far inside her, and all she ever showed him was sweetness and utter respect—that is, when she was not indulging his every, wildest, most outrageous or perverse sexual fantasy.

Master Sergeant McCandlish liked a curious mixture of aggression and submission, a woman who would do exactly as told upon a moment's notice, with no holds barred. Tomiko Oshita did that, reveled in it, recruited other women to provide the things her own damaged body ("she was kind of tore up down there") couldn't provide, and taught him things that he didn't know and never could have dreamed of. He envisioned a life of endless sexual variation once they returned to the United States.

It wasn't until after the first year back in the States that something went very wrong with his dream.

First, the former Tomiko Oshita, now Tomiko McCandlish, didn't like sex at all. She had used it, cultivated it, sharpened it on the streets and in the brothels of Osaka the way a samurai polishes his sword. She had then bribed her way into the most exclusive club she could afford, and waited to snare an American husband. She had zeroed in on Sergeant McCandlish, and had, as pimps say in the United States—Turned Him Out.

Second, there was something wrong with the Twins.

"Oh, not with their health," Duke McCandlish said. "In fact, they never really got sick. That was odd enough—not even childhood stuff. No measles. Mumps. Chickenpox. Nothing. But it was more than that. They didn't grow, you know? They stayed small, like they were growing at about half the rate ordinary kids did. Another thing. I couldn't ever nail her on it, but I had the feeling that she didn't . . . well, that she didn't really love them. It was the way she looked at them some time, when they weren't looking back. And the way she talked about some other children that she had with her first husband. Kids had died in the war. Almost had the feeling she blamed these two for what had happened." He took a long pull on his drink.

He swore that he loved Tomo more and more all the time. The little boy was bright, and loving. Cheerful—but Joy was his dark doppelgänger, a little black hole of emotional violence and trouble.

And she seemed to have an unusual connection with her mother. Joy adored her mother like nothing he had ever seen, which seemed particularly strange when combined with his suspicion that Mother Dearest didn't care for Joy at all. Although Tomo was never pushed completely to the outside, he noticed that the boy had far more urge to bond to the father, indeed, to try to make outside friends. Meanwhile, Mom and daughter spent more and more time together, talking—sharing. But sharing what? He didn't know.

Tomo was jealous of Joy. At times, McCandlish thought that he wanted to *be* Joy. "I used to catch him dressed up like his sister," he said. "He was a cute little thing." The old man's eyes were red and watery. "Looked better as a girl maybe than as a boy, you know?"

McCandlish shifted his eyes away from Jax as he said that, and Jax's stomach twisted.

Meanwhile, the sexual games with Tomiko continued, only now with a darker edge to them.

"A man can get hooked," McCandlish said. "I mean, she found my buttons, you know? And when I say she'd do anything, I mean *anything.* You can get taken out to a place where you don't belong to yourself no more. She'd go down on me and keep it going for hours, until I couldn't remember my name, you know? One hand on my balls and her finger up my ass and that tongue of hers . . . Jesus."

His forehead glistened with a cold sweat, as if it aroused him just to speak of it. Jax fought to keep his mind from forming an image, and barely succeeded. "I don't know, man. I ain't never experienced nothing like it before, or since.

"And after I dumped my load, she'd go over to the toilet and spit it out. Loud, gagging, you know? Make sure I *heard* her do it. Then she'd look at me with this big smile, and go and she'd whisper to that little girl of hers, you know?"

"Go? Go where? Outside or something?"

McCandlish watched Jax carefully, as if deciding how much to say. Drink had emboldened him, or increased their rapport to the point that his barriers were dropping. "Usually go over to the corner of the room. Tomiko made her daughter *watch.*"

Jax had never in his life used more self-control than he did at that instant, struggling to keep his face from revealing his utter disgust. He had a hard time imagining the twisted world view which had sustained this monster, but it was imperative that McCandlish continue to think that Jax shared it.

McCandlish didn't know how old the kids were when he had married Tomiko, but after they came to America, they began to grow. It was freaky—they didn't change at all, and then they exploded, and then stopped again, right about at what looked like maybe thirteen. They were only as big as their mother. And they went everywhere together. Couldn't pry those kids apart.

And as the girl began to mature, and their mother got more distant, Duke McCandlish began to look at the daughter, Joy.

McCandlish's lips twisted challengingly, perhaps expecting a reaction. Jax carefully controlled his revulsion, maintaining a neutral expression. "I mean, hell—she wasn't really my daughter, you know? And it isn't as if I came on to her. Her mother was teaching her, you understand? *Training* her. They used me. And that poor little boy. I mean, he knew what was going on, but he couldn't stop it. Tomo never could stop it. But he could touch you, take your hand, and know everything that was going on inside you, and he could heal. . . ."

The old man took another drink from the Snoopy glass, and continued. "You wouldn't believe the things I seen," he said. "I mean, I had this little dog. We got him from the pound. MacArthur, I called him, yeah, fluffy, even though he looked more like a drowned rat. Didn't matter none to me. I loved that dog. And Mac got hit by a car. Smashed his back side all to pieces. I thought for sure we'd have to put him down. He was suffering. I still remembering him crying. Well, I stayed up as late as I could with Mac, and Tomo asked if he could watch him while I slept. I said, okay, figured that the kid could say goodbye to the dog, we'd put it to sleep the next day. I must have cried like a baby that night. I don't know. But when I woke up the next day, Mac was all right. I mean, the leg was healed. No problem. Tomo told me that he loved me, but his Momma was hopping mad at him."

The corners of McCandlish's mouth curled up a bit at the memory, and Jax tried to imagine this monster. Humping his war bride's daughter, crying over his little dog's injuries. Somehow, he just couldn't quite get his mind around the vision.

McCandlish continued, growing drunker and more talkative as he did, as though the sluice gate had opened on his memory.

When the Twins were about fourteen the changes really began to accelerate. Tomo became increasingly withdrawn, even as Joy became more aggressive in every way, especially sexually. McCandlish still remembered the first night that the girl came to his bed. He was drunk, and maybe he could have told himself that he didn't know, didn't realize. He should have been too drunk for anything to have happened, but it did. Tomiko Oshita had always had a knack, an odd kind of body knowledge, a wisdom of the flesh, combined with an utter ruthlessness concerning its application. Joy Oshita had . . . something else.

It was as if she owned him, as if his penis and testicles were just tools she used to open him up. And once opened, she could reach inside and *twist*.

"That's how it started," he whispered. "But that ain't where it ended."

If it had been just that night, he might have pretended that it didn't happen. If it had just been Joy, or Tomiko, he might have gotten drunk enough to find them interchangeable. But they began coming to his bed together. And Tomiko . . . *taught* her daughter everything she knew.

"In heaven, earth, or the Devil's own hell, there never was anything like that girl," McCandlish whispered. A thin rivulet of spittle ran down his stubbled chin, and he wiped it away with one trembling hand. "I don't know. I tried to stop. God dammit, I did. I just couldn't. The hold that Tomiko had over me was *nothing* compared to what that girl did. And she laughed the whole time."

"And what about the brother?"

McCandlish blinked twice, slowly, like a basilisk. He took another drink, and stared at Jax. The corners of his mouth twitched up, once, and his eyes watered. Then his gaze shifted away. "He just slept in his room. Every night he must have heard what was going on. And in the mornings, he'd look up at me, and lean his head against me, and I really felt that he forgave me. He would try to get his sister to stay away from me, but it didn't work. And then their mother started finding girls for him, bringing them to the house. . . ."

His gaze went back to Jax, then shifted away again. And he took another drink. "Listen," McCandlish said. "It was out of control. All that there was in the whole world was my job, and coming home to those women so they could practice on me. And Tomiko started collecting books. Sick books, man, teaching 'em . . . teaching her daughter."

Jax stared at him, and *knew*.

It didn't stop with Joy, did it, you bastard? Just how drunk did Mommy have to get you?

The first time.

The air in the camper was suddenly like breathing through damp warm sickroom linens. "You said that Tomo could heal," Jax said, controlling himself. "Did you ever get the feeling that Joy had anything special about her?"

"You mean beside the way she got to me? You ain't been listening, mister—" he leaned forward, and his breath was like the stench from an open grave. "It wasn't nothing like anything you've ever known. Not before then, and I'd had a lot. After . . ." his voice drifted. "After, I guess I ain't had a whole lot of appetite for that stuff no more. I think they burned it out."

Jax interrupted him. "Was there anything . . . more?"

McCandlish emptied his Snoopy glass. "Yeah, there was."

"Like what?"

He looked down and shaded his eyes. "My sister lived on the other side of town, you know? She had a son named Sean. They were all buddies. Good friends. Best friends. 'Cousins Forever,' you know, that kind of stuff. They had a club. Some kind of club, blood brothers, all of that stuff."

"Blood brothers?" Jax said weakly.

"Sure. Poked their thumbs, you know. Anyway, that was right around the time that everything was heating up. I took my sister out for dinner, it was her birthday—and Sean stayed home. With the kids. Tomiko waving good-bye from the porch, and Joy with her arm around Sean. Tomo was so damned quiet. Anyway, we get back around eleven that night, and Sean can't wait to leave. He won't hardly say goodbye. His mother calls later, asks if anything was wrong—says Sean is upset, won't talk about it.

"Week goes by. Joy wants to see her favorite cousin, but he won't come over. She calls him, writes him. He won't come, and my sister is calling and saying something happened. Her son is terrified, and guilty, and that my wife is sick, and she's going to get Sean to tell her just exactly happened that night.

"And I talk to Tomiko, and she won't say anything, and I talk to Joy, and all she'll say is: 'He's mine. He's got my blood, and he's never going to say a thing.'

"Something went wrong at my sister's house that night," McCandlish said. "Fire. Something. Sean never had a chance. He burned right up in his bed, burned up and really didn't even set anything else in the room on fire. Killed him dead.

"I knew," the old man said. "He'd shared her blood. So she could reach out into him, even across town. He was hers. I'd only shared her fluids— no blood, but it was still so strong I couldn't stop. No matter how I tried."

Jax couldn't help but ask: "So how did you stop?"

"Easy," he said. This time, Duke McCandlish's grin didn't seem wholly sane. "I volunteered to go to prison."

seventy-two

Jax pulled his Bronco into the parking lot of the Motel Six just east of Palm Springs. A glance at his watch told him it was about six minutes to midnight. He felt utterly exhausted, and not just by the death, the disappointment, and the paralyzing lack of sleep. After three hours of conversation with Duke McCandlish, Jax felt as if he had been urinated upon by an old, diseased bear. All he wanted was to take a shower, and keep on taking it until dawn broke, or he fell asleep standing up, whichever came first.

Room 307 was on the third level, down at the end and around the corner, across from the courtyard satellite dish. Somewhere on the ground floor, a baby cried. The sound, ordinarily so irritating, now seemed blessedly normal. Embraceably average. He longed for the unremarkable . . . although when he peered up at the starlit sky overhead, he had the terrible feeling that nothing would ever be normal again, for anyone.

He collapsed onto the bed, and stared up at the ceiling. McCandlish was a small, stupid, corrupt, and evil man. *Oh, come on, Jax, don't mince words. Whatta you really think?*

He closed his eyes and put together what he knew.

McCandlish had found Tomiko Oshita. No . . . it was just the opposite. Tomiko Oshita had found him. But why? Why had she deliberately searched for a pervert like McCandlish? Someone to debase her own children? He couldn't even come close to an insight, but knew that the answer was out there, somewhere. For some reason, Tomiko Oshita had wanted to rip away the protective armor of social constraint. What was that insight he had received into the nature of premature sexuality? Something about flower petals torn away. For some reason, Tomiko Oshita had wanted to un-shield the nuclear core of her children's sexuality. To turn them into . . . what?

Jax just couldn't go further than that. He was beyond tired, and into the legions of the walking dead. He needed sleep. He promised himself that he would get up and take a shower. Take a shower.

Just close his eyes for a minute. . . .

Blackness.

In that void, Jax roamed in dream. Through one room in a vast and empty mansion, one war-torn world after another. Jax roamed freely through a world of pain and struggle, and occasional love. An often dark place, but comfortable because it was his. He knew it. He understood it.

Then . . . then something shifted, as if he had crossed a meridian, fallen across an invisible dividing line. The dreamscape looked the same but felt different, the colors somehow more intense and electric. He was suddenly in a different place. It felt foreign, and he suddenly realized what the alienness represented.

He had stumbled across the edge between his own dream, and some-one else's. This place was filled with strange, childlike images: Flaming hobby horses, twisted tree houses, a Daliesque landscape, with ropes, or something like ropes . . . stretching out across the ground in all directions. He bent, and touched one of the strands.

No. Not rope. A spider web. He noted that his feet didn't stick to the web, and wondered what to make of that. Did that mean that this was *his* web? Or that he was immune to its effects?

Turning to peer back over his shoulder, he saw something odd. It seemed that there were a series of blurs behind him, as if the web had ex-truded multiple Jaxes. He saw himself laying down, entering the motel room. Checking in at the main office. Bumping his car over the concrete lip of the driveway. Driving down from the trailer camp. And then meet-ing with McCandlish. . . .

Jax had the oddest sensation . . . as if he weren't the only one watch-ing. The succession of Jaxes went on about their business back into the dis-tant past, stretched out upon and across that infinite dreamscape. But he sensed that this was the moment most interesting to the *other* in his dream. He could sense it. He came closer, where he could see more easily. There was something which had been hidden only moments before. Emerging from the shifting patterns was an arachnid shape. He could see it clearly now. It was *huge,* and it was looking down on his memories as if they were stretched on the web like pearls of dew. Each pearl contained another moment, another memory. And the spider thing perched above and tapped into one of them. And as it sucked at one, the entire scape seemed to change. It was zeroing in. Yes. that was the only word that he could accept, the only word that seemed to make sense.

On . . . McCandlish. Again Jax found himself in the trailer park. It was cold and empty now, and he looked down at his feet, and he saw that he was following the spider. It was unaware of him. It had business ahead. Jackson Carpenter was of no moment to this thing. It had other . . .

Other . . .

Prey

Yes. That was the word. Other Prey.

Jax floated along, a ghost without a grave. Again he saw the courtyard, awash in beer cans. But as he did he had the uncanny feeling that he wasn't in his own dream any more.

No.

The feeling was (and here, his sense of thoughts, or awareness of thinking wasn't quite along its normal track) that he had strayed from his own dream world. That this thing, this thing which walked before him had used him, used him to hop from dream to dream to dream, looking for something . . . or someone.

He had a sense of this thing. He knew that it had been weaving its web for a very long time, spinning out its threads . . . looking for something. And it attached its threads, and each of the people it co-opted ventured out into the world, unwittingly assisting in its quest. And did this thing, whatever it was, gain access to their dreams, and the dreams of those they met, and so on and so on? How far did it go? He wasn't certain. All he knew was that as it had crept into *his* night visions, he now needed stealth to follow it into yet another dreamscape.

What was to happen next was not for his eyes. He felt it reaching back for him, like a little electrical buzz crawling back across the web, searching.

Jax became still. Very very still. Pulled in within himself, as he had learned to a long time ago, in another world. In the ground. In Vietnam. He was more than dead. He had never been born. He was a presence, a spirit never encased in flesh. And the crawling spark of awareness floated right past him, through him, over him, and was gone.

I'm not here, Jax said. *I'm not here at all.*

The spider thing seemed satisfied that it was not observed, that the night's business was as personal as it could possibly have wished. Private.

Some business was best done in the dark.

Like a ghost, he crept into the trailer, following the Hunter. Across McCandlish's beer-can-strewn living room. Through the kitchenette. Through a room whose walls and furniture seemed composed of nothing but old magazines, stacked in endless profusion. And finally, ultimately, into the bedroom.

Deep in dream, Jax held his breath. McCandlish was in bed, asleep, in the center of another web. The web's pearled nodes stretched out in all directions, each of them another precious moment in his internal world.

The entire trailer was twisted, darkened, but at the same time glittered as if coated with gold paper. The floors weren't quite real—his feet threatened to fall through them if he stepped too hard. This was McCandlish's world of fantasy. This was a world filled with his own self-justification, in which he was a great man of some kind, in which the myriad faceless enemies, the eternal "They," had plotted and failed to bring him down.

McCandlish Endures, the entire thing might have been titled.

The Hunter seemed uninterested in the tissue of dreams currently spun out of McCandlish's head. It picked among the dreams . . . so many of them, little gemstones scattered among the squalor. It sipped at one, and then moved with arachnid grace to the next, and sipped there for a while, tasting. Searching. And then it found one, and supped deeply. It grew black-red. Swollen. Immense. Enraged. And then in a single leap it was upon the sleeping man.

Former Master Sergeant McCandlish partially awakened from a dream that slipped away from him like a wet, dark, oily tide. "Wha—? Who's there?" he called that out hoarsely, not that he expected or wanted an answer, but because it was almost a litany to him at this point in his life. There was always someone there. Always someone watching. He knew that they would find him one day, he just didn't know when. Or who. Or even precisely who "they" were.

Coughing, he pulled himself to a seated position. He woke up so slowly these days, slipping back and forth from wake to dream, sleep-walking almost, as if the liquor guzzled the night before created an hour's window when reality and fantasy mingled. Sometimes he had to take a cold shower before he was at all certain where he was. He could fall asleep standing in front of his refrigerator, or sitting on the toilet. His head just didn't work right any more.

A huge amorphous mass of phlegm seemed to cling to the top of his throat. He tried to hawk it up, to cough it out, but failed. Blankly, he stared at the wall, watched it crawl with rainbows. He had more and more difficulty pulling himself back from his dreams. Duke McCandlish knew what death was, knew why so many people died in their sleep. They got lost in their dreams, and couldn't find their way back out again.

The night outside was warm and dry and quiet, the only noise the sound of McCandlish himself coughing out his lungs. He stared out, think-ing. Somehow, his life had gotten away from him. He wasn't certain how it had happened. A few steps at a time, he supposed. Just a few steps at a time. He really didn't need that Carpenter nigger coming around, talking, throwing his weight around. Hell, just because he knew a few people. Duke McCandlish was somebody, dammit. Duke McCandlish had stood up and done the deed, and he'd beaten the system.

But . . . had Carpenter really come? Or was that just another part of some damn fantasy? He rubbed a fist hard against his temple. This wasn't working. He just couldn't keep living like this. It wasn't worth it.

He didn't need to remember those kids. Hell, he hadn't wanted to do things to those kids, but Tomiko . . . she had a way about her, a way of get-ting what she wanted, and well, hell, he'd been drinking pretty bad. Be-sides, it was a way of giving love, wasn't it? He was only doing it for their own good. Anyone should be able to understand that.

The desert brush outside his door was just scrub, weeds, a dusty low-mountain-range assortment of miserable plants and bushes. This probably wasn't a dream. The breeze against his face felt real, and he leaned against the door jamb, let his mind wander, felt sleep steal up on him again. God, just a few more winks. Yeah, that felt great. Maybe life would be better somewhere else, someplace warm but not so damned dry. He would like to sell out, if he could find a buyer. Sell out . . . yeah, that was the ticket.

To the northwest, Palm Springs glowed in the night. He couldn't make out sounds now, but sometimes, if the wind was just right, he could hear things. Sounds like laughter, and people enjoying their lives. He remembered that. Remembered the way his life had been, before Tomiko Oshita and the brats. Duke shivered, and wasn't sure why: The air was warm.

Jesus. He had certainly never expected to talk about *them* again. The need for a drink suddenly struck him, so strong it was like an inner command. (And here he hoped he was dreaming, because in dreams, his refrigerator tended to stock itself with a much better quality and quantity of booze than he could afford in real life.)

It was cool, but the air seemed to be rippling, as if seen through a curtain of blistering air. The wind was still, but the dust at his feet began to roil. McCandlish watched, fascinated. What was he to make of this? He couldn't take his eyes off it. The wind seemed to be deliberately collecting motes of dust, swirling them into something that resembled dust-bunnies. He shrugged. It was a dream, then. Or too much drinking. Not enough sleep. Or vice versa.

McCandlish shambled back into his house, and thought about going back to bed, but couldn't quite bring himself to do it. This was all too strange. Ordinarily his dreams were quite mundane, but of late he had experienced very fluid, colorful visions, almost as if he had popped a vein in his head or something. They just didn't seem to be his ordinary fantasies at all. And there were other things about them that also created problems: They recalled memories that he didn't care to deal with. He had drunk much too much in the old days. Not that he didn't enjoy it, but there had been something about Tomiko that sent him into the bottle, and he had barely managed to get back out with his hide intact. He had memories of those times. Memories of tears, and small, lithe bodies bent before him, and memories of showing them things and doing things with them that . . .

His hands were shaking when he poured another glass. Hell. What in the world was he afraid of? Or ashamed of? There wasn't anything right or wrong in the world. Not really. Just actions that might feel good, or those that didn't. And he had only shared good feelings with the two brats, hadn't he? Raising the glass to his lips, Duke watched the clear, strong fluid tremble.

He must still be half asleep. Had to be, because the wind from outside was stirring the dust within his house. Churning it around, and around. He watched, fascinated. It wasn't a dust bunny. It was more like . . . well, a dust *spider*. He could make out the thickness of its body, and the legs. He steadied his grip on the glass. This was getting just too bizarre. This was the DTs. Or a dream, it had to be a dream, because the dust-spider was almost completely formed now, at least the outer shell was. But it wasn't composed merely of dust. He watched as it absorbed matter from a beer can . . . the can flattened and squashed and stretched until it was elongated and melded into the body of the spider, and it looked at him, and it had a face, and the face wasn't a spider's. He had seen that face before. He knew that he recognized it. It seemed absurd to see a human face where a spider's jaws should be. Absurd that it should be smiling at him, almost, damn near smiling *through* him, and absurd that the sight should fix him to the chair as it did. Crazy.

He wasn't afraid, not quite, because he knew he was asleep. Not when it scrabbled across the floor, and every tentative touch of its leg upon the floor had that absurdly delicate tarantula-like grace. It minced toward him, almost curtsying with each step.

Oh, Duke. You've finally gone over the edge now. You've finally shot the bolt. It's the rubber room for you. He had suffered DTs before, but never anything like this. Never anything so bizarre. . . .

Things had crawled beneath his skin before. Snakes and worms, and Duke wasn't surprised when the first physical sensation melded with the visual. It was all quite insane.

He closed his eyes, resting them, and just enjoyed the sensation of the spider's weight as it crawled up his leg. It seemed to be crooning to him, murmuring. What was it crooning? It seemed to be a lullaby.

Hush little baby, don't say a word—

It was up to his knee now. The pressure of its leg, its burr-footed step against the knobs of his knees scratched a little, and he was surprised at that. But that was all part of it too, he supposed. It was surprising enough that he was actually aware he was suffering from DTs. Most of the time you didn't understand it. Most of the time, you thought that the things which deviled you were real. That was what made it so terrible. If you just remembered that that wasn't true, that the thing that was calling to you, or crawling on you, or wriggling across the ceiling was nothing but a figment of your imagination, you were safe.

—daddy's gonna buy you a mockingbird—

He was safe.

The weight crawled forward, until it was crawling past his thighs, and now perched above his threadbare Fruit of the Looms. He opened his eyes. The eyes of the thing were still upon him, still watching him, still . . . grinning. It's lips no longer seemed human lips, and were becoming black, and shiny, and chitinous. Beaked. Hooked. Sharp looking. Edges like broken bottle glass.

—if that mockingbird don't sing—

Something dripped from them, and when it touched his skin, it burned. He whimpered, blinking hard. The spider thing seemed to settle itself in, like a fat man settling down to a sumptuous meal.

(And it was fat. Lord, he hadn't seen before now just how *fat* it was, the bulbous rear abdominal section swollen and glistening, even in the dim light. No. That wasn't right. It was glistening even where there was no light at all. So this had to be a dream, didn't it? Didn't it.. ?)

—Daddy's gonna buy you a diamond ring—

Except that for every moment that passed, he woke up more and more. He was awake. He *had* to be awake. It felt exactly as if he was awake, except that what he saw, the reality in front of him, and atop him, was something that just couldn't be. Couldn't. But as it settled its weight in

(Lord, its body glistened so)

—if that diamond ring don't shine—

One of its legs touched his robe, and he watched the cloth flow *around* the leg, absorbed *into* the leg, and the body of the thing grew heavier and elongated, he watched the robe unravel, like a silkworm spinning a cocoon in reverse. It was impossible, but there it was.

The thing smiled at him one more

(last)

time, and the lips that were not lips pulled back to expose a mouthful of daggers, and then they descended with sudden, savage speed, slicing through the Fruit of the Looms, slicing through withered thighs, seeking tender, yielding flesh. And finding it.

—Daddy's gonna buy you a Valentine.
Hush.

seventy-three

Jax awoke from his dream, face sopping with perspiration. No nightmare had ever been quite like *that* one. It wasn't just the imagery. It was the sensation, the certainty that he wasn't *having* a nightmare so much as witnessing someone else's. He swung himself over the side of the bed, and planted his feet firmly on the ground. According to the clock on the bed-side table, it was almost five-thirty. So he had gotten maybe four hours of sleep.

He performed a series of pushups and situps, stressing himself until the sweat gushed from his body in streams, and his arms grew leaden. Then he crawled back into bed, and tried to sleep some more. When he closed his eyes, images of Cat, and Tyler, and

(McCandlish. Dead, his lap a pool of slowly congealing—)

"Jesus." Jax's eyes flew open. Where had *that* image come from? Like a moment from the nightmare clawing its way into his conscious, waking state. But maybe not. Maybe he had just drifted off for a moment, and begun to dream again. He closed his eyes. Blackness. Comforting, blessed nothingness.

His heart rumbled in his chest. He had the information he needed. Maybe he should just check out and get going—there'd be no more sleep for him tonight.

Jax packed his few belongings, threw them into his overnight case, and left without showering. He should have, he knew, but couldn't bring him-self to strip off his clothing in this room. *Naked in a cage of glass, eyes closed against the film of soap, gushing water drowning out the stealthy tread of ap-proaching feet—*

God. What was happening to him?

He left the room, threw his key down the little orange night chute, and climbed into his Bronco. The roar of the engine turning over in the de-serted parking lot was a comforting one. Something was working in this world. The rest of the motel was still asleep. Somewhere to the south, the I-10 freeway was already purring.

He pulled out of the parking lot, turned left, and took the freeway off ramp, heading west toward Los Angeles. His mind was filled with thoughts of plane schedules, and weapons. Could he talk with Oregon law enforcement officers? And tell them what? That he had seen a woman who could make fire in the air? That would merely establish his presence at a multiple murder site. Joy and Tomo probably had alibis, and if they didn't . . . if they were confronted. . . .

He shivered, and thought of burned blood.

And of McCandlish. Why did he keep thinking about that man? And that dream. It was already slipping away. Something about a spider—

(how did Freddy die?)

And there was something else about McCandlish. . . .

He was two miles further down the road before it occurred to him. Brown hair, high forehead, prominent cheekbones. He looked like Freddy. Older, but Freddy nonetheless. Curious.

It took another mile before he realized that if McCandlish looked like Freddy, then he also looked like the transients, the dead homeless men from Joy and Tomo's early years.

Without completely realizing he had made a decision. Jax took the Bob Hope Drive exit, turned left, and reentered the freeway going east again.

His hands were tight on the wheel, his eyes fixed on the road ahead

If the dead transients all looked like McCandlish, and McCandlish looked like Freddy, then it might be reasonable to think that the transients died because they reminded someone of McCandlish. Someone with un-believable power. Someone who enjoyed killing.

Jax's hands were slippery. He felt a sour taste growing in his mouth. *How do they reach you? Oh, they talk to us in our dreams. They can find us through our dreams. They can see what we see. . . .*

Dear God.

Once they make you theirs . . .

Take, drink, this is my blood—

It's not my nightmare. It's like I'm peeking into someone else's. . . .

He remembered the offramp, and took it, and drove up toward the hills. He didn't get more than another mile before he saw the blinking lights up by the trailer camp. He turned off his engine, listening to the sounds drifting across the high desert morning air, and watched the little people scurrying around like ants whose hill has been disturbed by the care-less footsteps of a giant. . . .

Or by the deliberate, malicious act of a godlike child.

Someone who enjoyed killing. If not in their waking hours, then in their dreams.

Joy. Or Tomo. Or Joy and Tomo, because they were really one creature, weren't they? One single creature twisted by the mind of a woman named Tomiko Oshita. But . . . why?

And dear God . . . what in the world could he do about it?

seventy-four

Cat rose slightly from the saddle, urging her horse to greater speed, working hard to keep her lead. Although the ground ahead was fairly even, it had been years since she had sat a horse, and if the old skills returned quickly, still they required every erg of her concentration.

There was always the chance of an overhanging branch, or a stretch of uneven ground. It wouldn't take more than that to make the magnificent animal beneath her throw her off. Right now, that was the last thing in the world she wanted.

She took a chance, and glanced behind her, the wind throwing her yellow hair into her eyes. Tomo was only a few lengths behind her. Tomo loved horses, loved riding, and if he had a touch more ruthlessness about him, or a greater streak of competitiveness, he could probably have outridden her. But by the time that he realized Cat was out for blood, she had built up a substantial lead, and was unlikely to close the gap in the quarter-mile remaining.

A baton-bearing acolyte had been with Cat most of her waking hours. She was never alone with Tyler—undoubtedly the twins were concerned that the two of them might flee. This morning, Tomo had come to her personally, walking her out to the enormous blue barn at the east end of the encampment. Walking, they had gone down a steep, graveled grade past a series of fenced pens and log cabins. "We run retreats here during the summer," he said. "Children come from around the world, and we give them a week in the country. Martial arts, games, swimming, horseback riding . . ."

"And indoctrination?"

He smiled, and shook his head. "No, not really. Most of the staff moves out, except for Mother's support—she lives year round in the main house. The camp is run by one of our cover groups, through Manfred's chain of dojos. It's just a way of giving back. Once in a while I might show up, or Joy might show up . . . but the kids have no idea who we are, and we can just play with them."

He grinned at her in a surprisingly boyish way. Cat looked behind them. The acolytes were still there, just a few respectful paces behind. "So you do it to give some poor underprivileged inner-city kids a chance to breathe clean air?

He laughed again. "I'm not sure it's that altruistic. The truth is that we were under so much pressure when we were kids that we didn't really get much of a childhood."

"What kind of pressure?" Cat asked.

Instead of answering, he paused and his eyes defocused slightly, as if his mind had wandered down a darkened corridor. He continued. "I think that being a camp counselor for a week is a way of tapping back into that. Getting back some of what I was forced to give up along the way."

"Does it work?"

Tomo paused. He wore a plaid cotton shirt, sleeves rolled to reveal the slender strength of his arms. "It took a while, that first camp," he said, and entered the barn. It was a place of canted shadows. The ground was covered with straw. There were six stalls on each side, and only three were empty. He approached a beautiful Appaloosa, who nuzzled his right hand, seeking sugar. The sought-after lump was concealed in his left.

"We were up late every night. It was hard. Understaffed, actually, I mean, healing broken bones is one thing, but taking care of kids? Well, wow. Hat's off to the mothers of the world."

She almost giggled at that. She had a sudden, powerful urge to feel the wind in her hair.

"Three days in, I hit some kind of a wall. I had tried so hard to be perfect, to say and do the perfect things, and then one afternoon we were all by the swimming pool, and I was trying to be the perfect safety monitor. I remember Joy was working the pool too, and she had told a bunch of the kids to stop the horseplay, and three of them ganged up on her, and pushed her into the water."

Cat's breath froze in her throat. The image was almost mind-boggling. She repressed visions of child-sized charcoal briquettes bobbing in the chlorinated water, and could hardly get the next words out. "Ah—what exactly did she do?"

Tomo laughed. "Well, she came up sputtering, and then she got this kind of funny look on her face—"

I'll bet. Hey, kids, how do you like your ribs?

"—she dog-paddled over to my side of the pool, and held her hand out to me. I took it . . . and she pulled me in. I remembered belly-flopping into the water, and came up sputtering I think that that was when I finally felt like a real camp counselor. The rest of the week was easy."

They shared a deep, cleansing laugh at that, and some of her tension melted. Whatever Tomo was, he wasn't a monster. Whatever his sister was, she wasn't a goddess. What, then?

Tomo chose a mount for her, and saddled it, and helped her up. He swung himself easily up onto the Appaloosa, and they headed out of the barn, into the afternoon.

He took her for a slow tour of the twelve-hundred-acre ranch. There was plentiful raw forest area: western hemlock and Douglas fir, lacings of moss and dense sword fern, and an entire verdant mountainside, going up to about 3,400 feet. They wandered up a trail, until they were high enough for Cat to look down on the encampment. She watched the people playing in the rectangular pool, and a few ant-sized figures walking along the road they had just traversed. "How expensive is all of this?" she asked.

"About two million a year," he said casually. "We sell books, and tapes, and there are a few small business concerns, but most of the profits go to the people who actually operate them. No, what keeps us alive is interest on the investments, the stocks and bonds, and the donations we've received over the years."

"Donations?" To the tune of two million in *interest?* Her head spun.

"You have to remember that we have been doing this, very quietly, for over ten years. In that time, the word has gone out, again, quite discreetly, about who and what we are. People come to us. Many of the things that we do, we do at no cost. Some are a drain to us."

"Like the healing?"

He nodded. "And people whose children or wives or husbands we heal take care of us. We have many friends."

"You heal. What is it that Joy does? I mean in a positive sense."

"You do not understand. Few do. Joy and I are like a single creature. She is my power. I am her purity. There is no real separation."

She thought about it. For ten years, the whisper would have gone out along a private—and probably very wealthy grapevine. *There were real miracles in the world.* And even better than selling them outright would be providing them selectively, very carefully, to those who could be trusted not to talk. And to be generous. "Can you . . . share your power with others?"

He looked out over the retreat which their magic and majesty had built, and his head shook very slightly from side to side.

"Not at all?"

"We have tried," he said. "And there are some small effects which we can transmit. They fade." The two words contained infinite regret. "They always fade. But there may be another way."

"What, then?" she said. He didn't answer her. She tried another tact. "Tomo," she said. "Has your sister ever . . . killed before?"

He nodded. She felt her breathing start to go irregular, and fought herself, ordered herself to quiet. "When was the first time?"

"Defending me," he said. "Always defending me." He looked at her, and his eyes pleaded. This being, with all of his power, needed someone, needed her to understand his life, and what it had been.

"I believe you," she said finally.

His shoulders relaxed. Although his face tilted down into the valley beneath him, his dark, Asian/African face was lost in the past. "It isn't easy being different," he said. "We were always different."

She kept quiet.

"You know, all human beings are alone. And in some way we know that. And those of us who can fade into a crowd feel that loneliness and wonder if there is something wrong with us, if, in our . . . *apartness,* there is some evidence of sickness. But when you are marked by your gender, or your race, or your intelligence . . . this by itself is enough to account for the apartness, and I think that the same sensitivity which can induce a European among other Europeans to ponder existential loneliness can make a mixed-blood child among Europeans conclude that he is a bad thing. A twisted thing. An ugly thing."

He sighed. "It is more devastating if others help you maintain this illusion. Who are willing, or eager to tell you that you aren't one of them."

"You weren't white, and you weren't black," Cat said cautiously. "And you weren't Japanese, either."

Tomo stared, unblinking. His chest didn't move.

"Your mother said that your father died over Manchuria, or something. Implied he was Japanese. No mention of any other ethnicity. You've never answered questions about that."

As far as she could tell, he had stopped breathing all together. Something in the back of her mind said: *Shut up. Stop now.*

Instead of anger, or even addressing her second question at all, he began to reply to her first.

"There were two boys. Their names were Tyrone and Tyree, and they made my life hell."

seventy-five

United States Government RAIN FOREST Archive
Exhibit #3476
Oshita File. DO NOT PHOTOCOPY OR REMOVE FROM BUILDING

The following is a document removed from a computer verified to have been used by Tomo Oshita. Although it is impossible to verify authorship through graphology or fingerprints, it is likely that he is, in fact the author. It is speculated that he intended to publish the following account at some point in the future, perhaps after the event which they referred to as "The Unveiling."

It gives me no pleasure to write the following words, but I need to set the record straight. There are so many things about myself which I do not understand. So many which I may never understand. If I could have asked the world a boon, it would have been to be born a normal child, without the powers and abilities that mark me as an outsider in any company. If I could have been given a second gift, it would be to have been born black. Or Japanese. Either of these. But to be forever between has been to belong nowhere, and to no one. To be alone. Just me, and Joy, and Mother.

Almost as if someone intended it to be so.

I did say that the events in the biology class were a beginning. I didn't specify the manner in which this was most true. My earliest memories were of being *Kokujin,* half-black, in Osaka, during the conflict with Korea. *Kokujin* was a bad thing, almost as bad as it was capable of being. I remember playing during the day, just me and Joy, alone in the rubble of shattered factories. There, in the ruins, we would have our little games, and there we promised that no matter what happened in our lives, we would always have each other. And we dreamed of one day leaving Japan.

In Japan, we were less than totally human. There, we were products of our mother's shame. We knew that she was forced to work to earn our daily bread, but we didn't understand the true cost of her labors. We knew that something had died in her eyes, something that was only alive when she crouched in the corner and cried. She seemed angry with us all the time, and we never knew why. We lived in a tiny room in the back of another family dwelling, and the walls were so thin that in summer they served only to keep in the heat, in winter to preserve the cold. Once we lived on turnip soup with fish heads, and a little rice, for an entire month.

And mother worked. We were left alone, because no one would play with us. *Kokujin* were an abomination, but we didn't know why. We know now. Many times I asked my mother who our father was. And she would only say: "He died." He died. But once she said that she wondered what he thought, what he felt, and I knew that her story was untrue, but still I could not induce her to tell us the truth. Our father had not died over China. Our father was not Japanese. He may have been American, a black soldier, perhaps. Once, she said his name was Niles, and that he knew we would be different.

Mother never let me heal her. She never let me lay my hands on her. She had to ask for healing, and she never did, and I know why:

She didn't want me in her mind. There were things she didn't want me to know. And one of them was who my father was. But whatever he was, whoever he was, I believe that it is part of the mystery of who I am. I know that he was a tall man, very black, with scars along his face. I know that he was fascinated by my mother. He said things to her. The things that we teach in the workshops are gleaned from many different cultures, many different places. Every time we found a truth that matched the inner truth Joy and I perceived from early childhood, we brought it together, almost as if there were once a larger truth, something underlying all of the religions and philosophies of the world, something so huge and basic that it was almost unendurable. And that as human beings developed their languages and societies, they forgot this larger truth, and it fragmented into the magics and religions of the world.

I know that my father was a man of power. She said that he sought

her out because she was different. He said that she was as different as
he. He told her that there are Eight Great Powers in the world, and in
my studies I now know what he meant by this. The Celts, the Athabas-
can peoples of America, the shamans of Africa, the Shinto priests—
groups who still hold the magic, still access the true forces which rule
the universe. He said he was not truly American but African, one of
the few men who have not shorn themselves, neutered themselves.
Who still have the power.

He told her that he looked into her, and saw that she was a special child before she was a woman. That she had not known her spe-
cialness, but when she told the story of the Great Bomb, and how it
had killed everyone but her, and the hundred chemical weapons which
seared her body—which should have killed her a thousand times, but
didn't—he knew that she was special, and that she had a destiny, and
that he could awaken it within her.

He would open her eyes, so that she could see the world as it was,
all its brightness and cruelty. That he had traveled widely, lived longer
than she could believe, and that there were others like him—and when
they found each other, they mated. And that their children would
change the world.

He looked into her, and said that she had the power. And he paid
her money for the use of her body, and brought us into the world.

I know this much. But no more.

We never fit in. When the Marine—I will not speak his name—came
along, mother, who had already grown dark in her anger, took up with
him. She had carried Niles's children for years, and they had refused
to be born. Sometime during this time, her mind left her. It was just
too much. She thought he would return. He said he would return.

He never did.

She hated him, at last, for what he had given her, although she
loved us. She hated the country which had destroyed her native land,
helped the Chinese kill her husband, turned Nagasaki into the center
of the sun and infected her with God knows what. The country which
forced her to whore in order to survive.

She focused her anger upon America, and when her future husband appeared, she used every power at her disposal to induce him to
fall in love with her. She fed his every fantasy, became everything he

had dreamed—and not dared to dream—that a woman could be, until he could not help but take her away from the land which broke her heart—to the land which she hated so feverishly.

Perhaps she thought it would be a better life—if not for herself, then for her children. Although she never told us she loved us, we know she did. After all, she worked so hard to keep us alive.

Perhaps she thought she would one day forget her past, would begin her life anew, with her son and daughter at her side..

Perhaps she hoped she would meet our true father, and show him how we had grown.

My first memory of America is an image of the docks where her husband met us, in Long Beach, California, on October 14, 1953. Everything looked so busy, so industrious. The factories we passed as we drove from the docks were all swarming with life. The workers we saw crowding their gates looked like the Americans we had always heard of. This was the greatest country in the world, and we were here at last. Here, there would be room for us. Here, at last, we would find a home.

We had learned English from the GIs who lived and slept and whored in the house where my mother worked. Everything was A-OK, and Cool, and we were Hip Little Cats. The GIs were of all races, and all types. Some were smart, and some weren't, but most of them were nice to us, even if only because they wanted something from the women who worked there. For us, it was a world of dense smells and soft sounds, and we lived more there than outside, where the other children pointed at us and called us *Kokujin*.

Here in America, many things happened, some of which I spoke of in the pages of books already published. One thing which happened I have never shared:

The children somehow knew what we were. I don't know how. In some way that children often do, they knew that our mother was a war bride, that her husband was a Marine who worked too long and drank too much. And they knew that we were dirty, and told us as much at every opportunity.

The black children called us Jap. The oriental kids called us niggers, and the white children didn't waste the breath to curse. We were five years old at that time. Through the first twelve years of our lives, we grew and aged more slowly than other children, and mother delayed putting us into school for two years. We were seven, but looked five, another cause of ridicule. By the time of the events at Dorsey High School, we had begun to adjust to the world, and it to us. We had made a mutual accommodation, and if things had remained that way for the rest of our lives, I would not have complained.

The frog changed everything. Perhaps the other children in the room could believe that the frog had not been injured, that some trick of paint or fake blood had produced the grisly effect. Perhaps—just perhaps the teacher could convince herself of the same thing. After all—Miss Novokow was a rational woman, and what she saw, with the eyes of a biology teacher—a dying frog—did not match what she saw a few bare minutes later—a healthy frog. There was no answer for this, nothing that could explain that circumstance in any rational way. So it had to be a mistake of perception. The frog couldn't have been as badly wounded as it had seemed.

But Tyree, the boy who had driven the knife into the frog, and even Nadine Izumi, the girl whose hand had gripped the blade, knew different.

Nadine was afraid of me. That much was certain, and every time she looked at me, it was with that expression that marks fear. Tyree was the only one that understood her fear. Even though he was the one who had caused the pain, caused the grief, he was the only one.

A sweet irony, that.

Tyree had changed. He and Tyrone spent their lunch times sitting in the bleachers away from everyone else, talking and sometimes drinking something out of a brown paper bag. The boy was ashen, drawn, as if he had pulled away from the light that sustains life.

I don't know what Nadine felt. I don't know what they were saying. I do know that the gap between the Oshitas and the rest of the students began to expand. They didn't side with Tyree and Nadine. They didn't side with us. But the whispers had started.

Joy was beginning to develop an interest in boys. There is a strangeness here: Despite what we were being taught at home, despite what we knew of the energies which drive and compel human beings in their sexuality, Joy was still shy with the opposite sex. She was short for an American girl but straight, with long black hair and beautiful bronze skin. The promise of her future beauty was obvious to anyone who had eyes to see. The boys were beginning to appreciate her. In some ways she looked like a darker version of Nadine.

Joy and I have talked many times about what happened that night. I am the only one with whom she will speak of these things. In my poor way, I will try to convey what happened. Perhaps no one will ever read these words. But it is important that I put them down, to be able to have them in front of my eyes rather than behind them.

It helps me. It helps me to sleep.

Joy ran on the relay team, and as I said, she was bright, and quick, and her eyes saw things that others missed. The team was five girls, with three alternates, and a towel girl. The towel girl was often the worst runner, a girl who wanted desperately to run, but hadn't the skills or the strength. Sometimes, she would be allowed to race. Usually not. Towel girl was also a punishment position, given to a girl who ran poorly, or talked back to the coach, or whose grades fell too far behind. They ran relays in the two- to five-mile range. I remember watching Joy, her dark hair drawn back in a bun, and sometimes coming undone and streaming out behind her in a flowing ribbon. Firm brown legs pumping, face concentrated on the goal line, on running, running. The girls had accepted her more easily than the boys accepted me, perhaps because she was so obviously wonderful at what she did. They were so happy to have someone with her level of skill and drive on the team.

After the incident with the frog, everything started to change. Whispers circulated like leaves in a whirlwind. The other girls on the relay team began to pull away from her.

I think that this time was worse for Joy than it was for me. I had my books. I was used to living deep inside myself, in my dreams, and in my hopes. But Joy wanted to be accepted and loved. She had tried so hard. Now, the other girls gaped at her in the shower room, pointed at the scar along her side, and murmured. They heard things. They heard about the frog. They spoke of mother, who hid in the house most days, and was therefore seen as an erotic and potentially dangerous being.

Tyrone's sister Keesha was on the track team, a very dark, muscular girl with hard blunt features and a penchant for tight clothes. She tried to turn the other girls against Joy. After a time, her snide remarks, vicious rumors and manipulation began to work.

The girls pulled away. They didn't want to play with her as much. Joy was forced from primary relay runner to alternate, and finally to the position of towel girl. And I think that they would have forced her completely from the team, but she refused to be pushed any further.

I remember sitting in the library after school, reading by the window. The library looked out on the oval track, and I watched the girls out there, laughing and playing. I could watch Joy running, running in her laps around and around the track, with the sun glinting on her black hair, sometimes bound, and sometimes flowing. I dreamed of Joy running in city competitions, state competitions . . . and perhaps in the Olympics one day. God, she loped like a gazelle, as if the wind eternally embraced her and spurred her onward. The most beautiful thing that I had seen in my life was my sister running, face suffused with the ecstasy of extreme effort.

But other eyes were on her as well, and this I did not know, until it was too late.

When she became towel girl, it was her duty to run and fetch, and to hand towels to the girls as they came out of the showers, and to pick up the locker room. This last meant that she was the last one out of the building at the end of practice. Sometimes the coach was in her office, making plans. The track coach was a math professor, a stubby Irish woman named O'Hara who could sprint like a rabbit for about two hundred meters, or trot from sunup until sundown. She gave everything she had to the girls, but she had her own life. And sometimes, occasionally, the towel girl was the last coming out of the building.

And that was the final part in the recipe for disaster. Preparations for the meal were now complete. It now remained only to be served.

It was a Friday, after the annual intra-city track meet. Joy was unhappy not to be able to run with the other girls, but she knew that mandatory rotation would take her off towel duty next month. Even if Keesha and the other girls complained to Mrs. O'Hara, it would make no difference. Mrs. O'Hara hadn't seen a dead frog, and even if she had, it wouldn't have anything to do with running track. And she wouldn't be swayed. I think that Keesha threatened to quit. But Mrs. O'Hara said that would be fine. Joy ran well enough to replace two of them, and that was that.

I think that Dorsey was competing against Los Angeles High School, and Washington, and Hollywood. Students from all the schools were there. I think that Tyree had cousins who attended Washington, and that was another piece of the puzzle. Unfamiliar faces.

The crowd came out for the event, and I remember the day. Track was a big thing for our schools, and yellow buses pulled into Dorsey's parking lot, full of kids cheering for this or that team. Dorsey had a large field, and we could easily host six schools. The stands were filled, and it could have been a football contest between arch rivals.

In fact, I think that had been the specific intent by the faculty, an attempt to popularize sports which were "less conflict-oriented" than the barely sublimated tribal warfare called football.

Tyrone's sister Keesha had heard the frog story, and she was the one who pushed it. I despise dialect, so I render her words as: "I'm not running with this fornicating witch."

There was an argument, and they almost came to blows, but Mrs. O'Hara would not be intimidated. Keesha was suspended from the team. Joy was allowed to run, but she also had to hand out towels. If she was willing to accept dual duty, she would be able to compete.

She accepted.

The day of the race I knew that something was wrong, but to my shame, I had no clue what it might be. Keesha had a clique of girls who followed and loved her. Just as Joy's loyalty to me had led her into conflict with Keesha, Keesha's clique of followers obeyed her without question, and completed the circle of venom. And they had brothers and cousins, some of whom ran for the other schools, and some of whom watched from the stands, cheering, with all of the tribal fervor which makes the events so exciting.

And it was exciting that day. I remember the pole vaulting, the high jumping, the sprinting and the distance running. All of it going on like a three-ring circus, quite well choreographed, and the crowd cheering and yelling. A big digital scoreboard at the end of the field kept tally of the varied events. Dorsey was trailing by only a couple of points when Joy's event—the relay—came up for competition.

The crowd's tensions were high, because the competition had been so fierce that day. They were running a five-mile relay, each girl responsible for a mile of the distance. Joy was the anchor. She was strong, and solid, and competitive as the Dickens. She really wanted it.

The gun sounded, and the first girl took off. They virtually sprinted the first quarter mile, and then slowed, and began to speed up again for the last third, finally coming in at a blistering pace. It is hard to remember how these girls competed against each other. They were fifteen to seventeen years old, and although they had certainly experienced twisted ankles and maybe a sore knee, they were years away from any real sense of mortality, and they gave it everything that they had, everything poured into that effort, and were magnificent.

The second girl came into play, was passed the baton, and Dorsey was in third place, behind Los Angeles High and Century. She was a slender bit of black lightning named Terri, who ran as if chased by a lion. I think she must have almost broken something, because with the crowd cheering, and the band roaring in the stand, she brought the race into second place before handing it off. Second place now—neck and neck with Century. The third girl was solid, and ran the entire four laps at virtually the same pace. She seemed too slow at first, but what became obvious was that she simply refused to tire. Just wouldn't. And her efforts, as brave as any Olympian's, brought our team even to first.

How we all cheered! How proud we were of our team's efforts that day! The fourth girl was perhaps the weakest link, and with her, the efforts dropped us back into a tied position, and then slightly behind the front runner.

Then . . . they handed the baton to Joy.

She ran as she had never run before. Her shoes barely touched the ground, and her face was screwed to a point of concentration so intense that she might have been a bird of prey. Ahead of her, the runners from Los Angeles and Century were neck and neck. She needed to break that if she was to have any chance, and went for one of the outside lanes. The crowd was insane. The crowd was silent. I remember watching them cheering, jumping up and down. I remember cheering her name, but not hearing anything. My mind and heart were with her. It was *my* legs pumping down on the track, my eyes tearing with the sweat of exertion. It was my arms pumping. The wound in my side ached to join with her, to lend her my lungs.

I cannot read Joy's mind, but I knew what she was thinking. I cannot predict her actions, but I knew when the small intense frown on her face would blister into one of triumph. I knew . . . because she was running faster, and yet faster, and pulling up along them and then ahead of them, and in a few steps. . . .

And then something happened. She hadn't left herself quite enough clearance. Or the two girls, running together almost as if they intended to share the prize, lurched sideways with one mind, and Joy was caught in mid-stride, and went down.

She hit in a clumsy roll, and no one could doubt that she was hurt. The crowd reacted with a single disturbed whisper. Disappointment, concern, and from some of the boys and girls from Dorsey—unmistakable glee.

Joy rose to her knees, and shook her head like a boxer trying to shake off the effects of a brutal right cross. She stood, and almost buckled. The ankle was twisted. She saw victory disappearing in the dust.

She picked up her baton, and began to run.

There was no point in it now. There was no doubt that she would come in last. No one had any doubt that she was injured. She could have retired from the field. But *something* made her keep going. I winced with every twisted step, every pain-filled effort. It was terrible to see. My heart was in my throat, but it was impossible not to watch. It was impossible for the rest of the crowd not to watch. And although she lost by the widest margin of the day, it was Joy who got the biggest applause when she crossed the finish line.

I don't remember how long she leaned against me, and wept, after the meet. A long time. Until the meet was over. We were behind the stand, and she was utterly inconsolable. This had been her dream, and she had lost it. I told her that she had gained something larger, something more important, but I don't think that she could hear me. Her team had lost. Perhaps Keesha was right. Perhaps she hadn't belonged out there at all.

She still had clean-up duty to attend to, and I volunteered to help her. It was the girl's locker room, so I think that she was a little nervous about that, but perhaps she would have been even more nervous about it to do it by herself. I remember coach O'Hara asking her if she wanted to forgo her duties. Joy had run a hell of a race. Exceptions could be made.

But she wasn't having any of it. This was something which, for whatever reason, she wanted to do.

So after the girls had gone, we entered the locker room, and began to pick up the towels from the floor, the washcloths from the shower room. The yellow school buses had left, taking the kids back to their own districts. . . .

Most of them. We had seen a few, hovering around furtively. I couldn't quite distinguish faces. I had the impression that they might have been Tyree and some of his cronies. Maybe. They looked older than high school kids. I remember wondering what they were doing there. Once, walking across the field toward the gym, we passed a spot where a knot of them had clustered, and smelled alcohol. Looked under the stands, and saw some beer cans.

The locker room was still moist with steam, but beginning to cool. Towels were strewn everywhere, and we developed a companionable silence. We spent so much time together that being with one another was like being alone, only with company. Being by ourselves was like being shorn in half.

We didn't talk. Just worked, and in a half hour the room was neater. Joy wasn't limping quite so badly any more, and I remember the cleaning duty developed into a kind of freelance game of hide'n'seek between rows of lockers. I was picking up in one row, when I heard the door open, and then close. I wondered if Joy had left the locker room, because I couldn't see her. But I didn't call out. It was just like her to bluff me, so that she could spot me from my voice, and tag me first.

Then the lights went out.

The room didn't fall into an immediate darkness, but there was a moment in which I couldn't see anything. I heard the footsteps before I saw anything or anyone, but suddenly I was gripped from behind, and when I tried to turn my head to see whose hands had me so tightly, I was struck low in the side. Hard.

"Half-Jap" someone said, and I was hit again. On the other side of the room, I heard Joy cry out my name, and the sound of a muffled slap. I twisted, and am not ashamed to say that I sobbed. I caught one quick glimpse in a locker mirror, and saw my tormentor. He wore a mask of some kind, a stocking pulled over his face, and it turned his face into a nightmarish blank, behind which lurked distended nose and bestial, flattened lips.

The water in the shower was running, and steam beaded off the walls, filled the air, and I heard Joy scream as they dragged me back. "Don't wanna hurt you," one of them said. "Just heard so damn much about those scars. Just wanna take a look—"

They threw me down next to her. Like I said, we were almost nineteen years old, but could easily have passed for fourteen. Our development was slow. Even though Joy was like quicksilver on the track, she was a tiny thing, and so was I. Never had the disparity in size felt more real, more oppressive than at that moment. There were five of them. Three of them talked, giggled, laughed. Two were silent. They didn't want us to hear their voices. I knew who they were. One black, one white. Tyrone and Tyree.

I tried to crawl over to Joy, and one of them backhanded me across the face, and said "Get back over there, Half-Jap." I touched my lip. Blood beaded the back of my hand.

Joy's mouth was a pale thin line, tight with fear. This was spiraling out of control, and both of us knew it. What had begun with fear, and turned into a mission of chastisement and humiliation was now some kind of holy crusade.

"Take 'em *off!*" The biggest one roared, and there, in the shower, Joy and I were forced to strip. There was no one to protect us now, and we stood close together, our naked bodies pelted by the steaming water.

"Jesus, will you look at her? She ain't got no hair yet." Joy covered herself with both small hands. There may have been tears in her eyes. It was difficult to say, because of the steam and the hot water. Our faces were close together, and her eyes, ordinarily bright brownish-green, had gone emerald.

The boys were egging each other on, pushing each other further and further, and I realized that in a few moments things would go too far.

I had no idea how right I was.

"Please," I said. "Leave us alone."

There was a moment of sanity, a moment of silence. Maybe something in my voice reached them, got through to them. Maybe there was still a bit of decency left in their bodies. Or maybe there was something in the air that convinced them, on the deepest level, that this was nowhere for anyone sane to be. That they wanted to leave, that even *they* knew that things were spiraling out of control. But the worst part of a mob, even a mob of five, is that it takes on its own character, that even a quintet of cowards creates its own definitions and defining actions of courage, and that they will hold each other to that standard, even unto death.

None of them would be the first to quit. I think that it might not have been any more complicated, any more complex than that. None of them would be the first to quit.

And one of them—it must have been Tyree—kicked me in the groin.

Joy screamed. I remember the water striking her. I remember it boiling off her face. I remember the water around her beginning to foam.

I remember the boys screaming.

I remember thinking: *live steam.*

The stink of boiled flesh filled the locker room. I will never forget those poor boys, the withered flesh curled away from their faces, exposing broiled pinkish meat beneath. Their eyes staring, blood vessels burst from the heat.

There are many things that I don't remember about the time immediately following. One thing is the question of why I was unharmed by the heat, the flames. I know now that that was Joy, preserving me. I'm not sure I remember how I got out of that place, I only know that I was dressed in my sopping clothes, and that Joy held me. Heat radiated from her in waves, and in a few minutes the clothes were dry. We left that place of death, and locked it up, and went home.

The next day, Joy and I were called to the principal's office, where several police officers asked us questions. The questions were baffled, not accusatory. They asked us what time we locked up the gym. Did we see anyone? We had had time to devise our answers by that time, and I had already learned to live far back inside my head. I could answer "no" convincingly. Joy could do the same.

The entire school was abuzz: Five boiled corpses had been found in the locker room showers that morning. Not burned. There was no sign of fire. *Boiled.* As if a live steam pipe had ruptured. There was no explaining it: The peak water temperature in the shower room was far below boiling level. They couldn't have suspected us of anything, you see, because first they would have had to theorize how it had happened in the first place. An unsolved mystery. Five boys had entered the shower rooms late at night. Why, no one knew. Some bizarre homoerotic ritual was rumored. The alcohol levels in their blood—what remained of it—was very high. But no one knew, or could know.

But there was one inevitable result. There was someone who knew, oh, yes. Keesha told the police that the boys had gone after us, on an errand of revenge. Retaliation for slights real or imagined. And she swore that we were freaks, that we had killed her brother and her cousins and friend. And I will never forget the look in that girl's face, her black skin shining with fear and loathing. We sat in that office, and I remember the principal, and the police officers looking at us, and not knowing what to say. I remember Keesha being taken out of school, and I remember never seeing her again. I think that she was transferred to another school.

But the one thing that I know is that from that time on, no one at Dorsey High School bothered us. Or bothered with us. Or sat next to us at lunch. Or spoke to us unless it was absolutely necessary. It didn't matter what we said, or what we did. From that time on, we walked apart.

seventy-six

Tomo finished his story, the fatigue and pain in his eyes terrible to behold. Cat reached out and took his hand. "That was the first time you knew?" she asked. He nodded.

There was another question that she didn't want to ask. Didn't quite dare ask. *It wasn't the last though, was it?*

He seemed to shake himself out of it, and suddenly grinned at her. "Come. I'll race you the rest of the way."

The trip down from the mountain was potentially hazardous, with steep drop-offs and low overhanging pine branches, but the horses were sure-footed and picked their way cautiously. Only when they drew to within half a mile of the barn did their mounts seem to realize that they were on the downside of a circuit, and began to sprint. All Cat could do was hold on for dear life. Between gasps for breath, she noticed a thin line of acolytes straggling toward a long low building, white bundles slung over their shoulders.

She beat him to the barn by two lengths. Breathing hard, he swung down from his mount, damp circular sweat-stains beneath his cotton shirt. His grin was pure youthful pleasure, all angst forgotten. "That was fun." He blushed suddenly and lowered his eyes. "Do you like it here?"

She avoided his gaze. "I saw people going over to a low building. What was that?"

He glanced at his watch. "Oh that's Manfred's afternoon class. Would you like to watch?"

"Very much."

"Then let's go."

seventy-seven

The dojo was a long, low shed of a building, constructed of pine logs with an arched, reinforced tin roof. Twin roof turbines vented heat in summer-time, and a double rack of solar panels warmed in the winter. Long slit windows admitted a small amount of natural light, but aside from that, the illumination was provided by four sets of fluorescent tubes.

The gym was actually larger than it looked from the outside. Concrete steps led down to a full-sized basketball court with collapsible bleachers.

The far end of the gym was dominated by a stage large enough for a decent production of *Camelot.* A scratched and slightly battered black piano stood over at that end, as well. Low doors beneath the stage hung open, and students were busy extracting long pieces of foam matting, fitting them together like jigsaw puzzle pieces to create a twenty-five-by-fifty-foot workout area.

When the entire surface was in place, they worked in concert to pull an enormous canvas sheet over the entire foam surface, then neatly tucked the edges in.

Cat counted twenty-seven students here for the class, of all ages, and physical conditions. Some were as young as eighteen, and looked tennis-fit. Others were in their fifties and sixties, with discreet pot bellies, graying hair, and spindly legs. Kolla and one other girl were heavier than most. But the rest of them were trim, fit, and alert. When Tomo entered the room they paused, came to attention and then bowed deeply from the waist, as one might to a revered instructor in any Japanese-style dojo anywhere in the world.

Tomo excused himself and went off to the dressing room. Cat found a bench at a side of the room and pulled into herself, trying not to draw any attention as the students rolled and jumped, flexed and stretched, preparing themselves for their hour of exercise. The bodies flew through the air, and landed making satisfying *thwacks* against the canvas, then bounced back up and kept going.

That was something that she had always admired about Aikido classes. They truly understood how to take falls without murdering themselves. Cat had a personal, passionate hatred of falling down.

Manfred Gittes emerged from the dressing room wearing white *gi* and black *hakama* skirt. He took position on the mat, facing away from her and toward a framed photograph of a wizened old man she recognized as Morihei Ueshiba, the founder of Aikido, said to be one of the great warriors of the twentieth century. Gittes now seemed not European at all, but an odd incarnation of some ancient Asian warrior-saint. His every motion was ritualistically precise as he clapped his hands together, and bowed before the picture. The class fell into place behind him, also kneeling and bowing.

He bade them stand, and led them through a series of carefully judged warmups, until the slit windows above them dripped with condensation.

Gittes carefully supervised as they flexed and twisted their wrists. He led them through circular footwork drills, worked on backward and forward rolls, duckwalking, leaping, and partner stretches across each other's backs. Then he began the actual workout.

He extended an arm. Kolla leapt to her feet and attacked. Cat noticed that he didn't specify any particular attack, allowing her to improvise. Kolla flew forward with speed which utterly belied her mass, bladed hand flashing for Gittes's head. With that almost slow-motion contemplative quality which marks the true master, Gittes lazily moved out of the way, seemed to blend with the attack, and spun her to the mat. Cat winced, expecting a bone-jarring impact, but instead there was a muffled *shush* of a collision, and a blur, and Kolla was pinned. A half-dozen times, he motioned to this or that student. Each attacked him in turn, and all efforts ended the same way: evasion, blending, throw, pin. Devastating efficiency and lyrical structure in physical form.

There was a whisper of moving wood on the left side of the room and Tomo emerged, wearing a *gi* and *hakama*. He walked fluidly—or perhaps the *hakama* conveyed a certain plastic beauty to his motion. Ordinarily, there was a quality about Tomo that suggested the ethereal, as if he was all too ready to separate from this mortal clay and just float away. Here, he seemed lower to the ground, and more centered.

He exchanged bows with Gittes, and entered the mat area. Gittes's smile was that of a proud father as he asked: "Would you care to demonstrate?" Tomo sparkled, the little boy within him more present than at any other time in Cat's experience. Tomo took the center of the mat, and Gittes walked smoothly to the side and sat, watching. Tomo gestured, and one of the students rose. Tomo extended his arm, and when it was accepted, he twisted, did a kind of skipping step forward, and then moved backward at a low angle against his attacker's shins. The man flew high through the air, and hit with a lovely *thwack*. Tomo moved left and right, as lightly as a flower drifting on the wind, and every time he did, another student flew.

Cat stole a glance at Manfred Gittes's face. Throughout it all, he watched approvingly. It was clear: In this arena, Gittes was the master, Tomo the student. The two of them taught class for an hour and a half, and took the students through sword and knife drills, working them until their heavy cotton *gis* dripped with sweat. Then they concluded with a generous cooldown exercise, a three-minute meditation, and then dismissal. Most filed out in a kind of sensual afterglow, leaving Manfred, Tomo and a couple of the senior students behind.

Tomo strode across the mat to Cat, projecting yet another personality.

The little boy was gone. This was a young warrior, proud of his skills. "So," he asked, wiping a hand across his forehead. "What did you think?"

"Very impressive," she said honestly.

"You've seen Aikido before?"

"Yes, a few times. You have wonderful skill—and Manfred is just magic." Gittes inclined his head graciously.

"You're too kind."

"I understand that you have training," Gittes said.

She nodded carefully. They waited, but she didn't volunteer any more. One of the senior belts said: "What art?"

"Kenpo," she said. And again, declined to continue.

"What rank?" Manfred finally asked.

She sighed. *Here it comes.* "Fourth degree black. BKF style." She couldn't quite repress a chuckle at that.

Manfred inclined his head. "Excuse me? I'm not sure I recognize that? Is that branched from Mitose?"

"By way of Ed Parker, yes. BKF is the Black Karate Federation. Sort of an inner-city variant."

"I see." He seemed to study her blond hair for a moment, and one of his thin eyebrows lifted. "Isn't it a bit unusual for you to have trained in something like that?"

"When I was LAPD, a couple of the Black officers used to go down and train with the Brothers. As a joke, they took me along once." She shrugged, some part of her not happy with this conversation. "I liked it," she said finally.

"Would you be kind enough to show us some?" Gittes asked.

Cat sighed. There was no getting out of this. She could only hope that she wouldn't be making things worse for herself.

"On the mat?" Manfred said politely. She considered the wisdom of declining. The mat was *their* domain.

"We generally worked out on a concrete floor. Shoes on." *That* raised an eyebrow. "I've used it maybe thirty times in the line of duty, and I was never barefoot."

"Fair enough." Manfred pointed to a tall man, wearing a black sash around his waist. He moved like an advanced student. "Julio."

All right. She wasn't warmed up, she was in her street clothes, and she wasn't entirely certain what the game was.

The two of them stepped onto the mat, and Julio waited for her to make the first move.

"Ah . . ." Manfred said. "Aren't you going to attack?"

"Why should I? He seems a nice enough guy." Julio turned toward Manfred in frustration, and in that moment, Cat slid forward. When he flinched, she swept his right ankle with the inside edge of her left foot. As he scrambled back, fighting for balance, she was already on top of him: eye jab, hammer fist to the groin, throat strike, never giving him a chance to catch his breath. The strikes were barely touches, but so fast and precise that they triggered a panic response. Then she was behind him. His balanced destroyed, it was easy to sweep his ankle from the rear and take him down, miming an elbow to the back of the head.

Julio gawked up at her. "That wasn't fair."

"No," she said. "It wasn't. Sorry."

He scrambled back up. "Let me try again—"

Gittes considered her thoughtfully. "No, I think not. Mariah? Would you honor our guest with your energy?"

Mariah had watched Cat with intense, almost feral interest. She was a lanky brunette who reminded Cat of a humming dynamo. Incredible focus. When she rose to her feet and faced Cat, everything else in the world seemed to disappear.

If Aikido is a highly sophisticated grappling art, most noteworthy for its development of timing, sensitivity, and balance, Kenpo is a perfection of high-speed hand- and foot-strike combinations. While Aikido bases much of its theory on a total defensive posture, Kenpo's basic tactic is one of testing the opponent's periphery with brief sallies and sorties, searching out weak spots in perception and position, and then wearing the defender down with pain and damage. Speed is favored over power, until initial damage has been done—only then are the more powerful, but slower tools brought into play. In many ways, it might be considered knife fighting without the knife.

Mariah shifted her hips, feinting, and then lunged with a powerful reverse punch. Cat's combat computer flashed the message *Shotokan,* a power-oriented Japanese style, and used a lateral motion to defeat the forward drive. When Mariah adjusted her footwork, Cat flickered a whiplash back-knuckle strike at her head, knowing that Shotokan's "One punch One Kill" philosophy instills contempt for such showy techniques. The feint drew a brushing block and an almost inevitable reverse punch, Shotokan's version of boxing's right cross.

Cat pivoted so that the punch slid by her ribs, and brought her right elbow up vertically, touching Mariah's jaw just enough to clack her teeth together. Mariah's eyes opened wide and she tried to backpedal. Cat thumped her hard in the stomach with a back-heel strike, and then swept her to the mat. The lanky girl thumped, not rolling quite as gracefully as she might have hoped.

Ouch.

Manfred looked politely at Tomo, whose eyes were wide with delight. "Would you care?"

Tomo bounced up, and extended his arm to Cat. Reflexively, she reached for it, breaking contact barely in time to keep herself from being thrown. Over and over again, he entered into her space, and she had a very curious feeling of being ensnared in a slow motion syrup, only her alertness and experience snapping her out of it. Tomo's energy was intoxicating, playful . . . but not at all dangerous. He was a superb Aikidoka, and there were things about his mind and the way that he projected his intent, his *ki,* which made him fascinating to work against, but his energy was all implosive, not destructive or even percussive, and the interaction was just plain *fun.*

But Gittes, now . . .

Gittes watched. He had taught these three, and she knew that his skill went far beyond them. She fervently wished that Jax were present (and realized in that moment how desperate was her hope that he still lived). Jax, though no more skilled than she, had the mass and technique to make a grappling-range attack overwhelming. She just knew that if Gittes wasn't satisfied with the outcome of the present engagement he would step in personally. If necessary, he would make the exercise an unpleasant one.

So she waited a moment too long, and Tomo trapped her wrist, twisted and swept, and she went down. He had her in a lovely pin, her cheek pressed hard against the mat. The other students applauded them both, and everyone was pleased, Dojo honor satisfied.

Manfred watched her, his eyes speculative.

When the others went to dress, Gittes motioned for her to follow him. To the side of the dojo was a cubical with a futon couch, a desk and three chairs. He unlocked the door and waved her in, indicated that she should sit. She felt minuscule as Gittes sat at the edge of his desk, looking down

at her. Considering their relative heights, the maneuver was hardly necessary, if intimidation was his aim.

He said nothing, just watched her. She took the time to gaze around
the room. A filing cabinet, a magazine stand with a copy of *Aikido Today,*
and a little shrine in the corner of the room.

The shrine was about three feet in height, of hardwood and intricately
carved ivory in a horseshoe shape just large enough to accommodate one
kneeling supplicant. On that shrine were candles, incense burners, and a
dozen photographs of Joy and Tomo. Tomo on horseback. A rare, perhaps
singular photo of Joy on the pyre. Tomo playing with children in the
swimming pool. Joy standing naked on a mountaintop, perfect athlete's
body glowing in the sunlight, head thrown back as if intoxicated with existence, her hair blowing like smoke in the wind.

"This is where I sleep," he said. "My life is simple. I need my art. I
need a place to rest. And I need the Twins." He said the words as if they
were an article of faith, like a Christian pilgrim might have spoken of
Jerusalem.

Cat felt her breathing grow deeper, hotter, and fought to remain centered as he leaned over her. "Could you have escaped Tomo's hold?" he
asked quietly. His eyes burned.

"Maybe. There was nothing to gain."

"Nothing to gain," he said. And then, for the first time, his mouth
softened. "I hope that you are not an enemy, Ms. Juvell. I love Joy and
Tomo more than my own life. I brought you here so that you might understand." He paused, searching for words. "They give so much, and there
is almost no way for anyone to give back. They let few in—really in. And
those they do often betray them."

"Why would that happen?"

"Supplicants see gods. They come closer, and find out Joy and Tomo
are human, and become disillusioned. Do not betray their trust. It wouldn't
be safe."

Cat moistened her lips, and swallowed, forcing herself to stay calm.
"Do you remember someone named Tony Corman?"

Manfred nodded fractionally. "He stole a motorcycle, and left. We
were very disappointed."

I'll bet.

"I'll remember that," she said.

He pursed his mouth thoughtfully and then nodded, indicating the open door. Cat stood and walked out. After a dozen steps she turned and looked back at him. Manfred Gittes was staring at her expressionlessly, those enormous, flat fingers drumming slowly on the desk.

It took every ounce of her self-control not to run.

seventy-eight

It was another time and place. Perhaps two years before, in the home Cat shared with her husband. And again, another again, another endless again, they were arguing.

"What am I asking for that's so damned much?" Jax raged.

Cat's face was sunken in her hands. "I'm sorry," she muttered. "I'm just sorry." She looked up at him, eyes wet. "Is that what you want me to say?"

He slammed one of his huge hands down on the table. "No—I want you to be with me, not lay there like you're dead."

She stiffened almost as if he had struck her instead of the table. "I give as much as I can, Jax. If that's not enough . . ."

He reached forward to take her shoulder. She pulled away from him violently. "Don't touch me," she said.

His eyes softened, and he made a low, miserable sound. He released her shoulders, staring at his hands as if they belonged to a stranger. "I'm sorry. I'm so sorry. . . ."

Another image, earlier still. Perhaps six years before.

She wasn't just seeing it—she was feeling it, living it all again. The police station. Freddy King was introducing her to an enormous detective, a man she had seen slouching around the station at a distance, but had yet to meet. He was at least ten years older than she, but possessed an awesome vitality. She smiled coolly and shook his hand.

"Jackson Carpenter," he said. "Cat, meet Jax." The broad dark planes of his face creased in a smile. She caught a southwestern twang to his voice, but couldn't quite place it.

"Porsche Juvell. My friends call me 'Cat.' I guess we'll be working together on

the Vasquez case." She liked his eyes. They didn't lie, and in her world that was no small thing.

"Juvell!" someone called. "Line one!"

"Good to meet you," she said. "We'll nail that bastard."

She went to get the phone, and conducted her conversation lucidly, but one ear was peeled to the office behind her. In spite of herself, she wanted to hear what Jackson Carpenter was going to say.

"Forget about that one," Freddy said.

"Meow," Jax drawled.

"Porsche Mew-zette Juvell. Friends call her Cat. We usually just call her 'PMS.' "

She remembers dying inside. Just a little.

Just enough.

T he images explode, implode, re-form.

She is younger still. A teenaged boy sits at the edge of a manicured expanse of grass, in a wheelchair. It is Tyler. He is watching her, as she plays a pickup game of football with boys who outweigh her by twenty pounds.

She tackles the quarterback, a redheaded chunk of a boy with no lateral motion. He goes down hard, then bounces up and pushes her.

"What the hell's the matter with you?" he snarls. Strange. She can't remember his name. Back then, everybody knew him, admired him. Now she can't remember his name at all.

"Can'tcha take it?" Tyler asked from the sidelines.

The quarterback turned to Tyler, embarrassment turning into pure venom. "Who asked you, Crip?"

Anger flares. Unreasoning. Ferocious. Cat launches herself at the quarterback, smashing him to the ground and pummeling him. Two other boys pull her off. The quarterback wipes at a bloody nose.

"God, Porsche," he says. Fear strikes sparks in his eyes. "Can't you take a fucking joke?"

A nd back a little further now. She doesn't want to go further back, she is getting too close to something that she doesn't want to pry open. Too close to

(treasure chest)

and she can't go there, can't go there—

───────

Twelve-year-old Porsche with eleven-year-old Tyler in his wheelchair at the play-ground. Sitting, eating by themselves. Kids playing basketball next to them. They scream for Porsche to join them. She looks at Tyler, and he nods "go ahead," grin-ning. Cat bounces up, grabs the ball, makes a beautiful lay-up shot, glances back at Tyler, who beams. It is for him. All for him.

Blackness. Utter and complete.
The void.

Then: another memory. Cat and Tyler playing on the schoolyard. Tyler perhaps ten years old. Running on strong, healthy legs.
Laughing, chasing a soccer ball. Tyler, chasing a ball
Tyler, running on healthy legs.

seventy-nine

In the shadowed canopy of Tomo's bed, Cat drew back from her lover, trembling. If the room had burst into flames, she doubted she could have made it to the door.

"He could walk," Tomo said.

Her voice sounded weaker than her legs felt. "Yes."

"What happened to him?"

The bottom dropped out of her stomach. *Treasure chest? Jewel Box?* "Accident?"

Tomo moved his hips against her. She fought the wave of pleasure, fought the thinning of her ego walls. "The memory is blocked," he said.

Not blocked. Locked. "I don't want to know."

"What happened, Cat?"

"Please," she whispered.

"What happened to Tyler's legs?"

"I . . . accident."

"Why don't you remember, Cat?"

"I . . . Tyler . . ." weakness ebbed, and she struggled with an almost overpowering urge to rise and run, to get the living hell away from him.

Gently, with almost surgical precision, Tomo plucked at the snarled emotional thread. "What about Tyler?" he asked.

The words stuck in her throat. *She closed her eyes, and the image of a tiny golden chest came to her. Tomo's gentle probing words, his healing energy, materialized a key in the lock. And turned it. A brief flash of light from within, then the lid closed again.* The truth bubbled up like vomit. "He's not . . . my brother."

Tomo nodded. "He's your foster brother, isn't he?"

"Yes."

"What happened, Cat?"

"I don't remember."

"Do you want to?" he asked.

She shut her eyelids tightly, and found no darkness to hide in. "Yes," she said.

eighty

Tuesday, July 4

The morning clouds above Portland International Airport glinted pale steel as Jax left the terminal, duffel bag light in his right hand. He scanned the airport, the cars and buses and taxis, remembering another airport, not so long ago, thinking how he had no idea at all where it would lead, or what in the world might happen.

Would he have gone to Santa Cruz, if he had known? No, certainly not.

But still . . . but still . . . *something* had happened there. And if they survived all of this, it would have been for the best. He hoped. But that was too far in the future. For now he had to rent a car, and drive like hell.

eighty-one

Joy sat alone in the precise center of the yurt, a stick of incense in her hand. She wore a white silk gown. Her long, perfect legs were crossed in a full lotus pose. Her posture was perfect, the strong, dark contours of her face completely relaxed. Cat thought that she was the most beautiful women she had ever seen in her life.

Compared to her, Cat felt like a boy. At that moment, it was hard to remember the true nature of the being she faced. At this moment, it was easy to think of the half-breed girl Joy had been. To remember the child playing in bomb-torn streets. Growing up in the brothels of Osaka. In the inner cities of Los Angeles. Never fitting in anywhere, with anyone. Forever an outsider, and cursed with the greatest powers any human being had ever known. At least, the greatest powers of anyone Cat knew of. God in heaven—could there possibly, even credibly, be more than this? Cat shuddered to think of it.

Joy beckoned her to join, to sit next to her. Cat did so, and for a long time, perhaps eight minutes, Joy was silent. Then finally she said: "You and my brother have bonded."

The comment seemed to require no answer, so Cat said nothing. "You know much about us," Joy said, "and yet we have just met. Tomo took you into his confidence, and into his heart." Her eyes narrowed. "Who are you?" she asked. It was the question of a woman who had always protected the ones she loved, who was terribly aware of the burden she carried. Who was the goddess of a new religion.

"I hope you will be good to him," she said.

"Tomo has had . . . other loves," Cat said timidly.

"You are special," Joy said. "You have a place deep inside you, that he cannot reach without permission. You learned to wall yourself off, didn't you? Probably in childhood. It is a thing that some of us learn, in order to survive."

Joy made a small, sad smile, not at all the kind of expression Cat would expect from a woman of power. "I hope that you are different. Are good for him. He has tried so hard with so many to create some kind of bond, and his failures have hurt him."

"You have bonded to Tyler . . . ?"

Joy shook her head slowly. "No, I haven't. I've never been able to bond to any man."

"What about Manfred?"

"He is a great man, and I love him. But not the way he loves me. I have had loves. And lovers, but they all go, in time, with my blessing. And I have made my peace with that." She stood, and from behind herself drew out a broad shell holding an inch-thick bundle of cedar. She raised her forefinger, then closed her eyes. The air around the finger began to glow. She drew a line of fire in the air, then touched her fingertip to the cedar. She walked the yurt's rim and drew the smudge through the air, leaving a trail of smoke.

"Mother drew us into sexual magic because she knew America was repressed. She knew that would keep us out of the mainstream, keep our ranks from being infiltrated by officers of the law. We searched the world for any teachings that related to sex, or sexuality, or the human energies. Because we needed a shield, something to hide behind."

She waved the shell in the air, drawing a feather across the top of it. Smoke rolled toward the walls in pungent little puffs. "Many people have come into our circle, but none know as much about us as you do, or came with your intent. We know that you meant us no harm. That you came to help Kolla. It is not your fault that you were lied to. You caught Simon's eye, and when he bedded you, he verified that you are . . . special. And told Tomo. You have caught Tomo's eye."

"Special?" Cat said weakly.

Joy waved the shell, leaving a contrail of smoke. "Some of us are, you know. By birth, or intent, or force of will. We are special. And there is no more sin, no more vanity in admitting to it than there is in admitting to being taller than average. In fact, there is a very real bit of reverse egotism in refusing to take responsibility for your uniqueness."

She had almost finished circumnavigating the room. "If the tribe, through genetics, or teaching, produces a unique and valuable creature, and that creature refuses to accept its responsibility to be a role model, to be a leader, does the tribe not suffer? Is that leader not stealing from the tribe?"

Cat thought about that, and then nodded feebly.

"Yes. And yet we are taught and encouraged from the very earliest age not to acknowledge our greatness. How foolish. I am special. And my brother. And you, in your way, are special." She had finished with the room, and came to sit before Cat now. The aroma of burnt cedar was comforting and somehow delicious. Joy reached out her hands. As Cat took them, she saw that they were strong, the fingers unusually blunt. She searched Joy's deep, almost impenetrably dark green eyes, and she saw something else.

Joy knew that the only man in the world she could ever mate with was her own brother, and that could never happen. What she could do, instead, is recognize in Cat a woman who could hold her brother's heart, and offer that woman a bond.

"Why me?" Cat said, already knowing the answer.

"Because Tomo is lonely, and you are lonely. There aren't really answers beyond that. You can spend decades wondering why, or you can have each other. The choice is up to you. For me . . . I offer you sisterhood, if you will have it."

But Jax. Jax might still be alive. . . .

She thought it, but didn't say it. For multiple reasons, she decided to keep that thought to herself.

Cat looked down at Joy, unconquerable, untouchable, and saw the vulnerability, saw who this woman truly was, and her heart melted. Tomo was his sister's other half. Joy loved him completely, and she craved friendship with a woman who might take him away.

Their fingers locked tightly. "I . . . don't know what's happening," Cat said. "There is so much to be done. So much to do. I care about Tomo, who wouldn't? But how can I love someone who keeps me prisoner? And don't tell me I'm wrong. We both know that's what it amounts to. The man I married, and divorced, and found, and lost . . . is gone." *Yes, leave it at that.* "I don't know what to feel."

She looked at Joy, and realized that this woman understood. Oh, God, she understood. Mirrors. Everywhere, mirrors.

"None of that matters," Joy said. "The future doesn't matter. All that I care about is right here, right now. I ask only your love. Your sisterhood."

Cat felt some sharp weight breaking in the center of her chest. "I've never had a sister," she said.

"Neither have I," the goddess replied.

She leaned forward, and they hugged.

eighty-two

Seated cross-legged on an inch-thick woven mat, Cat and Tyler faced each other in the hollow womb of the yurt. Both wore bathing suits beneath their saffron robes. Tyler's back was braced by an anchored stack of cushions. His dark soft eyes pleaded with her. "If there's any part of you that doesn't want this, please don't, Cat."

Cat's voice was quiet, contemplative. "Most of my life I haven't known what I've wanted—but I want this."

They sat at the center of a circle. Joy and Tomo were positioned at the north and south. Kolla sat crosslegged at the east. Simon, who had arrived only this morning, sat in the west.

Cat knee-walked forward, sat in Tyler's lap, and with a vast sigh, pressed her stomach muscles against his. Tomo had shown her the contractions of upper and lower abdominals, the proper breathing patterns. And she knew that Joy had taught Tyler in a similar fashion.

She began to roll her breathing, bringing it up from deep inside her, and Tyler joined her—more clumsily at first, then with growing confidence and ease.

Their mouths were only a whisper apart. She fell into his eyes, and through them.

Blackness within his eyes. Darkness as deep as the space between the stars. And sitting swathed in velvet, delicate and mysterious, a tiny golden jewel box. Repository of something precious. Something locked away, beyond the reach of friend or foe, or even her own questioning mind.

Then the blackness shattered, like a painted mirror struck with a sledgehammer—

And she was *in* Tyler's mind, now. In Tyler's memories. In one crucial area they dovetailed with her own.

The treasure chest opened.

eighty-three

Within that darkness, behind it, a small boy prowls through a house bound in darkness and secrets. Afraid, alone, he seeks the source of muffled cries.

He has been in the new foster home for six months. He loves it most of the time. His foster sister, Cat, is a walking dream. The foster parents are O.K.—when the MAN isn't drinking. The mother spends a lot of time working two jobs, as secretary and waitress, he thinks. Sometimes he thinks that she does that to be away from them. She leaves them alone with the MAN so much, and Tyler spends some of his time hunched in his small room, jumping at the smallest little sounds. There is something wrong, something *very* wrong, and Cat is a part of it.

He can see it in the way the MAN touches her. Hugs her, says things like "that's my girl," and tries to get her to kiss him on the mouth.

He can tell by the way Cat stays away from the house as much as possible, stays out late playing, eats her meals as fast as she can, and then hurries up to her room to sleep. Something is wrong in that house.

But Tyler loves Cat. And so when he hears the sounds, he wakes up, and comes out of his room, even though the Man has told him to stay in bed, *right, Tiger? Right Tiger? You just stay in your room, Buckaroo.*

No matter what you hear.

The sounds are muffled. He isn't sure what they are. He isn't sure *who* they are. But his stomach fists up, and his breath tastes like sour milk. That is why he took the steak knife from the dinner table, hid it in his sleeve, and carried it to his room.

Which is why he has it in his hand now. Tonight, this house is not a home. This is a place of deep shadows and hidden secrets. It is a house of fear.

He can hear the MAN's voice now. *"I feed you,"* it says. *"This is* my *fucking house. You belong to* me.

"I know you're hiding. I know it, and when I get my hands—"

Tyler checks Cat's room. It is empty. She is gone. Fled. And where would she be? From where do the voices descend?

The attic.

At the end of the hall, and to the right is the MAN's office, where he works at night. Just above the office door, a trap door is cut in the ceiling. An A-frame ladder stands under the open trap. Yawning blackness is pierced by a wavering light.

A voice. A girl's voice, filled with some twist of emotions Tyler can not name. *"No. Please. Don't."*

A sound, the sound of a hand striking skin. Tyler climbs up the ladder, one unsteady rung at a time, holding the knife in his hand. The attic smells like chalk.

He peeks up into it and sees—

The MAN. He has trapped Cat in the corner. He stands in front of her, and he is trying to force her to do something. Tyler can see her face, just enough of her face, an oval pale as a ghost. On the floor beside her, spilled onto its side, is the tiny golden box which holds finger and earrings, tiny precious pendants, all the beautiful things she owns, including the pin Tyler won her at the grabber machine in the mall. She had always laughed that the little gold box was safely hidden away, that no one could find it.

The man shifts his weight, and his heel comes down blindly on the golden cube, and it splinters into fragments. Bits of paste pearl and faux diamond skitter across the floor.

A scream. A MAN's scream. *"You little bitch! You bit me! I'm bleeding!"*

The sound of another blow. Harder, this time.

Tyler has no thought except for Cat. He rushes into the attic, knife in hand. He slashes, furiously but weakly, and the MAN roars, spinning, hand lashing out and Tyler sees stars and falls back, stumbles back, tries to catch himself, falls through the hatch—

Falls forever.

Impact. Then numbness. He feels twisted, senses pressure, but not pain, and is afraid.

He lies at the bottom, feet up on the ladder, wondering if he is dead. He can't feel anything. The MAN stares down at him, face framed in darkness. Then the MAN screams, and there was is another struggle. Cat has lunged at the MAN from behind, and they fall together. Two bodies fall out of the attic and crash into the ladder, and then onto Tyler.

The MAN, his head twisted at a new angle, and Cat, her beautiful head bruised. Slammed down onto Tyler. Something in his body surrenders with a kind of sigh, and he slides away and away into blackness.

eighty-four

Cat sat at the center of the ceremonial circle, holding Tyler's hand tightly. Twin tear-tracks sparkled on her cheeks. "I lay there for hours. All of us."

Joy nodded. "You . . . and Tyler . . . and your foster father?"

"No," Cat said. "Tyler is my foster brother. The man was my father."

For a long moment, there was silence in the room, and then she continued. "I can't remember much of what happened. I was in the hospital for a month. Tyler longer. He should have died, but didn't. My mother . . . she was never much. She never really recovered. Tyler and I . . . stuck together. I never remembered what he did for me, but from then on, he was just my brother."

Tomo said: "Tyler?"

"I love her," he said. "I always have." He looked shyly at Cat. "I just wanted to be with you. That's all that mattered."

Cat kissed Tyler's hand, holding it as if she were touching it for the first time, and realized that perhaps she was. She had never let herself really see him, really acknowledge the price he had gladly paid for her. The price of his silence over the years, his willingness to let her heal at her own pace.

But another part of Cat had known fully well. And that was the part which had driven her into the martial arts, into basketball and weight training. Into the police force. It was that part that shared her victories with Tyler, which did everything within her power to be his legs, to be the athlete, the warrior, the protector that he had once been, and could never be again. God, no wonder she had never had room for another man. She lived for Tyler, and Tyler lived for her, and theirs was a love that lived in a distant palace, in a realm far beyond consummation.

Jax had never had a chance.

"This is a place of truth," Joy said. "You have made a choice. For truth over comfortable lies. For pleasure over pain."

She touched her finger to her cheek, streaking the tears. "You heal bodies and minds? You heal hearts?" She struggled to force words past the wonder. "What kind of creatures are you? How can the world be so cold and dark while lights like yours exist?"

"Few are ready to receive that light," Joy said, as if speaking to a child. "You have seen more than most. You know what we can do."

"You have another choice," Tomo said. "Will you be ours? Tyler has already made his decision."

Startled, Cat jerked around. "Tyler . . . ?"

He set his jaw defiantly. "They can give me back my legs," he said. "You know they can, Cat."

"You sound very different than you did a few days ago."

"I didn't know then what I know now. What are *you* going to do, Cat?"

A band of pressure pressed at Cat's temples. She needed time to *think*. "I don't know. I really don't."

"Tyler," Tomo said. "We will have a very special meeting next month. Can you wait that long? A medically documented case such as yours would be very useful. We are in a new time. . . ."

"A time when miracles can be shared," Joy said fervently.

"I can wait," Tyler said.

"If I join," Cat said. "I will have to take your blood, directly from your veins."

"Yes."

"This meeting next month. You're going to reveal yourselves to the world, aren't you?"

"Yes," the Twins said in unison.

"And what else?"

"Are you ours?" they asked.

All eyes were on Cat. Tyler gripped at her hand. "Cat. Please."

"We'll see," was the only answer she had.

Cat wheeled Tyler back toward their quarters. He looked up at her imploringly. "Cat," he said. "Would you stay with me?"

"I need some time, all right?"

He nodded. She leaned down and hugged him. She started to wheel him on, and he gripped her hand. "No," he said. "I'll do this myself." His smile wasn't hurtful or challenging. She stood in the quad and watched as he wheeled himself toward the dormitory, a small and solitary figure, spine straight, head held high.

Tyler, her brother. Her friend.

And God, what else?

eighty-five

Joy and Tomo left the ceremonial yurt, heading back to the mansion, and their personal quarters.

They never noticed that one shadow separated itself from the others, and followed them as they walked to the great house. They never saw it follow them through the doorway, floating silently. They never saw it retreat and ghost about the periphery, until it found the room where Tomiko Oshita sat, precisely as they had seen her last, her red kimono flowing like a fiery shroud.

Without raising her withered eyelids, Tomiko said: "So?"

"The woman is strong," Joy replied.

They never noticed the flexible, whisker-thin probe entering the corner of a window. Even if they had noticed, there was little chance they would have recognized it as a fiber-optic camera

"Very strong. I think we have found someone special. As our father once thought you special."

"I trust you, Tomo. You are a good boy. You have always been a good boy." Despite the affectionate words, her eyes were cold. "We need the specials. The other girl . . . Kolla is her name?"

"She signs the papers next week," Joy said. "Her brother is dead. It is possible that she now owns the entire company."

"A quarter of a billion American dollars. Good. Good. We must own the children who control America's future. Money is all this country understands."

Tomo's gaze slid from mother to sister and back again. His beautiful face was haunted. "Mother," he said. "I am troubled."

Outside and below the window, Jax connected the camera to his black backpack, and slipped a pair of goggles over his eyes. A virtual video monitor shimmered to life in front of him. In it, he could see part of the room. He wiggled the camera until the room was properly framed.

There. Joy, Tomo, and what could only be Tomiko Oshita.
Mommy Dearest.

"What troubles you, my son?"

"I did not know how great Joy's power had grown." He seemed to choose each word with infinite care.

"She needs you more than ever."

"It frightens me, mother. She . . . *destroyed* those men." The image reflected in his eyes was a blazing, capering horror. "That is not why we came here."

"I know, my son. I am certain it won't happen again." There was a quality of dismissal about the words, reinforced by those which followed. "Tomo. Why not see to our new guests? I must speak to Joy."

Tomo stood. He paused, waiting for mother or sister to speak. As if needing them to say something. When no words were forthcoming, he rose, bowed politely, and left the room.

When the door closed behind him, Joy smiled. "He is such a child, sometimes."

"Tomo's spirit is still young. It is nature's way that women mature more quickly." Tomiko Oshita smiled slyly, the tip of her tongue flicking, leaving a glistening sheen on the dull brown stumps of her teeth.

"Yes, Mother." Joy said.

"America will suffer for what she did to your poor dead brother and sister." She leaned forward an emphatic half-inch. "For what I was forced to do to feed and protect you. Your brother must be sheltered, protected. Until the scales have dropped from his eyes."

"Yes, mother."

"Electric computers," Tomiko Oshita hissed. "Media. Steel. Oil. We have use of almost five billion dollars. After the broadcast, the world will know what you are. They will be afraid, as they should be. And they will try to destroy you. You will need the money and power to protect your brother, and yourself. And you will gather unto you the children of the world in their millions, inoculate them, and create my army."

"Yes, mother," Joy said patiently, the tones of a child faced with an aging parent. "You've told me a thousand times."

"Insolent, useless girl!" Mother Oshita screamed. "You'll hear it a thousand more! Until you use the money and the power heaven gave you, to destroy this spiritually bankrupt . . ." she sputtered passionately. ". . . bring death to the killers . . ."

Mother Oshita began to convulse, and she lost the thread of her speech. Joy blanched. "Mother . . . Tomo! Wait, mother. I'll fetch Tomo."

"No." Mother Oshita shuddered, but still shook her head adamantly. "If he heals me, he will feel my mind. He will know—I cannot keep him out, as you can. I am so tired. I have had to ask you to do so many things. . . ."

"I never complained, mother."

Joy took a deep breath. "We faced and conquered the Iron Shadows yesterday, mother. And they were not the great power you warned us of. They were just men."

Her mother's red brocaded arms levitated as if raised by puppet strings, and gripped her daughter's shoulders. "No!! Do not relax. Not ever. They are not men. They are everywhere. They live. They kill. They hide in the husks of the dead. You can kiss them, and not taste the rot in their spit. If you relax, even for a moment, they will have you." Her entire body shook like a leaf in a whirlwind. She must have been horribly frail beneath her robes.

Joy held her mother in her arms, crooning. Her eyes were closed tightly, and she never noticed the tiny camera as it slid silently from the corner of the window.

eighty-six

Cat reared up, golden in the firelight, her face lightly dewed with sweat. She smiled and lowered herself to Tomo's mouth. Their shadows melded again, and in the gloom Tomo's eyes glowed, not with reflection as an animal's might, but as if a fire burned deep within them. The warmth of that flame touched her heart.

"Cat," he said. "You are special. You have so much within you."

"Don't talk," she said. "Please."

"I could heal you," Tomo said. "I know it."

She stretched luxuriantly, still gripping him within her. His lovemaking burned her, and she willingly, urgently, rushed headlong into the flame. "I'm not broken," she said. "If I was, you and Joy have healed me."

"No," he said. "Not yet. But perhaps you are healing me. I saw your dream. Your memories, and they touched me deeply."

His hands dug into her with strength that she wouldn't have credited his slender body. "I need something I can't have, Cat."

"What are you talking about?"

"Sometimes," he said in a small, flat voice. "I see things that are to be. Just flashes, bits of a future. And sometimes merely deeper into the present. You are so strong," he said fiercely. "So used to making your own fate. We don't all have that option, Cat."

"What are you talking about? If we don't control our fates, who does?"

"You, more than most, should understand that our past controls our future."

She considered arguing with him, but realized that he was trying to tell her something, and almost breaking with the effort. "You remember what I said about the Gordian Knot?" he asked.

She nodded assent.

"I think I may have found a way to cut it—with your help."

Suddenly, and for no reason she could determine, she was suddenly afraid.

"I can heal you," he said. "But you have to ask."

"Ask . . . what?"

"Trust me, Cat. You're my only hope."

"What do you want," she asked, her heart beating terribly fast now.

"Someone," he said. "Some one person I can trust. Everyone needs one person."

"You have your sister. And you have yourself."

His eyes were haunted, sunken. "Please. Ask me in. I can't, I won't enter without your permission."

"What do you want?" she whispered.

"Ask me, Cat."

"I can't."

"Porsche."

She felt that hollowness inside her, knew that it grew stronger every moment, knew that if she didn't speak, didn't do something, and do it now, she was going to die inside. "Please," she said finally.

"Cat Juvell. Are you mine?"

Tomo's eyes glowed, and she tumbled silently into them.

eighty-seven

Half an hour had passed since Tomo had returned to his own quarters. Cat sat at the edge of her bed, head cradled in her hands. She examined her image in a wall mirror. She still looked much as she remembered—a pretty woman with soft blond hair and a face which was softer and more open than it had been in years. Perhaps ever. She wore a white silk gown—another present from Tomo—and found that she didn't automatically flinch at the sight of its frills and ribbons. Strange.

Too many choices. Too much had happened. What did she believe? Her senses, or logic? Logic said that there was something wrong, something still *hidden* in all of this. But her senses said to trust, everything within her said that at this moment, she stood at the living heart of the most momentous occurrence in human history. And what was the rational response to *that?*

A scratching sound at the window disrupted her reverie. She looked up, confused and surprised.

Jax Carpenter's face stared back at her, and for one terrible moment, she feared she was seeing a ghost. Then his broad, flat features split in a grin, and the ice in her chest melted.

She threw the window open, pulled him in with explosive, almost convulsive strength, and crushed herself against him. God, his solid reality, the smell and sight of him, was intoxicating. Only in that moment did she realize she had never really expected to see him again, and how much his living presence meant. His raw immediacy was almost overwhelming. The night chill on his clothes, the slight dew dampness, the molten core of heat burning within him . . . these blotted out all rational thought, cast her adrift on a sea of sensation. "Jax," she whispered. "I thought you were dead."

He smoothed her hair, sighing. "Hell wouldn't have me. Tyler?"

"Down the hall."

"We need to get you out of here."

Her fingers clutched at him. "Jax. I don't know. I think that I've changed my mind about the Twins."

"Again? Which way is it this time? You change your mind more often than you change your underwear. You need to see this."

He took an 8mm video playback unit out of his belt pack, and placed it on the table. Cat backed away, until the backs of her knees hit the bed's edge, then sat. "No," she said, staring at the ground as if she had found something terribly interesting there. "I don't want this."

"You have to."

"I don't have to do anything," she said irrationally. She tilted her head up shyly, and reached for his hand. "I've found something here, Jax. Stay with me."

"Cat," he said patiently. "You need to look at this. Now."

Cat snatched her hand away from Jax, and cocked it as if to strike. He glared at her until her she relented and snatched the sunglasses. Jax pushed the button as she slipped them on.

She watched in a strained and painful silence. Afterward, Cat said, "It doesn't prove anything."

"Not by itself," he admitted, and then told her of his conversation with Duke McCandlish. And of the dream. "It's a big lie, Cat. And the whole thing is a time bomb. Who the hell knows what those kids actually are? Or how many people Joy has killed? Joy probably doesn't know herself, after what she went through with her mother. And that poor kid Tomo— Jesus, this whole thing is as sick as it gets. Tomiko Oshita hates her life. Hates men. Hates America. Hates sex. She's twisted and warped those children for forty fucking years. Her daughter is a walking talking H-bomb, and we've got to get the hell out of here, and somewhere where we can think."

To Cat, the night outside the window seemed so peaceful. A curtain concealing . . . what? A hundred yards out, two saffron-jumpsuited acolytes patrolled the perimeter fence. A lonely moon sat fixed in a starless sky. A single, evil eye.

"Damn you, Jax" she said, and slapped him, hard. Jax made no attempt to dodge or block, and her palm cracked across his cheek with a sound like a rifle shot. Cat stared at him, then burst into tears, her shoulders slumped. "I'm sorry. God, I'm so sorry." It took her a full minute to gather herself, but one piece at a time, she came back to herself, remembered who and where and what she was, and finally leaned her head against his chest. "All right. We need time to think. Away from here."

Jax shucked his backpack, and extracted a duplicate of Cat's Glock 9mm, handing it to her. As she checked its action, he rubbed his cheek without rancor. "Now we're talking."

eighty-eight

Tyler sat staring sightlessly, inner eye trained on the wall of his mind. A few minutes ago it had just peeled right open, and he knew that Joy had been thinking of him. Tyler shivered at that thought. He wanted, he craved, he *needed* Joy to think of him, to open her heart to him. He could feel their connection, even now, knew that he was one node on a web which stretched around the world. Distantly, he sensed the presence of others connected as he was connected, souls linked by blood and love to the most amazing woman who had ever lived. His entire world, both his concept of the past and hopes for the future, rested in her hands.

If she would only open herself to him, just for a few moments, the pain would go away. When she actually accepted him into her bed and body, she lifted him to a peak of ecstasy beyond anything a man could dream. He could tolerate waiting for that moment, however long it might take, if only the pain would cease.

He hoped that Cat would make the right choice. The *only* choice . . .

His thoughts were interrupted by a quiet knock on the door. He wheeled up to it, and opened carefully. Cat, in a black pullover, denims, and rubber-soled shoes. And . . .

"Jax?!" he squealed in astonished delight. He wrapped his arms around the big man's waist and hugged him. Tyler shook, literally trembled all over. "I never thought I'd be so happy to see your ugly face."

"Are you all right?"

Tyler wrapped his arms around himself, groaning. "I'm . . . hurting, Jax. I don't know."

Cat's expression was artificially perky, her undertone on the bright edge of controlled hysteria. "Tomo can fix this. Really."

Jax snorted. "They can fix everything, can't they, Cat? Salvation by the pound. Just toe the party line. Come on. We're getting him out of here."

Tyler's eyes snapped open. They were too bright, and lacked focus. "I don't know. I don't know, Cat." He shivered like Chris Zimmer, the boy from the secondhand shop.

"What is this, Cat? This something about their blood? Something about having sex with them?"

"No," Cat said quickly. "Tomo is good. . . ."

"I'm not talking about Tomo. I don't know *what* Tomo is. I'm talking about his fucking sister. They're both twisted, but she's twisted and violent. She got into your body, into your mind, and she gets off on the fact that you need her now."

Cat kneaded Tyler's shoulder gently. "We'll get out of here. Then we'll take care of Tyler, and take some time to think."

Tyler shivered, and when they put hands on him, he jerked out of their grip, and screamed at the top of his voice: "Help! Help me!"

Jax was a moment slow to react, but Cat slapped her hand across Tyler's mouth. His teeth nipped at her fingers, but stopped short of actually tearing flesh. By the time Tyler could pry her arm free, Jax had already ripped a pillow cover off the bed, fashioning it into a crude gag. Cat held his arms down onto the wheelchair. His fingers lashed at her, as if only now understanding the strength of their resolve. Jax tore strips from the bed and bound Tyler's arms tight to the wheelchair. Tyler glared at them over the gag, tears streaming down his face.

Jax snarled, *"Now* do you see? We have to get the hell out of here."

They wheeled Tyler out into the hallway. An saffron-jumpsuited guard rounded the corner. "Hey! Who are you?"

Jax's good right arm blurred. The jumpsuited young man went down bonelessly, his face barely registering the pain.

Cat stared at the crumpled body, and winced. "I wish you hadn't done that. Come on."

They each took one side of Tyler's wheelchair, helped it down the stairs. Cat signaled for Jax to wait. She peered out first, then signaled them to come on.

Another guard appeared, a large thick-waisted blonde woman. "Miss Juvell. You're not supposed to be on the grounds after dark."

"Why not?"

"Those are just the rules."

"I'm making new rules," she said.

The guard took her arm, gently. Cat countergrabbed the arm, whirled the guard to her knees and into a lock. She twined her arm around the woman's neck and, as gently as she could, choked her into unconsciousness. The guard didn't look angry or afraid, or peaceful. Just . . . surprised. Cat gritted her teeth, filled with self-loathing.

"Well, that tears it," she spat. "Dammit! Come on." She waved to Jax and Tyler. Jax ripped away the binding sheets and picked Tyler up, running across the grass with him. A triangular section of fence was clipped and peeled to the side: Jax had been busy.

A maroon Toyota sedan waited on the other side, hidden in shadow. They hustled Tyler into the back seat. He no longer struggled. His eyes were tightly shut. He moaned softly, like a lost spirit.

Their car pulled away, crunching gravel bitterly beneath its wheels. Behind them, an alarm split the night air.

eighty-nine

There were no lampposts on the road, and Jax drove without headlights. Their car slewed and juddered, plowing blindly through the night.

He managed to get his left arm working enough to steer, and stretched out his right to fumble open the glove compartment. He handed Cat a folded map. "There's a logging road about half a mile ahead." His voice was clipped and precise, almost devoid of emotion. "McManus Road. See if you can find it."

Jax snapped his right hand back to the wheel and jerked it hard to the left as a Plymouth Fury pulled out ahead of them, trying to cut them off. "Somebody took a shortcut." Jax hit a soft shoulder and lost traction, then shifted gears and made the tightest turn he could, gouging his way back onto the road. The Plymouth slammed into their rear bumper. Cat's teeth clicked together hard, nipping her tongue. Behind them the attacking car fought for control, spinning to block the road.

In the back seat, Tyler lolled loose-limbed as a puppet, suddenly almost comatose.

Panic clawed at Cat. She fought the urge to care for Tyler, and managed to focus on the task at hand. By the dim light of the glove compartment reading lamp, she studied the map.

There, printed in almost indecipherably small blue script, were the words *McManus Road.* She glanced up in time to catch a glimpse of a sign reading Cotter Way, and verified that it was the last turnoff before McManus. Good.

"This way!"

Wheels grinding against gravel, they pulled off to the left.

Tyler's head snapped up as he felt Tomo and Joy *slam* into his mind. His own personality, his *is-ness* was driven into a dark corner, where it crouched, shuddering and afraid. He felt totally out of control. His head and eyes moved despite his screaming orders that they stay *front.* To his right, he saw a sign reading: MCMANUS ROAD.

The corners of his mouth twitched upward in a smile that was not his own.

ninety

Jax's Toyota bounced along the dark, rutted road. Clouds parted in time for a sliver of moonlight to reveal a fall of aspen on the road ahead. He slammed on the brakes, slewing the car to the side just fast enough to prevent a collision.

"Jesus wept," Jax said. Dead end. Behind them, headlights were coming up the road. He killed the engine. "Shit!"

"Out!" Cat yelled.

Jax and Cat helped Tyler out. He trembled, his pupils dilated painfully wide. Then he spoke, but when he did, it was an odd and completely disturbing meld of his own voice, and Joy's. *"Cat,"* he said. *"Cat. Stop now."*

Jax cursed under his breath. His right arm took the brunt of the load as they worked Tyler out of the back seat. Tyler was oddly passive at first, but as a second car pulled up behind them he began to buck and struggle.

Two guards exited the cars, holding hands up, palms out. "Please," one pleaded. "Come with us."

"Just turn around and go back," Jax said, "and there won't be a problem."

"I can't do that—" the guard said, and reached for Cat's arm. Her leg cocked almost to her chest, and she exhaled sharply, driving her heel into his solar plexus. The guard crumpled to the ground, diaphragm paralyzed. Cat turned. Jax had the other man up against the car, pinned by a forearm against the throat. The second guard would be unconscious in a moment— but that wasn't what captured her attention. She stared, open-mouthed, at the sight beyond him.

Tyler floated in the air like a marionette suspended from invisible strings. His legs hung slackly, limp toes dangling six inches above the ground. His mouth was open, his eyes very black.

"Oh, God," Cat heard herself say.

His mouth worked, opened and closed, but only a *huhn-huhn-huhn* gibberish sound emerged. An envelope of air around his body emitted a violet glare, and within that glow a network of crackling blue-white lightnings crawled, fine as wires, hot enough to singe the eye. The electrical discharges knitted together until they were like tiny cilialike threads. When they touched the grass beneath his feet the blades were drawn up, braiding together, knotting together, sucking up ponderosa pine cones and needles into tendrils of living plant, writhing out toward Cat and Jax, who stared in disbelief. The cords kept knitting and reknitting, and Cat had the unmistakable impression that they were forming into tiny hands, little woven fingers and thumbs which grasped at the air, stretching toward them hungrily. Lengthened into little thin childlike arms. Grasping.

Tyler's mouth worked again, but this time they were finally able to make out human language. "Cat . . ." he groaned. "I can't. Stop . . ." The field continued to expand, ferns and huckleberries beneath it ripping up, joining the mass of writhing green and brown arms.

Her eyes locked to that impossible, hideous sight, to the forest of tiny impish arms woven from grass and sticks, from soil and sand. Cat froze a bare moment too long. The first fingers gripped at her ankles, the first arms lashed themselves around her calves. She startled herself out of the trance and ripped her way free. Torn hands devolved to strands of plant matter, fluttered back to the forest floor, and were again incorporated into the rippling horror.

"What the hell—?" her attention snapped back to Jax as he struggled away from the car like a man wading through a tide, the little green hands crawling up his calves, digging at his thighs, scratching and clawing at him.

But although the leaves and vines beneath their feet still trembled, they no longer seemed capable of forming into limbs and questing digits. Whatever the hell this madness was, it seemed to have a limited field of effect. Beyond about fifteen feet the tendrils lost their strength.

Tyler's eyes were open, as if he was finally able to engage his mind, able to see what was happening, able to exert some small measure of will upon the energies funneling through him. It was like a resistor on a line, though—he screamed as if scalded. But the glow began to diminish, and then die down. Then it was gone.

Very cautiously, they approached him. "What happened?" Cat asked. She looked like a woman picking her way through a mine field.

Tyler pulled himself to a seated position. "They argued," he said. "They weren't sure what to do about us." He looked up at Cat. "Tomo loves you. Joy thinks you betrayed them. That's all I know for sure."

His head lolled forward on his chest. Cat held him. "You don't have to know any more," she said. "That's enough."

ninety-one

"Come on," Jax said. "I don't know how much time we have."

Less than a mile behind them, another car climbed the rutted road. Jax picked Tyler up, slung him over his right shoulder. Tyler was groggy now, almost completely unaware of what was happening around him.

Cat shut her mind to his soft, almost inaudible murmurs, and lead the way into the woods.

They walked for close to an hour. During that time Jax felt Tyler's weight shift from a burden to a burning hell in calves and shoulder, but refused to rest. Every step was an agonizing struggle. He dared not turn an ankle. He

dared not even consider stopping. The only thing to do was to compart-
mentalize the fatigue, and keep going. Push the strain into a deeper
and darker portion of himself, and keep going. Even when the fatigue part,
the molten lead of his suffering became the largest part of him, and there
was a smaller and smaller man left to walk onward, he dared not think
of it.

> *The woods are lovely, dark and deep,*
> *But I have promises to keep . . .*

He felt giddy now, and with a start, became alarmed by the giddiness.
That sensation was the edge of the dark place which grew within him like
a giant cyst, encapsulating the deadly fatigue. He kept his eyes on Cat, who
blazed a path for them.

There was no trail here, and she trudged through the vine maple and
damp falls of old man's beard, relying on glimpses of the moon to mark
out direction. They had agreed to head north for Bend, but had to avoid
main roads. If they could cross the open mountain range, they might have
a chance to get down to a side road, someplace where they could catch a
ride. Find a bit of farmland or an outlying house. Maybe steal a car. Something.

But meanwhile, it meant that Jax had to carry Tyler's hundred and fifty
pounds, and not let it kill him. Not think about what might happen if the
Twins exerted their hideous powers through Tyler again. He couldn't let
himself think about that. That way lay madness, and even worse, despair.

So instead he watched Cat. He carried the burden of Tyler's weight,
but she carried the burden of his soul. And there was something else between them. In some subtle manner the balance between the three of them
had shifted again. He hadn't had time or nerve to ask either of them what
had happened to them at the camp. He wasn't completely certain that he
wanted to know.

She looked at Tyler differently. Not with more or less affection, more
or less concern . . . but with a different . . . *awareness.* Yes. that was the
word. Some tiny primitive part of him, in the very back of his mind,
screamed that it knew exactly what that meant. But Jax wouldn't, couldn't
listen to it and keep walking at the same time.

A question rose up in his mind like a sea serpent cresting a wave,
gaining momentum steadily. Never letting him see it completely, hiding

from him just enough to avoid taking complete form in his mind, neither allowing him to cope with it or banish it. It hung there, just out of reach, like a recurring fragment of a terrible nightmare.

The moon was still high above them, a sliver of pale orange, clearly visible through the thin cloud cover. It was dark, and they were satisfied for that to be so. They were also cold—they dared not light a fire—and that was far worse.

The three of them crouched in the sheltering dark of three ponderosa pines, clustered at the lee of a hillock. The night wind whipped through the trees, carrying distant sounds—a dog howling for its mate, an indecipherable buzzing sound, a distant car horn.

Tyler shivered, turned on his side against the mossy roughness of a pine trunk. He was exhausted, and more than that, terribly shamed. "You should leave me," he said. "Without me, you have a chance."

Jax thought it was odd. He was weary in his every joint and bone, but Tyler looked even worse. "We're all getting out of this," he said.

Cat smoothed her fingers across his face. "Tyler," she said. "You just keep saving me."

"I'll try not to make a habit of it," he said.

Cat turned to Jax. "I'll take first watch," she said. "You try to get some sleep."

Jax nodded, then a horrible thought came to him. "Cat—I don't know if that's a good idea. They move through dreams. I don't understand it, but that's what their followers believe, remember? That's what their book says. And I think they found their father through me, through my dream. And killed him. If I sleep . . ."

Cat cursed viciously. "Of course. Damn. Oh, Jax . . ." she buried her face in her hands for a moment, and thought hard. "There has to be a way out."

"They came through while I was conscious because I didn't resist. I'm sorry." He looked utterly ashamed. "I didn't realize the threat. Now I know—and I can block it consciously."

"But you were awake," Cat said. "How the hell do we do that in our sleep?"

"Maybe. Maybe an idea," Jax said. "I think that this thing they sent into my dream . . . it kind of crossed from my dream to McCandlish's. I don't understand. But when it did, I was behind it, and it didn't sense me. I was pulled into myself." He hesitated. "There's a dark place inside me. It's like a grave, almost. I found it a long time ago, in Vietnam. I found it again during that cave-in."

"A private place? You can look out, but people can't see in?" Cat asked.

He nodded, and suddenly the air between them almost crackled.

"Jax," she said. "Do you have conscious control over it?"

He shook his head. "No. It only happens when I'm threatened. Then some part of me seems to take over on its own."

Cat smiled for the first time in an hour. "Same here. I learned it a long time ago." The smile vanished. "My father taught me." There was more, he knew there was more, but she declined to offer it. "No control over it, but I go there sometime, under threat. Some parts of me hid there for twenty years. Maybe . . . just maybe we can learn to hide there in our dreams."

"Oh, great," Tyler said. "Do either of you have experience in lucid dreaming? It can take months or years to learn. We've just got tonight. What do you think the chances are?"

"Not good," Jax confessed. He felt despair chewing at him again, and then brightened. "But here's something else. Just before you began to channel that force, the light around you bent a little. At first I thought it was a trick of the shadow, but now I don't think so. I think that it's a precursor."

Cat nodded slowly. "I saw Tomo doing that once, while he was asleep. He was in the Dream Time, and something was happening. You have sacred paintings from all over the world showing light effects around saints and magicians. I don't need to understand it or rationalize it. But maybe we can use it. What do you know about lucid dreaming, Tyler? Anything fast and dirty?"

He concentrated for almost a minute, and then started talking. "You can look for a mirror in your dream, and when you see your reflection tell yourself you're just sleeping. You can count as you fall asleep, and try to keep counting all the way into your dream. Ahh . . . you can ask yourself all day 'Am I dreaming *now?*'" And if you ask yourself that question enough, you'll eventually ask yourself in the dream."

"So what do we know?" Jax said. "We know that dreams are the conduit. But that a conscious mind can fight off the possession, or whatever you want to call it. Maybe trying to be lucid will help. Maybe not. The possession might be preceeded by a light effect around the sleeper. That may be enough. We might be able to beat it by just rotating sleepers. Somebody stays awake and if they see anything . . . *anything,* they wake the glowworm up. Fair enough?"

Cat's face was tense. You could hear the motor hum. "Looking for problems. Could it really be this easy?"

"Nothing easy there. But it still might work."

"All right. Your idea. You take the first nap."

He started to argue with her, but realized, once again, that there was something left unsaid about the relationship between Cat and Tyler, something that simply did not, as yet, involve him. Jax grunted assent, and crawled over to the furthest pine. The ground beneath it was matted and soft with needles. He curled up into a ball, and shut his eyes. Fatigue overcame cold and discomfort and dread. He fell asleep in seconds.

Cat held Tyler, stroking his hair. "It's strange, you know?" She said. "I've known you most of my life, and I feel like we're just getting to know each other." She paused. "I'm just getting to know myself."

"Must be strange," he said.

"There's no hurry. We have a whole world ahead of us," her voice was studiedly merry.

Tyler paused before answering. Perhaps listening to the wind sweeping through trees. Perhaps listening to something within himself.

"Right," he said finally. "Yeah, I know. I . . . you didn't remember about your father. Just tried to forget about it—there wasn't anyone to talk to about it, and I didn't want to tell you anything you didn't want to know."

The wind cut right through her jacket, and she clung more tightly to Tyler, perhaps seeking warmth. "Some part of me knew," she said. "Some part remembered what you did for me. What it cost you. Maybe there was a part of me that went out and lived for you. Wanted to be your legs."

"Nice legs, too."

She glanced at Jax, sleeping not ten feet from them. "What are we going to do?"

Tyler smiled at her gently. "I think it'll work out, somehow. Things always do."

"Yeah. Somehow." She leaned her head against his shoulder. Tyler looked out into the darkness, and watched the stars.

Distantly, he saw searchlights making their brief, yellowish brush strokes among the trees.

ninety-two

Wednesday, July 5

The sun had barely crested the eastern mountains, and as yet the shadows still concealed them. It was Jax's watch. Cat lay curled in a knot at the base of a pine, her head on her arm. Tyler was stretched out on his side, a heap of pine needles for his bed, covered with Jax's blue windbreaker. Jax sat up, his back propped against a ponderosa trunk.

Jax's eyes were closed. He had dry-swallowed half of a Tylenol caplet with codeine. That, plus his fatigue, had forced him to close his eyes for just a moment, just a few seconds. . . .

Which turned into the better part of an hour . . .

And he never saw the first sparks as the bluish glow began around Tyler's inert body. Jax finally began to stir as Tyler's hands knotted into fists, and beat at the earth. Then his eyes snapped open.

"Found you," Tyler whispered, in a voice not his own. His mouth stretched into a painful smile, and the cords stood out in his neck and face, a parody of sensual *extremis*. "Found you, *bitch*—"

Cat curled up and awakened almost instantly, taking in the situation at a glance. "Wake up, Tyler" she said urgently. "For God sake, wake up."

He writhed, gasping. Then his eyes snapped open. The blue glow didn't fade—instead, it actually grew stronger.

Jax watched, aghast. "Shit. It came through the dream, but it's here now. He's not waking up. Tyler." Desperation flattened Jax's voice. "You fought it before, and you can do it again."

Cat held her foster brother tightly. She felt a sensation like heat forming, some odd combination of fire and electricity. Her arms were numbed, her joints flamed, but she couldn't let go. The sensation was like an orgasm, sustained until it went completely beyond pleasure, until all of the charge was discharged, and the body responded in a raw, wet, spastic fashion, all ecstasy forgotten.

Jax tried to grab his other hand. Tyler's sleeping arm swept up. With a violent discharge of blue sparks, Jax flew back, smashing against the trunk of a young pine tree.

Tyler's eyes rolled up and his hands scraped at the needles and pine cones. Cat fought to focus, to come to herself and fully deal with what was happening here, but her mind was filled with a low, crazed buzzing, a droning that grew louder as she tried to ignore it, but receded when she focused. Where was her gun? She had dropped . . . her Glock. Her hand cast about for it, but couldn't find it. Where . . . ?

She turned her head, and saw Jax laying near her, his elbows crooked, and eyes closed. His big chest rose and fell as slowly and powerfully as the turning of the tide. She intuited that he was all right. And Tyler—

Oh yes, Tyler.

She turned over onto her belly, and watched him with growing horror. He sat on the ground with his back against a tree stump. His legs were spread wide, and he stared at the ground between then with unfocused, sleeping eyes. Something, *someone* else looked out through those eyes, at the ground in front of him.

The ground was *alive.*

The leaves humped, writhed and crawled together like a clump of worms, breaking, crumbling, re-forming into . . . what?

Instinctively, she knew that Tyler was in no danger. With the same deep intuitive knowing, she realized that she and Jax were very close to death.

She crawled over to Jax, and shook him, calling his name. No answer, no movement. She shook harder, although her own limbs felt leaden Cat looked back at Tyler. His eyes were stretched open, and vibrated side to side rapidly, like a dreamer deep in REM sleep.

The thing between his legs had assumed a shape now, a form, even if an embryonic one. It looked like the head of a gigantic spider. She saw the faceted eyes now, composed of leaves and twigs, of dirt, and it was crawling, seemed to be forming and re-forming itself, swirling, as if it were energy more than solid matter, more than pattern than substance. It was almost hypnotic, buzzed like a swarming colony of bees or ants, a sound like grease sizzling in a pan.

She fought a burst of sheer panic, and shook Jax, hard. He muttered, mumbled, sagged back into stupor.

Cat bit his ear.

Jax roared, sat up violently and tossed her off, flinging his arm clumsily like a bear awakening from a winter's slumber.

She rolled with it, and managed to exhale as Jax's arm crashed into her. Her head spun again, and she looked back at the thing growing out of the ground. Her heart raced. It was larger now, and in the morning light cast its growing shadow across the clearing. The thing was almost completely born now. Its rubbery hide glistened with mud and night damp, its eight pipe-like legs were formed of twigs and bits of earth, its eyes of pebbles. It turned and snarled at them, a stinking wind churning with jealousy and rage, frustration and blood hunger. It was as large as a doberman, with fangs half a foot in length. Even across the intervening distance, its stench turned her stomach. It's face was not completely arachnid. It had a woman's eyes, its leathery black mouth somehow defining a woman's face. It grinned at them

Oh, God.

There was a crackling sound in the woods behind them, and Cat turned in time to see . . . two truncheon-bearing acolytes enter the clearing. They weren't looking at Cat and Jax. Or even at Tyler. They were watching the Thing, the thing growing and shaking itself slowly to life between Tyler's knees. And were afraid.

The two of you create a third, imaginary entity we call "The Prey." The Prey is the orgasticness, the ecstasy, the pleasure you both crave. Together the two of you create it, chase it, and feed upon it. Feed your hungers.

And what was this? If they were the Prey, this thing was the Hunter.

The Hunter had almost completely emerged from the soil between Tyler's legs, and the acolytes stared at it with superstitious awe.

"Iron Shadows," one of them whispered.

"No," Cat said her voice urgent. "There *are* no Iron Shadows. There never was. It's a projection of their own fear and darkness. This is Joy. She's going to kill us. She'll kill anyone who stands in her way."

They looked at each other, clearly confused, and afraid. The spider-thing pawed at the dirt and took a single clumsy, halting step forward . . . then its legs folded beneath it, and it tumbled back to ground. Understandable: It was a babe, and newborn.

Cat grabbed Jax and pulled him back, fought to get up on her feet.

The two acolytes were ashen. "You . . . you stay where you are," one stuttered.

"It's going to kill us!" Cat said.

"It's some kind of . . . of big crab. . . ." the taller one said, and picked up a rock, throwing it. It hit the thing between the eyes, and the Hunter snarled.

The Hunter leaped, and the acolyte went down, screaming as it ripped through robes and skin. The acolyte still screamed and thrashed weakly, then shrieked hideously as its fangs sank into his back. Something milky white drooled out of the wounds. With a single spastic convulsion, the acolyte died.

The second guard took a single glance at the carnage, and screamed, fleeing into the trees.

Cat bent deeply from the knees and slipped her arms around Jax's waist from the rear, struggling to raise him. The Hunter was coming. It was finished with the acolyte. Its bloodstained fangs glinted black in the shadows. Its sides heaved and sucked as if it were a bellows. She looked into its eyes, deep into its eyes, and saw cold hatred. "Joy," she said desperately. "Please. Don't do this."

The beast stopped, its head tilted sideways a bit, looking at her. It smiled. Its head began to melt like blood-blackened tallow in a raging fire. Then the slagging mass reversed direction, and it re-formed into Joy, the head of the woman upon the body of the beast. It snarled at her. "Go ahead," it said, in a voice that was a mockery of Joy's mellifluous tones. "I give you until the count of ten. One . . ."

Cat struggled to heft Jax's bulk, groaning beneath the load. "Tyler," she sobbed. "Please. If you can hear me. It's coming through you. You can stop it. Only you."

"Two . . ." the Hunter grinned at her. "See Cat. See Cat Run. Run, Cat, Run."

"Tyler!" Cat screamed, and pulled at Jax again.

"Leave the big one for me," the Hunter said seductively. "You'll live a little longer. Not much, but a little."

Like a legless man crawling up a burning staircase, Tyler fought his way up from the depths of the trance. Blazing fingers, claws, talons gripped at him. Dream. All dream. Keep . . . going. Keep going.

Up above him was the light, was the world he belonged to. This seductive darkness was a tempting hell, but he wouldn't let himself succumb
to it. Up above him, his friends were fighting for their lives. As he neared
the door, he saw through it into the forest, and redoubled his efforts. He
could not fail. He dared not.

"Seven," the Hunter was saying.

He felt that he was not alone in his body, and knew who was there with
him, shocked and dismayed by the answer. When he closed his eyes, he saw
through the eyes of the thing, the hideous thing that hunted his friends
through the woods.

(Hunter)

Yes. With a deep and horribly certain knowing, he understood what
this thing was. What had Cat said about the sexual exercises? The "Prey"
exercise. The transformation of sexual energy into the mental projection of
an animal form. Which, in turn, evoked a predatory response from the
practitioner, shutting down the forebrain logic circuits, freeing something
deeper and far more primal. God help them.

He watched as Cat hauled Jax out into the woods, and the Hunter
crawled off after them. Walking tentatively at first, testing its legs, and
then crawling rapidly, then its eight legs a blur. He sensed its hunger,
knew its lust, saw through its mind the intent to rend and tear, knew that
in a few minutes the people he loved most in all the world would die. He
cried for shame at his inability to help them, knew that their lives were for-
feit because they had tried to save his.

Then he saw, half-buried in the leaves, Cat's Glock.

And Tyler's world went very quiet. He almost laughed, realizing the
answer, the only answer. Without him, Cat and Jax could disappear into the
woods. For him, they had risked everything. He was the weak link. He had
opened himself to Joy, and in doing so had lost his ability to resist. Had Cat
opened to Tomo? He thought so. But she had resources he did not: gifts of
the fire through which she had crawled as a child.

Heat and pressure create diamonds. Cat was a gem, and he was a fucking zircon. He didn't have the resources to fight a thing like this—which
was why it had chosen him.

Tyler pushed himself onto his side, clawed his way forward. The morning would have been a good one. A cluster of pink and white flowers concealed the Glock. Their slender brown stalks swayed in an imperceptible
wind. All around them, the dirt was ripped bare by the Hunter's search for

substance. He recognized the flower: wild rhododendron. It would be nice to have remembered some obscure fact about them, or to recall that their name meant something poignant and tragic in Greek or Latin. He couldn't remember a thing. They were simply the last flowers he would ever touch, that was all.

His hands closed around the Glock.

Tyler wished that there was time for more of a goodbye. A poem, perhaps. Or some pithy observation. No time for anything. How about: "Dying is easy. Comedy is hard." Who was it, what actor had said that? God, how true. Every time he watched Cat and Jax together touching, and laughed at them, it had been like dying. Watching them fall in love. Marry. And then watching them dissolve. And all the time, playing court jester.

Hah. Hah. Hah.

"Last laugh, Cat," he whispered.

ninety-three

The gunshot rang through the woods like a crack of thunder. The Hunter stopped, trembled. The Joy-thing atop it devolved back into insectile form even as Cat watched. She watched the life leave its faceted dead eyes, saw it crumble into a heap of brown needles leaves, twisted branches, dirt and dust. A golem returning to the elements from whence it came.

She stared at the pile of organic matter for a long moment, and then said: "Tyler?" as sudden, horrible certainty ripped through her.

Jax was only half-conscious. "Wha—" She sat him down gently on the ground. "It's all right," she said. "You'll be all right here." She couldn't look at him. "I'll be right back."

Before he could phrase a question, she was gone.

She approached the clearing carefully, barely able to breathe. Tyler was sprawled on his bed of pine needles, a spreading dark stain crimsoning his chest.

Cat crossed the clearing with a heavy tread, and collapsed beside him. She cradled Tyler in her arms. He stared up at her, the light in his eyes already dimming.

He turned his head sideways, nuzzled it up under her arm like a puppy seeking warmth. Blood bubbled from his mouth as he tried to say something. His eyes were urgent. His fingers, so strong they seemed the talons of some predator gripped at her. She could understand nothing, knew nothing except her own grief.

His mouth opened and closed, like the mouth of a baby bird. No sound emerged. Christ. What was he trying to say?

In his last moments, Tyler realized he had made a terrible mistake. There was one last thing that Cat needed to know. She had been unconscious at the mining camp. Hadn't seen Milton Quest's thug try to shoot Joy. Had never seen the bullets bounce away harmlessly. He knew what Cat would do next, and needed to tell her somehow that it was futile, that to try to kill Joy would be suicidal. . . .

To try . . .

It was all going dark and cold. If he could just get that one thought out.

Just that one . . .

Cat tried to speak, but grief constricted her throat. There was nothing she could say, no words to take the pain away from him, none that would stave off the approaching cold. Even now, he struggled to speak to her, to give her some last measure of himself. Whatever this final message, it was so important that he would spend his final breath trying to impart it.

And when the vitality left his eyes, when they didn't close, but just grew still, and his chest ceased its struggle to clear itself of fluid and speak whatever final words he had struggled to convey, there was nothing in the world for Cat but pain.

She held his cooling body, her heart like a great, raw wound.

Jax limped into the clearing. He watched, but did not speak. After some time, Cat wiped her sleeve across her face, streaking it with dirt and tears.

Only then did Jax have words for her. "What do we do now, Cat?" he asked quietly.

She said nothing, but her eyes burned.

ninety-four

Tyler ran at her side through the sand, his legs strong and muscular, his freckled face glowing with health. Cat smelled the sea breeze and turned to admire him. He was tanned, and perfect. The sea rolled ceaselessly against the shore behind him. Ahead of them, Jax stood at the cooler, holding a beer in either hand, his laughter spurring them on. Cat bore down and pumped her legs harder, feeling her soles slapping against the sand, feeling her toes digging in, hearing the breath roaring in her chest.

She wanted to laugh, wanted to sing, wanted to cry for

(Joy)

that life could be so good, so full. They would race, and race again, and drink ice cold beer, and laugh. Sitting on the picnic blanket behind Jax was Freddy King. And next to him . . .

Cat, bearing down on her running, struggled because suddenly it felt as if her legs were being sucked into the sand, pulled down into its sodden depths. Confusion clouded thought.

. . . next to him was someone that Cat had never seen, but looked just like Freddy, only older.

Duke McCandlish . . . ? But he was dead, wasn't he?

Confused, but still determined to win, Cat ran on, and turned to look at Tyler—

Who must have spilled something on his shirt. Raspberry sandwich filling? But he hadn't been wearing a shirt a minute ago, and the ocean rolling against the shore was no longer blue and white but red, thick and crimson. When she looked over her shoulder, the footsteps in the sand weren't traces of human passage at all, but clawed and knobby imprints, although there was nothing to be seen, spurts of sand were puffing up into the air in galloping rhythm, faster and faster now and—

Am

She looked back at Jax. He was screaming at her, words that she couldn't hear, and the faster she ran, the more she stood still and the sand flowed backward beneath her—

I

The sun was blue, wavering blue light all across the horizon, as if it weren't a ball of yellow fire but a ribbon of flame, stretching at the very periphery of sight in three hundred and sixty degrees—

Dreaming

—almost as if something were screwing off the top of her dream, something larger than her dreaming mind, and she felt the sensation of pulling and stretching and oh my God in heaven someone is here, is here and Jax is screaming and—

Now?

ninety-five

Friday, August 4

Cat awakened sputtering, water filling her nose and mouth. She scratched and flailed, and finally sat up, her sopping blond hair streaming down over her face, sobbing for breath. She shivered, but that wasn't surprising—the tub of ice water beside the bed was slopped half onto the floor after Jax's emergency actions.

It took about four breaths for her to orient herself: A motel room with two beds and a cheap television on a pivoting pedestal. The shades were drawn. The room had to be dark: They had learned that the very first and earliest signs of invasion were the tiny blue discharges, visible only in total darkness. Jax flicked the lights on.

"I was about to go, wasn't I?" She didn't need an answer.

She hadn't had a full night's sleep in two weeks. Jax looked as if he hadn't slept in a month. His wounds were healing poorly. They didn't dare go to a hospital. Didn't dare use anesthetic. One of them had to remain awake at all times, and watch. Watch to see if the other was the victim of a dream invasion. The instant it began, the instant any sign of a glow developed, or abnormal tossing and turning, any distress at all—into the ice water.

His face was terribly haggard, but concerned. "What happened?" he asked.

"I could feel them," she said. "Coming. Searching for me."

Jax nodded his head. He knew the drill, all too well. She had been forced to awaken him three times a night from dreams in which Jax had to hide as soon as the dreamscape began to shift, as soon as he had the feeling that he was not alone. He knew places to hide in his mind, had found them under extreme duress in a life lived long before. And if he had forgotten those lessons, he had learned them again, in Santa Cruz.

Cat had a place, had always had a hiding place, since childhood. Perhaps that was what they had seen and sensed in each other, from the very beginning. Each of them had learned reasons and methods to hide. At least they were no longer hiding from each other, and that was a very genuine blessing.

Cat ground her palms against her eyes. "I don't think I can sleep any more tonight," she yawned. "Why don't you try to get some rest?"

He lay down on the bed, feeling her residual warmth in the sheets. He folded his hands behind his head. Strange. Books written by the Twins clearly explained how to lucid dream. That, and what they had learned in the workshop, and their own natural protections had, so far, kept them alive.

Strange.

"Two more days," Jax said. He had never looked so exhausted.

"Two more days," she replied. "And then, one way or another, its over."

ninety-six

Sunday, August 6

Sixty-six thousand people were packed into the Los Angeles Memorial Coliseum, a large town, a tiny nation whose citizens had been born in two dozen countries, and every state in the Union. Searchlights stabbed up into the night sky, and helicopters from local television stations circled the gigantic bowl like eagles protecting a nest. From the air, individual human beings were spots, specks, spots of red tunic and blue scarf and thousands of golden robes. The stadium fluttered with banners, illegible from a height. At the very center of the field were an enormous stage, a landing zone, and a twelve-foot-wide, two-hundred-foot-long mat of burning wood, as attendants prepared the largest fire walk in history.

No voices could be distinguished from a height, but there was a general pace, a rhythm to the motion of individuals and groups. Excitement sizzled in the air. This was a special day, a very exceptional day, and everyone there knew that when this night was over, nothing in the world would be quite the same, ever again.

Cat washed her face carefully. For the third time she scrubbed and scrubbed, until her cheeks were bruised pink by the pressure. She gazed at herself in the mirror, and didn't recognize the woman who stared back at her. The eyes were darker than the eyes she had been born with. The hair was stained dark, and clipped short.

She hadn't slept in fifty hours, and exhaustion pounded a jackhammer rhythm in her bones. She refused to feel it. She just wouldn't—until this was finished. Until it no longer mattered.

She hitched the corners of her lips up into something that bore a superficial resemblance to a smile, but contained no trace of humor. She thought to herself: *I look like a corpse, with a live woman's face stapled to its skull.*

From the hallway behind her came a cry: "Ten minutes! We've got ten minutes to show time!" The message was repeated in German, in Spanish, in Japanese, and then in French.

She tucked her blouse in, arranging her coat to hide any trace of a holster's bulge; the Glock nested beneath her left arm like a sleeping spider. She adjusted the rectangular plastic badge affixed to her gold vest. Obtaining the badge had been relatively simple. This event was very special, a once in a lifetime, once in a century, once in a millennium event. Because of its importance, every major Golden Sun enclave from Sri Lanka to Switzerland had provided support. Crowd control, security, communications, press relations, hospitality, transportation, setup and breakdown crews were all carefully internationalized. Due to that diversity, no one knew anyone.

Finding one acolyte had been easy. The only question had been: Would it be a man or a woman? To whom would the terrible duty fall?

Luck of the draw, Jax. A woman it was.

Cutting Leah Van Ness out of the pack and rendering her unconscious had been simplicity itself. For Cat, insinuating herself into the crowd of supplicants proved only slightly more onerous. She knew what must be done. Knew where she needed to be. She also knew what this would cost her.

She could do everything, anything that needed to be done, if she was willing to lose her soul in the process.

In one hand, the world. In the other your soul. You can only save one. Which will it be?

Once again, she examined the haggard creature in the mirror. *Oh God. How had things come to this?* She yanked that smile back into place. It was a death's-head leer. She splashed cold water on her face. It didn't wake her—she still felt like roadkill. Only now, she felt like wet roadkill.

She walked out into the hallway, joining the flow of effervescent, glowing, beautiful, golden robed young people sprinting toward the field. They cheered, chanting *hup* with every upswept knee. Their chests were high, heads back, eyes bright, smiles and voices proud. These were the children of the Golden Sun. This was their moment. At double-time, they marched down the rectangular concrete tunnel, toward the shimmering light of the field.

The Korean boy next to her grinned broadly, eyes wide. This was a moment when faith, when works, when years of sacrifice would be rewarded. This was the dawn of a new age. They left the corridor and entered the arena's glare, the lights so intense she was almost blinded.

The crowd roared like an animal with a million hearts and a single throat.

The central stage, six feet of steel and plastic and wooden support beams, stood in the exact center of the field. Towering banks of sodium arc lamps transformed nighttime to high noon. Mobile relay trucks from every major television station in the Greater Los Angeles Metropolitan area circled the parking lot outside the coliseum. Their cameras perched at the edges of the field, feeding cable relay stations and satellite dishes. How many countries currently received this feed? Sixty? Eighty? A hundred? How many people were watching this? A hundred million? Two hundred? Eight? A billion and a half?

She didn't know. She hadn't seen the latest figures, and didn't want to. What she wanted, more than anything in the world, was to be anywhere in the world but here, and now. This was no place for anyone sane to be. This was nothing for anyone sane to do.

That mattered little—she was beyond sanity now. Beyond right and wrong. There were no rules.

The metal spider beneath her arm whispered to her: *When you have principles, you don't need rules.*

She giggled at that, a tinny, twisty sound. She bit her tongue to stop herself, and was shocked from her stupor by pain and the thick salt taste of blood.

How many times had she spoken those eight words? Hell, she'd damn near built her life upon them. And now, they seemed words that could have been spoken by Hitler, by Torquemada. By Lee Harvey Oswald.

None of that changed what had to be done. And God help her, there was no one else in the world to do it.

Ten, twenty, thirty members of the Golden Sun circled around the landing pad, linking hands, gazing drunkenly up into the night sky. A blazing naked moon glared above them, Polyphemus' pockmarked eye.

Finally, faintly, came the steady *whop-whop whop-whop* of approaching rotor blades.

The crowd swelled, roared, stomped like some mindless super-stimulated organism. Thousands of streaming banners and a hurricane of multicolored confetti erupted from the stands. The great gold and silver Bell executive transport crested the arena. It hovered at the lip for a dramatic moment, like an eagle levitated by an updraft. Then it began its slow and graceful descent.

The four searchlights found it, caressed it as if they could support it with beams of light. Slowly, very very slowly, as the loudspeakers blared the theme from *Rocky,* it settled in for a landing. It settled into the precise center of a huge silver X to the left of the main platform, waved down by four ground-crew techs wielding huge silver flashlights. The crowd roared its approval, then shushed into a reverent silence.

The rotors materialized out of a blue atop the copter, slowing, slowing. Stopping.

There was complete quiet in the arena, a state that held for almost two minutes, until a hushed murmur began to build, and then build, excitement, anticipation, a demand, a hunger. Feet, at first patting the ground in individual rhythm something soft and eccentric. The beat was picked up by neighbors on all sides, slowing and speeding up, swelling and cresting, becoming a roar, a single animal sound washing from one side of the arena to the other, catching, lifting, growing as if it were a living thing.

The doors opened.

Silence. Then—

Joy and Tomo emerged.

Joy's hands were raised in triumph as Queen's "We Are the Champions" filled the stadium's bowl, and then lifted to the stars. There was something in her face, some calm certainty, that had never appeared there before—at least, never in public. And around her flickered the faintest trace of an aura, something silver and red, something flashing to catch the eye and freeze the breath. And for a moment the sound of the music seemed to stutter and die, as those facing the open side of the helicopter saw this display, and those behind it saw the giant figures projected on the titanic video screen. And saw the reflection of the lights, washing across the grass, glimmering in the night.

Somehow they knew that this night was very special. That this night they were attending the coronation not of a queen, but of a Goddess.

Fingers locked and raised high with hers, Tomo stared at his sister's face as if he had never seen her before. He seemed pale, uncertain, shrunken, as if the thing coming to life within his sister was simultaneously eating him, devouring him alive as a means to gain its own sustenance.

Confused and uncertain, he looked out and then down at the ground crew.

And saw Cat.

How exquisite they were. How incandescently beautiful. The gun beneath her arm burned like a live coal.

From a hundred loudspeakers, Queen's anthem swelled to embrace the coliseum. Pace by measured pace, arms linked, the Twins dance-stepped from the helicopter to the speaking platform.

This was the moment. *Now, now. Do it, now, while they are focused on the crowd.*

Cat's face was turned away. She couldn't risk meeting Tomo's eyes. Or Joy's eyes. Even with the contact lenses, the hair paint, they would know her, and that would be death.

She repressed another mad giggle. *Death before dishonor?*

No, the spider whispered. *Dishonor first. Then, who gives a fuck?*

They mounted the steps, spun in concert and faced the crowd again. This was the moment, this was the time. The spider beneath her arm stirred in its nest. It whispered to her: *Take me. Take me. Point me. I am yours to command. Align the metal notch at my back with the red dot at my muzzle. Brace me with your left hand, right shoulder back, your right arm straight like a rifle stock.*

Its call was mesmerizing, a deep and irresistible comfort to her weary spirit. She had come so far, and it was almost over. In completion she would find peace. She wanted it to be over. She longed to exhale, then inhale and hold her breath. To squeeze the trigger slowly.

A fleeting thought: *I'm sorry, Jax. To come so far, to finally find each other, only to end like this. . . .*

And even as she thought those things, as those images and feelings danced on the stage of her mind, her body moved as if it had a will of its own. Perhaps it moved in obedience to an internal command deeper than thought, or perhaps the entire universe suddenly tilted, and she was just rolling down a karmic slope, moving inevitably to a preordained conclusion.

It's bigger than both of us, Babe. Hell, it's bigger than all *of us.*

In one smooth motion, the automatic aligned on the center of Joy's head. For Cat, arm, hand, notch, dot, and intent all coalesced. All thought, all breathing, her very heartbeat itself ceased. For a moment, the universe itself was nothing but silence and potential. Then, she squeezed the trigger.

And in the moment before the night filled with fire and anguished sound, through peripheral vision she glimpsed Tomo's face. And his eyes, deep, dark. Afraid . . .

Cat fell. Her mind collapsed within itself, into a gap between seconds, between heartbeats. Tomo. *Where have you been, Tomo? What is the truth here . . . ?*

A hundred thousand tiny facts and suppositions collided, crashed, coalesced and crawled across the web work of her mind. Who killed Tony Corman? Who had a reason to? Who was Chris Zimmer's lover? The look on Zimmer's face. Cat had said "Joy's lover." Not Zimmer. He agreed. *After a pause.* Tomo was bisexual, and uncomfortable with it. Why? On some level, he saw himself mirroring his stepfather's abuse. Dear God.

Click, click click. Things fell into place one after another after another. The string of deaths in L.A.'s east side. *They look like you, Freddy.* Tomo was killing his father, over and over again. Tomo had pursued his lovers across a dreamscape.

Her friend. Her healer. Her lover. *We have so much in common. So very much.*

The deaths: the transients, Freddy King, Duke McCandlish. All killed for revenge? But why Cat and Jax? Why Tony Corman? and what about the Twin's young cousin. . . .

What if there was a single pattern behind all of them? If Tony Corman had been Tomo's lover, and had left him . . . and if Duke McCandlish, Daddy dear, had fled to the safety of prison, like the cousin had refused to return to the fun and games . . .

Oh, God. They weren't just revenge killings. They were pure jealous rage. Revenge for *abandonment.* A Daddy's love, in whatever twisted form, was still a Daddy's love—especially when Mother withheld her own.

Cat wanted to vomit.

Dear God in Heaven. Joy was an angry Goddess. But Tomo, darling, damaged Tomo, was a smiling monster.

C at Juvell turned a fraction of a degree, and now the gun was aimed at Tomo. Her face was pure fury, pure vengeance.

Their eyes met, and she flew down a tunnel of energy, and was within him. She felt it, and felt in that instant his shame, his anger, confusion, chaos—the broken heart beneath the shield of rage, within the shell of bliss. This was the man she had come to love. There was no time for more. No time even for *this.* It was imperative that she act.

His lips moved. What was he saying?

Then she heard the words, as if the crowd sounds were nothing, as if in all the world only the two of them existed.

"I forgive you," Tomo said, before the sin had even been committed. He spread his arms wide, exposing his chest. There was the smallest flicker of doubt in her mind, but before it had fully registered, her finger squeezed the trigger.

ninety-seven

Cat backed away from the helicopter pad, the Glock still smoking in her hand. There was the sensation of pressure as somebody tackled her. The automatic was wrested away. Pain darkened her eyes, shattered her consciousness into slivers.

It didn't matter. What happened next was of no consequence. It was over.

She thought.

Joy cradled Tomo's body, fingers tracing the contours of a face more familiar to her than her own, paralyzed into temporary silence. "Tomo . . . ?" her voice was a low rasping sound, coming from some deep cavern within her, barely passing her lips.

His eyes flickered open. They focused on her, then clouded again. "Tomo," she said. All of her former hautiness, all of her certainty had vanished. All that remained was a girl who had been given only half of her humanity, and had always trusted another human being to complete her. A woman, who saw that one, singular Other slipping away from her into a void where she feared to follow.

"I'm sorry," he said, the wisp of a sad smile softening his mouth. "God made a mistake. We weren't meant to be here, Joy. It wasn't the right time."

"Tomo?" The question was there in the single word, and her eyes and voice and face were no more than a child's, filled with the uncertainty and fear that only a child feels when the foundations of her life are revealed to be, not impervious pillars, but splintered timbers, vulnerable to wind and rain. "Don't. Please. Heal yourself."

"I didn't want this," he said. "I'm so sorry." His voice dropped to a whisper. "I'm bad." He shivered uncontrollably.

"Tomo?" This third time that she said his name, it was different. The doors of her heart had been flung wide, and all of the pain and rage and loneliness of a twisted lifetime were boiling to the surface at once, like an injured squid venting a cloud of ink.

"We won't be apart long, I think," Tomo's words were a wet rasp. "Forgive me, please. Forgive . . ."

She held him for a time after he was gone, her eyes closed. Then . . .

The entire coliseum had grown hushed. If Tomo had been a pope or a president, the aftermath of that shot would have been utter bedlam. But this was something different, and if their conscious minds didn't completely comprehend that difference, some other level understood quite clearly. Thousands watched, and waited for the inevitable.

Joy's aura began to glow again, a pale yellow intensifying to dazzling gold, and shifting toward darker, more violent hues.

The faithful who surrounded her heard a dull throb, a humming sound which slowly began to build . . . and then to amplify in a cycling pulse, increasing in strength.

Suddenly, and without warning, Joy's corona flared like a star going nova. For a radius of fifteen feet around her, suddenly everything and everyone *flashed,* disappeared, and in their stead appeared a solid wall of flame.

No warning. No chance, just sudden, massive death. In a single searing instant every human being in that first circle was transformed from a living, breathing, worshipping human being into a flaming, screaming unstrung marionette. Some screamed only once—then inhaled fire, transforming lungs into charcoaled sacs. Then no more screams, just pain and death.

Her aura imploded into darkness.

For almost twenty seconds, the crowd watched in stunned silence. The circle of guards and faithful who had subdued Cat suddenly froze as the light and the screams and the wall of heat turned a night's celebration into sudden horror.

The smell of singed meat filled the air, and somehow, that sickly smell made everything suddenly real, drove it home to their hind brains like an icepick in the ear.

Out of silence, another scream from somewhere in the stands. Then the chaos began.

———————

Jax ran toward them, cursing himself for letting Cat talk him into letting her take the shot. In some odd way, he understood her reasoning, even understood why she had taken the shot at Tomo instead of Joy. He didn't understand why Tomo had let her do it, but there was no time to think about that now. He tried to fight his way through the crowd, and clubbed two or three spectators to the side, pulling them off Cat, before strong arms found and held him. A fist struck him in the center of the face, and he thrashed without winning release. Too many days without sleep. His arm throbbed in agonized protest. The world was spinning—

He kicked someone in the crotch, satisfied with the solid thump as the shoe drove home.

He took another blow across the face, and began to lose consciousness.

Then he heard a scream, a shriek that sounded beyond rage, beyond pain, beyond hatred, beyond anything human. It was the wail of a goddess gone berserk.

"*Bitch!*" Light flared as if someone had ignited a thermite bomb. A tidal wave of blazing air slammed across the field. A small brunette in a flaming bundle of tattered robes sailed past him, almost completely consumed in flames. The ground beneath his feet shook, trembled, *crawled.*

Her aura expanded explosively, crackled across the field, scattering the faithful like blazing tenpins—

"*Whore!*"

The single word had more venomous than a coral snake. Joy stood in the midst of a patch of flaming grass. At least a dozen blackened human figures lay about her feet, in agonized cruciform postures. Some still clawed at the ground, moved their arms and legs in the spastic manner of half-crushed insects.

Joy's eyes locked onto him, and she came for them. Light erupted from her body. When she slammed people out of her way, their singed and flaming bodies flew like wind-whipped embers.

Jax fought his way to Cat and picked her up with his good arm, running with her. Behind him, the glow of Joy's force field grew until it resembled a fire-tinged tsunami.

The field was strewn with screaming people, patches of burning earth, twisted corpses. The flame crawled out ahead of Joy, and where it touched the grass, the blades twisted, turned and knit into patterns like a grotesque spider web. Grass gnarled itself into strings, into ropes and tentacles. Burning, falling apart, re-forming. Where it touched human bodies they came apart, just disassembled. Human sinew and bone, gut and hair knit together, wood and steel and flaming cloth all woven into the web. Joy stood at its center, screaming and laughing as the crowd in the bleachers struggled to flee this place of death and madness.

Jax hauled Cat up, kicked another screaming supplicant out of the way—an action hardly necessary at this point. All anyone desired now was to escape the thing which looked like a woman surrounded by a fluctuating, flaming obscene webbing of flesh and bone and metal. Her impossible tendrils disassembled anything they touched and reassembled it into more knitted strands. Here they touched grass, gouging troughs in the earth. Where they touched luckless human beings—

S imon stood, staring at his mistress, unable to speak, to move, watching the final moments of his life passing without any of the deep thoughts or profound revelations that he had always supposed might come to him at such a time. Here he was, with a phenomenon such as the world had never seen bearing down upon him, and all he could think, the cosmic totality of his final revelation was:

I've pissed myself.

Then the first of the tendrils reached him. He felt the skin tear off his hands and legs, felt his muscles taken apart one strand at a time, felt himself *unravel,* and had time to scream before his veins popped out and lashed into the burning cables. His blood sprayed the field, dampening the flames not the smallest iota.

C at and Jax limped through the stadium. Jax paused, looked back at Joy, who appeared like nothing so much as a human spider in the midst of a flaming web. Security guards, loyal only to the arena itself, dropped to one knee, raised sidearms, and fired at Joy. With a contemptuous gesture she flung them screaming, blazing, through the air.

They melted as they flew. One tumbled directly at the mouth of the tunnel where Cat and Jax stood. He hit the ground and burst, the wet dark contents of his body sizzling.

The stench of burning human flesh choked the tunnel. Jax backed up, thinking *She's going to kill us all. She's going to kill the world.*

But with every life Joy stole, every fireball she threw, her aura darkened through red and toward the black.

"Tomo!" she shrieked, a cry which became more of a sob with every word. "Tomo! My brother! Heal me! I need you. . . ."

The need for a security supervisor in the main video trailer had saved Manfred Gittes's life. At the moment he heard the explosive crack of a handgun, even before Tomo fell, his eyes went instantly to the crowd. Camera three had picked up a small figure in saffron coveralls.

The attempt to disguise meant nothing. The false hair color, the masculine clothing, neither of them obscured for even a moment the identify of the assassin: *Cat Juvell.*

He immediately began to operate the remote cameras. Cat. And without Jackson Carpenter, who must be guarding their escape route. One of the main service tunnels, no doubt, and he focused in. Four tunnels serviced the field, and two of them lead directly to guard stations. On a hunch Gittes excluded them, and zeroed in on tunnels One and Three. And there was Jax, limping across the field to rescue his co-conspirator. All right. Tunnel Three.

Gittes vaulted the metal guard railing on the ramp outside the trailer, and landed in perfect balance with barely a whisper of sound. The trailer was in the arena parking lot, blocked on all sides by cars. Gittes pressed through a flood of panicky devotees, fighting his way through the crowd.

Tomo, sprawled and bloody on the ground.

Oh, God. The image had flashed to mind, ripping through his calm and focus.

Manfred Gittes felt a jolt of sheer panic. He knew, without exactly knowing how or why he knew, one absolute truth: Joy would go berserk unless the one who had damaged her brother was brought down, brought to justice. That was his only hope. He had failed, and only capturing Cat Juvell offered any hope of salvation.

Gittes went after them, not knowing what was happening in the arena, not really paying attention to the flashes of light, the arcs of flame that played like low fireworks displays above the edge of the coliseum. The crowd screamed and roiled, a churning hysterical mass that fought to escape.

Something exploded ahead of him as he clawed his way through the human tide. It was all coming apart. Everything that they had fought for, and dreamed of. Tomo was dead or dying. The holy child Gittes had nurtured as his own brother, the salvation of a wounded world . . .

He hated as he had never hated in his life. Feared as he had never known fear.

Manfred Gittes ran, his long legs eating up the distance between himself and his quarry, moving through the crowd with unnatural facility, as though he didn't really see the people, but rather saw the spaces *between* the people, and automatically slipped into them.

Then he was in the tunnels. He would find them. He would stop them, and lay them at Her feet. And if necessary, he would kill them. He hoped that wouldn't be necessary—that was not his place. He considered himself to be a man of peace, suddenly and horrifically thrust into war.

Which way out?" Cat whispered. She could barely think any longer, let alone plan. Her sides ached, and her head rang ominously. Her vision was a smeary blur.

The concrete tunnels beneath the stadium were a maze of rectangular passages, with steam pipes twisting across the ceiling overhead. Metal-mesh-shielded lightbulbs glowed yellow, chasing away the dark. They stank weakly of oil and sweat, with a faint tang of urine from some nearby, underserviced urinal.

Jax had laid out an escape route. Two escape routes, actually. But somehow they had missed both of them, and were currently in a part of the arena they didn't recognize.

What they *did* know was that the noises filtering down to them were cries of terror, pain, confusion . . . And inhuman screams of rage.

Jax held Cat in the shadows, felt her arms around him, and tried to think clearly. This wasn't anything that he had wanted. But it was the only way she would have it. Why she had changed targets at the last moment, he wasn't certain. In retrospect, it made logical sense, but . . .

The sounds were distant echoes, murmuring like water falling in a distant cave. They moved out of the shadows.

And right into Manfred Gittes. Almost without thinking, Jax balled his fist and threw it, and until the very last instant was certain that it would land. Then Gittes slipped to the side, and the point of his elbow impacted directly in Jax's right fist, splintering bone. The pain obliterated rational thought.

He lashed out with a kick. Gittes brushed it aside, stepped in and clotheslined Jax, hitting him in the throat with his forearm, and his feet flew from beneath him. The world spun, and he went down hard.

Gittes pivoted as Cat came at him with a length of pipe. He took the blow on his arm, countergrabbed the offending arm and spun. Cat went down, hard. Jax was struggling to get back up, was levering himself up onto his hands and knees, when Gittes kicked. It wasn't particularly fast, but was perfectly timed: Jax didn't see it coming until the very last instant, and barely managed to turn his shoulder into it, felt the left side of his body go numb.

Jax stayed down, tried a sweep, actually caught Gittes on the calf. Gittes didn't try to resist it, went with it, seemed to collapse into a ball, went down, bounced up, and stomped, and Jax's knee splintered. Jax's muffled scream sounded like a prayer.

Cat struggled back to her feet, but Gittes turned the knee stomp into a pivoting cross-step, bridged the distance between them, and hit Cat precisely under the jaw with the heel of his right hand. She collapsed bonelessly.

He walked to her, vengeful as a god, sure and certain of his powers, and grabbed her arm, and then her hair, and yanked her to her feet. He turned her face up to his and gazed into her eyes. He shook her until her senses began to return. "Do you have any idea at all what you have done?" She glared at him, exhausted, blood trickling down her cheek.

Then the light changed. He turned around, as the tunnel filled with light. Glowed as if filled with frozen fire. Gittes's stone mask cracked, and what lay beneath it was sheer terror.

The thing coming toward them in the tunnel wasn't a human being. Not a man, or a woman. Not even a goddess. It seemed to be a pattern based loosely on a human form, condensing and dissolving and recongealing, a flowing, churning mass, as if the strain of exerting or channeling her destructive energies had driven Joy to the very edge of her abilities. She filled the tunnels and yet at the same time seemed somehow shrunken. The blazing bones of her skull shimmered through her skin. Her glowing eye sockets scanned the three of them, Cat and Jax and Manfred Gittes.

"Joy . . ." Gittes said. She turned slowly toward him, and there was nothing approaching human recognition in her eyes.

"My brother . . ." she said. Her voice sounded like a release of compressed air. "You killed my brother. . . ."

Gittes said. "Joy . . . let it end. No more death. Please. You're undoing all the good that you have done."

He held his hands up palms out, as if to attempt to reason, to cajole, perhaps to remind her of obligations or commitments. His hands were broad and strong, incomparably skilled. At times they had been loving.

They were the first part of him to disintegrate. The breadth and length of him was suddenly transformed into a man-shaped wedge of fire. There was a single, searing, yowl, agonizingly prolonged, and then Manfred Gittes was gone.

Joy turned, the murderous fires within her burning at peak now, ready to take the lives of the two who had betrayed and destroyed her—

Cat and Jax were gone.

Dread swelled to fill Cat's entire universe. Until this moment, fear, at its very worst, had existed as a sour weight somewhere inside her body, a small, gnawing creature burrowing its way through her mind. This was something very different. This was a cocoon spun of pure mortal terror.

Above their heads, the pipes hissed and bled warm water. The tunnels beneath the coliseum were as warm and damp as a womb. Gasping for breath, she pulled Jax to the side, and yanked his Glock from his holster. It was fully loaded, but that was scant comfort. She no longer believed that physical force would make any difference at all.

Screams still echoed through the concrete hallways, and oily smoke hung in the air like a shroud.

She could still hear, or imagine that she heard, the dying screams of the best fighter she had ever seen in her life. Ultimately, all of his skills had meant nothing. Nor did the fact that he loved Joy Oshita with all of his heart. Perhaps the real Joy was already gone, as if she had never existed at all.

And perhaps, in some terrible sense, she hadn't.

Sound. Something was coming toward them now, something which used to be human, but was now all fire and fury.

Cat held Jax upright, staggering a few more paces through the gloom. The lights flickered, and then died. Her mind raced, trying to find a way out of the trap.

"Please, Cat," Jax said. "For God's sake, get the hell out of here." He coughed. She wondered if a lung was punctured. "Without me, you've got a chance."

That was as far as he got, as far as his strength could take him. Both were operating in some resource twilight, stripped of anything, everything except the will to live. And now, perhaps Jax had even lost that. She held him, pressed her cheek against his, cursing herself for waiting so long to open herself to loving him.

Only now. When it's too late.

Shit.

"Go on . . ." he began.

"To hell with that," she said, and slammed the clip back in. The moment of fierceness swept away the cobwebs. If this was the end. If this was death, if the creature coming to take their lives could not be stopped, then by heaven she would die fighting, rather than spend the rest of her life wondering if she could have saved him. Saved the man she loved.

Damn you, Cat. Did you even tell him? Have you ever told him?

Even now, you can't can you?

"You're right, you know," she said. She stood, but had to brace her back against the tunnel wall to balance herself as she pushed her way up. She took the Weaver stance, aiming at the corner not twenty feet away. Already, the unholy light was lifting the darkness. The temperature was rising. Death was on its way. "We should have let Sinclair keep his damned money. We should have left the Twins alone."

"Bitch! Where are you . . . ?" the voice was only barely human. Not much time remained.

Cat bent, and ran the tips of her fingers along Jax's stubbled cheek. Despite his injuries, the corners of his mouth lifted in a smile. "You never listen, do you?"

She kissed him, softly, her heart breaking. *Say it, dammit. Say it at least once, before you die.*

She stood, tears streaming down her face, struggling to find her voice.

The heat was baking now, and sweat streamed down her face, plastered her dye-darkened hair against her forehead.

"I just wanted you to know . . ." she began to say.

"Shut up," he said. "I know. I guess I've always known."

She bit her lip, and nodded, relaxing her shoulders, taking a bead on the corner as the floor boiled with flame, as if a pool of blazing oil was spilling down the corridor. She glimpsed a leg, an arm, a face shrouded with fire, and her finger tightened on the trigger.

I love you, Jax.

And hopelessly, she fired.

The bullets never reached Joy. Little bursts of flame flared in the air eighteen inches away from what had once been her skin. Drops of molten lead slagged to the ground.

By Joy's dreadful light, Cat could see her phalanges naked through the flesh of her hands. This, then, was the moment of death. This was what all beings prepared themselves for. She was beyond fear now, feeling only a stab of regret that she had, finally, run out of time.

She shielded Jax with her body, without any real hope that the effort would prolong his life by more than a moment. She inhaled. Her final breath. Wishing that it wasn't soured with the stench of urine and burnt flesh. Wishing that it could have been clover or fresh sea air. Holding that breath, wanting to exit her life consciously, and not just slip mindlessly into whatever gap or void existed between worlds. For a long moment, the tableau was unchanged. Then . . .

Joy's eyes widened in surprise, and she studied Cat carefully, as if she saw something she had not expected to see, something within Cat. Within her heart? Her mind? Her . . . ?

The face of the goddess softened, and for a moment there was another, gentler expression, as if in recognition of something precious and lost, something more important than her rage. But . . . what?

Joy's gaze burned into Cat, the eyes of the most powerful being who had ever walked the earth, the eyes of a creature who should have been loved and perhaps even worshipped, but instead had been twisted and broken before she was strong enough to defend herself and her brother. Lost eyes. Burning eyes. Cat met them squarely, with nothing left to defend herself or her actions but honesty.

And barely, almost imperceptibly, the goddess nodded.

Nodded . . . what?

Joy's entire form shimmered, disintegrated, reintegrated as she tried to control it, but could not—she had expended too much, and needed the brother who was no longer there to heal and purify her. She took a step back, and suddenly flew apart like an image fractured in a kaleidoscope, expanded into a sphere of light—

—then re-formed into a woman again, barely managed to hold that shape for even a second before she came apart—

—and then congealed into human shape one last time. There was a question on her face. She looked around as if uncertain *where* she was, *why* she was. As if she were awakening from a long dream, and couldn't quite recall *who* or *what* she was. Then there was a sudden, heartbreaking moment of remembrance on her beautiful face, and she screamed: *"Tomooooooo!"* as if to announce her coming.

For an instant she became a being of pure, radiant light, woven of some finer stuff than flesh. She expanded to fill the entire world. In all existence, there was only Joy.

Then she was simply gone, as if she had never existed at all.

ninety-eight

Sunday, August 13

Rain fell in dark, warm sheets as Porsche Musette Juvell and Jackson Carpenter pulled up to the gates of the Golden Sun camp east of Bend, Oregon. The gates hung open, unguarded. There was no one in sight. Cat twisted the steering wheel to the right, found a patch of flat ground, and killed the engine.

Without speaking to each other, they left the car, and began to walk through the thickening mud. Jax's crutches and splinted leg made his passage unsteady; from time to time he was forced to lean on Cat.

For the first few minutes they spotted no one, then Jax pointed out a group of three acolytes sitting on a porch, near the great house, the former lodgings of their masters.

They turned, looking pasty-faced at Cat and Jax. She recognized one of them. Kolla Sinclair. The girl looked beat to hell, discouraged, lost.

"What happened here?" Cat asked kindly when they were close enough.

"Everyone left," she said. "Everything's just . . . come apart. Everyone's scared." Kolla had little of her old air of pride and confidence. She seemed only a sad, heavy girl with a lovely face. "I heard that you left. That they went after you."

Cat nodded.

"It was just to protect you, you know. It was close to the Unveiling. Iron Shadows would have come after you. Tried to get to you." She paused. "And they did, didn't they?"

There was something in Kolla's eye, something flickering there for a moment. What did she know? What had she heard? The guard who survived the Hunter in the woods escaped alive. Would he have talked? And to whom? Rumors would have spread . . . but of the spider-thing with Joy's face? And would he have known that it was Tomo, masquerading as Joy? Probably a sleeping Tomo, a dreaming Tomo, his damaged emotional core no longer under his conscious control. A jealous, damaged, fearful godling, desperate for love and respect and unable to receive what he needed so badly. What did Kolla know?

A single tear welled in the girl's right eye, spilled down the pudgy cheek. And Cat suddenly was quite certain: Kolla knew. She knew more than she wanted to know, and needed a word from Cat. The others beside her waited as well. At this moment, Cat had the power to destroy them. Or to set them free?

Cat looked up into the sky, the rain beating down upon her face, wishing that she had more answers. All she really had were questions, and many of them would never be answered. What was truth? What was lie? And did she have the right to offer a painful truth rather than a comforting fable?

Jax had been traveling the same mental road, because he spoke the words she thought. "It was Iron Shadows," he said. "They came after us. They killed Tomo. And Joy died destroying them. It's over. You're safe."

A shaggy-haired boy nodded his head, rain-darkened hair flapping. "She died for us, man." And the three of them clung to each other, crying.

———————

Mother Oshita sat in the middle of the mat, in the middle of the room. Alone. A dozen of the dolls which had stood in glass cases were now scattered around her. She had pulled the heads off, twisted the arms and legs until they seemed parodies of human figures. At least one of the origami dolls had been shredded.

She looked as if she had aged decades in the month since Cat had seen her last. The room smelled terrible, reeked with all the exudates of an aging body losing control of its most basic functions. Her cheeks were more sunken, now, as if the very air were thicker, heavier around her, more burdensome.

Behind her, a sliding wall was pulled aside, so that she could be seen all the way back into her sleeping chamber. It was like an animal's den, the lair of some beast too old and sick to care about fouling its own nest.

"Go away," she said, blind eyes searching for them. "I have told you to leave me alone. I will die here."

"Mother Oshita," Cat said, and the old woman finally seemed to focus on her.

For a few moments, there was puzzlement, but Cat could very nearly hear the file cards flashing in the old woman's head. "You," the old woman said finally. She paused, and then said: "I know who you are. I know why you came here. I am not afraid of you. Kill me."

"No," Cat said. "Someone will be coming soon. They'll take you to a hospital."

The woman's slack mouth snapped shut, and there was sudden steel in her voice. "No. I refuse." Her face was twisted into a parody of a stubborn, petulant child.

"You don't have a choice," Cat said. "It will be clean, and you'll be taken care of."

Jax finally spoke. "Why did you do it?"

She didn't even pretend not to understand the question. "I have a right to my revenge."

"The atom bomb was a terrible thing. But all war is terrible," Cat said.

"You can't know," Mother Oshita whispered.

"But out of that special pain came two unique children," Cat said. Her voice was very patient, measured, and somehow that deliberateness made the words more terrible. "The man who gave you those children did not do it from love." She paused, watching Tomiko Oshita's face. There was a measure of cunning in it, like an animal peeking out of a maze. "Did he?"

She was silent

*S*he would not speak to these people. No one must ever know.

He had seen her. The Man who came from America, who before America had come from Africa. He said he had lived a dozen lives, and would live a hundred more. He saw her, knew her beauty and her power. Without being told, he knew she had survived the Bomb. He knew she had survived the biological weapons. He knew that her ancestors had been priests and holy women. Knew that she was special.

He had come with the Americans, after the war, but was not truly one of them. He spoke perfect Japanese, and Chinese, and a dozen other languages. He told her that after a war there are many, many dead, and many who go missing. And that he had come to harvest life, that he traveled the world harvesting life. Wherever there was war, or disaster, or famine, he could reap, and thereby continue to live, as he had for hundreds of years. He needed only a few miserable souls who would not be missed—and a child of his own blood.

She was beyond judgment. Something in the atomic fires, in the days fever had burned out her heart. She wanted only revenge, and deep within herself, she knew this man could gain it for her. She asked him to let her learn his secrets, but he laughed at her, and told her not to desire those things which might destroy her. And she thought that once there had been another woman who had learned his secrets, and that this woman had betrayed him, but could never get him to speak of it.

There was fire in his words, and in his touch. He knew her children had died. He knew Tomiko Oshita wanted revenge. At first he was a customer, he used her body with a power and control that no other man, certainly not her husband, poor dead Shintaro, had ever possessed. He redefined sexuality for her. He painted symbols on the walls and floors of the apartment that he rented to shield their actions from the world. He used her body among the coiled loops of paint and animal blood . . . and blood that was not, she thought, merely from animals.

He made her pregnant, and at first she was afraid that he would harvest her child, use this pregnancy to extend his own life. But he said, no: that he was interested to see what the two of them might create together, that he knew it would be special. He said he would return some day, to see.

But she knew. She knew from the moment he planted his seed in her that these children could be the instrument of her revenge. That they would be like no other children. And to mold them, she needed only to harden her heart. To remember that they were not her real children. That they were nothing but demons in human form. And to treat them so.

It was hard, especially with little Tomo, who never wanted more than to be held and loved. Little Joy, who tried so hard at everything, seeking approval from a mother who gave it only in response to corruption. To make a sword you must heat, and bend, and fold it a thousand times, and pound it flat, and heat it again, and pound it flat until there are a million layers, until the sword does not know itself, knows only its intent. And poor Tomo didn't even know that. He could never admit that he was a killer, could only let that darkness prowl in his dark and bloody dreams.

It is easy to make a sword, if you thrust your own heart into the flames.

Cat watched as the single tear wound its way down Tomiko Oshita's withered cheek. Just one, which never quite reached her chin before it dried. The old woman's lips trembled, and at last she spoke.

"Kill me."

Cat could think of nothing to say to this creature. It was impossible even to feel anger. She wanted only to reach her, to touch her, to in some way impress upon her the enormity of what she had done. One last, final time, she picked her words with infinite care, and spoke. "They could have been gods," Cat said. "Joy and Tomo might have been the children we've awaited for fifty thousand years. They might have led us out of darkness and into the light. Out of war and to some deeper peace. They healed hearts and bodies with a touch. Taught and moved through a world of dreams. And you destroyed them. They never had a fucking chance. I think . . ." She gripped Jax's hand hard, fighting to find the right words. "I think that this might be the worst thing anyone has ever done."

Then, and only then they turned, and left the old woman alone with her thoughts and her grief, and her broken, headless dolls.

ninety-nine

The Los Angeles skyline was placid. It was home to three million people, few of whom realized how close the world had come to changing forever. Most of them knew about the incident at the Coliseum. Special effects gone berserk, most speculated. Some kind of fire trick. There were a thousand conflicting stories, a dozen descriptions of someone who had fired a shot. Most agreed that the killer had been a man, a short man. A lone nut, the kind who had killed Kennedy, and Kennedy, and King.

No arrests had been made. Over a hundred dead—burned and broken and crushed.

In her Malibu Apartments condominium, Jax and Cat made love. There was a special tenderness and intimacy about it, one springing more from a newfound wonderment than Cat's concern for Jax's wounded body. Ever more easily, Cat touched the place within herself that Tomo had shown her—

She burned. In her mind and heart came images of the time in Santa Cruz. The workshop. The sexual exercises. The lovemaking.

And Tomo. Beautiful, golden as a sunset, warm as a sunrise. Tomo, who opened the golden jewel box where she had hidden away her heart, and set her free.

They held each other, and in the aftermath, lay and breathed each other's breath, a spark between them.

"Are you ready to talk now?" Jax asked finally. She said nothing. "Why didn't Joy kill us?"

Cat turned her face to the ocean, listening to its eternal voice as it rolled ceaselessly against the shore.

"He gave you a gift, didn't he," Jax said.

"He tried to give us all a gift. He healed me," she said, and though he waited patiently, explained no further. Nor was any further explanation necessary.

"What do we do?" he asked.

Cat considered. "Maybe what they taught was artificial, but they made it real. There *is* magic in the world now. I see it and I feel it. And some of it was good. Some was bad, but it wasn't their fault. But somewhere in the world are people who use that evil deliberately. I don't know who they are or what they plan. I only know that if we let this spark die, the world may have no chance against them. People have to know, Jax. I know what I have to do."

"What?"

She was silent. Then, still without a word between them, began to make love again.

one hundred

United State Government RAIN FOREST Archive
SUMMARY NOTATION
Oshita File. DO NOT PHOTOCOPY OR REMOVE FROM BUILDING

A new element has arisen, in connection with the Oshita woman. Although she was retrieved alive from the Oregon camp, Tomiko Oshita refused to speak to doctors or interviewers, fell into an apparent coma, and died nine weeks later. Autopsy revealed nothing extraordinary. Ova were salvaged. They were remarkably robust, and may prove viable.

Copies of the autopsy, ova analysis, and a catalog of Tomiko Oshita's personal possessions can be found elsewhere. As to the events which took place at the Coliseum, brain and tissue samples from Tomo Oshita's corpse reveal nothing—and in actuality, there is no evidence that he had any powers at all. His sister's body was never found, although some experts believe that she may have spontaneously combusted (!). The identity of the assassin was never determined. There were thousands of people in the arena that night. There are no clear pictures, and no two descriptions match. Videotape images suggest a woman of small stature, but there are literally thousands of possible suspects, many from foreign countries. The assassination weapon has been identified as a Glock 9mm automatic, available the world over. (See relevant documents for additional data on all above subjects.)

The major concern of this summary is the African Letter.

The letter was discovered at the Oregon site, on the floor of Tomiko Oshita's room. It had, apparently been folded into the shape of a doll, in the Japanese style called "origami." The doll had then been cut and torn to pieces, such that a complete reconstruction was impossible.

It was signed "Niles." This is, of course, the same name used by the man who disappeared in Malibu on May 15, 1994, after kidnapping and apparently sacrificing numerous persons. According to eyewitness reports, paranormal phenomena similar in intensity, if not in nature, occurred at that time and location. His true identity was never determined, but he is assumed to be the same man Tomo Oshita referred to as "the African," the man the Oshitas believed to be their blood father.

It is presumed that "Niles" is dead, although no corpse was ever found. What can be determined of his history is daunting: It is determined that before and after WWII, he traveled to Europe, Northern Africa and Japan. At least one photo exists, which shows a very dark, tall man of African extraction, with scarred cheeks. Amazingly, he appears to be the same age in this photograph, circa 1950, as in a passport photograph taken in 1987!

We do not know how many others there may be with his abilities. How many variants there are. How many students he may have taught, or children he may have fathered. The Twins seem the result of a cross-fertilization between the African's powers and those of a woman from another tradition, another gene pool. A wild card.

Although a fragment, this letter may yield the greatest insight into the nature and scope of the situation. Note that "Niles" was unaware that Tomiko Oshita's pregnancy had resulted in the birth of twins. Note also his closing comments, in reference to the designated title of this archive. "Niles" suggests that psychic powers controlled in one culture can be devastating in another—a situation similar to that biological time bomb awaiting as diseases like Ebola emerge from the rain forests into the modern world.

(Note: before the following transcription was performed, the original was verified to be the handwriting of the man called "Niles," or "The African." Deletions and illegible passages are clearly indicated.)

—the first time we met

(deletion)

—promises that no one could take seriously. Still, I have an obligation
to the child you carry, although I find myself startled that I would care so
much. This may be because I sense that your love for your first children
may prevent you from loving him

(deletion)

—not as other children. The money accompanying this letter is for his
support, and not intended as a reminder of the actions you were forced to
take in order to survive. It comes late, perhaps, but you will never have to
suffer such

(deletion)

—discover who and what he truly is. I know that the magic runs in
the blood, but that it is impossible to say whether children or grandchil-
dren will bear the stronger gifts. He should be taught, but I will not be
there to teach him. You must do this—and you now have ample monies to
fund

(illegible)

You must protect him. All human beings have some of the gifts our
child will possess, but most deny them, or shut them away. Such powers
can cause madness. At the least, our child will deal with loneliness beyond
that which most can comprehend.

(deletion)

—for these reasons and others, the paths leading to true power have
been deliberately corrupted and compromised. Religions in all cultures and
lands operate at least partially to control or repress these

(deletion)

—abilities and skills developed over a course of tens of thousands of
years in widely separated sections of the planet. In the last few hundred
years, people have been interacting more intimately and across greater dis-
tances. Christianity and Judaism are vulnerable to the "Magicks" of, say,
Asia or Africa. African religions cannot control the forces which evolved in
Europe. Asian mystics are vulnerable to the African disciplines. When Europeans came to the new world, they brought with them diseases which had
already run their course on the Continent, but which devastated the native
peoples. I think this situation may be the same.

(illegible)

—is something special in your blood, as there is in mine. When these two combine, anything might happen. I will not be there to see it. It is best if I leave you and your child alone, if I not know where he is, until he is grown. Today, I am sated. Tomorrow I may be famished, and my mind may change. Take this money, and hide yourself away, hide your child away until he is strong.

I never offered you love—such an emotion is not mine to give. But I can offer you honesty. Our child will be extraordinary, and you must keep him from me. Do not seek me out. I give you this warning only once. If you ignore it, his blood is on your hands.

—Niles

epilogue

It is a quiet day in Gallup, New Mexico, the dusty town where a man named Jackson Carpenter once misspent his youth.

Down in that town, people still make the bulk of their money serving the tourist trade. Indians, stripped of their dignity by the same unyielding forces which stole their lands and heritage, turn the symbols of their faith and gods into plastic knickknacks sold to visitors from California and Florida. They wander the streets at night asking for spare change. They still get too drunk, still spend Saturday nights in jail with the cowboys who have lost their own way. Cowboys and Indians still stare at each other across the bars of ammoniated drunk-tanks and dimly recognize the funhouse mirror their respective cultures have become.

The sun is still high above the horizon.

In a sheltered resort in the mountains of Gallup, two dozen cars are parked on a spacious, graveled lot.

The central course room is packed with couples. People of all ages, all races. They are here by invitation only. Some pay, but to ensure the ethnic mixture, others are given travel vouchers, and some receive full tuition.

A black man and a blond woman sit in the middle of the room, and they speak easily, freely, of things that they know and believe and have experienced. Of magic and miracles. Of passion and healing, and the truth that love is a binding force in the universe. That while good and evil may be only perceptual constructs, there are truly forces of creation and destruction at work, and we must ultimately decide which we serve.

That the emptiness of dead space is mirrored by the emptiness living within us, and it is our job, our quest, our duty as conscious beings to not feed soul or flesh to either void.

The man is twice her size, but despite her smaller stature, the strength and certainty in her voice and every motion transfixes the room, transforming four wood and plaster walls into a temple.

"You are here to learn about yourselves," she says. "And you will. All your life, you've been told that your sexuality isn't yours. That your body belongs to your country, or the church, or your wife or husband, or your parents."

"It's an evil, manipulative lie," the huge man beside her says. "It's yours. You own you. No one has the right to do anything other than support your magnificence. But be careful—living from this space makes you as dangerous as hell to those who would control you."

"Don't believe anything we say. Try the exercises we show you. Listen to our words. For the next few days, empty your cup and simply see if we are correct. Keep what is useful, and discard the rest. If it doesn't prove out in your experience—"

"Forget it."

"Hear, and doubt," she says. "But see, and believe."

The day progresses. *There are exercises, and lectures, and when they break for their private work in the low, curtained cabins, lovemaking so exquisitely sweet that it makes all that has gone before, all sexual memory or fantasy, no matter how intense, a mere preamble.*

At the end of the day, the large man and the small woman join hands and walk back to the cabin they share. They are met at the door by a large, beautiful woman with straight black hair and an angel's smile.

"Kolla," the man says.

The girl gives them each a quick hug. "Tyler's sleeping," she says. "Tracy woke up a minute ago."

The two approach the back of the cabin, and the crib snuggled there against the wall. The small woman bends, lifts the girl child, sits and unbuttons her blouse. Sleepy lips find their warm target, and she begins to nurse. The woman hums contentedly.

Tracy's hair is brown, her skin dark olive, as is her brother's. Their eyes and cheekbones are Asian enough to make them achingly lovely.

As Tracy nurses, her sleeping twin purrs contentedly. He turns over once, and if he dreams, his dreams are peaceful. In fact, the man and woman have noticed that it is calming to sleep in his presence. Almost as if there is something about him which banishes nightmares. They will give Tyler and his sister love, and protect them, and fill their lives with all of the good things that loving parents could hope for their children. And then, they will see.

"He gave you a gift, didn't he?" the man had asked.

"He tried to give us all a gift," the woman had replied. "He healed me."

The whole world will see.

The boy burbles in his sleep, cherub cheeks pooching just a little. His tiny mouth pouts in a smile. And at the same time, his darkly golden skin emits a pinkish aura, warm and comforting but so soft that, were the cabin lights not turned low, there would be nothing to see at all.

VANCOUVER, WASHINGTON, MAY 26, 1997